CW00400901

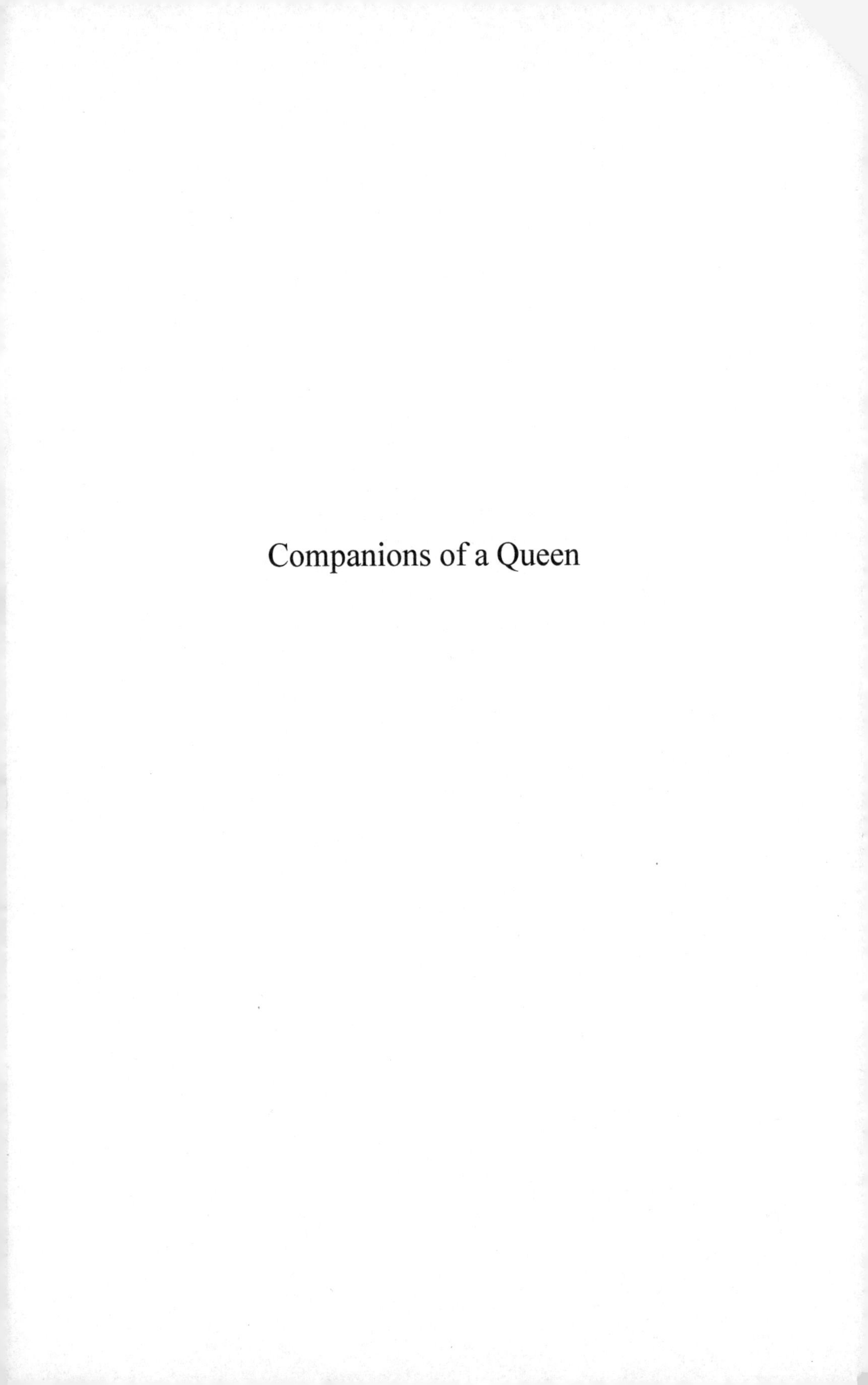

Companions of a Queen

O.A. CHILD

Companions of a Queen

Vanguard Press

VANGUARD PAPERBACK

A CIP catalogue record for this title is
available from the British Library.

ISBN 978 1 80016 375 1

Vanguard Press is an imprint of
Pegasus Elliot MacKenzie Publishers Ltd.
www.pegasuspublishers.com

First published in 2023

Vanguard Press
Sheraton House Castle Park
Cambridge England

Printed & Bound in Great Britain

For my family:

Elizabeth Mary Cannon

Anthony Joseph Child

Carol Ann Stagg

Edward Davies

Michelle Ann Davies

Harvey Charles Sarsfield Child

Lois Elizabeth Child

Anna Caroline Child

Tabitha Margaret Child

1

The Archer

The kingdom of the North Hanuli an enormous castle, surrounded by hills and mountains, covered in thick, white sheets layering the land, as light silver flakes sprinkled from above. The castle was built from grey stone, forging high walls and asymmetrical spires poking from every tower and turret. Every window was fitted with stunning stain glass windows, which dazzled in the afternoon sunlight, which peeked from beneath the thick cloud.

Inside the walls of the castle, tents swarmed the sides of the grey stone paths that twisted and curved through the kingdom, selling to the people that flooded to the gardens at the back of the kingdom.

In the vast gardens of the Hanuli kingdom, crowds flocked around the few men and women that lined a few metres in front of round targets in the centre of the fields. The men and women that stood lined together each faced their own wooden painted targets, holding bows in their hands and quivers on their backs.

Inspecting the archers was a man with long raven hair swaying underneath a shimmering silver crown. Proudly, he patrolled like a gazelle and eyed the archers like a hawk. His black cloak glided behind him and covered his silver armour, as a white outline was carved into the armour of his chest, revealing a large unicorn on its hind legs, sparkling in the sunlight. The man slithered between the archers and stopped beside the last, as the crowd produced whispers and waited for the archers to fire.

The end archer with long white, straggly and curled hair tied into a plait, squinted at the target ahead ignoring the man at their side. The archer's grip tightened around the bow relaxing at the side of their body, which they held in their palm, patiently waiting to fire an arrow from the brown quiver strapped against their back. The archer was quiet, listening to the whispering crowds and the other archers conversing with their caddies.

Behind the archer, a woman waited and held a quiver of arrows. There was long and wavy dark hair laying over her shoulders, as hazel eyes sat underneath thin, ebony eyebrows. Her cheeks blushed a pale pink in the biting snow and she shivered despite the thick fur over her blue cloak that covered her brown dress.

The young woman stepped closer to the archer's and hissed, as her eyes watched the crowned man dressed in robes inspect the archers and the targets from the side. "A coward be he, Tatiana."

Tatiana breathed, "Bidelia, be quiet."

"Sister, you are the best archer in all the North. Yet, every year, he chooses the winner that gives him the most money." Bidelia spat, as her arms folded across her chest. "Does King Hunter favour his disciples over his people?"

Tatiana's brown eyes lowered, as she turned her head to look over her shoulder and softly smiled, "Wouldn't you favour the people who give you money, over those who do not?"

Bidelia stepped back with a huff, returning to the edges of the crowd. She eyed her sister, as King Hunter came to inspect the archers one by one.

King Hunter stooped over Tatiana. He paced around her and examined her tall physique. He chortled. "Why do you insist on partaking in these events?"

Tatiana grappled her bow and remarked, "One day, I hope to win my Lord."

King Hunter stopped pacing and stood in front of her, glaring. He mentioned, "Then, you shall have to pay me."

"My Lord, I do not want to win with money, but with skill."

"You are skillful with a bow," he admitted. "But I suggest you use your skill for another purpose. Like, putting food on the table for you and your sister."

"I am aware I have very little."

The wrinkles on King Hunter's forehead appeared as his eyebrows narrowed towards his nose. His nostrils flared and his teeth bit the insides of his cheek. His eyes lingered on Tatiana, before he paced across the field and along the archers again.

As soon as King Hunter left, Tatiana Green planted her feet in the ground, with one foot slightly in front and her torso twisted to the side. She raised her arm and stretched her bow in front of her, clenching her muscles and tightening her grip around the wood. Tatiana lifted and placed her arrow against the bow, curling two fingers around the end and tugging the string to rest at the side of her cheek. Her bright brown eyes glistened and locked onto the white target in the distance of the enormous white fields of snow.

Tatiana was eased as her focus turned to the target ahead. Tatiana waited for King Hunter to shout and begin the tournament, prepared to hear strings slinging and arrows smacking into the bark of the targets with a *bang*, followed by an applause of the crowd behind.

With a loud voice, King Hunter called, "Fire!"

The strings of the archers sprang from the sides of their cheeks and launched the arrows at various heights towards the targets in the distance. The arrows flew slowly at first, meeting the air, before curling round and plummeting down to the targets on the ground, as arrows slammed into the wood, or bounced from the targets and were flung into the snow.

The last arrow to be fired was Tatiana's. She ejected her arrow into the air as soon as the man beside her had shot. Tatiana tugged her two fingers that held the end of the arrow and the string, pointing her bow slightly higher than the other archers had and aiming.

With a deep breath, Tatiana released the string of her arrow and propelled her arrow, which warped slightly as it sparked in the sunshine that blinded Tatiana and gradually lowered. Tatiana watched her arrow lower above the target, as the point faced downwards and at the centre of the target, it landed.

Silence swooped over the crowds, as the archers lowered their bows and eyed their arrows, which had either failed or succeeded to hit the targets. The archers stepped away from their stance and relaxed, as the quiet crowd finally burst into a cheer.

King Hunter paced across the archers, eyeing them, as he decided the winner. He inspected every archer and the arrows they had flung, instantly passing the archers that had missed their targets and moving quickly to the next, until he stopped in front of an archer and stretched out his arm.

He declared the winner! He stood in front of an archer that had slung his arrow just left of the centre. The crowd cheered and the archer was awarded a heavy bag of coins as he lowered to kneel before his king.

As soon as the King congratulated the winner, he paced from the fields and returned to the castle walls with his knights that had waited at the front of the crowd. They circled him as the crowd dispersed.

Tatiana fixated on the winning archer. He reveled with his friends and juggled the bag to listen to the golden coins clanging inside. His cheers were heard even after he left the field towards the castle village.

Tatiana laughed with disbelief and strung her bow over her back. She joined her sister's side and slowly walked away from the targets towards the castle gates.

Bidelia slapped the strap of the quiver over her shoulder and huffed, "Why do we keep doing this over and over?"

"It keeps us safe," Tatiana answered, "It has kept us safe!"

"I long for the day that the Southern kingdom is restored and I can walk beside the castle walls of Cahercasey again."

"We were babies when we fled from the Necromancer and his army! We don't remember what it was like living in the South. So do not be longing for its restoration," she growled, "Our home is the North and we are safe here."

"I am tired of being safe and I want to go home!" Bidelia cried, "The only way we will ever have a chance to go home is if you stop being a coward and fight the Necromancer to claim what is yours!"

"You are not my mother! You are not even my real sister. So don't tell me what to do."

Bidelia swerved in front of her sister and raged, "The Necromancer killed your mother. He killed your father and your brother! Your entire family was slaughtered, and you were nearly murdered too. But it is all okay because everyone believes your dead and it means nothing to you!"

"The North is my home. This is where I feel safe. This is where I am happiest and most at peace." she spat, "You want to start a war which cannot be won even if all the kingdoms came together. The Necromancer is too powerful, and he cannot be killed. It is not worth dying for."

"You have not searched for a way to kill him so how do you know he can't be killed?"

Tatiana breathed, "If you know a way then enlighten me!"

Bidelia tugged the quiver strap and flung her hands around it. She thrust her arms forwards and smacked the quiver against Tatiana's chest. Her body spun to storm across the remaining field and paced between the crowd toward the castle gate.

Tatiana sighed as she placed her quiver which she had been clutching at her chest onto her shoulder. She strolled across the field and merged with the crowd unaware she was being followed and using the main path around the castle.

The Leader

A man with chartreuse eyes and golden skin was hiding under the hood of a raven cloak and shadowed Tatiana. He stepped lightly and moved rapidly over the snow to follow Tatiana. He danced to hide behind people and gawked over their heads to watch her from afar.

He followed her along the castle path through the market stalls and into the main courtyard. He slipped into the shadows around the edges and used the stalls to remain hidden as he watched her approach her horse tied on the far side.

Just as he stood, hiding among the crowd, something cold was pressed against the side of his rib and something sharp pierced his skin. He was tugged by the collar of his cloak and his head spun to meet a scowl.

The man was grappled and held with a knife pressed to him by Bidelia. Bidelia spun him behind the nearest stall and tugged him closer. Her grip fastened tighter around her blade as he squirmed to free himself.

Bidelia interrogated, "Why do you follow my sister? Do you wish to kill her? Are you really like what they say you are?"

The man's brash voice scoffed, "I am flattered! I don't need to introduce myself."

"There are many stories about you and they might not all be true," Bidelia's blade pushed a little deeper into his rib, "but there is one thing they always mention. Beware the murderer with the green cat-like eyes."

He grinned.

"What are you doing here? Why are you following my sister Barnabas Mint?!"

"If she knew what you truly were do you think she would still think of you as a sister?" he asked, "Does she know you come from the sky and shine brightly as the Star you truly are? Does she know your only duty is to keep her safe and to protect the kingdom as she rules? Is she aware you have reached the age when you stop growing and your face will never age?"

"You were once a kind servant boy in the castle and then you disappeared. Yet here you are before me, and you follow my sister. Why?!"

"I want to go home Bidelia. I miss home."

Bidelia removed the knife from his ribs and released her hand from the material she had plunged into his neck. She shuffled back and muttered, "You will not be able to convince her Barnabas! She doesn't want to go South."

"Even with all the power of starlight you cannot convince her. What happens if she dies and still hasn't returned home? Will you spend your eternal lifetime here on earth and never go home to the skies because you have not completed your task?" he questioned, "Is that what you want Bidelia?"

"No." Bidelia shook her head and pulled her cloak further over her shoulders, "Barnabas I want to go home too."

Barnabas lunged forwards. His hand raised from clutching his sword and he pressed two fingers underneath her jaw. He elevated her lowered face towards the sky and examined her, but her watery eyes lifted to glare at him.

After a few moments, Barnabas removed his fingers from beneath her chin and his hand returned to clutching his sword. His heart thudded in his ears and the warmth of her skin was imprinted into his fingers not allowing them to touch the frozen handle of his sword.

He uttered, "Do you still live in the village on the outskirts? If so, I shall return with a small companionship, and we shall try to convince Tatiana!"

Bidelia lips curved into a smile and her head bowed at Barnabas. Slowly, she turned from him and paced across the snow. She lifted the hood of her cloak as icy winds started to whip and as a dusting of snow fell from the sky, following the path to the stables to fetch her horse and return home.

Barnabas'stare followed Bidelia. He watched her blue cloak whisk behind her and catch the falling snowflakes as she darted through the crowd . He observed her until she twisted at the bend of the market and he eventually lost sight of her.

The corners of Barnabas' lips lifted, but his softened stare quickly returned to a scowl. He turned to lean against the pole of the stall behind him, as soon as Bidelia had disappeared. He reached for the pipe inside his belt pocket and placed the wooden rod between his lips. He took a pinch of crushed herbs from a pouch on his pocket and heated the end of his pipe with a match. He breathed in the grey swirls of smoke as soon as the herbs had been heated and waved the flame of his match until it had gone out.

Barnabas resumed watching Tatiana under the shadow of his hood. He observed her readying her horse and beginning to mount whilst using the end of his pipe to warm his reddening and frost-bitten fingers.

For a few minutes more, he eyed Tatiana, until he pushed away from the wood he leaned against and stealthily strode into the crowds of Hanuli kingdom. Barnabas hid beneath his hood, as his black cloak whipped behind and paced rapidly to become lost in the crowd.

Barnabas strolled to the public stables just before the courtyard. He staggered slowly towards a slender horse that was tied to the outside pole of the small stable with a short piece of string lapping loosely around its neck. The tall and muscular horse's white hair glistened in the small rays of sunshine that broke between the clouds. It camouflaged among the falling snowflakes and on the colourless blanket covering the ground.

He gently greeted his horse, stroking his horse's hair as his hand glided down the front of its nose. Barnabas glared into his horse's dark brown eyes and removed the rope from his horse's neck and paced to the side of its body. He jumped and swung his body over his horse's back with a grunt.

Barnabas lifted the reins of his horse and lightly tapped his horse. His horse trotted forwards and he steered his horse through the courtyard heading to the open castle gate.

The Seeker

Barnabas rode underneath the iron gates of Hanuli and galloped across the bridge above the icy moat.. Barnabas gripped the reins of his horse and lightly heeled the side of his horse's stomach, asking to be carried faster along the vast snow-covered land and heading towards the cloud-covered mountain peaks in the distance. He travelled with the wind, as his black hood stayed afloat on top of his head and shadowed his stern stare.

Not too far from the gates of Hanuli, Bidelia waited for Barnabas. She was mounted onto a stationary deep brown horse and watched Barnabas arrive from underneath her blue hooded cloak. Her cheeks red from waiting in the snow and her breath appearing as blue swirls.

Barnabas guided his horse and slowly met her as he approached. His voice shrilled, "I thought you had already began riding home. Why do you wait?"

"I had hoped you had not left the castle yet and thought I would offer you somewhere to stay!" Bidelia grinned, "The outskirts are a days ride and I assume you have nowhere to stay once you reach there. My sister will not be home for at least two days. She hates to ride home on the same day she arrived at her destination. Offaly settlement has been a great home for us. I can provide food before you leave to gather your companionship. Should you wish to stay."

"I most definitely shall take your offer," he remarked, "but you shall be providing shelter for my brother and a companion too. They are on their way to meet me here."

"I can provide for them also." she remarked, "It has been many years since I saw your brother last. I hope you have not caused him too much trouble! And who might your companion be? Have we ever met?"

"I have not caused any trouble for my brother. He has been well." laughed Barnabas, "My companion you have met only once. You may not remember him. Maybe, you do. But he is like a brother to me."

"The journey we intend to take will make us all brothers and sisters in the end."

Barnabas smiled and relaxed the reins of his horse. He eyed the distance in the south and saw through the white fragments falling from the sky. Clumps of snow was collected by his cloak, but small particles were blown onto the strands of his hair that caressed his forehead as his eyelashes were dusted.

Bidelia guided her horse and waited beside him. She turned her face away from the southerly wind and clasped her cloak at her chin. Flakes of snow were whipped towards her eyes, and they were forced to close. Her lips were deeply reddened, and she trembled She waited silently with Barnabas for the arrival of his companions.

Across the white fields and travelling over the hills, two riders came. Swiftly, horses galloped through the thick falling flakes and stamped their hooves into the freshly fallen snow. The horses fought the howling winds and carried their riders from the direction of the mountains.

Two men raced towards Bidelia and Barnabas, steadying their horses as they approached closer. The two men walked their horses to Barnabas and greeted him.

The first man to speak had long and dark brown hair straggling at his shoulders. His greenish brown eyes bore at Barnabas and his body stayed tensed even as his horse stopped. He muttered and quickly glanced at Bidelia, "I see you have met an old friend already."

Barnabas huffed and looked over his shoulder at Bidelia,"You remember my brother, Wylie."

Bidelia squinted through the snow and smiled briefly at Wylie.

"You may also remember our companion, Free Stellam." Barnabas added,

Bidelia examined the straight postured man beside Wylie. She just glimpsed his face from underneath his hood and met a large pair of sparkling brown eyes as his white strands of hair were whisked by the wind. She smiled, "I remember now. I remember your eyes."

"Bidelia Lovet! The only Star left on this earth." Free exclaimed, "The only Star who did not abandon us when the Necromancer attacked. A pleasure to meet you again."

Bidelia's smile dropped, and she sighed, "I only remain because the Necromancer attacked before I could help Tatiana onto the throne. I failed my only duty."

"No one predicted the Necromancer would wage war on the South. He had a kingdom of his own. A nameless kingdom but still a kingdom." Barnabas insisted, "You blame yourself and you say your own duty is to help Tatiana onto the throne. But have you ever thought your destiny is to help us as well? We need your help. I need your help."

Barnabas's appearance became blurry in Bidelia's eyes as water gushed. Her eyes flooded and singular warm tears fell down her frosty cheeks. The corner of her lips curled, and she let her tears roll till they fell from her chin.

"You are the most important companion in this companionship!" Barnabas added, "You are the only one on this earth that can help Tatiana return to the throne, restore the Southern kingdom and help us find a way to destroy the Necromancer! Not a moment more should you blame yourself."

Bidelia nodded as her tears dropped from her chin. She tugged her cloak tighter under her neck and nodded again. The water inside her eyes remained and stayed smiling.

Wylie nagged his brother, "Now where do we go? Do we find the rest of our companionship?"

"Our companions reside further South. We shall head to the outskirts of the North and stay with Bidelia for at least a night before we travel any further." he answered.

Barnabas clipped the side of his horse with his heel. He lifted the reins from his lap and his horse trampled the snow underneath him. Barnabas led his horse into the vast swirling winds of snow and across the white plain.

As soon as he had moved, Bidelia, Wylie and Free hustled their horses to follow him. They clipped their horses and they hurried to ride beside Barnabas. Their horses trotted across the snowy ground, and they travelled towards the outskirts of the North.

The Loving

Across the North, the skies were covered with deep grey clouds and the sunlight vanished. The beams of yellow disappeared rapidly, as grey puffs merged over the blue skies and fizzled the light. From the dark clouds, heavy ice dropped. The winds twisted every white flake into spirals and everything in the North vanished among the white blanket that had fallen over the land.

Riding through the North, trudging through the white lands, Barnabas, Bidelia, Free and Wylie continued to ride. They collected their cloaks in the grips of their hands and kept the material close to their icy bodies. Fragments of ice clustered and stuck to the hairs on their faces and they could barely see the ground in front of them.

As they rode, Wylie called to Bidelia, "Do you not have the power to do something about the weather?!"

"Brother! Stars do not shine," Barnabas hissed,
"rather they burn!"

Wylie glimpsed at Free. He stared and waited for Free to explain what Barnabas had meant. Free added, "Bidelia can kill herself by using her power. Using her power too often will kill her and she will burn."

"How useless!" Wylie spat, "She is suppose to be a Star and yet she cannot control the weather?"

Barnabas and Free argued with Wylie. They rode on through the snow as Wylie insisted Bidelia use her power to stop the storm. Barnabas and Free hissed, though Bidelia was no longer beside them.

Bidelia stopped her horses as soon as Wylie had asked her to change the weather. She abruptly stopped her horse by pulling on the reins. Her hand released her cloak from her neck and her hood fell from her head. Bidelia examined the snow swizzling around her and felt the ice scratch her skin as her companions marched on.

Her hazel eyes which were heavy with ice on her eyelashes fell. A small smile creased her cheeks. Her shoulders dropped and the reins slipped from her hands as her arms dangled at her side. Her horse was obediently motionless as her stirrups fell from under her feet and she sunk into the saddle.

The winds around her stopped dragging strands of her hair over her shoulders and softly blew wispy strand lost on the surface. The roars of the wind transformed into a siren's call and the voices of the arguing men were suddenly echoing. The snow a few feet above the ground continued to land, but the snow high in the air, hovered. The low clouds parted in front of them and the white ground at their feet was visible.

As the weather altered, a white light shimmered around Bidelia's entire body. A twinkling spotlight streamed down from the dark snow clouds and encased her.

Suddenly, Barnabas, Free and Wylie's voices trailed, and they pulled the reins of their horses. Their eyes looked to the sky and examined the floating ice particles which stopped a few feet from their heads.

They released the reins and reached forwards to touch the hovering flakes. Their arms stretched and knocked the surrounding looming flakes, which plummeted to the ground with a single touch. Freely, they glanced over their shoulders without being attacked by swirls of air whipping towards them and seeing the white ground at their feet.

Slowly, Barnabas, Free and Wylie turned on their horses and stared behind them. They followed the blinding white light from the sky and gasped as they saw Bidelia, radiating a silver light around her.

Bidelia's eyes fluttered open. She looked up and saw her companions twisted on their horses. Bidelia laughed and her white light flashed a little brighter. Her horse carried her forwards and the white torch from the sky, followed her, as she arrived beside her companions and knocked flakes of snow at her side.

Bidelia's cheeks reddened, and her head tilted lower. The white light continued to blaze the outline of her body, but the torch started to dim and retreated into the clouds. Her lips curled and she focused on Barnabas' widened green eyes.

"Have you never seen such magic?" She chortled,

Barnabas shook his head.

She glanced over at Wylie and Free and exclaimed,"Have you never seen magic either?!"

They both shook their heads.

Gradually, the lining of light around her body faded. The light shimmered one last time before being drawn back into the pores of her skin and disappearing. She exhaled, "A small insight."

Though impressed, Wylie sneered, "I would like to see much more!"

If you would like to see more, then we must stay as a companionship!" Bidelia retorted,

Wylie growled and marched across the snow. His body pushed through the hovering snowflakes and knocked them to the floor. He staggered in front, as the others followed.

Barnabas, Bidelia, Free and Wylie trudged towards the outskirts of the North, passing through villages dotted across fields. The snowfall continued to halt mid-fall as the companions entered new areas of land and surprising villagers that were able to glimpse Bidelia's power. They were sheltered by her power, and they paced in silence towards the outskirts of the North.

The day darkened and night drew in. The clouds loomed above their heads and streamed across the sky. The outline of the moon glimmered through the thick cloud covers and small specks of light flickered in the darkness.

It was almost dawn by the time companions arrived at the outskirts of the North and came to Bidelia's village.

Ahead, smoke drifted from pocket squares amongst piles of straw that covered small wooden houses. Glimmers of orange fires standing on tall wooden torches, were plunged in the ground and circled along a tall stone wall around the clustered houses. Underneath the snowy ground, there were trails leading through the small village.

At the entrance of the village, there was a stone keep. The keep entrance faced the east and the opened doors led to the village. The foot of the turret was guarded by armored Northern soldiers, as guards stood at the very top of the tower and searched over the lines of the North.

The companions staggered to the keep, as the falling snow they saw ahead, halted. The winds ceased and the snowflakes hovered above their heads. The flames of the torches stopped blowing and swayed peacefully on the wooden poles buried in the ground.

The guards at the keep, stared at the snow and pulled their swords from their sheaths. They lunged forwards from the entrance and pointed their blades at the approaching companions.

Bidelia rode out before her companions and approached the soldiers at the gate. She stopped her horse a metre from their blades and entered the light of the torches they held.

The guards viewed Bidelia and the forthcoming companions following her. They lowered their swords and inspected them as they waved the flame of their torches in front of their faces.

In the light of the flame, the guards were alerted. They captured Barnabas' infamous green eyes, Wylie's resemblance to his brother and Free's long white-blonde hair. The guards whispered the companions' names under their breaths, as they gathered in front of the companions and stopped them from entering.

Bidelia quizzed, "Is there an issue here? Why do you keep us from passing into the village?"

"You return home to the Northern Keep with despicable men! Why do you bring them here? Why does a Star bring such dangerous men here? They may not slaughter you, but they will slaughter us!" a guard declared, "Do you know how many they have killed?! They have killed noblemen and women! They have killed children."

"It was one child and it was an accident." Free sighed,

"Do not speak 'man-lover'! You are the worst of them!" the guard latched onto the handle of his sword, ready to pull the blade from its sheath again and shouted,"How dare you come to the Northern Keep and stain King Hunter's name! How dare you mislead the last Star we have!"

Bidelia pulled her feet from the stirrups and dismounted from her horse. She jumped onto the snow and passed the lead of her horse to Barnabas. Bidelia stepped in front of the companions and before the guards.

Bidelia lunged forwards and stared down the guard in front of her. Her eyes flared with silver lights that forked like lightning among the hazel iris. A fluorescent glow grew from the strands of her hair and from the surface of her skin. Her radiation burned the torch fire and reduced the flame to nothing more than a spark.

Her hand whipped from her side and wrapped around flesh. Her nails pierced into the guard's warm neck, and she felt him gulp in the palm of her hand. She lifted the guard and raised his feet from the ground, as his hands scratched across her hand.

The surrounding guards jumped back and grabbed their swords, but did not pull them from their sheaths. They waited unsteadily.

"I can kill you. I want to kill you. I have been abandoned by the Stars and left to live with vermin like you. Why shouldn't I kill you? I will not be stripped of my powers, and I can kill all of you with a single blast of burning light!" she cried, "Does my hand feel warm? It will burn your flesh if I don't let go soon! My power cannot keep me warm in the cold, but it can warm you till your blood boils! My companion awaits an apology."

The guard stared at Free and gagged his apology with a frantic smile.

Free kept a stern glare.

Bidelia's voice lightened, "Now, let us through!"

The guarded nodded in her grip and waved his arms at his guards, flicking his hands to make his guards move to one side.

Once the guards had stepped away from the companions, Bidelia dropped the guard from her grip. She spun to her horse, as the guard flopped on his back and howled. Bidelia took the lead from Barnabas and led her horse towards the entrance of the keep.

The light around her diminished and the glimmers of the torches around the keep grew back to form flames. The lightning strikes in her eyes deceased and her green streaks returned.

Closely, Barnabas, Wylie and Free hurried and followed her into the village. They followed her through the arch of the keep along the snow path, into the walls of the village.

In the village, people crossed the paths, dressed in thick layers and moved with torches in their hands. Outside the houses, horses were stationed in stables and covered in blankets but were in darkness. The lit torches hung along the paths on the walls of houses and smoke blazed from chimneys.

Inside, Free rode to Bidelia's side, as they followed the quiet paths around the village. Free breathed,"There are not many people who show us the kindness you have. There are not many who show me the kindness you have. Thank you! But do you really hate us?"

"Yes," she took a moment before speaking anymore, "I do. But, I also don't. I hate you because you are what I have been left with: ignorant, stupid and angry people. Yet, I have been left with something and I should be grateful. The Necromancer could have destroyed you all and I would be living his darkness, unable to return to the sky still!"

He insisted, "Soon, you will be in the sky again and you can watch over us. You can hate us from the skies. Have faith!"

As Bidelia and Free conversed, Barnabas slowly staggered behind and eyed Bidelia. He watched her face animate as she confidently spoke. The corners of his lips lifted from his pout and his heavy eyes lifted..

Wylie's elbow knocked his brother's ribs, as his eyebrows raised at Barnabas' small smile and gleaming eyes. Wylie watched Barnabas struggling to pull his eyes away from her, chortling at Barnabas when his eyes finally looked at him.

Wylie whispered, "Though her face be friendly, she be not overly pretty. Rather, she be scary."

Barnabas' lips tightened into a pout and stared down at his brother, as his hand raised to slap the back of Wylie's head.

Wylie growled, causing Free and Bidelia to quickly glance back and then forwards again, as he continued whispering to Barnabas, "Well, at least you know I do not find her attractive..."

Barnabas smacked the back of Wylie's head again, causing Bidelia and Free to turn again and scowl at Wylie rubbing his hand through his hair after a small cry, but turning to face the front after neither Wylie nor Barnabas spoke.

Wylie smirked at Barnabas with a raised brow. He watched Barnabas turn and avoid his stare. Wylie saw Barnabas' eyes frantically scan around the village, deliberately looking in the direction of Bidelia and discreetly watching her.

Bidelia led Free, Barnabas and Wylie to the back of the village., She led them to a small house with boarded windows and no light shimmering from inside. It was attached to another house and faced a dark empty stable, but it was the last and pressed against the wall of the village.

Bidelia stopped and dismounted, jumping into the snow. She lead her horse to the empty stable and opened the door, gesturing the others to do the same and guide their horses inside. The companions removed the saddles and gear from the backs of their horses, which rested on the hay.

Once the horses were resting and the companions laid the saddles to the side, they followed Bidelia to the door of the house on the end.

Bidelia and companions crowed their necks underneath the wooden beams of the roof. Still crouching, as Bidelia lifted the plank of wood hanging across and throwing it beside her. Then, placing a key from her pocket inside the lock.

The wind threw open the door and slammed it against the wall on the inside. A wide and short path of the night appeared through the doorway in the pitch black of the house.

The companions lingered and peered into the dark, as Bidelia stomped inside and removed the snow from her boots. She crossed the wooden floor beyond the stretch of light that appeared and disappeared.

After a moment of Bidelia disappearing, Barnabas strolled through the doorway. He stopped at the edge of the path and squinted in the dark, just faintly seeing the outline of Bidelia's body and her movement towards something at the edge of the room, which she lowered too.

There was a zipping sound and a sudden flame of light appeared in Bidelia's hand as she held a small piece of wood between her fingers.

Quickly, she threw the flame away from her and onto the ground in front. The single flame burst into many and swarmed around burning logs inside a fireplace. The rapid-fire breathed light into the rest of the room and the companions entered.

The companions had entered a circular room, with dark wooden floorboards staggering to the centre from the bottom of dark brown walls. The ceiling ran with thick beams, as a candlelit iron chandelier hung at the middle, glowing over a long rectangular table and chairs. There was a fireplace at the far side of the room, already crackling with orange flames, with an adjacent door and a closed shuttered window beside. Around the room, on the shelves of wooden bookcases, there were thousands of wild plants growing from glass jars and rising towards the beams, encasing them with dark green vines and hanging low from them, as flowers bloomed.

Wylie and Free ran towards the fire. They slid down in front and removed their boots to warm their frozen feet over the flames. They moved so rapidly, Bidelia had almost just stepped away before they crashed onto the floor.

Barnabas slammed the door of the house and barred it shut with the plank of wood Bidelia had thrown on the outside. He shuddered the frame and propped the plank, before slumping down onto the stool closest to the fire.

Bidelia gathered mugs dotted around her home and scooped rum from the barrel at the corner of the kitchen. Then, handing them to her companions and joining Barnabas at the table, sitting beside him.

Barnabas gulped his rum, "There is a man I want to join us. He lives in Cheslyn. He can be found at the tavern."

"Do I know him? Is he prepared for the journey ahead of us?" Bidelia growled as she swirled her drink in her cup, "Does he know me?"

He nodded.

"What value is he?"

"A knight of the South! A knight who still wears his armor. A truthful and trustworthy man," he remarked, "though he may drink a lot."

"When do I meet him?"

"In a few hours, we shall ride to meet him. You will stay here." he grinned,"Get some rest. I will return you and Tatiana."

The Knight

Cheslyn. A Southern settlement, located west of Cahercasey castle. With more than a hundred people encircled by tall, stone walls, the settlement was heavily guarded as the chimneys of Cheslyn smoked throughout the night. Inside, the streets stayed quiet, as wooden houses emitted little light from the gaps underneath doorways, leaving an absence of light until the centre of Cheslyn.

At the centre, there was the tavern. Music radiated and voices shrilled from inside, as yellow hues beamed through the windows and into the streets. The door of the tavern was shut, only opening to allow stumbling men and women to leave. Laughter and joy did not cease till the early hours of morning, even as voices shrilled and fights commenced outside.

Inside the tavern, in the corner of the room, amongst the noise, there was a man. He was alone, swigging his drink, which ran down the curve of his lips and fell from his chin. Despite his eyes beginning to shut, he continued to drink, as his head rolled and he slurred his words. Though alone, he did not cease to ramble to the men and women that crossed the tavern. His name was Sir Terrence Prisca.

From underneath the hood of his cloak, which he always wore, a pair of dark brown eyes peered around the tavern, as bags drooped down his cheeks. He leaned forwards with his legs perched under the table almost touching the underside with his knees. Despite a slim stature, with little fat and little muscle, he consumed vast amounts, sitting at the table with two large, cooked pigeons, which he picked with his hands that quickly became greasy. Continuing to babble, he did not swallow his mouthful first, as pieces of pigeon flesh sprung from his mouth, landing across the table. His voice travelled throughout the tavern, over the music and laughter, stuttering every word he mumbled, addressing the tavern, which ignored him.

He called out into the tavern, gulping pints of alcohol and spitting food from his mouth. He slurred, as his hands erratically raised to point at strangers in the bar, accusing and insulting them. "Ye sillerness sorners. Ye dastards. Ye live quietly in comfort, to have never seen war. The King Oistin of the East shelters ye from such darkness which still exists in the South. Cheslyn be a settlement of the South, not the East! Yes, the South. The forgotten kingdom, which all have let fallen into despair. All have forgotten the kingdom and its greatness. All have forgotten the heir, which was born before the Necromancer attacked, cowering still! May the Stars gleam upon the South and the heir."

The entire tavern hushed Sir Terrence, as the tavern owner, from behind the bar, yelled. "Keep thy mouth shut. I shall throw thee into the mud, outside, into the freezing night! Thou will not sleep here tonight, if thy behaviour continues, Terrence."

"S-S-Sir Terrence! My name is Sir Terrence. Previously, a knight of the South. The youngest there be. Sir Terrence Prisca, a knight of

Cahercasey." He bellowed. "With my own eyes I saw the last living heir escape. Ye do not believe me. Ye shall believe me. I saw the babe. The babe, I saw!"

The tavern resumed, ignoring Sir Terrence, as a stealthy figure strode towards Sir Terrence and joined him. Sir Terrence fell silent, surprised to be joined and surprised to find the figure did not mock his rambling.

The figure's name was Barnabas Mint. He had travelled, from the Offaly settlement. Barnabas had arrived at Cheslyn to try its famous stimulants, which he smoked through his pipe that sat between his lips. He had been relaxing at the far side of the tavern, ignoring everyone, except from Sir Terrence's loud voice, hearing the most intriguing words. Barnabas smoked on his pipe of weed before Sir Terrence, as Barnabas' green eyes scowled from underneath the hood of his cloak.

Instantly, Sir Terrence recognised the man before him as the infamous killer he was. Sir Terrence sobered, as Barnabas' eyes saw through him. "Barnabas Mint. An honour to meet the most wanted."

Barnabas propped his feet on a spare stool and leant into his chair, continuing to smoke his pipe.

As Barnabas moved to be comfortable, Sir Terrence spotted four men a few feet from them, sitting around a table, drinking and eyeing Barnabas. The men sat upright against their chairs, sitting in silence as they observed.

Quickly, Sir Terrence flicked his eyes to glare back at Barnabas and quizzed. "Hath thou killed someone, recently? Art thou being hunted?"

Barnabas eyed the men from the corner of his eye and grimaced, as he blew smoke from between his lips. "Yes. Yes."

"It be many years since both thou and I conversed last. Why did thou find me?"

"An easy man thou art to find."

"Dost thou wish I help thee?"

"No."

"Then, why dost thou join me so?"

"Ah! Finally, the question I have waited for," he exclaimed, pulling the end of the pipe away from his teeth and lips. "Everything thou know about the South, I wish to know, also."

Sir Terrence chuckled. "Why dost thou need to be informed, when thou wert already there, in the kingdom, as a boy?"

"For I need to be informed, as I never knew there be a living heir. The South needs to be restored, though Cahercasey is no longer thy home," he answered. "It be right."

"Dost thou wish to find the heir? Be the most violent man asking me for help?" Sir Terrence smirked.

"Wipe the smile from thy face! Before I begin removing the flesh from thy bones," Barnabas hissed.

Sir Terrence's smile faded. His eyes glazed over at the men still gathered around the table, watching them abruptly raise and stride towards them.

Still watching the men, Sir Terrence panicked. "Those men are heading towards thee."

Barnabas cackled. "Fortunately, thou art being chased alongside me! Those men are heading towards us."

Slowly, Sir Terrence turned to look at Barnabas and frowned. "Absolutely not! I shall not be chased by association to thee!"

"Seemingly, thou hast no choice," he argued, releasing the last blow of white smoke from his lips and lowering his legs from the stool, before clicking his neck from side to side. "Now, do not stumble. Do not persist to be in my way!"

Sir Terrence barked, "Why dost thou always find pleasure in trouble?"

Barnabas did not answer. Instead, he heard the flat and loud footsteps from the men behind him, and rapidly twisted to raise and lift his chair and threw the chair at the man closest, knocking him onto his back. The legs of the chair smacked into the man's chin, as Barnabas snapped a chair leg after the closest man fell.

Using the chair leg, Barnabas whipped the wood against the man's head, listening to his groans. The man did not fall as easily as the first. He smacked the wooden leg against the man's head, splintering the wood and dropping the leg to the floor, before smacking his fists into the man's nose and receiving the same punch.

Stumbling backwards, Barnabas caught the blood falling from his nostrils with the palm of his hands. He fell on the top of the table, as the men surrounded him and Sir Terrence, who remained comfortably sitting. Barnabas dropped his bloody hand to his side, flicking the scarlet drops on the floor, before rising. With blood still running from his bruised nose, he continued fighting.

Lunging forwards, he jumped onto the man who had bruised his nose and wrapped his limbs around his body. Barnabas arched his mouth open and grappled the man's ear with his sharp teeth, tearing his ear from his flesh as blood splattered into Barnabas' mouth and across the floor of the tavern.

The initial commotion went unnoticed at first, until screams travelled through the tavern as Barnabas tore the man's ear. The music and laughter were silent, as the people stood watching Barnabas spit the man's ear to one side and jump down to release him, as the man tumbled to the floor clutching where his ear once was. Spurting blood forced many to vomit, but as the fighting continued, many fled the tavern, including the owner, and the tavern became empty.

There were two men which Barnabas was left to fight, as Sir Terrence remained sitting and watching. The two men staggered forwards to push Barnabas against the table again, as they drew their swords from their sheaths.

Already exhausted, Barnabas waited a few moments before he rose again. From his mouth, blood seeped, but it was not his own, as he viciously glared with bloodshot eyes. Barnabas' fists clenched, as every muscle in his body tightened. He leant backwards, before throwing himself forwards and tackling the closest man to the ground.

Barnabas landed on top of the man, grunting, as his knees smacked against the hard wooden floorboards. Though pained by his throbbing knees, he ignored the pain, smashing his fists into the man's now bloody face, which splattered across Barnabas. Barnabas would not stop till the man was silenced with death, watching him choke on his own blood.

As Barnabas battered the man to death, the last man swept behind Barnabas with his sword, swooping his blade through the air. Barnabas was unaware the man behind him had whipped his sword to slice through Barnabas' neck.

Sir Terrence watched the man attempting to slice Barnabas' throat. Mostly, Sir Terrence wanted to let Barnabas die. Yet, no matter the hatred and annoyance he had for Barnabas, he would not let him be killed by anyone except himself. Sir Terrence groaned. He raised from his chair and paced towards the man with the sword.

Sir Terrence charged forwards and disarmed the man of his sword. He whipped his sword from his sheath and slashed his blade through the air, slicing through the man's wrists and removing his hand which still clasped the sword. The man dropped to his knees clutching his wrist, which spurted with blood over Barnabas and the man he pinned down that he had just killed. Finally, Sir Terrence decapitated the man, hurling his head across the floor of the tavern.

After Sir Terrence wiped the blood from his sword, he helped Barnabas to his feet. Sir Terrence grabbed Barnabas' bloody hand and yanked Barnabas to stand, staring at his crimson liquid face with a sigh of relief. Sir Terrence tucked his sword back into his sheath.

Once Barnabas stood, he wiped the blood away from his eyes and lowered his hood to brush his dark hair away from his forehead. Barnabas clicked his knuckles and neck, before stretching and breathing deeply to relight his pipe.

Sir Terrence questioned, returning to rest in his chair with an exhale, "Whom did thou kill now?"

"Truthfully, I cannot tell thee. For I do not know." Barnabas smirked. "There are so many I have killed and I begin to lose my memory."

"Truly, thou art unstable," Sir Terrence admitted. "From such a young age, thou hast always killed."

Barnabas cackled. "Yes! It has always been joyous to kill!"

Sir Terrence grinned. "What dost thou wish to know?"

"Tell me where the heir of the South is!"

"Ah! I can only assume the heir was taken," Sir Terrence remarked. "The heir escaped to the Northern kingdom, Hanuli. The heir was taken there by Ezra. The old man from the castle. I believe that is what thou used to call him."

"Then we shall find Ezra!" Barnabas concluded. "Come, quick. My brother and companion wait for us outside."

Sir Terrence nodded. He gulped the last few mouthfuls of alcohol left, slamming the cup against the table and following Barnabas through the bloody tavern to leave. Barnabas stormed outside into the village with

Sir Terrence beside him, meeting two men standing beside four horses which they cared for.

The first man was Barnabas' bastard brother, Wylie. Wylie was younger, resembling their mother, almost looking exactly alike. Greeting his brother, Wylie did not speak simply passing him the reins of Barnabas' horse to him and mounting his own horse, as Barnabas and Sir Terrence approached the second man.

Free Stellam was the second man. He had been friends with Barnabas and Wylie since they were children. Free and Sir Terrence were not strangers either, arresting all three of them on multiple occasions when they were younger. Free had confided in Sir Terrence for his love of men and Sir Terrence accepted him anyway. Instantly, Free was recognised by his long, glowing white hair.

Kindly and timidly, Free greeted Sir Terrence with an embrace. "My friend, hello. We have not met since I was a child, and thou look well."

"After the fall of the South, I was saddened. Except I was delighted not having to arrest thee anymore!" Sir Terrence smiled. "Always, thou wert in trouble."

Free faintly smiled. He twisted to mount his horse, glancing at Wylie, as they waited for Barnabas and Sir Terrence to mount also. Free and Wylie waited silently.

Sir Terrence glared at Barnabas, as Barnabas gave him the reins of the fourth horse. Sir Terrence watched Barnabas step to the side of his horse and asked, before Barnabas mounted his horse. "Shall, I question why thou wish to save the Southern kingdom? Solely, thou cannot want to save the kingdom to be right?"

"If we do not save the kingdom, no one else shall!" Barnabas huffed, lifting his body onto the back of his horse and looking down at him. "We shall be the ones to save the kingdom and so shall thee."

Seeing the glimmer in Barnabas' eyes was enough to convince Sir Terrence to join him. The glimmer was the same glimmer Barnabas had when he passionately killed. He trusted Barnabas' desire to find the heir.

As soon as Sir Terrence was convinced, he threw himself on top of his horse and strapped his boots into the stirrups. Sir Terrence guided his horse to follow Barnabas, Wylie and Free through Cheslyn and into the darkness of the night, heading North to find the heir, travelling beneath the moonlight.

2

The four companions travelled throughout the night, for many hours, riding on the backs of their horses. The night began with clear skies, but shortly, the moon was covered by thick, black clouds. From the clouds, water poured heavily, drenching the companions and drowning the land. Following the fall of rain, thunder began to roar and blinding lightning flashed. Falling temperatures and violent winds forced the companions to stop their journey earlier than expected.

A settlement, not too far from Cheslyn, was where the companions stopped. The companions sought refuge in Bhile, a much larger village, located further to the North. Bhile attracted many, as the village had been built around an ancient oak tree, which was unusually tall and was wider than most, with thick roots sitting on the surface. Being the most influential settlement across the land, Bhile was almost a kingdom, where the most wealthy dwelt and the poor served. There was one man in charge of Bhile, General Xanthie, who had previously served for the kingdom of the East. He was rarely sighted by the people of Bhile.

The companions arrived at the fortified gates of Bhile, which were heavily guarded by men that inspected the companions as they waited before them. At the gate, through the hatch, the companions were questioned by the guard on duty, identifying them and creating detailed drawings, as the companions were strangers to Bhile.

Finally, the gates were opened and the companions trudged into Bhile, as the doors locked behind. The companions headed to the inn as the rain continued to fall.

Inside the walls of Bhile, a stone path covered the ground and was brightly lit by candle lanterns hanging from the walls of houses. The stone and wooden houses were narrow and tall, with smoking chimneys, even as the rain fell. Emitting from all the houses there was light. Hues from fires and candles radiated, as the streets laid bare and cold. Every path eventually led to the centre of Bhile, where the oak tree stood, which shadowed the settlement with its roof of leaves, catching the droplets of rain.

At the far side of the settlement, far from the gate, there was the inn. The inn was wider than majority of the houses, with two floors and made entirely from grey stone. There were shutters on every window, which were locked, as the chimney puffed and small amounts of light seeped from underneath the low-bearing front door. The inn was silent, as horses rested in a nearby stable and as a tavern was attached to the side of the inn, deafening the entire settlement with music, laughter and smashing glass.

The companions led their horses to the stable and laid them to rest in the warmth. The companions headed into the inn, ducking their heads underneath the doorway. They entered a large room where a frail, old woman sheepishly stared at them as they entered. Through the walls and above the silence, they could hear the commotion coming from the tavern, which was behind an adjoining door that remained temporarily shut.

Approaching the woman, who sat at an enormous table, the companions' feet echoed against the wooden, black floorboards. The companions stood before the woman under the dim lighting of the lanterns, which hung from the beams of the room. They waited for the woman to address them, as the companions did not want to wake her from her sleep haze.

After a few seconds, eventually, the woman spoke. She asked with a slow and sweet voice how many rooms were needed for their stay, glaring down at the tattered book in front and grabbing a quill.

"If the beds sleep only one, then we will need four. If the bed sleeps two, then we shall only need two," Barnabas answered, harshly.

The woman checked available rooms, flicking through a few pages, before yawning her response. "The room in the attic is spare. It is one room with five singular beds. However, as there is a spare bed, I shall provide the spare to a lone traveller if required. Would ye be willing to share?"

"Yes," Barnabas growled, impatiently stretching out his hand for the key she had not taken from the hooks behind her, nailed to the wall.

"Now, I shall need a name," she remarked. "Whose name shall I use?"

The woman dipped the end of her quill into a pot of ink, placing the point against the paper of her documents, ready to write. Her eyes glared down, as she waited to hear a name. Except the name she heard struck fear, as her eyes widened and as her quill slipped from her shaking grasp. She looked up at the companions, examining them, searching for the one that had roared his name. Her eyes landed on Barnabas, who smirked.

She trembled, looking down at her documents and avoiding Barnabas' violent glare. "I do not want trouble. I do not want to die. Please, I only have so few years and I would like to live them! Do not kill me. I beg thee. I beg thee, Barnabas Mint!"

"Currently, I am not in the mood to kill. I am far too tired to kill thee." He grimaced. "In the morning, I shall be well rested and perhaps, I shall kill thee then."

"Hopefully, thou shalt change thy mind, after I mention the room is free." She gulped, directing the companions through a passage and to the staircase, passing Barnabas the key with her shaking hand. "Please, any drinks in the tavern are on the house for thee and thy companions! Enjoy thy stay."

Pleasurably, Barnabas snatched the keys from the woman, grappling them in a tight grasp and twisting on his heel. Barnabas strode towards the passage, as Sir Terrence, Free and Wylie followed behind, avoiding the eyes of the woman, who could not help but stare.

Quickly, the companions rushed to their room, climbing the spiral stairs and unlocking the door. They entered the low-bearing attic, with beams stretching across. A single, circular window sat above two of the beds, which were staggered on the same side. The attic was lit by few lanterns and smelt damp, but there was little dust and the sheets were clean.

Wylie and Free strode to the farthest beds, throwing their armour and small belongings to one side. They collapsed onto their lumpy beds, being too exhausted to be uncomfortable and sighed. Free and Wylie relaxed, as they closed their eyes and slipped off their shoes, before climbing between the sheets.

Slowly, Barnabas headed to his bed. Barnabas hung his bag over the side but did not remove any amour and kept his sword at his side, resting upright and keeping his shoes on. His eyes closed, but he did not fall asleep, listening to his sleeping companions and the silence within the inn, as music and voices blared from the tavern.

As Sir Terrence entered, he inspected the room and watched his companions rest. He stood at the door for only a moment, before declaring he was leaving for the tavern, slamming the door behind him before he could be persuaded to stay. Sir Terrence stomped downstairs, crossing the entrance of the inn to enter through a side door which led to drunken chaos. He drank quickly but did not return for hours.

In the early hours of morning, Sir Terrence returned. Barnabas heard his stomping feet climb the stairs a while after the tavern fell quiet. Sir Terrence opened the door of the room, leaving the door partly ajar and stumbling to his bed. He collapsed onto his bed, landing on his stomach and tilting his head to one side and snoring heavily and loudly. Sir Terrence fell asleep, muttering, but making little sense.

Yet, as Barnabas' eyes stayed closed, he heard the door shut and scowled. Barnabas had not heard any previous steps leading to the door or following Sir Terrence as he entered. His eyes flicked open and he examined the darkness of the room.

Through the darkness, he saw a figure striding to the last empty bed, dropping their bag gently on the floor and resting on the bed. The figure did not remove their shoes and laid on top of the blankets, facing away from Barnabas as he sighted curly black hair.

Over the silence, a woman's voice called softly, "Art thou to stare all night?"

"No," he responded.

"Barnabas Mint. If thou wish to kill me, do so already. Death shall be more comfortable than thy stare," the woman on the bed hissed.

"I shall not kill thee." He yawned, closing his eyes and relaxing his tense body.

"Dost thou wish to know who I am? A stranger shares a room with thee and thy friends! Does a stranger not scare thee?"

"No. I am not scared. I have never been scared."

"There is a tremble in thy voice. Dost thou not hear?"

"No! I do not hear!"

"From now on, thou shall regard the tremble in one's voice after I have mentioned so. Now, my name is Tasmin Berry. I met thy friend in the tavern. He explained the journey and invited me to join the companionship. Here I am." Tasmin rolled to face him and he noticed her dazzling, deep brown eyes. "Do not dismiss me for being a woman. I am not weak!"

"Never. Never would I dismiss anyone for being a woman, for loving the same or having different skin," Barnabas mentioned. "My best friend is a man who loves man."

Tasmin propped her arm against the pillow and laid her head against her hand to stare closely at Barnabas, over Sir Terrence's sleeping body. Her brown eyes gleamed, as Barnabas' stare continued to harden. She remarked, "I may be very young, much younger than thee, but I can see thou art kind."

Barnabas hissed. "Still, thou art only young."

Tasmin's eyes rolled, dropping her head onto her pillow and groaning. She closed her eyes and muttered, clearly, "At least, a woman is safe beside just a killer."

Barnabas grinned, as glimmers of orange radiated through the window above his head. In the hues of dawn, Barnabas rested for only an hour before waking again. He was not disturbed by Sir Terrence's snoring, nor by Tasmin's heavy breathing, allowing him the rest he needed to begin the new day ahead.

In an hour, the first companions woke. Wylie. He awakened to Sir Terrence's snoring, abruptly covering his ears with a pillow. Wylie rose to look over at Sir Terrence laying on his stomach but overlooked him to scowl at Tasmin. He wondered when she had appeared but looking over at Barnabas and being comforted by his light sleeping, which would have awoken him as Tasmin intruded to question her, he ignored her.

For the time being, he overlooked Tasmin, as Sir Terrence's snoring became deafening. Wylie swung his legs over the side and stormed to Sir Terrence's bed, stooping over him. He still held onto his pillow, removing it from covering his ears and slapping the pillow against Sir Terrence's head till he woke.

Wylie screeched, waking Free and Tasmin from their slumber. "Thou drunken bastard! Wake! For I cannot endure thy snoring anymore! I wish to rest further."

Tasmin and Free raised to watch Wylie beat the pillow senselessly against Sir Terrence till he woke. They watched for a while, listening to Wylie's grunts that had awakened them, as their tired eyes squinted to focus.

Sir Terrence woke with a grunt. His body moved before his eyes even opened, throwing himself onto his feet, which hung off the side of the bed and nearly knocking Wylie over too. He burped, stretching his arms above his head, tucking his top from his trousers and opening his drowsy, puffy eyes. Alcohol continued to linger on his clothes and his breath, and he continued to slur, though he was only muttering his companions' names.

As soon as Sir Terrence stood awake, Wylie returned to his bed to sleep for the next hour or so. Wylie slapped his pillow down and submerged himself underneath the covers, as Sir Terrence collapsed onto the bed and remained partly awake. Sir Terrence did not snore and Wylie fell asleep almost instantly after landing in his bed.

From the far side of the room, Tasmin sheepishly called to Free and introduced herself, as she rested against the headboard. "Hello, there. I am Tasmin Berry. Thou must be Free Stellam."

Free nodded, avoiding her stare.

"Ah! I was told thou rarely spoke. May I ask why?"

He shook his head, still looking away from her.

"Already, I have been informed thou art a man, who loves man! An old friend was the same."

Free blushed, as his eyes lowered with shame.

"Terribly, I am sorry. There are many times where I continue to speak so truthfully that I embarrass everyone, including myself," she apologised. "Profusely, I speak a lot."

He nodded.

"Truthfully, I did not to intend to offend thee. I am sorry, Free!"

From the bed in the centre, Barnabas groaned, keeping his eyes shut. "Silence, Tasmin. If thou art to be a part of our companionship, thou must learn to be silent."

"Yes. Yes, of course. Always, I have been told to learn when to be silent."

Rapidly, Barnabas' eyes opened and he glared at her, seeing her eyes lower. He mentioned, "Surprisingly, I have changed my mind. Do not be silent. Do not cease to speak. Rather, thy voice is comforting."

For the first time, Tasmin was left speechless. She avoided Barnabas' stare, as a small flood of tears filled her eyes. Tasmin sunk into the covers and faced her new-found companions, who were resting, before closing her eyes.

In an hour, the companions would wake and gather their belongings, before retrieving their horses from the stables. They left the village of Bhile, continuing to head to the North, as Barnabas led the way, hearing Tasmin babble and the small groans of the companions, who listened to her. Swiftly, they moved.

3

For the companions, it would take two days until they would arrive at the next settlement. The companions would travel as fast as their horses could carry them, across the meadows and through the forests ahead. Mostly, the companions encountered wildlife, running across the picturesque scenery silently. Yet soon, they heard screeches travelling along the wind.

The howls of torture grew louder as the wind strengthened and from the grey sky above, rain started to fall. Heavily, the rain fell, soaking the companions instantly, bringing forth the cold. The companions shivered and their teeth chattered, as their cloaks and hoods were blown from their shoulders. The companions continued to travel through the raging storm.

Travelling brought the cries closer, as the companions spotted moving figures in the distance, as lightning zapped and thunder growled. The companions crossed the meadow, catching the men and women that stumbled on their feet, keeping a young girl captive. The young girl was dragged in chains, struggling to free herself and screeching until her voice began to strain.

The companions trotted beside them, examining their rags of clothing and extremely dirty faces, as they hid under the hoods of their cloaks. In seconds, the companions started to call to the men and women.

Tasmin yelled, “Why dost thou shackle the young girl? Has she committed sins? Art thou listening? I do not speak to the wind! Though I have spoken to the wind often in the past. The wind cannot answer.”

Barnabas trotted ahead, as Tasmin’s babbling rambled. He led his horse to stand before the men and women, cutting their trail and forcing them to abruptly stop before him. The men and women glared viciously at him.

The woman at the front addressed Barnabas, shouting over the thunder. “Why dost thou care for the bitch? Dost thou know her?”

"All which has been asked by my companions is why she is shackled," Barnabas stated, after dismounting his horse and squelching through the mud to stop before her, drawing his sword also. "A question does not harm anyone."

"The girl is wanted by a wealthy family in Brill. We shall be rewarded greatly!" She grinned.

"We will accompany thee. I and my companions are heading there also," Barnabas declared.

"There is no need to do so. The girl shall return to her family," the woman hissed.

Behind the men and women, the young girl begged Barnabas, dropping to her knees and clasping her shackled hands together. "Please. Save me! Please."

Annoyed by the girl's pleas, the woman turned and ordered. "Keep quiet. Otherwise, there will be another beating! Ungrateful girl. A loving family waits for thee."

Helplessly, the young girl sunk into the mud and wept further, as the aged woman before Barnabas turned to face him. Feverishly, she smiled. "There is no reason for thee to accompany us."

Barnabas placed his sword in his sheath and faked a smile. "No. There is no need to accompany thee. Seemingly, the girl is spoilt and ungrateful for privileges, which we have not been given."

"Precisely. Now, we will be on our way. Fortunately, we may meet again in Brill." She smiled, as Barnabas stepped to one side, letting them pass, as the young girl screamed as she was dragged.

Barnabas returned to his horse's side and watched them leave. As soon as they had vanished into the distance, Barnabas mounted his horse and gathered his companions. For a moment, he brooded, which was enough time for his companions to discuss and question him.

"Why didst thou let them freely roam? I believe they were lying. Surely, thou knew they were lying. For I do not believe what thou hast allowed," Tasmin exclaimed. "The girl was shackled. The storm raged. The thunder was deafening. The poor girl!"

"Brother, why dost thou brood?" Wylie questioned. "Brother? Brother Barnabas?"

Gulping a mouthful of whiskey from his flask, Sir Terrence slurred, “Dost thou not wish to kill those people?”

“Enough!” Barnabas ordered, silencing his companions. “Before further conclusions are insinuated, I shall first explain the plan. All of us shall kill them once we have arrived at Brill and freed the girl.”

“Oh goodness. We thought too fast. In future, we shall wait to believe our thoughts. Though, we shall not know what our future thoughts shall —”

Tasmin stopped, as Sir Terrence drunkenly spoke over her, spitting his drink into her face. “How will we kill? When will we arrive and where are we going? At least, I —” He chuckled, but lost his train of thought and grabbed his flask to drink again.

“Come,” Barnabas ordered, hearing Tasmin groan. “For the rest of the journey, we will not bicker. Understand?”

The companions nodded, before following Barnabas across the meadow and through the strengthening storm. They followed the men and women ahead, quickly being able to sight them in the distance once again, hearing the screams of the young girl. From a distance, they observed the men and women, hearing their yells being carried by the wind and above the thunder.

Beside Barnabas, as he led the way, Free was at his side. Free listened to Barnabas, as the companions followed and as Tasmin and Sir Terrence bickered constantly, even as Wylie insisted they stop.

Barnabas addressed Free in a hushed voice. “Tell me what thee suspects is going to happen to the girl.”

In a quiet voice, which was barely heard, Free stated what he thought. Free was not heard by his other companions. “Honestly, I believe the girl will not return to a loving family. She will be abused.”

“I agree.” Barnabas nodded. “Now, tell me a successful plan to save her.”

“Follow the girl to Brill. We will wait till the night and we shall attack the men and women, which have taken her. I do not believe they will return the girl till the next day, wanting to bargain for more money than they deserve,” Free whispered. “Thou art our leader. Thou shalt be the one to finalise the plan.”

“Yes. However, I desire the advice of my companions.”

"He does not need the advice from his companions. For we shall follow him till the end, no matter the duration or the destination," Free remarked. "We have known one another for years and those we have recently met have little and no home to return to."

Barnabas sighed. His head bowed and he looked down at his horse. "Is the only reason why I am followed due to my companions being homeless? Do my companions not follow me for my leadership?"

Only Free listened to his lowered and trembling voice. Free politely explained what he thought. "Forgive me, Barnabas, but thou hast thought a twisted opinion from thy words! Here is the truth. The companions follow thee not for thy leadership and not for being homeless. Instead, we follow thee to become our home."

Instantly, Barnabas raised his head and stared at Free with gleaming eyes. A rare, small smile appeared. "Thou must stop being so kind to me. Otherwise, I shall blush and I shall not be scary to many."

Free tittered. "Even when thou smile, thou art still frightening!"

Taking pride, for being terrifying, Barnabas trotted ahead, as his companions followed, quickening their pace. Barnabas concealed his smile, hiding his happiness from Free's warming compliment behind a stern pout. He led his companions through many meadows, still stalking the group ahead and eventually arriving at Brill in the early hours of morning.

Brill was a relatively small settlement. The settlement was neither poor, nor rich. It was somewhere in the middle. House sizes varied, as the rate of money did. There were those who had no house and slept in the streets, outside in the doorways of the closed shops. Few clues were seen on the villager's clothing about their wealth, as clothes were unimportant, with the size of the house establishing wealth and status. Mostly, the village was clean, but drugs and crime swarmed through Brill, as bodies appeared almost every day and as traces of drugs appeared on the side of the streets.

Having very little, the companions were safe, as they entered through the tall gates and followed the group ahead through the streets.

The muddy streets of Brill bustled with people, music and voices that migrated across the settlement to create muffled and ear-ringing noises. Throughout the village, the companions travelled unnoticed, dismounting from their horses and shoving their way through the enormous crowds and nearly losing sight of the girl they wanted to save. The companions followed the girl, whose screams had been silenced from the material which covered her mouth, towards a small house located at the back of the village and next to the inn.

The men and women scurried into a dark house, where the shutters were locked against the windows and many locks were on the front door. The slabbed roof was drained from any colour, as the wood from the house was stained black with mould. The tall chimney smoked, as the wide house remained silent against the chaos outside. The young girl was dragged through the doorway, as no light radiated from the inside and the front door slammed shut, locking again.

From afar, the companions observed. They watched from a nearby corner, as crowds continued to form along the streets, creating continuous noise. The companions stood silently, together. Through very few words, the companions created and finalised their plan to save the young girl.

After the door of the house had been shut, the companions headed to the large inn, which sat beside the house the young girl had been taken into. The front door of the inn immediately led the companions to the tavern, which was humid and filled with a sickening aroma. Intoxicated men and women stumbled across the room, spilling their drinks, as their voices shrilled. There was music from a band in the corner, which slurred every lyric, as they were also drunk.

The companions placed their horses in the warmth of the stables outside and adjacent to the inn before entering. In the doorway, the companions stopped to observe.

Inside the inn's tavern, the companions stood amongst swaying and clumsy men and women. Their ears were pained by the yells that screeched across tables and their feet stuck to the sticky floor. The companions' noses crinkled, as the pungent smell reached their nostrils and churned their stomachs. The music which flooded the tavern was most irksome to the companions, except for Tasmin and Sir Terrence, who staggered to the bar and ordered rounds of drinks.

Leaving Barnabas to stand alone, Wylie and Free headed to the table in the corner and rested their tired feet, propping their legs onto spare chairs and leaning back, as their eyes closed.

For Wylie and Free had not intended to leave Barnabas alone, but they had. Barnabas still pondered, still examining his surroundings, only relaxing once they were safe. Surrounding men and women eyed his still stance, looking over the rim of their drinks, watching till he moved.

Eventually, Barnabas stepped forwards, pacing towards the table where Free and Wylie sat and scanning the entire width of the bar. Yet, he did not walk for long. A strong and sweet aroma swept over the alcohol, starving his empty stomach and creating a fuzzy warmth which reminded him of his childhood, sniffing strong, indulgent nutmeg.

Twisting on his heel, Barnabas followed the aroma, which carried him through the tavern, arriving at a door towards the very back. The door was closed, but Barnabas could still smell the nutmeg seeping underneath the door and pushed the door open to reveal a darkly lit kitchen.

The dark kitchen, was small and lit by a single lantern hanging from the ceiling. There was a long and wide table in the centre, as narrow surfaces were pushed against the walls with cupboards above. A large hearth was at the far side of the room, where a wide, circular pot hung over the flames.

Quietly, a man scattered through the kitchen, preparing ingredients for delicious meals, a man with a large stomach and a belt holding his trousers, which were tucked into his boots. He sweated from the heat of the room, noticing Barnabas at the door, after he had been watching for a while.

The man called to Barnabas. "This is not the place to piss! Go outside!"

"I am not here to piss."

"Then, leave. I am cooking."

"I smell nutmeg!"

"Yes. I have baked a sticky nutmeg cake."

"I want a slice."

The man chuckled, still holding his knife, which he had been using to chop vegetables. "Thou want a slice? Well, thou shall have to wait, just like everyone else."

"I want a slice, now!"

Finally, the man focused on Barnabas. Previously, the man had only seen him from the side of his eyes. Now, he saw Barnabas, dropping his knife and trembling with fear. The man had heard the description of the infamous Barnabas Mint, being tall with dark hair, peached skin and the most intoxicating pair of green eyes. The man dropped to his knees and bowed his head before Barnabas, apologising.

"Barnabas Mint. Sir, I am sorry. May thou have all the nutmeg cake thou desire." The man grovelled. "There are a few minutes before I can remove the cake from the fire."

"Fine. I shall wait. When the cake has cooled, please bring it over to me. I shall be waiting in the far corner," Barnabas stated, stepping backwards and closing the door, before heading to the table in the corner where Free and Wylie dozed.

Barnabas relaxed at the table, resting his arms on the table and facing the tavern, watching everyone, even as Tasmin and Sir Terrence returned, carrying drinks in their hands. Tasmin and Sir Terrence carried more drinks than necessary, placing them on the table and joining Barnabas to relax.

Tasmin slid a drink towards him, gesturing him to drink with a small nod. "Barnabas. Relax, for a while."

Barnabas took a single sip from his cup, soothing his sore throat and watching the tavern again. As Barnabas refused to drink any more, other than water, Tasmin and Sir Terrence started to drink, becoming rowdy and drunk, waking Wylie and Free from their sleep. They began to drink slowly.

Moments later, as Tasmin and Sir Terrence argued, Barnabas spotted the man from the kitchen. He paced through the tavern holding the entire nutmeg cake in his hands and avoided the surrounding people, as he searched for Barnabas. The man from the kitchen spotted Barnabas and quickly paced towards him.

The man laid the cake gently before Barnabas and announced, "Sir Barnabas Mint, please enjoy. Share amongst friends."

Barnabas looked up and glared. "I shall not be sharing."

"Ye dastard! Thou cannot have the cake all to thyself!" The man snapped, before clutching his mouth and fearing what Barnabas would do, as Barnabas frowned. "Please. Please, forgive. I did not mean to be rude. I am sorry. Do not kill me!"

After a while, Barnabas chuckled. "I will not kill thee. Thou maketh delicious cakes."

"Thank ye." He bowed. "I do not earn much for baking or cooking."

Taking a piece of cake, tearing the piece with his hands and popping a small handful into his mouth, Barnabas' mouth watered. His eyes closed, as the sweet nutmeg reminded him of his younger years, when he was happier. Still chewing, he remarked, "I shall pay thee double from what thou earn here. If thou journey with us."

"Where dost thou head?"

"My companions and I journey to the North, searching for the heir of the South. We wish to restore the throne," Barnabas stated.

"Are the stories indeed true? Truly, is there an heir? Can the South be restored?" He sighed. "I was only a young man when King Moryn and Queen Gwendolen reigned. Oh, how those twenty and six years have passed."

"The stories are true!" Sir Terrence declared. "I am a fellow knight of the South and saw the heir escape."

Barnabas smirked and looked back at the man frowning at Sir Terrence. "Join us."

"Double, ye says?" He deliberated. "Then, yes."

"Good." Barnabas insisted, as he handed over a pouch of money. "Tell me thy name."

"Darrel Ormond. Who are the rest of ye?"

"Brother Wylie. Free Stellam. Sir Terrence Prisca. Tasmin Berry." Barnabas introduced, as they waved as their names were mentioned.

"Welcome to the companionship!" Tasmin slurred, raising her mug above her head, spilling her drink over her legs, before slamming the mug down on the table and spilling her drink further.

Darrel grabbed a chair and sat between Barnabas and Tasmin. He saw Barnabas was troubled by a man that he had watched entering the tavern. Darrel explained, "Ye should not stare at him. Or anyone he is with. Him and the others are wicked. An incestuous family, snatching girls to sell them on, for all purposes."

"I am going to kill them all."

"Did they take someone close to ye, Barnabas?"

"No. They have taken no one from me!"

Tasmin sneered. "A girl, much younger than I, was captured by them. We are going to save her."

"Ah! Ye speak about young Helen. She belonged to a wealthy family, but they were not loving. They hurt her. Her parents are willing to pay diamonds," Darrel mentioned. "Do not save her. I enjoy my life and wish not to be chased."

"Do not cower, Darrel!" Tasmin hissed. "The companionship will not be chased. For we shall kill them. A slice of the throat. A twist of the neck! I cannot wait. They deserve what will come. I have not been this excited in a while. Well, since my last kill, which was only a few weeks ago now that I brood. Again, why did I kill him? Ah, yes! He was —"

"Thou hath a deluded mind!" Darrel commented.

"Thou cannot leave the companionship, now!" Tasmin giggled, gulping more alcohol, which made her sleepy.

Barnabas addressed Darrel and added, before Darrel returned to cooking in the kitchen, "Once the tavern has closed, meet us by the barn. Be swift. Bring a weapon. We aim to kill tonight."

Darrel nodded with a prolonged huff. He returned to the kitchen to cook and bake until the tavern closed, meeting the companions inside the barn.

4

Gathered in the barn of the tavern, the companions stood. Swiftly, they had left the tavern as soon as it had closed and headed to the barn, greeting their horses which they prepared to ride, as they waited for Darrel. The companions waited in the entrance, looking onto the silent and dark tavern, as well as the house it sat beside, where Helen was kept.

From the tavern door, Darrel emerged with more belongings than the companions had collectively, entering the barn to greet the companions. On his belt, there was a sword and an axe, which had not been there previously. He passed the companions and loaded his belongings onto his horse, before enduring a further conversation with the companions.

Tasmin quizzed Darrel, after he had loaded the bags onto his horse and approached them again. "Why doth thou have so many belongings? Thou should not have so many. Besides, I shall not carry them for thee. I have enough already. Though, being only a small bag that I carry."

"I do not need thee to carry my belongings."

"Why doth thou need so many?"

"If I am to create splendid food, then I shall need my utensils, my ingredients and spices. Dost thou wish to eat well?" he questioned.

Tasmin nodded with a grin.

"Now, what is the plan?" Darrel asked Barnabas, scowling.

"There is little planning. It shall be spontaneous," Barnabas remarked. "The only information which has not been gathered is how well thou can use thy chosen weapons."

"I have used a sword and an axe since I was a boy. I shall be fine!" Darrel spat.

"Good! Thou can enter through the front door with Tasmin. Wylie and Free shall climb the roof. I shall be with Sir Terrence and we shall enter through the back door of the house," Barnabas explained with a small gleam.

Tasmin cheered. "Let us leave!"

Tasmin pushed through the companions and left the barn, storming silently between the falling water, underneath the moonlight. Already, her sword was drawn and a glow appeared in her brown eyes, as she eyed the house ahead. She stopped just after the tavern, before turning to gesture the companions to hurry with a grin.

Barnabas smirked, following her. He drew his sword and waited beside her. Shortly, the companions followed, with Darrel being hesitantly last.

Darrel muttered to his companions, before they parted to position themselves around the house. "This is barbaric. We are all going to die!"

Tasmin groaned, tugging Darrel to the front door, as the companions ignored him to begin their plan. She hissed. "Negativity will not help us. Please, be quiet until relevant thoughts come to mind!"

Darrel fell silent, as Tasmin continued to haul him until they came to the front door of the house. Tasmin insisted for Darrel to draw his axe, as the companions readied their weapons to forcefully enter. The small footsteps of Free and Wylie tiptoeing across the slabs of the roof, which were weak, informed the companions they were ready.

Loudly, Barnabas whistled.

Crashing through the roof and smashing through the doors, the companions arrived in the same, dark room, rampaging inside with their weapons, only to find each other. The rectangular room was small and empty, smelling foul, with a small fireplace located beside the rear door. Other doors, leading to other rooms, were shut, but the companions could hear movement and circled to view every inch of the room, gripping their weapons tight.

In minutes, the doors around the companions, swung open. Men and women stormed into the room, wielding their weapons and instantly recognising the companions. Without hesitating, the men and women viciously attacked the companions, jabbing their blades at the flesh of the companions and roaring loudly.

The companions charged forwards to fight their oncoming opponents. They sliced their weapons to cut through the air, before smashing their opponents' blades. The companions screamed just as loud, wrestling to scout through the house and to find Helen.

As the companions fought, Tasmin throttled her opponent unconscious. Tasmin's sword had been kicked from her hand. She heard the metal of her blade clang against the wooden floorboards, after her handle had slipped through her fingers. Her opponent's sword flew towards her, swooping towards her neck.

Tasmin's eyes widened as she watched the blade swing towards her. Her heart thumped against her chest, tugging her to move. Tasmin ducked underneath the sword that continued to sweep the air and lunged forwards, rising inches from her opponent and glaring with her calm, chilling eyes. Tasmin threw her fist forwards, her knuckles slamming into her opponent's neck and watching her opponent tumble to the ground. Tasmin stood above, smiling, as her opponent struggled to breathe. Yet, Tasmin's smile only grew larger, as her foot slammed against her opponent's head, stopping their thoughts.

Slowly, Tasmin stepped away, eyeing her lifeless opponent and still smiling. She twisted to explore the house, as her companions continued to fight, searching for Helen. Though the house was silent, the roars and thuds clouded the quiet, even as she distanced to furthest corners. Frantically, Tasmin raided, praying her companions would fight until she rescued Helen.

Suddenly, as Tasmin scattered through the house, she heard faint muffling screams. At first, the screams seemed to echo from every room, twisting Tasmin through the house, until she was forced to stop as the rooms began to spin.

Listening to the screams, she slowly followed, closing her eyes that still saw spinning rooms. Tasmin paced into a room she had already scouted, seeing the beds she had flipped against the walls, which now rocked on their sides. Her eyes opened, scouring for what she had missed.

There, in the dark, in the corner of the room, was a hatch. Perfectly, the hatch camouflaged with the same wooden floorboards of the room with a faint and thin outline. The screams she heard were almost deafening as she fixated on the hatch and ran towards it.

Sliding onto her knees, she stopped before the hatch and lifted the lid, leaning the hatch door against the wall behind. Tasmin glared into a bleak pit, seeing white ovals gleaming back at her, still howling through the material that covered their mouths.

The young girls, trapped in the pit, wiggled, as their hands were tied behind their backs, calling for Tasmin to help. Tasmin reached for the closest girl, hauling her by her armpits and cutting the rope, which had burned her skin. She lifted eight girls from the pit, with the last being Helen.

Tasmin reached for Helen, watching tears fall down Helen's cheeks. She lifted Helen and placed Helen beside her, cutting the rope from her aching hands and untying the material from around her mouth. Tasmin held Helen in her arms, as Helen threw her body into Tasmin's chest, thanking her.

Tasmin lifted Helen as she ordered the other weeping girls towards the window. With her hands, Tasmin tore the shutters from their hinges, stumbling back as the wood fell at her feet. The natural darkness of the light entered, lightening the room, as Tasmin opened the windows and instructed the girls to climb through.

The girls followed Tasmin's orders, throwing their bodies through the window and running into the night, disappearing through the village. Tasmin watched the girls vanished, eyeing Helen, as she began to slowly climb onto the window ledge.

Helen climbed to sit, turning to look over her shoulder and glaring at Tasmin with her silver eyes. She smiled, briefly through her tears. "Did thou come for me? Did thou come to rescue me after sighting my pain?"

Tasmin nodded.

"Thank you." Helen breathed, turning to glare at the village ahead, which still stood in absolute silence.

Tasmin stepped closer, looking at the village with her, seeing the same darkness and emptiness that Helen sighted too. Tasmin asked, "Dost thou wish to venture with us? Does thee wish to join the companionship?"

Without hesitation, Helen nodded. "Yes. Please, take me from here. Wherever, the companionship goes, I shall follow."

Tasmin snatched Helen's hand and hauled her from the ledge, pulling Helen through the house, returning to the companions, as the house fell silent. Helen stayed hiding behind Tasmin, as Tasmin staggered slowly with her sword, through the darkly lit house. Tasmin was ready to swing an oncoming opponent, but hearing her name being called through the darkness, her weapon lowered, hearing Sir Terrence's voice bellow.

Tasmin and Helen entered the room where the companions had fought, sighting the companions standing over bodies and blood that scattered and stained the floor. Minding the flowing crimson liquid, the companions met in the centre of the room.

Tasmin declared, sternly, to her companions, "This is Helen!"

"Helen Hobart." Helen smiled to the companions before her.

"Welcome," Wylie insisted, taking a small bow, which made her blush as the companions copied him.

Quickly, Barnabas moved from his companions to stand in the doorway, barely welcoming Helen. Barnabas glared into the empty streets of Brill, which would swarm with people. He gestured his companions to follow, as he stepped outside, wanting to leave Brill rapidly, before being convicted of murder.

The companions waited no further, rushing to the tavern barn, squelching through the mud and leading their horses into the night. Through the settlement, Darrel overtook Barnabas and led the companions towards the gate, as villagers flocked from the homes and piled into the streets, after hearing the raucous noise of the fight. The villagers began to flood to the house beside the tavern, where the front door was left open and the village sighted the bodies in the moonlight.

Darrel led the companions through hidden passages. He heard the voices of the villagers and the silence of the companions that trusted him to successfully escape from Brill, arriving at the gates.

Grinding to a halt, the companions stopped just after the passage they had galloped through. The companions viewed the gates, from the corner of the alley, which were heavily guarded and were kept shut after the news of murder had spread through the village. The guards did not sight the companions yet, but if they continued to wait, they would surely be noticed.

Barnabas insisted to his companions, jumping down from his horse with a thud, "Dismount! Dismount from the horses and release them."

"Why, brother?" Wylie questioned, as he threw himself from his horse, as did the other companions.

“We need to be on foot,” Free remarked quietly in his soft voice, standing beside Barnabas.

“Why?” Wylie asked, before releasing his horse like his other companions already had.

“Brother, Wylie! Do as I order!”

Wylie refused to release his horse, awaiting an explanation. Barnabas continued to stand silently, as his eyes examined the gate. Free had said too much, whilst Sir Terrence was still too drunk to think.

Darrel stated, “It is the only way to escape. We will not escape with the horses.”

“Why not?”

As Darrel and Wylie bickered, the lead slipped from Wylie’s hand. The horse remained still, until Tasmin dismissed the horse, which began to sprint through the alley, following the other horses.

Wylie twisted to see his horse sprinting, but he did not stare long. He spun and snapped, “How dare thee, Tasmin!”

Tasmin’s eyes rolled, already having a plan to escape. After sighting a tall ladder, a few feet from the gate, she knew climbing over the wall was the only way for them to escape. She did not want to hear Wylie questioning any further, leaving her companions as she silently staggered to the ladder, with Helen ghostly pacing beside her.

Without the guards sighting them and as their companions watched onwards, Tasmin and Helen arrived at the bottom of the ladder. Insisting Helen climbed first, Tasmin waited, watching Helen climb fast and quiet till she arrived safely to sit on top of the stone wall, waiting. Helen watched as Tasmin climbed shortly after, also arriving at the top and gesturing their companions to follow.

Hurrying to the ladder first was Darrel. He charged forwards, noticing more guards arriving at the gate and hearing the commotion of the villagers rising as they came closer. Being incredibly light on his feet and observing the guards, he came to the bottom of the ladder and watched the guards, whilst impatiently insisting his companions followed.

Sir Terrence, Free and Barnabas stormed ahead, as Barnabas dragged Wylie behind him. Quietly, Sir Terrence and Free came to the ladder and rapidly climbed to join their companions on the ledge of the wall, as Barnabas and Wylie lingered.

Barnabas and Wylie bickered below, as Barnabas continued to haul Wylie through the mud, creating footsteps much louder than the other companions'. Wylie fought against his brother, as his voice started being dangerously loud, pulling the attention of the guards away from the village commotion.

From the corner and from the gate, the guards scurried. They heard Barnabas and Wylie fighting, as their voices shrilled, turning the corner to observe the squabbling brothers. Instantly, the guards recognised the infamous Mint brothers and without hesitation, the brothers were convicted of murder.

Immediately, Barnabas and Wylie stopped arguing and twisted to glare, as the guards sprinted towards them with their swords raised. Barnabas tightened his grip around his brother's clothes and dragged him to the ladder, as the guards chased them. Wylie did not fight his brother, glaring at the men that sprinted towards them.

The guards called their names through the dead of night, as Barnabas shoved his brother further on the ladder, scrambling after him. Quickly, Barnabas and Wylie sprinted onto the wall, wobbling the ladder, as the guards climbed closely behind. Barnabas and Wylie threw themselves onto their companions, kicking away the ladder from underneath their feet, which tumbled with some guards falling too. Their legs dangled as their companions heaved them onto the wall.

As soon as Barnabas and Wylie toppled onto the companions, Tasmin directed the companions to jump. Tasmin swept Helen into her arms, before glaring over the side of the wall, already feeling the pain of her injury, but being her only way to escape. With a small shuffle to the edge, Tasmin dropped to the ground, stumbling to her land on her feet with small screams, as Helen fell from her arms and rolled onto the grass.

Almost instantly, Darrel leapt from the wall, pouncing from his feet. Landing beside them, with a small groan as his feet thumped against the earth, Darrel rosed rapidly from his crouched position and turned to watch his fellow companions fall also.

Sir Terrence grabbed free, as they remained sitting, sliding to the edge and falling with their eyes shut. Free and Sir Terrence screamed as they descended, landing on their stomachs, roaring loudly, as Darrel, Tasmin and Helen rushed to their aid, moving them, as Barnabas and Wylie fell after.

The companions heard the gates opening and the roars of the guards charging from Brill and storming around the bend of the wall. The companions urged Barnabas and Wylie to jump.

Barnabas and Wylie separated to jump, as Barnabas' grip loosened and as Wylie shifted. With a little sprint, Wylie and Barnabas jumped simultaneously from the wall and down to their companions. Tumbling through the air, Barnabas and Wylie crashed before the feet of their companions. They stumbled, but their companions heaved them to their feet.

The companions paced into the long strands of meadow, racing away from the guards, which filed from the gates of Brill. Together, the companions sprinted into the night, losing the guards which chased them and fell silent.

After a while, the companions stopped running. Collectively, the companions ground to a halt, gasping for air and collapsing to the floor with sweat soaking into their clothes. They lay on their backs staring at the full moon and eventually falling asleep, waking with dawn.

5

Waking at dawn, the sun gleamed on the faces of the sleeping companions. A small breeze crossed the land, as fresh frost stuck on the yellow strands and on the leaves of the trees in the distance. The companions rested underneath a clear, blue sky, as the land was bare, golden and chilly.

Consecutively, the companions awakened, but the first, was Darrel. Awakening with fright, Darrel screeched, waking often from night terrors. His screech awakened his other companions, who were spread a few feet from him. Through the strands of yellow meadow, Darrel spotted his companions, as his screams faded and as sweat rolled down his face. Sighting his waking companions, Darrel eased, deeply inhaling and falling to lay on his back, watching the blue sky and the soft clouds which floated.

Immediately after the companions had awakened, they rosed to stand and gathered closer to Darrel, almost stooping above him. Standing quietly, the companion waited for Darrel to stand also, as Barnabas impatiently waited a few feet behind his companions with his arms crossed. Tasmin embraced Helen at her side, as Wylie and Free stood together and as Sir Terrence drank from his flask.

Darrel exasperated. “How can thou sleep so peacefully? Thy mind is so vivid, I cannot sleep.”

Stretching out his hand, Wylie reached for Darrel, grabbing his hand and hauling him to stand. Wylie grunted, as Darrel faintly smiled. “Imagination cannot be tamed, even when there are bad dreams.”

As Wylie lifted Darrel, Barnabas stormed towards his companions and ordered before Darrel had stood. “Let us leave. The companionship must arrive North, hastily!”

“Brother, lead us then!”

Barnabas paced through the meadow, heading to the North and storming ahead of his companions. He led his companions by foot, stumbling in the golden light, where his eyes became a bright and envious green, dazzling against his olive skin. Barnabas moved with his cloak flowing behind, as his hand rested on his blade.

Close behind, Wylie followed. Wylie mimicked his brother's proud and long stride, sometimes tripping over the uneven terrain. His hands swung beside his body, bathing in the sunlight as his deep brown eyes and gleaming gold skin sparkled. Wylie's footsteps were heavy, trampling strands under his feet, creating a trail of crushed meadow.

Following, passing Wylie to pace beside Barnabas, Free strolled lightly. Free was silent, staying very close to Barnabas, almost touching his shoulders. He travelled in Barnabas' shadow, dimming his white hair and diminishing his bright eyes. For the entire journey North, he did not speak, even when he was addressed.

In pairs, Darrel and Sir Terrence travelled, with Helen and Tasmin pacing behind, constantly talking. There was laughter echoing through the gales of wind, as their cackles grew louder. Sir Terrence shared his flask, easing his companions, who began to wobble and hiccup.

By the time midday arrived, Darrel, Sir Terrence, Tasmin and Helen slurred their words and their eyes were ready to close, as their heads rolled. Their voices were extremely loud, shouting endless nonsense, which Free, Barnabas and Wylie ignored. Their footsteps thumped against the ground, almost falling over their feet, continuing to follow their focused companions.

When nightfall came, the companions stopped to rest underneath the moonlight, still within the meadow, but sighting hills in the distance. The night was frigid, as crickets rattled and the winds vanished. Amongst the black sky, there were glistening dots of light, sparkling with blue and white hues, which were not overpowered by the moon. There were billions of lights, which bewitched the companions to glare.

Before nightfall, as the companions travelled, Helen had drunk herself to sleep. Helen stumbled across the meadow, as they arrived at their resting place, watching the sun resting at the horizon with pink and orange ombre streaking the sky. Seeing the brightest star glowing before her relieved her and her vision blackened. Falling away from Tasmin's side, Helen hit the ground without a squeak.

As soon as Helen had fallen, balancing as she crouched and trying not to fall, too, Tasmin placed Helen in her arms and against her shoulder, carrying her lightly till they stopped.

Once the companions stopped, Tasmin knelt to place Helen on her back to sleep for the rest of the night. Tasmin rested at Helen's side, holding her tight and wrapping her cloak over them, keeping each other warm. Her eyes did not look at the stars, instead she sealed her eyelids to dream.

Beside them, Sir Terrence toppled to sit, swigging his flask and drinking the last remaining mouthfuls of his alcohol. Sir Terrence swallowed the last drop, before plummeting to lay on his back, clutching his flask to his chest and closing his eyes. He drifted deeply into his sleep, already beginning to snore.

Quietly, Free and Wylie laid next to each other and beside Sir Terrence's feet. Both rested on their sides, facing away from each other, but both staring into the glittering night sky above, letting small smiles seep across their lips. Into the late hours of the night, Wylie and Free stayed awake, until their eyes shut, falling too heavy to stay open.

As the companions slept, Barnabas remained awake with Darrel laying at his feet. Barnabas gazed at the starry night, losing all thought and ignoring the restless sounds of his companions. Deeply, Barnabas breathed white swirls from his lips, as he smoked his pipe of weed, letting any pain escape. Though focused on watching the stars and smoking his pipe, he could not ignore Darrel's whispering voice speaking to him.

"Barnabas, dost thee not ever sleep?"

"No." He chortled, quietly.

"Why dost thee not sleep?"

"I do not wish to see what my mind imagines, when I have already witnessed true horror!" Barnabas sighed. "For it is best for me to be awake, when so many chase me."

"I would not like to be chased. A simple life I have lived. Travelled far, but never with intention to cause chaos," Darrel explained. "Always, to bring comfort with my food!"

"Such a life seems absurd to me! It would not be a life I would want." Barnabas chuckled. "To lead a simple life would be most tedious."

Rising to view Barnabas, eyeing him with a scowl, Darrel growled. "My simple life has been far from tedious! An honest life I have led. It has been wonderful. A lovely wife I had and a child I adored. Though taken from me, I would not have changed. Though little friends I have had, the ones I have met have been most caring and loving. Before thou judge my life for not being extraordinary, I suggest thee thinks again!"

Barnabas pulled his pipe away from his lips, wanting to speak, as Darrel's eyes bore. Before Barnabas pronounced a word, Darrel dropped to lay on his side and rolled away from his new companions. Not knowing whether Barnabas was about to apologise or insult him further, Darrel's eyes closed tightly.

Once Darrel had returned to his slumber, Barnabas gripped the wood lightly with his teeth. His eyes sparkled green in starlight, as his eyes flicked into the night sky, again. For most of the night, he thought on Darrel's words, trying to picture his life without chaos. As much as he imagined, Barnabas did not find peace.

Arriving shortly was the morning. The companions did not wake early, sleeping further into the day. Their aching bodies forced them to retire longer than anticipated, remaining still in the silence of the morning and soaking the early sunlight. Even Barnabas had fallen asleep, with his pipe still resting against his mouth.

Suddenly, the sunlight darkened. The companions could still feel the sun's warmth against their skin, but a dark shadow cast over them as they slept. The sudden bleakness was enough to disturb the companions and wake them from their slumbers.

Standing above the companions, in direct sunlight, there were two women. The women were flustered, panting and sweating, as their hands rested on their hips, where their axes were kept on their belts. The women were much older than the companions, with aged skin and wrinkles, as all the strands of their hair had transformed grey.

The taller woman stepped forward, hesitantly addressing the companions and insisting they should begin moving. "A force comes from the South. They persist by horse and shall kill us all if we are not hidden."

The companions stood, but they did not move, continuing to gape at the two strangers before them.

Darrel, whose frightening dream ended before he could scream, asked the strangers what they had seen. "What is so terrifying that has caused thee to run?"

The second woman, who was incredibly short, declared, "The Necromancer's men travel North, searching for the heir to the South. Seemingly, the rumours are true and the truth spreads quick!"

The companions' eyes quickly glanced at Sir Terrence, whose constant drunken blabber of the heir, had surely been the reason for the Necromancer knowing. The companions looked back to face the two women, scowling.

Barnabas demanded, "Show us!"

"Why would thee want to be so risky?" the first woman questioned, before answering her own question. "Ah! Thou art the companionship which searches for the heir. Thy names spread fast amongst the land, companions. The Necromancer shall surely follow thee."

"Show us!" Barnabas repeated.

The two women nodded, deciding to hide amongst the trees ahead, leading the companions hastily. Amongst the bushes and trees, they were able to examine the entire meadow, sighting everything through the small gaps of the leaves and between the trees. The companions and the two strangers waited in silence.

In the distance, riding through the meadows on horses, were a group of black-cloaked riders, racing to the North. The hooves of the horses pounded on the ground, as they galloped, kicking mud behind and trampling the meadow strands. The riders were ordinary men, layered with armour and equipped with many weapons. The riders could not see the watching companions, viciously whipping their horses to quicken with small shrieks.

The two strangers faced the companions, eyeing them, as the companions watched the riders race into the distance ahead. The two women waited for the companions to speak.

Barnabas turned first and hissed. "This proves nothing."

The short woman spat. "Thou art an idiot!"

Sir Terrence howled, as he knelt behind Barnabas and faced the two women, spitting, as he said every word. "Does thou not know whom thou speak to? This man is the infamous Barnabas Mint. Dost thou wish to die?"

The women exchanged looks, searching for an answer from the other. They scowled.

"Dost thou not know him?"

The two women shook their heads.

"How does one not know?" Tasmin exclaimed. "It seems thou art too old to know the young. Art thou ignorant, also? He will kill thee. Well, he would have done so, if thou did not have such valuable knowledge, helping us on our journey. Ah! Would thou wish to join our companionship? It is most likely thou will die. More so than before, as the Necromancer also searches for the heir!"

The companions twisted to glare at Tasmin, who immediately apologised, persistently. Tasmin did not cease till Helen muffled her voice by covering Tasmin's mouth with her hand. The companions turned back.

"Truly, we do not know who thou art," the first woman admitted. "Truly, we are sorry. Where has one resided, so we may ignite our memories?"

"As a boy, I lived in the Southern kingdom, Cahercasey. Since, I have never resided anywhere long, travelling alongside my brothers." Barnabas answered. "I wish to return home, to the South and restore the throne."

The two women still did not know Barnabas, but were delighted by the passion of his stare, which intrigued them. Introducing themselves to the companions, as Orla Dyel and Ainsley Rodia, they asked to join the companionship.

"Why?" Wylie quizzed.

"The South was once our home too, a very long time ago," Orla stated, as she rose to stand with Ainsley. "We wish to have a home, again."

The companions welcomed Ainsley and Orla, beginning their journey North. Barnabas strode ahead with Free and Wylie behind, as the other companions collectively walked in a group, bursting with excitement and laughter.

6

At last, the companions arrived at the furthest settlement to the North built only a few miles from the kingdom of Hanuli. Violl. A tiny village with no walls or gates and no guards, allowing the companions to enter freely. The village houses were small, with straw covering the roofs and chimneys smoking from the enormous hearth inside. There were crops, stretching for miles, around the village, which were being harvested.

The companions entered the village as Sir Terrence led, taking them to Ezra's home, who had taken the heir with him. Sir Terrence had been to Ezra's home, once before, not realising that one of the two children he lived with was indeed the heir to the forgotten kingdom of the South.

As the companions passed, they received stern glares from the surrounding villagers, who stopped to observe. The companions' eyes lowered and their heads bowed, striding closer together and quickening their pace to arrive at Ezra's home.

Somewhere, in the middle of Violl, there was Ezra's home. A small home, with a closed front door and opened shutters, as a chimney smoked in the early frosty morning. The rest of the village was mostly quiet, with few chirps from passers-by, whilst Ezra's home blasted with chatter and chortles. As the companions approached the door, they smelt sweet and musky herbal scents originating from inside, hearing tea being slurped through the thin wood.

Sir Terrence stopped just before the door, raising his fist and knocking, loudly. The laughter and voices died, as there was sudden pause, before the companions heard movement shuffling towards the door.

The door swung open, rapidly, revealing a man. The blue-eyed old man, dressed in long robes and leaning on his tall staff, eyed the companions. He used his entire body to block the entrance of his home, questioning the companions with a low and bellowing voice. "Who art thou? Why dost thou stand before me? What thou want will not be granted by me."

"Ezra! It is I, Sir Terrence. Dost thou not remember a familiar face?" For a second, Ezra saw Sir Terrence as no more than a stranger, but looking past the wrinkles and aged skin, he saw his old friend and smiled. "My friend! Forgive me, it has been many years since I saw thee last. Yet I welcome thee warmly."

"Do not be so willing. For, thou dost not know why my companions and I venture here."

"I am not a fool. Already, I know what thou seek. Rumours travel as fast as the wind, echoing across land and sea. What thou seek is the heir. The heir of the South, is what thee seeks. Is it not so?" Ezra raised his eyebrow and waited a reply.

"Yes, it is so," Barnabas declared, stepping forwards and addressing Ezra. "Thou know where the heir hides and we wish to seek!"

As Barnabas' voice rose from the darkness behind Ezra, a young woman appeared. The young woman eyed his companions with her amber eyes, raising her crossbow just below her chin and balancing the end of her bow on Ezra's shoulder, aiming for Barnabas.

Barnabas met the glare of the woman standing behind Ezra and smirked, as the swords of his companions were raised. He chortled. "Thou art not going to kill me."

Standing silently, the woman did not relax. She continued to point her bow at Barnabas, until Ezra told her to lower her weapon, as did the companions.

"Forgive my granddaughter. She has rather a temper and will kill thee. Be blessed, she has spared thee, for now," Ezra remarked, moving to one side with his granddaughter and gesturing the companions to enter.

Firstly, Barnabas entered. He passed the young woman with a smirk, which had only appeared after his back was to Ezra. Barnabas' eyes examined the woman, who was tall, with a muscular physique, as she stood wearing trousers. Her stern expression did not fade, pouting further. Barnabas felt her piercing eyes follow him through the house, even as the companions followed.

Ezra's home had one enormous living area, which the companions immediately entered. There was a large fireplace at the far side of the room, with comfy chairs before the cackling fire. A small kitchen was in the corner, with a long wooden bench. Dotted on the walls, there were many paintings and drawings, mostly of stunning landscapes, but with few being of two young girls, including Ezra's granddaughter. An iron chandelier hung at the centre with lit candles, which had been burning for hours.

The companions headed towards the long table, sitting comfortably, as they dropped their belongings and leant against each other, almost falling asleep. As the companions seated themselves, Ezra came to stand at the head of the table alongside his granddaughter, eyeing them.

Before an uncomfortable silence could occur, Tasmin questioned Ezra, sitting at the other end of the table and staring over at him. "Is thy granddaughter the heir? Is she the heir thou hast been hiding all these years? What is her name?"

"Stop, please," Ezra remarked. "My granddaughter Bidelia is not the heir to any throne. However, the heir does live here. Yet, I have many questions for thee. Firstly, what is thy plan?"

"Truthfully, we shall head to the South and fight," Darrel declared.

Ezra chuckled. "Fight? Thou wish to fight the Necromancer without an army? Art thou mad?"

Bidelia laughed, also. "There must be more to thy plan! Thou cannot enter the Southern kingdom without an army."

"A plan to make the heir publicly known is how we shall gain an army," Barnabas insisted. "Every kingdom wants the heir to return to the South and to revive Cahercasey again."

"Thou will need more help than thou have imagined," Bidelia added.

"Admittedly, we have witnessed the Necromancer's men already travelling North and searching villages to kill the heir!" Orla spat.

"It is important for the heir to be given refuge by the other kingdoms," Ainsley hissed.

Ezra and Bidelia turned to each other with wide eyes, concerned for the heir they had been hiding for so long. They stepped close together, whispering before the companions who were unable to hear their rapidly spoken words.

Darrel asked, purposefully interrupting Bidelia and Ezra, "So, where is the heir?"

For a moment, Bidelia and Ezra paused. They turned to glare at the companions, knowing where the heir was, but not wanting to cause any fear.

Wylie hissed. "Where is the heir?!"

"The heir has gone to the Northern kingdom, Hanuli. The heir will not be returning till two days' time," Ezra stated. "The heir sells in the market."

"We must head there, immediately," Barnabas growled, rising abruptly and causing the bench to move slightly. "The heir needs protection from the Necromancer's raid."

"The heir is in the safest place possible. King Harold of the North will not let those riders pass through the gates," Bidelia argued. "We will wait till her return. Dost thou understand?"

"I am Barnabas Mint. Do not belittle me."

"Already, I was aware who thou art. Yet, I do and say as I please, so listen well, Barnabas Mint," Bidelia snapped, raising an eyebrow as she passed, beginning to stride across the room and leave through a passage leading to her room, slamming the door shut.

Once she had left, Barnabas lowered to sit on the bench. Proudly, he eyed his companions and looked to Ezra, who focused on the ground, brooding.

"Ezra. We shall be staying here tonight. The companions and I shall sleep on the floor. Then, we shall leave tomorrow," Barnabas announced.

Ezra nodded, looking at Barnabas and then at the rest of the companions. He escaped his thoughts and insisted the companions to make themselves comfortable. Swiftly, Ezra left the room, beginning to ready some belongings for their journey tomorrow.

When Ezra left, the companions rose and dispersed across the living area. The companions headed to the fireplace and relaxed on the chairs and the floor before the flames. Orla and Ainsley stooped over their fellow companions standing beside them and warming their cold bodies, as Free and Barnabas continued to sit on the bench, quietly, as their companions chattered.

Free smiled. "At least, we have arrived, safely. We know where the heir is and we shall meet them tomorrow."

Though Free spoke about their journey, Barnabas' thoughts were elsewhere, asking unrelated questions. "Is it I, or was the girl very annoying?"

Free chuckled, but Barnabas continued to pout.

"How dare she speak to me like so." He huffed. "An incredibly young girl should not be so vicious to someone like me. I may just have to kill her!"

Free continued to grin as he observed his friend. He listened to Barnabas' complaints, watching his eyes beam with an unusual delight. Free and Barnabas relaxed, as the chatters of their companions around the fire started to fade and their eyes closed as night came.

8

The heavy rainfall ceased. A gigantic black cloud lingered in the sky, as the wind howled. The air, travelling across the land, was frigid and continued to drop. The ground was soaked with pools of mud sitting on the surface, squelching underneath Tatiana and Midnight's feet as they travelled home, after leaving the forest where they had taken refuge.

In the distance, Tatiana spotted Violl. The settlement was noticed easily amongst the many smiles of fields ahead, as smoke rose above the houses and into the dark cloud. There were few houses, but Tatiana sighted many people, with some tending to the fields. Tatiana walked beside the crops, as she smelt small amounts of burning wood and the smell of warm, fresh bread, which was sweet.

She headed into the settlement with Midnight at her side, as her stomach twisted with excitement, ready to inform Ezra of Prince Hunter's generosity. Her pace quickened, tugging slightly harder on Midnight's reins.

Tatiana arrived at her small, cosy home, leading Midnight to the stable at the side of the house first. She tended to Midnight, giving him water and food ensuring he was warm, also. As soon as Midnight rested, she left after placing a blanket over his cool body.

She raced from Midnight's stable and towards the front door, flinging herself inside and stumbling into the living room, leaving the door open.

After entering the living room, inspecting the familiar objects of her home, she instantly halted. Inside, she did not see familiar faces, lounging on chairs and around the table in the centre of the room. She sighted strangers, instead. She drew her dagger, examining the men and women who slept, screaming into the silence of her home. "Who are ye?"

Abruptly, the companions woke. They jumped to their feet and drew their weapons, positioning to fight. The companions waited for Barnabas' command, as they eyed the girl with flowing white hair.

Barnabas stepped closer with his sword, sweeping his blade through the air and disarming Tatiana. His blade tapped the handle of her dagger, which was enough to knock her weapon from her loose grip. Barnabas raised his blade to her neck, eyeing her and waiting for her to grovel.

Though Tatiana's dagger had fallen with a clang, she stood fiercely before Barnabas and gaped at his cruel green eyes. Tatiana hissed. "If ye wishes to kill me, then do so already. Do not ponder!"

Just as Barnabas was about to address Tatiana, he heard a shrilled voice bellowing his name, followed by pacing footsteps. Barnabas glared over his shoulder to see Bidelia storming from the doorway, after hearing the commotion.

"Barnabas! Barnabas, drop thy weapon! Now," Bidelia screeched, as she paced to stand at Tatiana's side, reaching for Tatiana's dagger and returning it to her.

Slowly, Barnabas lowered his weapon, as the companions did also. Barnabas questioned, "Who is this child?"

"Tatiana Green," Bidelia snapped. "The Queen of the South!"

Quickly, the companions approached, stopping closely to her. Their eyes beamed with wonder, as Tatiana stood in the light of the doorway, reaching forwards to stroke her cheeks and strands of her hair.

Tasmin was silent. Her excitement forbade her from speaking, as she observed Tatiana lovingly. Tasmin still held young Helen at her side, who smiled, cheerfully, as they both greeted her.

From afar, Wylie and Free beamed. Their fellow companions suffocated Tatiana with their bursting excitement, as Tatiana faintly smiled and her eyes watered. Free and Wylie were not noticed by Tatiana, but they knew they would have their chance to speak to her.

Orla and Ainsley reached for Tatiana's strands of white hair, examining its glow in the light that entered through the doorway. Their happiness blinded them from seeing Tatiana's uncomfortable whimpers, as they whispered cruel words.

It was Darrel and Sir Terrence who scared Tatiana the most. Their excitement could not be contained, as their voices grew to deafening volumes, cheering for Tatiana. Darrel and Sir Terrence bowed before the Southern Queen, forcing their lips on her hands as they greeted her. They did not sense her tugs, attempting to release her hand from their grasp. Darrel and Sir Terrence continued to gush.

Standing further away from Tatiana than the rest of the companions was Barnabas. Barnabas allowed his companions to swarm, pushing him away, for he did not share the same excitement. He was overwhelmed by Tatiana's young and hideous appearance, as his stomach sunk deeply. The malice in his green eyes vanished, as they lowered to the floorboards. Barnabas turned from Tatiana and his companions, as he stumbled to sit before the fire, feeling light-headed.

Barnabas bowed his head over his knees, resting his face in the palms of his hands. His behaviour was noticed by Free and Wylie, who strode over to sit at his side, hoping to catch the eye of their other companions, which they eventually did, calling them over. The companions joined Barnabas and left Tatiana alone.

As the companions joined Barnabas, Bidelia stepped away from Tatiana to close the front door and to address the companions. Bidelia stood before the companions, frowning and crossing her arms over her chest. "What is the matter? Is there a reason why ye stays so silent?"

"Brother Barnabas has concerns," Wylie stated, as Bidelia continued to stare at Barnabas.

"Do share, Barnabas!" Bidelia spat.

"She is young. Too young, to be a queen," Barnabas muttered, looking over at Bidelia and Tatiana with his green eyes. "She has not lost her virginity yet!"

"Virginity or not, it does not determine maturity!" Bidelia's eyes rolled. "If he is thinking of intimacy, maybe he should relieve his self!"

The companions tittered, as Barnabas' cheeks flustered and Bidelia remained composed.

Barnabas growled. "How can she rule the Southern kingdom?"

"What did ye expect? She had aged only a few months before King Samael attacked the South, which was twenty-five years ago!" Bidelia howled. "Truthfully, she cannot alter her age!"

Tasmin babbled before Barnabas could speak further, "Her age is not an issue. She will make a fine queen! Happily, we will help her reclaim her kingdom."

"Yes! However, we will need to teach her to fight!" Orla added.

"A blade needs to be wielded well, as a bow needs to be used accurately," Ainsley mentioned.

As Tatiana was praised and cheered, she stormed towards the companions, stopping before the semi-circle they created as they rested on the chairs by the fire. She scowled, as her fists clenched and her cheeks flustered, shouting through her home. "Before any other words are shared, may I speak? May I share?"

The companions nodded, as Bidelia stepped back to allow Tatiana to speak.

"I do not desire the throne. I wish for the life I have held here with Bidelia and our grandfather." Tatiana sighed. "Dost thou not believe I would have already attempted to reclaim the throne if I had wanted so? I do not wish for the South. I cannot rule. For I am too young, as Barnabas has already stated!"

"Absurd! My companions and I did not journey here for thee to turn us away," Ainsley exclaimed.

"Besides, the Necromancer's riders have already journeyed North and pillage every settlement till thou art found. Word has spread. There is no returning to the life thou had before," Orla informed softly. "Please."

Tatiana shook her head. "I have not asked for a companionship and I do not want the kingdom!"

In silence, the companions stared. The companions' eyes filled with water, as their mouths gaped open. Their eyes flicked back and forth from Tatiana to Bidelia. They waited to be consoled by her, but she stayed quiet.

"Deeply, I am sorry," Tatiana apologised, slowly retreating from the living area and rushing to her room, closing the door silently behind.

Bidelia stepped away from the companions, slowly walking to grab the kettle already filled with water and hanging the pot over the flames. She offered the companions food, which she lined on the table, including a freshly baked nutmeg cake. Bidelia called the companions to sit, hoping food would comfort them.

The companions rose as soon as they called, but they did not rush. They plodded to the bench and slumped on their seats, picking at the food laid across the table. The companions needed a few persistent shoves from Bidelia to drag them from the fireplace.

Bidelia joined the companions as soon as the tea boiled, placing the steaming kettle at the centre of the table. She placed herself at the edge of the bench, sitting opposite Barnabas and beside Wylie. Bidelia said very little to the companions, but she connected with each of them, especially Barnabas, who she stared at with wide eyes.

9

Tatiana's room was spacious, with two separate, singular beds, perfectly positioned underneath the windows, as the evening sunset glowed through. Between the two wooden beds, there was a chest of drawers, which was shared by Tatiana and Bidelia, whilst the rest of the room remained bare. Hanging on the walls there were paintings of the South, mostly of Cahercasey Castle.

In the silence of her bedroom, Tatiana curled on her bed, laying in the hues of orange and pink sunlight. Tatiana laid above her covers, curling her knees further into her chest, pimples appearing on her skin. Magnificently, her chestnut eyes turned golden, as they lowered to fixate on the wooden floor, bathing in the light.

Before Tatiana could dwell too long, her bedroom door silently opened, and a tall and slender man entered. He wore a blue robe, which gathered at the floor, as he leant on his brown staff that helped him walk. His wrinkled and heavy eyes observed Tatiana as he stopped in the centre of the room. The man's long, white hair was covered by his hood, but the sunlight was still able to glimmer the strands falling over the front of his shoulders.

The man approached Tatiana, perching at the end of the bed and looking over at Tatiana. He placed his staff in front of his legs, still gripping and leaning, as he sighed. "My Tatiana. There is no need to be ashamed from not wanting to reclaim the throne. It is a huge responsibility!"

"I did not wish for this birth," Tatiana cried. "I did not want to sit upon a throne. Nor did I wish for a kingdom."

"I understand, my Tatiana. I do. However, I believe thou art upset due to being conflicted. Thou dost not want the responsibility of a queen, but thee refuses to disappoint, even those thou dost not know."

"Ezra, what shall I do?"

"Honestly, I believe thee should reclaim the throne. For that purpose, it is why I have kept thee safe." Ezra admitted. "Yet it is thou who shall make the final decision."

"I do not want it!"

"Then, at least, help the companions that have travelled to find thee reclaim the South," Ezra suggested. "The companions would despise thee less if thou did. The South is their home and they wish to return without King Samael ruling there."

She sighed with a small nod, sliding to the side of the bed and letting her legs dangle. Tatiana eventually rose, stretching her hands towards Ezra and lifting him to his feet. Though she raised him to stand, Ezra guided her from her room and into the living room.

The companions gathered around the bench with Bidelia, still filling their empty stomachs and soothing their dry throats. Deafening laughter and constant chatter swarmed between the companions, sharing stories and explaining bizarre dreams. They shouted over each other, sometimes arguing too. Yet, every look and every smile warmed the room.

Tatiana entered with Ezra, stopping just after the doorway to scan the companions that did not cease to amuse themselves. Too distracted by their flowing and hilarious conversations, the companions failed to notice her and Ezra watching them.

Until Barnabas looked over at Ezra and Tatiana, the companions stopped to stare. Barnabas had been distracted by Bidelia's golden eyes, which locked onto him, watching his lips form and hearing his musical voice speak. He had stuttered almost every word, blushing as his smiling companions eyed him.

When Barnabas saw Tatiana, he scowled. His flustered cheeks faded and his voice lowered to growl. "Why dost thou smile, Tatiana?"

Tatiana's lips pouted and hissed. "I smile at thy blushing cheeks, which redden for my sister's beauty!"

Barnabas flustered, grinding his teeth together, as his companions tittered and Bidelia's head bowed, hiding her blushed cheeks.

"I smile for I will venture with thy companions to the South," Tatiana admitted proudly, though her heart became faint as she mentioned the Southern kingdom. "Yet, I wish to make my feelings clear. I will not reclaim the throne and I will not rule. However, I will help ye fight the Necromancer and do whatever it takes to see the kingdom prosper again. I understand the South is in thy hearts and I wish to keep it there!"

From her seat, Tasmin jumped from the bench and exclaimed, twisting to Tatiana with a smile. "Ah! We are delighted the Queen of the South shall venture with us! We shall restore the throne."

"At last, the darkness from the South shall retreat and we will return home!" Sir Terrence declared, joining Tatiana to stand and facing Tatiana. "Hail. Hail. Queen of the South!"

The companions cheered, clapping and letting their voices bellow. They rose to welcome Tatiana, surrounding to embrace her, still yelling their delight, despite not listening to her fully.

As the companions praised and danced, Barnabas stayed silent. Barnabas watched his companions, as Bidelia stayed seated before him, observing the companions also.

Above the celebrations of the companions, Barnabas roared, "Be quiet!"

The companions fell immediately silent. They separated from Tatiana, releasing her from an embrace and forcing their smiles to fade. Slowly, the companions returned to their seats, continuing to eat and drink, silently listening to Barnabas yelling at Tatiana.

"Thou shalt need to prove thyself before any further praise is received from my companions. Thou art a coward! Thou art frightened to rule!"

"Why art thou so rude?" Tatiana snapped.

"I am concerned my companions and I are wasting time on a young child, which knows not how to grow," he spat.

Tatiana stepped closer to the bench, leaning over her fists that clenched against the table and glaring at Barnabas. Her lips parted, preparing for her voice to project every word with a growl.

Just as Tatiana pierced her lips, the hairs on her arms rose and a shudder climbed her back. Her body chilled, as a repetitive and loud bark of a dog rang through the village, followed by horses galloping through the silence of the near distance.

A sudden burst of screams flooded the village, as villagers left their homes and raced amongst the chaos. Despite the village screams and pounding feet, trying to flee, the hooves of horses were still heard, growing louder.

Tatiana stared through the window at the head of the bench, watching the flocks of villagers pass, screaming, as they fled. She fixated on the villagers running in different directions, slipping across the mud, before sighting a tall shadow trotting through the village, which made her lips tremble.

From the side of the opposite house, a stealthy and tall black horse elegantly walked, carrying a figure on its back. The figure sat upright, as flowing black hair blew in the small gale of wind and piercing blue eyes searched the village. The figure held the reins of their horse tightly, till their knuckles burst through their skin, keeping the head of their horse upright. From the lips of the figure, they bellowed their demands.

Tatiana had sighted the figure before, and struggled to turn from the figure, despite her rapid heartbeat and her sweating palms. She heard the companions rushing to stand, gathering their belongings and sighting them from the corner of her eyes, but unable to move her glued feet. Her name was called through the house by the companions, urging her to move, as their voices reached outside for the figure to hear.

The ocean eyes of the figure stopped searching the village, after listening to the frantic voices of the companions that were heard above the screams. Devilish eyes sighted Tatiana through the window, as the figure's hand raised to point, shrilling an order to her riders which pillaged.

"She is here! The filth of the South. The Queen! Kill her. Kill her," the figure screamed, as horses neighed and galloping hooves followed.

Still, Tatiana did not move. Though she saw hooded shadows storming to the house as the figure still glared upon their horse.

Suddenly, a pair of strong hands grasped Tatiana's waist, heaving her back. Tatiana grunted and was hauled into a flat chest, being lifted from her frozen feet and twisting her from the window. Tatiana was turned from the window, her body was lifted higher till her head almost touched the ceiling and she flipped to face the figure, who placed her over their shoulder.

Briefly, Tatiana met dazzling eyes and long white hair of her fellow companion, Free. The corners of Free's lips raised, despite Tatiana sighting the front door forcefully swinging open and the shadows charging through the house. Free placed Tatiana against his large, muscled shoulders and carried her on his fast feet towards the rear door of the house.

Losing sight of the figures, Tatiana was carried from her abode and taken into the village. A sweet and pungent smell of smoke climbed through Tatiana's nostrils, as black clouds curled above her head and bright, orange flickers raged on the roofs of the village, growing high. Slowly, the screams faded as the villagers successfully fled and the companions were some of the few left to escape, as the companions crept quietly to the outskirts.

In the village, there was still one figure searching, which the companions had not yet seen. The azure-eyed figure still lurked, hunting for Tatiana and the companions, who crossed the village, stopping behind the corner of a burning house after sighting the figure that halted before the border of the village, where the house finished.

Abruptly, Barnabas stopped at the corner of the house, feeling the heat of the flames sweltering his skin and covering his mouth with his hand, as swirling grey clouds attacked his lungs. As he halted, he stretched his arm behind, gesturing for his companions to stop, also. Barnabas and his companions stayed motionless and silent, as they examined the pondering sapphire-eyed shadow that continued to rest on their horse.

Once the companions stopped, Tatiana forced herself from Free's grip and gently placed herself on the ground. Faintly, Tatiana smiled at Free before turning to view the foreboding figure with the rest of the companions, standing behind her sister, Bidelia.

As Tatiana stared, she whispered to the silent companions, "Who is she? I have seen her once before!"

At first, she was not answered by the focused companions, but after a while Tatiana heard Barnabas' aggressive voice reply. "She is Belladonna. The Necromancer's witch. Hated by all, including by me."

Tatiana gulped. "How dost thou know such a woman?"

Barnabas fell silent, again. His green eyes lowered from Belladonna, as water filled them. He brooded for only a moment, which was enough to cause Barnabas to tremble. The lowering of his head was sighted by his companions, copying his bow with small sighs. His companions did not know why he was pained, but they sensed the gut-wrenching churns of his stomach.

Before too long, Ezra stepped in front of the companions to view Belladonna and searched for an escape. Ezra scanned the village surroundings, seeing very few successful plans to escape all together.

After, Ezra addressed the companions, declaring his plan. “Dearest companions, our time together has been short and I believe it is time for us to leave one another now! Separately, we must escape and meet South as soon as possible!”

Barnabas hid his tears and raised his head. He agreed with Ezra, turning to his companions. “Yes. My companions, we must depart. For now, we shall travel apart. Yet, we will meet again in the South. Visit kingdoms and gather armies before our arrival. My fellow companions, be safe.”

The companions nodded, forming small groups to escape from the village and to begin their journey ahead. The companions did not wish one another farewell in the hope they would see each other again.

The first companions to depart were Helen, Tasmin, Sir Terrence and Ezra. Swiftly, Ezra hugged Bidelia and Tatiana goodbye, before scampering quietly through the village with his companions that were already ahead. Belladonna’s horsemen were beginning to block the exits, forcing the companions to move fast. Sir Terrence led Helen, Tasmin and Ezra to safety, leaving the village quickly.

Following, there was Ainsley, Orla, Darrel and Wylie. Wylie departed to leave the group without saying goodbye to his brother, moving and ordering his companions to leave in a different direction than the companions that had left before. Only Darrel wished his companions farewell, praying for their safety, as he embraced everyone. Ainsley and Orla were like Wylie and left in a hurry, as Darrel had to chase them.

Tatiana waited quietly behind Barnabas, Bidelia and Free, scanning her surroundings and stepping further away from Free, who was in front. She heard Barnabas, Bidelia and Free murmuring as they discussed a plan, but Tatiana did not speak. Tatiana had many plans and ideas, yet she stepped away from the companions and stared at them from the corner of her eyes.

Whilst she looked, Bidelia twisted on her heel and slipped passed Free to stand before Tatiana. Bidelia exclaimed, delightfully, as Free and Barnabas turned also. "Please, Tatiana, will thee ask Prince Hunter to aid us? Surely, he will!"

Tatiana's eyes rolled and growled. "I do not want to ask any favours from him!"

"Please. Prince Hunter may give us an army!" Bidelia pleaded. "I understand thou dost not wish to return to the kingdom, but thou have been found by Belladonna and the Necromancer. Once news spreads about thee, more shall find thee and more shall want thee to reclaim the throne or wish for thee to die."

Tatiana huffed. "Let us hurry to the North and ask Prince Hunter for aid!"

She snatched Bidelia by the wrist, slipping around the bend of the house, rushing towards her home. Tatiana twirled Bidelia, as Barnabas and Free scurried, slipping in the mud. Tatiana led the companions towards the outskirts, attempting to escape to the North.

With haste, avoiding the riders that searched and hiding behind the walls, Tatiana successfully led her companions to the edge. They were not seen by the riders as they crossed the village, which continued to blaze auburn.

Striding North, Tatiana and the companions deserted the village, hearing Belladonna's orders and the neighs of the horses behind them. Eventually, the smoke cleared from the skies and cleared from their lungs, as the village became small, losing sight of the flames. The companions travelled fast towards Hanuli, seeking help from Prince Hunter.

10

Since the companions departed from one another, Ezra, Sir Terrence, Helen and Tasmin journeyed South. The village had quickly disappeared behind them, rushing through the meadow, as ash layered their hair and clothes. The companions removed their clothing they had pulled over their mouths, as their faces were lined with soot and inhaled the clean air, as the clouds passed over their heads. Their legs shook, as their muscles tightened and as their eyes began to close, still travelling quickly, as Ezra led Sir Terrence, Helen and Tasmin, who followed closely behind.

Tasmin called to Ezra, quickening her pace to stride at his side. "Where shall we head? We cannot enter the Southern kingdom alone! We shall be killed. So what will we do?"

"Ah! A boy is whom we will meet," Ezra declared. "King Samael Cain's boy. The heir to the Lost Kingdom if he chooses to reclaim the land."

"A boy? Never did I suspect the Necromancer to have a boy!" she exclaimed.

"Nemo, the coward boy," Sir Terrence mentioned. "He was a young and kind boy."

"Then, who is his mother?" Helen quizzed.

Ezra admitted, "Till today, I believe he be not knowing who his mother be."

"Where will we find the bastard?" Helen questioned.

Ezra chuckled at Helen's stern question and answered with a smile. "The bastard resides South. He shall help Tatiana, favourably."

"Has he met dearest Tatiana?" Tasmin asked.

"Yes. Though he met her many years ago. Yet he writes almost once a month," Ezra responded, marching ahead of his companions who stumbled slightly behind.

Tasmin and Helen travelled beside Sir Terrence, arguing as they shared Sir Terrence's flask of liquor. They shared a pipe, to smoke their weed, as Ezra smoked his own pipe. Helen, Tasmin and Sir Terrence soon stumbled, as their eyes stared blankly and their limbs waddled at the side of their bodies.

Quickly, the sun hit the horizon. A dark sky sat above their heads with small stars appearing, as the sun lowered in the West. The golden light had disappeared, as they travelled under a blue hue with few glimpses of sunlight catching the strands of their hair. Rapidly, the companions became cold with the absence of the sun, continuing to smoke and drink, fighting the chill. Eventually, the companions were buried in the jet-black night, having to stop.

The companions halted in the middle of the meadow, burying themselves into a pit and hiding amongst the night. Ezra, Helen, Tasmin and Sir Terrence shuffled against the soil walls, resting beside one another and using each other's shoulders to sleep upon. The companions gazed into the twinkling sky, as the land fell silent.

The companions watched the Stars. A race of mystical beings, which had watched over the land for millions of years. The origin of the Stars was unknown and very few had been so luck to sight a Star in human flesh, wishing they would.

Helen snuggled against Ezra's chest, which inhaled deeply, as she stared at the Stars above. She asked, as Ezra watched the sparkles of the rayed dots also. "Who leads such a race of beings?"

"It is uncertain! As constellations, the Stars have names, but individual Stars do not," Ezra answered, still looking at the sky. "No Star ever shines brighter than others. If one does, it can only be due to the others being further away."

"Are Stars born?"

"All Stars were once like us, mortal. Very few and very special persons are selected. It is not known how, or why, the Stars choose, but with every new invite, another Star is added to the sky!" He beamed. "To never die and to never fight, a nirvana."

Sir Terrence mumbled, overhearing Ezra's kind words, "Yes, the Stars have their nirvana. Yet, the Stars leave the lands to rot in bloodshed and pain. The Stars may glisten, but their hearts falter!"

"Many, many, years ago, the Stars helped. Since, the Stars have left us to perish against the greatest darkness, including the reign of the dark, when the Stars deserted us!"

"I have heard such stories, which present the Stars as loyal and humble." Helen yawned, as she closed her eyes to sleep in Ezra's arms.

Instantly, Helen fell asleep, laying on Ezra's chest and listening to his calm heartbeat. Falling asleep beside Helen, Ezra closed his eyes, after gazing at the Stars above, which allowed him to sleep without fear.

Throughout the night, Sir Terrence and Tasmin drank from the silver flask they shared. They watched the night sky until their eyes were forced to shut, as their lids drooped and darkened the world around them. Peacefully, the companions slept till morning.

The sun rose over the horizon, brightly golden. The meadow and grass glistened indefinitely amongst the land. The sun raised silently over the companions that slept. Warmth surged the air and there was little wind whipping through the companions' hair.

Yet, as the companions slept in the small ditch, ten black clouds blocked the sun and left the companions to shiver. The clouds blocked the sun and left the companions to shiver. The clouds stooped over the companions, waiting for their eyes to open from their dreams. They remained almost lifeless, standing still with silver, sharp wands stretched towards the companions' necks, even as they awakened.

The companions awakened from their slumbers. Their eyes widened. They gulped, as a cold pointed edge rested against the flesh of their necks. The companions were silent, as Helen screamed, bursting into waterfalls and hiding in Ezra's chest.

From behind, the masked and black statures parted to reveal a hooded figure, wearing navy. Striding towards the companions, blue eyes examined them, stopping just before and observing the silver blades on their flesh.

The navy-cloaked figure, cackled, as their head rolled back and addressed the companions. "Ah! The disciples. A wizard. A drunkard. A duenna. A child! All of thee, I know. Yet, thou have never met me. I am Belladonna! Many have heard my Tenebrous Tower, which resides south-east. The screams from my prisoners travel far across the plain. So many screams, but my favourite scream is a disciple and they are not here. Suppose I shall have to make thee all scream!"

"What does thee want, hag?" Ezra snapped, clutching Helen tightly into his chest.

"I want the Queen of the South. For many years, thou have hidden her. Being not too long ago, the Necromancer and I, did not know her existence," Belladonna sung. "Soon, we heard the chirps of the drunkard in Cheslyn and we followed the bird as it flew with all of thee. Eventually, the Necromancer and I would soon grasp her, and we will!"

"The heir does not want the throne," Tasmin mentioned, as Belladonna turned to listen. "She wishes to be home."

"Enough!" Belladonna hissed over Tasmin's soft voice. "Whether the heir wants the throne or not, it does not matter. If an heir is alive to the throne, there will be a war against the South. All kingdoms shall fight against us! This will not happen. The heir will die before she reaches the South!"

Randomly, Sir Terrence laughed, just after hiccupping. His boisterous and high-pitched laugh saw Belladonna's eyes grow and heard her teeth clench.

"Seize them!" Belladonna ordered, turning from the companions and storming to the horses behind the hooded shadows and mounting her horse, waiting for the companions to be chained.

The hands of the hooded figures grappled the companions, hoisting them to their feet and forcing them to stand. The companions' arms were strung behind their backs and tied with rope burning their wrists. Pieces of cloths covered their mouths, muffling their shrieks as they struggled to free themselves, as they were made to walk behind each other, following the hooded figures and Belladonna.

Across the land, the companions stumbled behind, as a rider tugged at the rope which joined them all together. The companions bled from their burning restraints, tripping over uneven terrain and slipping in the mud. The companions were dragged underneath the rising sun, passing few travellers, who screeched sighting Belladonna and the riders, avoiding them, though they saw the companions had been captured.

When nightfall came, the horses were exhausted. Belladonna and the riders dismounted to allow their horses to rest. They led their horses to lay in the centre of the now rocky terrain, letting their horses sleep underneath the moonlight, as Belladonna and the riders rested beside them.

By the time Belladonna and the riders had stopped, the companions dropped to their knees, smashing against the rock with clicks. Gasping for air, either bowing their heads, or searching the starry night, they slumped onto the wet ground and inhaled the pungent damp air. It had fallen cold, as Belladonna and the riders shivered, exhaling blue air, as the companions sweltered.

Eventually, the companions rested to lay on the cool ground, laying close to one another, as Belladonna and the riders slept beside them. The companions laid silently, hearing the riders murmuring, as they whispered to each other. Ezra, Sir Terrence, Tasmin and Helen watched the twinkling Stars, looking endlessly and unhinged by the close howls of wild wolves. The companions stayed still, as their bodies palpitated and sweated, waiting for their eyes to temporarily close throughout the night.

As the companions remained awake, they heard the words shared between Belladonna and the riders, as they huddled beside their horses and the companions.

A rider remarked, leaning against a horse's side with folded arms and crossed, stretched legs. "Why do we have to bring them before the Necromancer, my mother?"

"My son, Nemo." Belladonna grimaced, as she sat opposite curled on her side and facing him. "Is it not strange the old man has not recognised thee? He does not care for thee!"

Once Ezra had heard Nemo's name roll from Belladonna's tongue, his eyes widened and looked over at him. Ezra watched as the rider removed his mask, sighting his glowing golden eyes and instantly recognising Nemo. Nemo's eyes did not catch Ezra watching, as Ezra turned to face the Stars, with lowered eyes.

Nemo answered, still unaware Ezra had watched and heard him reveal himself. "Mother, will the disciples be punished?"

"Yes!"

"Will my cousin be punished, too?"

"Yes. As soon as she is captured, once the land has darkened, she will experience pain that will kill her!" She smiled. "Finally, we are close to her death, after so many years writing and visiting her, our wait is over, mother."

Nemo exclaimed, "Is it not funny the companions blame the drunkard for her existence being known, when we have known for years?"

"Yes, my son. Talented, thou wert at deceiving them," she remarked, as her eyes closed and as Nemo placed his black, metallic mask over his face.

Belladonna and the riders fell silent, as did the companions, underneath the starry night.

11

Since escaping Violl and parting from the other companions, Orla, Ainsley, Darrel and Wylie travelled towards the South, crossing through the East. Orla and Ainsley led Wylie and Darrel after leaving Violl and departing from the rest of the companions. Mostly, the companions were quiet as they travelled, rushing to the South and hoping to meet the rest of the companions.

As the companions journeyed South, marching through the meadow, they came to a forest. The companions stopped a few metres before observing the tall and bleak forest, which stretched far across the horizon ahead. The trees stood with grey trunks and mountains of veins raising from the soil, as the thick wood twisted around others. The treetops almost vanished in the grey clouds with long branches stretching downwards and bearing no leaves, as the clouds morphed black. A strange warmth radiated between the trunks, capturing and drawing the companions to enter.

The warmth which embraced the companions continued to grow, as the companions moved between the trees. Inside, the companions stepped on dry ground and travelled underneath a grey light. The woods were silent with no tweets echoing and no sightings throughout.

At the centre, they halted. The companions dropped their bags beside their feet, as the companions flopped their exhausted bodies against the trunks of the trees, resting closely together. The companions stretched their legs, before curling their bodies and attempting to keep warm.

Ainsley and Orla slept beside one another, with a small blanket resting over their legs, as Darrel and Wylie rested opposite and leant against each other's shoulders. The companions exchanged glances, as Darrel shared his rationed food.

The clouds rapidly darkened, almost becoming night. The warmth started to fade. From the clouds, a dusting of snow emerged, sticking to the wood, which had already frozen. Slowly, the tiny flakes fell, lighting landing on the clothes and heads of the companions, soundlessly.

Though the companions saw their breath rising before them, as their teeth chattered, they did not cease to speak.

Wylie stuttered, keeping his arms folded across his chest and shuffling closer to Darrel, clinging onto him as his hands froze. "Snow only falls in the East! We have travelled too far. Surely, we will die."

Darrel hissed, as his companion clung tightly to his clothes. "Possibly, we will die. Yet, it is not definite."

"Do not sleep. The beast waits for us beyond the snow. She uses fire for a show. Forced to slumber, so she can eat and keep!" Ainsley mumbled with wide eyes, staring through her companions.

"A beast? Art thou expressing utter nonsense?" Wylie snapped, as his eyes rolled. "There are no beasts."

"Yes. Yes, there is!" Orla argued. "Soon, thou will see. Yet, the beast Ainsley speaks of is a beast we will not seek and will move as soon as a little snow sets!"

"I shall sleep for how long I wish to endure." Wylie yawned with a smirk, as his eyes tightly closed, falling asleep instantly. His companions scanned the surrounding forest, watching the snow fall, ready to move, before the white sheet thickened on the ground.

For a while, the companions remained awake. Yet, the companions' eyes closed, as a flame sparked just at their feet, flickering from the invisible air and growing as nearby twigs and grass caught fire. A small, controlled fire began to grow and warmed the companions to forcefully slumber, deeply, as the snow became thick.

Only Wylie had not seen the fire, which bewitched his fellow companions to sleep. Wylie heard snapping wood from the flames that danced and loud movement travelling through the trees but did not wake. He remained sleeping, though his body was heated as a warm, brisk and constant air layered his skin. He waited to wake, listening for his other companions to stir.

Soon, Wylie realised his companions would not wake easily. The thudding from the trees became deafening, hearing trees crashing against the ground, after snapping from their roots. He heaved his knees into his chest, as his legs began to scorch, tearing his clothing away from his skin. His eyes whipped open.

Tall and dancing auburn shadows surrounded the companions, growing between the trees. The orange and yellow hues blinded Wylie's sight as they wickedly swayed underneath the night sky. Above, the leaves burned, falling with the snow, reaching the ground as nothing more than grey dust. The moving flames cackled, shredding the branches and tearing down the trees, burning through Wylie's clothes and reddening his skin.

At Wylie's feet, a small fire still blazed, but snow had piled thickly. Wylie examined his companions, sighting their heads poking through the white flakes which covered them. Quietly, the snow clung to their hairs of their bodies, sticking to their lips. Yet the snow, was not melted by the devilish flames around them.

Rapidly, Wylie twisted and grappled Darrel's shoulders, shaking his entire body and ordering him to wake. Wylie's voice trembled, as he screamed, wanting to see the eyes of his companions, open wide.

As Darrel's eyes stayed shut, Wylie shuffled towards Ainsley and Orla, perching between their bodies. He stretched forwards, tapping their shoulders with his fingers and screeching their names as they slept soundlessly.

Suddenly, Wylie's fingers stopped thumping against the bones of his shoulders. His fingers froze, as did the entirety of his body. A sharp and vicious shiver climbed his back as a low, bellowing roar travelled through the woods as a bright light lit the sky above.

Slowly, Wylie twisted from his companions, as brisk and heavy warm air was blown against his back. Wylie's eyes firmly shut, as his heart pounded against his chest and his breath quickened. Wylie looked over his shoulder and above where Darrel rested, sighting what he feared.

From the darkness, a pair of ovals, glowing white with black irises, feverishly locked onto Wylie from above. A parted mouth with sharp daggers growing from pink gums and an orange hue glowing from its throat breathed warm air. Glimmering white scales appeared in the light of the fire, covering a long, swooping tail resting behind its enormous body. It stood between trees, as its body caused them to lean, standing on its large feet, with silver talons lacing the snow. Its height shadowed Wylie and darkened the flames, growing above the trees.

Fearfully, Wylie whipped his sword from his sheath, pointing his blade at the snow dragon. Wylie shuffled to his feet, bending his knees, as the dragon's neck lowered to him. Wylie yelled with a stutter, gripping his sword tighter. "Stay back! Stay away from my friends and me! I shall kill thee, foul beast!"

The snow dragon crept forwards, though its feet still pounded against the ground, shaking the ground Wylie stood upon and knocking him onto his knees. The dragon stooped over him, peering with his white eyes and breathing heavily through its nostrils.

In a low and honeyed tone, the dragon spoke, after its tongue slithered to lick Wylie before retracting inside its mouth. "Such taste. A divine treat. Thou and thy friends shall be so sweet. My belly roars."

Wylie begged, as his sword slipped from his grip. "Please. Spare us! There is a journey ahead, which is greater than thou and I!"

The dragon's body slumped to rest on its feet, as its tail continued to slither between the trees. The beast hissed. "What journey is greater than a starving dragon?"

"The return of the heir," he explained with a tremor in his voice, as he cowered in the snow. "The Queen of the South!"

The beast lowered further to Wylie, wanting to listen more. "Thou must speak, if thou wish to live."

"My friends and I are travelling South to reclaim the throne, preparing an army," Wylie remarked, relaxing slightly. "The Necromancer must be destroyed. Too many years have passed as all reside in the dark."

"What is the Queen's name?"

"Queen Tatiana Green."

"Will thou show me her?"

Wylie nodded.

"Then I shall help."

Wylie nodded.

"Wilt thou not ask why?"

Wylie shook his head.

"Good." The dragon sneered. "First, thou must bring me food. Thy friends will not be released till their bodies are replaced, including thee."

"Yes. Anything to spare our lives." Wylie nodded, rising to his feet and grabbing his sword from the ground.

"My name is Bathilda and I shall be waiting for thee," Bathilda growled, laying down her head, as the fires continued to swarm.

Wylie nodded. He was reluctant to leave his companions, but as a path through the fire emerged for him to walk, he marched through the forest and towards the nearest settlement. Wylie moved quickly, fearing Bathilda would grow hungrier and swallow his sleeping companions whole.

Wylie began to sprint through the forest, sighting a path of collapsed trees and knowing Bathilda had passed through. He followed the path, reaching the exit of the forest quickly, after rampaging over the fallen trunks and branches which resided in the snow. He could barely see through the dark, with only the moon as his light.

An hour passed before Wylie arrived to the outskirts of the nearest settlement, Elba. The houses were shadowed by the moonlight, as small torches flickered around the perimeters to form a circle. A small watch wandered between the houses, with weapons and shields made from wood, whilst the doors and shutters of the houses remained shut. Paths through the settlement had been made, as shovelled snow stayed at the sides, leaning against the walls.

Wylie walked through the snow on the outskirts of the village, stumbling towards the clear paths and halting, before falling. He examined the path before him, which was dimly lit with houses either side and snow toppling on the exposed ground. The watch had passed already, leaving Wylie to enter almost freely. He treaded quietly to enter the settlement, searching for an open door or window.

Wylie moved rapidly, as his companions slept beside Bathilda, who was growing hungrier. His heart thudded against his chest and his soaked palms were unable to grip his sword. He swallowed the water which fell from the top of his lip, soothing his dry mouth, as his hair became glued to his face.

Swiftly, he moved through the settlement, heading to the centre. Elba stayed quiet, as Wylie heard the whispering voices of the watch, communicating behind the walls of the houses he passed. The moon continued to shine its light, causing the sweat on Wylie's body to sparkle, as the droplets appeared like falling diamonds.

As Wylie's eyes glowed within the moonlight, ahead, there was a window. The window was at the end of the path, with its shutters still opened wide, opening outwards and into the street. Inside, Wylie only saw darkness and heard silence, as he came close, beginning to peer in and standing before the window.

A closer look and he found, five sleeping bodies sharing a small blanket and a bed. The five bodies slumbered deeply, facing the window, as their limbs stretched across each other. Nearly being all the same age and being much smaller than Wylie, he was able to carry them with ease.

Wylie lifted his body with his hands leaning against the windowsill and heaved his body to sit, before swinging his legs through to the inside. He slithered down, landing gently on the wooden floorboards and creeping towards the side of the bed. Wylie stooped above them, examining the sleeping bodies and listening to their soft breathing from their parted lips and nostrils with a smile. He lowered to watch their breathing chests expand, as the rest of their bodies stayed motionless. He rose.

He searched the rest of the room, which was bare, and sighted a pile of blankets in the corner. Wylie strode towards them and picked the largest blanket from the pile, which he laid on the floor. After, he approached the bed again and stood above the bodies.

Slowly, he reached for the closest body, letting its legs fold over his arms and resting its head on his chest. He carried the body over to the blanket and laid the body down gently. Wylie placed the head of the body down first, before lightly letting its legs fall too. He carried all five bodies over to the blanket, covering their mouths with cloths, before wrapping the blanket around the bodies, tightly.

Once he began moving the blanket and the bodies inside, his grip tightened, as the bodies began to squirm. He saw their limbs slamming against the blanket and felt their bodies toppling over each other. Wylie heard their screams through the cloths that he had tightly fitted over their mouths, picturing their tears that fell.

Before the bodies made any more noise, Wylie climbed through the window. He threw his body through first, landing onto the path and tugging the blanket over the sill. Wylie placed the bag of bodies over his shoulder, scanning the path ahead and the ones at his side. He could hear the whispers of the watch becoming closer as his feet started to move briskly on the path ahead. The sudden rise in the voices of the watchers heard the whimpering bodies which Wylie carried, echoing through Elba and awakening the sleepy settlement.

Violently, Wylie flung his body forwards, moving his feet faster along the grass and avoiding the crumbling snow. Wylie clambered onto the bag over his shoulder with both hands, hoping to reach the outskirts without being caught. The screams of the bodies were growing louder, as Wylie heard the footsteps of the watch charging through and sighting lights from the gaps of the doorways as the settlement began to stir.

In sight, there were the outskirts of Elba. The torches were still lit and the thick snow had not been cleared, stretching into the distance, as the moon glimmered from behind Wylie. Wylie quickened towards the torches and bounced into the snow ahead, immediately fighting through. He distanced from the settlement, as a chilling shriek, echoed through the land.

For only a moment, Wylie stopped, as shivers flew through his spine and as a small churn deepened inside his stomach. The scream lingered inside Wylie's mind, long, after it had passed, but he continued his journey ahead. He stormed through the snow, carrying the bodies and arriving at the forest, finding the path with the fallen trees.

Wylie entered. He headed towards the orange lights he could see between the trees and felt the heat against his skin, which scorched as flames started to rage around him. Wylie saw Bathilda resting in the shadows of the fire, as her scales glowed and as her eyes stayed closed. He heard her deep breathing vibrating the ground, moving subtly as she rested.

With delight, Wylie smiled, entering the clearing and seeing his companions still asleep amongst the snow. The snow had not deepened and their faces remained seen as they leant against the trees, warmed by the flames and Bathilda's warm breath. His companions were soundless and would soon wake to greet him.

Wylie stood before Bathilda, throwing the bag from his back and onto the ground before her. He watched the bag roll, as the bodies inside squabbled to free themselves, still hearing their cries. Wylie called to Bathilda.

"Bathilda. I have given thee what has been asked. Now, free my friends!"

Her eyes whipped open. She viewed him, before glancing down at the moving bag and raising her head to lower further, inhaling the divine smell of flesh, which caused her to purr. "Ah! Thou hast brought me five to replace four! Thou hast given me more than I asked. Yet I only wanted four."

Wylie's lips parted, as he watched Bathilda delicately tear through the bag and peer inside, sighting the five bodies which screamed. The cowering bodies remained inside what was left of the bag, as Bathilda picked the first body to eat.

She lunged, devouring the bodies, as blood splattered from her mouth and over Wylie, as she swallowed the first body. Then, another. Until, her teeth drizzled in crimson liquid and ran down the sides of her mouth. Bathilda purred again, as her eyes rolled and as she leant her head backwards to bathe in the moonlight.

Wylie watched her from below, as her neck raised above the treetops and rested for a moment. Yet, his eyes caught the bloody bag at his feet, beginning to move. He heard quiet cries and approached quickly, flinging the bag to one side and sighting a living body, whimpering against the ground.

Grabbing the hair on the head of the body, he dragged the screaming body before Bathilda and threw the body against her chest. The body bounced from Bathilda's stomach and rolled beside her talons, which did not move. The body hid within the snow, as Wylie scowled at Bathilda, who continued to rest under the moon.

"Eat!" Wylie demanded. "Why does thee leave one to waste?"

Simply, Bathilda replied. "I am full. I asked, only, for four bodies. I cannot eat five."

"Thou must eat!" Wylie roared, stumbling forwards to stand underneath her head.

Suddenly, Bathilda's head swooped down and shadowed over Wylie, almost touching his sweating face with her nose. She hissed. "Then, thou should eat."

"No. I will not eat. I want my friends to wake and we shall be on our way." Wylie planted his feet in the snow, stupidly arguing with Bathilda.

"Then let the body live. There is no harm."

"No. The body is too old. It will remember what I have done!"

"Then kill the body."

Wylie shook his head and begged, "Please. Kill her. I will not kill!"

Bathilda breathed deeply. She tilted her head towards the body, which cowered at her feet and tapped the body with her talon. Her gentle tap cured the cries of the body that slowly raised to stare into her white eyes, which calmed the body. Bathilda raised her leg to stroke the body's cheek with her talon, feeling warmth radiate from its flesh.

Afterwards, Bathilda turned the body to face Wylie. Wylie stood underneath the moonlight. His features were undeniably clear and his hazel eyes bore through the body, which glared back at him. Wylie's tall and slim stature was noticed by the body, even as his clothing hung over him and as his shoulder-length hair clung to the sweat on his skin. The body identified him through its tears, remembering him.

Wylie sighed and turned from the body and Bathilda. He stared at the moon, unable to glare into the brown eyes of the body that he had taken and almost fed to Bathilda. The world began to spin, as he breathed heavily to calm himself, gripping his fists and sinking in his tears.

He cried, "Please. Let us leave, now."

Bathilda's body swooped to turn, taking the body with her. She eyed Wylie one last time, as he stood under the moonlight, before returning to the darkness of the woods. Her body stealthily moved through the trees, breaking the trunks and causing the trees to fall. Yet, her exit was brief and Wylie could not hear her stomping feet, nor feel the shaking of the ground. Bathilda had disappeared into the night.

As she left, the surrounding flames lowered and fizzled. The warmth vanished, as did the light, leaving Wylie to stand in the blackness of the night. The blanket he had used to carry the bodies was burnt away by the small, lingering flames, leaving nothing more than a pile of ash, as the last flames fled.

Wylie still watched the moon, as his knees sunk into the snow and he breathed even deeper. His mind still turned and his stomach still twisted, trying to forget what he had done. However, in the silence of the forest, his thoughts radiated and became as bleak as the night.

Suddenly, Wylie heard his name being called. The voice was soft but overpowering and demanded for Wylie to turn. Wylie waited for his tears to dry before turning to see his fellow companion, awakened and unhurt. Yet, the gloom upon Wylie's face caused his companions to worry instantly.

"What is it, Wylie?"

Wylie raised and slumped towards his companion, dropping beside him and falling against his companion's chest. He grappled the clothing of his companion as his lip quavered. "My Darrel! I am delighted to see thee."

"What has happened?" Darrel questioned, seeing Wylie's lips trembling, as Darrel laid his hand against Wylie's shoulder. "Why dost thy lips wobble?"

Wylie's eyes closed. His voice was quiet, as tears formed underneath his eyelids. "I cannot speak. I do not wish to speak."

"Sleep, my friend," Darrel whispered, rubbing Wylie's shoulder and watching as tears slid from under Wylie's eyelids. Darrel stayed awake for a few moments, before closing his eyes again, seeing his companion fall asleep with incredible guilt.

12

In the North, underneath the sunlight, Hanuli castle stood tall. The sharp, spires staggered into the sky, almost reaching the clouds, as monuments of past kings and queen were honoured. The colourful glass, which decorated the long and wide centre window, dazzled across the meadow, shining over the high walls. The gate was opened, as a bridge balanced over a deep and wide moat, with guards standing at the sides, wearing silver armour and holding shields pictured with unicorns.

Across the meadow before Hanuli, there were four figures approaching the castle on foot. The figures moved quickly through the long and yellow strands of wheat, storming to the bridge.

At the front was a woman with long white hair. She was followed by a tall and fierce woman, an angelic man and an aggressive man, pacing in silence. They had not spoken for their entire journey, prevailing hostility amongst the white-haired woman and the aggressive man behind.

Tatiana, with her white, long hair flowing behind her back, crossed the bridge. She visited Hanuli so often that she was known to the guards of the castle. Tatiana smiled, as her companions followed closely behind, eyeing the castle, which Free and Barnabas had never seen before.

Free and Barnabas' eyes widened, looking up at the castle that shadowed them. Their eyes followed the dazzling rainbow lights which shone from the window above as they headed underneath the gate and into the market.

The market was filled with stalls. People bustled across the courtyard, selling and buying, their voices bellowing. Pungent smells of fresh-baked bread streamed through, followed by the subtle scents of dried herbs and fruits. Warmth spread throughout the market.

Tatiana led her companions through, stopping just after the gate and looking into the courtyard. Above the noise, she heard the shrieks of girlish giggles, followed by a deep voice of a man. Tatiana listened thoroughly, twisting on her heel and following the laughter, as her companions followed too. She scurried around the edge of the market, turning corners until she came to the very far side and slowed her pace.

Ahead, there was a group of young girls. Their hair was beautifully pinned on their heads and they wore elegant makeup, as they cheerfully smiled. The girls wore long and presentable gowns, draped with jewels around their necks and hanging from their ears. They surrounded a tall and dark-haired man, talking deeply and flirtatiously towards the girls, who laughed.

The man caressed the soft cheeks of the women he was surrounded by, whispering his honeyed words from his forked tongue with a grin. His eyes held the gaze of the women, staring deeply, until the women blushed and smiled.

Yet, his eyes departed from their stare, sighting Tatiana from the corner of his eye. The man's obnoxious smile faded and his pale cheeks reddened. Quickly, he moved away from the young girls to greet Tatiana, stopping close to her and tilting his head slightly downwards to view her. A small glaze of sweat rested on his top lip, as he became lost within her eyes.

He stuttered, "Tatiana! Dost thou still feel ill?"

She shook her head. "No. I am fine, now. Thank ye."

Silently, the man stood. He waited for Tatiana to speak, seeing her lips part and her eyebrows frowning.

"If thou art not too occupied, I need thy help. Please, Hunter," she begged with tears pouring from her eyes.

Hunter's hands raised to rest on her shoulders, lowering his body to be level and looking closer into her watering eyes. He whispered, "Come with me."

She nodded, looking over her shoulder and gesturing her companions to follow. Hunter and Tatiana paced beside each other, as Bidelia, Barnabas and Free stumbled behind. Hunter led Tatiana and the companions to the side of the market, stopping abruptly and swivelling.

Tatiana stood before Hunter and leant against the wall, as Bidelia, Barnabas and Free surrounded them. Tatiana waited for her companions to stand at her side, before revealing to Hunter what she needed to say.

Tatiana began to speak, softly. "Hunter, my time has come. I have been found."

"Thou knew this day would come," Hunter mentioned. "The day thou would have to take responsibilities for a kingdom."

"I am being hunted. The Necromancer and Belladonna search for me. They wish to kill me!"

"What art thou proposing?"

"I need refuge."

"We need an army!" Barnabas declared, pushing in front of Tatiana and scowling at Hunter, standing above him. "We want Cahercasey returned. We wish to fight for the kingdom."

Hunter pouted and frowned, disliking Barnabas instantly. "Dost thou not know who I am? I could have thee killed!"

"I cannot be killed easily." Barnabas chuckled. "Besides, would Tatiana be impressed by my death?"

Hunter fell silent, as Tatiana stepped in between them and elbowed Barnabas to step back. She addressed Hunter, sternly, as he continued to gape at Barnabas. "Please, Hunter. Wilt thou help?"

Hunter's eyes lowered. "I shall need to ask my father, first. He is sure to help thee."

Hunter gestured the companions to follow him back through the market, avoiding the young girls he had been flirting with, who called to him. He scampered underneath a main archway, greeting fellow villagers and hurrying to the servant door at the side of the castle. The side of the castle was clear from the villagers, as Hunter paced to swing open the door.

Hunter entered the castle kitchen, where the divine smell of bread entered through the companions' nostrils. They were warmed by the heat of the fire, which danced at the far side of the room, where a large pot hung above. There were long tables spread across the room with utensils hanging from iron hooks, as the castle servants bustled, carrying pots and already cooked food.

As soon as Hunter entered, the servants bowed. Instantly, they stopped and dropped to their knees, holding pots and food in their hands. Their voices softened and silenced, as their heads lowered into their chests, looking down at the ground.

Hunter paced through. He dodged the servants who bowed between the tables, heading towards the stairs at the side of the room, which led to the rest of the castle. Frantically, he paced up the stairs, as the companions scurried behind, seeing the servants rise as soon as Hunter left and continue their work.

Finally, Hunter led the companions to the throne room, after detouring through the hallways of the castle. They arrived at brown and tall doors, which were closed, with gold unicorn handles that Hunter used to throw open the doors before him, striding into the throne room with Tatiana, Free, Bidelia and Barnabas behind.

Inside, there were enormous, golden columns standing either side of a long red vertical carpet, which covered the grey cobbled flooring of the room. From above, white and golden banners flew, embellished with unicorns, just past the columns of gold. The throne room dazzled with deep blues, greens and reds from the windows at the far side of the room, where subtle hues of yellows illuminated from the painted glass just over the guards that stood beside the four thrones ahead.

Waiting underneath the glass windows, sitting in the golden thrones, which were cushioned white, there was a king. The king rested proudly against his throne with a small slouch, as his hands rested over the sides of the armrests and as his fingers were weighted by huge ruby rings. A golden and diamond crown, which sparkled, sat upon his slick, dark hair that fell below his shoulders, whilst he wore a silk cloak around his shoulders.

The king was joined by his queen, who sat to one side. Her straightened back rested firmly against the throne, as her hands clasped together, carrying twinkling rings on her fingers and heavy bracelets on her wrists. She was also draped in silk, wearing a silver cloak around her shoulders and a white dress underneath. Resting on her curled blonde hair there was a crown. It was just as large as the king's, lavished with more diamonds. The queen pouted alongside the king, watching Hunter and the companions approach.

Hunter bowed with the companions just before the king and queen, dropping to their knees and lowering their heads. They awaited the command of either the king or queen before they rose, waiting eagerly in silence.

The king's voice was deep and brisk, bellowing through the throne room and vibrating the ground. He ordered. "Prince Hunter, my son, rise. Rise from the ground."

Hunter rose slowly before the king and greeted him. "Hello, father."

"Why hast thou entered so urgently into my throne room?" the king growled.

"Father, I seek aid from thee. My friend, Tatiana Green, is already known to thee as the heir of the South. Yet, time has brought the Necromancer and Belladonna to know her existence. She is not safe, Father," Hunter pleaded.

"Rise, Tatiana Green. Rise, Tatiana Green and friends!"

Tatiana rose, as her companions closely followed, keeping their heads slightly lowered. They waited to be addressed by the king, examining the jewels that covered him.

"Tatiana Green, listen. When Ezra came to my kingdom, those twenty and five years ago, seeking my help, I almost sent him away. The chaos caused by the Necromancer doomed thy kingdom. My kingdom suffered, like all kingdoms. However, I did not lose my son and he did not lose his father or mother. When Ezra entered thy kingdom, sharing thy loss, there were tears falling from my eyes. I had lost two friends, thy mother and father. I almost lost thee, too. I wanted to send thee away, knowing the Necromancer would come for thee one day soon. Yet, I remembered promising thy father that I would care for thee, Tatiana Green, if such circumstances were to happen, as which they did," the king insisted. "I hope I have done so."

Tatiana smiled at King Umut. "My king, thou art just."

"Thou ask for more. I do not believe I can give more, without causing a war!" King Umut admitted. "My kingdom is prosperous, but all I have achieved cannot be allowed to end just for the Queen of the South."

"Thy kingdom will not end!" Barnabas shouted, pushing Tatiana to one side and stepping before King Umut and Queen Ioana.

The guards whipped their swords from their sheaths, stepping before King Umut and pointing their blades at Barnabas. Barnabas stumbled back, as the swords flew towards him, returning to stand with his companions behind Tatiana who had remained still.

With a wave of Umut's hand, the guards placed their swords into their sheaths and returned to their motionless positions. King Umut hissed. "Ah, Barnabas Mint! In my kingdom, men like thee are silent. Otherwise, tongues shall be removed from mouths."

Barnabas gulped, closing his parted mouth and lowering his head, as his cheeks started to blush.

"Now, I cannot help, Tatiana Green," King Umut shared. "I shall send word to the other kingdoms that thou seek aid and thou seek an army. I shall pray they give thee one."

Tatiana sighed a little and nodded. "Yes, my king. Thank you. Thank you, Queen Ioana."

Queen Ioana gently nodded.

Prince Hunter, whose mouth parted widely with dismay, after seeing his father dismiss Tatiana and the companions, glared over at his mother. His brown eyes widened with sadness and disappointment, as he wished for his father to change his mind.

Queen Ioana continued to stare at him, as her chin lowered and she smiled a little. "My son, be sure to arm Tatiana and friends with armour and weapons."

Hunter nodded, twisting on his heel and storming along the red carpet. His feet pounded to echo through the throne room, nearly leaving through the double doors before the companions had even moved to follow him.

The companions bowed at King Umut and Queen Ioana, before turning and scurrying behind Prince Hunter who had almost left the throne room. They quickly left to run through the halls of the castle, chasing after Hunter, who had almost disappeared.

The companions followed Hunter towards the far side of the castle, entering through an arched doorway and into another large room, which was also dimly lit. The room was shelved and hooked, as thousands of weapons were hung and stacked before them. There were swords resting horizontally across the walls, reaching to the ceiling, with ladders at the sides, as shelves stacked arrows for the bows which rested on the sides of the cases. Shields had been placed to one side of the room, ranging in sizes and materials methodically. Axes were placed inside opened boxes that were also placed inside the same casing as the arrows.

Hunter gestured the companions to search and take the weapons they liked. The companions hesitantly stepped forward, beginning to search through the thousands of weapons and shields before them.

As Tatiana split from the companions, Hunter snatched her wrist and tugged her to one side, leading her to the far side of the room. His grip was tight and reddened her wrist. He stopped in the corner of the room and before a chest. Hunter's hand loosened and he was eager to open the chest before him and to show Tatiana what was inside.

Hunter rested the lid against the wall as he crouched over to retrieve an object that he swept into his arms. Slowly, he raised the object from the chest, turning to Tatiana as soon as he had lifted the weapon above the chest lid and straightening his back. He revealed what was inside the chest with a glimmer in his eye as he examined the object which weighed down his arms.

Hunter held a bow. A gigantic heavy silver bow that shined. The string had not broken and the silver metal had not aged. He held the bow gently, stretching it towards Tatiana for her to take.

Tatiana traced the silver bow with the tip of her fingers, feeling the chill from the metal through her arms. She stroked its smooth coating, before gently touching the string, which cut through the fingers of her flesh. Her fingers retracted, as she jolted with pain and gazed upon the dribbles of blood that came from her slitted wounds.

She looked up from her fingers and back at the bow. Tatiana exclaimed, looking away from the bow and at Hunter, fixating on his beaming brown eyes, "It is beautiful."

"It is yours to have, Tatiana." Hunter grinned, placing the bow against Tatiana's hands, as the blood from her fingertips quickly dried.

Thankfully, she took the bow from Hunter and was given a matching silver quiver with silver, sharp arrows inside, which had been sitting on Hunter's shoulder. Tatiana placed the quiver over her head and rested the strap over her chest to rest on her shoulder, as she grappled the silver bow in the palm of her hand and at the side of her body.

Rapidly, the companions gathered around Tatiana and Hunter. Bidelia had attached axes to her belt with daggers at the side of her boots, and a crossbow and a quiver sat strapped against her back. Free and Barnabas had renewed their old swords with shining new ones, which were heavier and longer, but stronger. They returned with smiles, admiring what they had chosen.

Hunter addressed the companions, sadly and apologising. "I suggest thee head to the West and I advise thee to stay. Thou must be tired."

Barnabas shook his head. "No. Our journey awaits us."

"We shall head West as ye suggest. Ensure word is sent to the kingdom of the West and thank ye, Hunter," Bidelia added, stepping forwards and embracing Hunter, tightly. "Thank ye, for everything. I do not believe we shall see thee for a while, but I hope thee remains safe."

Hunter thanked Bidelia, after parting from their embrace and wishing her well. As soon as Bidelia pulled from Hunter and returned to Barnabas' side, Hunter quickly stared at Tatiana. He stated, "Do not cower when there is sadness and burdens that thou cannot bear. Be resilient against the Necromancer and Belladonna, as the journey will be incredibly long and dark! Please, save the kingdom of the South and ignite its rule again."

"I shall be fine." Tatiana smiled at Hunter, turning with her companions and leaving the room without Hunter following behind. The companions strolled through the castle with their weapons and headed to the gate, leaving the North as quickly as they had entered.

Tatiana, Bidelia, Free and Barnabas passed underneath the gate and over the bridge, crossing the moat and entering the fields ahead. They stormed South, as the early daylight continued to glimmer, beginning their journey to the West.

13

In the forest, where Wylie had found and fed Bathilda, the companions still slept. Wylie still rested against Darrel's shoulder, and Ainsley and Orla laid opposite. The snow had stopped falling from the grey skies above, but the ground was still covered in thick, white blankets. It was frigid and a howling wind whipped between the trees.

Wylie was the first to wake. He opened his eyes to view his surroundings before lifting his head from Darrel's chest and slowly removing Darrel's arms from his head. Wylie pressed his back against the tree, as his neck turned to stare at the spot Bathilda had shadowed over him. His eyes were crimson from the tears he had cried and he was haunted by her glare.

Opposite from where he sat, his name was whispered through the forest by Orla. Orla had watched him bear at a spot in the forest, examining his scarlet eyes and pink cheeks with a small smile. She called to him till his eyes looked over at her, already seeing tears form.

Orla scurried over to Wylie, gently moving away from Ainsley and dropping to her knees before him, where she cupped his cheeks in her hands. She caught his tears with her thumbs, stroking his face. "Why dost thou cry so?"

Wylie gulped. "I cannot tell thee. Thou would hate me, forever."

Orla sighted Darrel peering over, after awakening from his slumber and remaining silent. Orla turned to Darrel and wondered. "Dost thou know why he cries?"

Slowly, Darrel shook his head. "No. He would not tell me. If he still does not want to tell, I will not be asking again."

"Darrel, there be no need for brutality." Orla scowled, before turning to Wylie and continuing to console him. "If thou dost not wish to tell me, then please dry thy tears."

Wylie nodded, breathing deeply.

Orla gently removed her hands from his cheeks, before raising to her feet and stretching her hand towards Wylie for him to take. She grasped Wylie's hand and heaved him to stand, as he wiped away his falling tears. Orla did not leave Wylie till all the drops of water had disappeared from his skin, returning to Ainsley's side after she had awakened.

Darrel, Orla, Wylie and Ainsley continued their journey, beginning to pace through the rest of the forest. The companions marched through the falling snow, heading South, leaving the forest and straying further from the East, where the snow began to lift, beginning to cross over mountain terrain, with frost still lingering on the ground.

Darrel, Wylie, Ainsley and Orla halted. They had travelled far over the hills surrounding the snowy mountains, which were to the left of the companions, sighting something ahead. There were shivers spiking over their bodies, as they stared onwards.

Ahead, underneath layers of frost, there were huts, circling an old fire in the centre. The wood had been scorched black and the huts still smoked from the fire they had been burned with. A pungent sulphur smell swarmed through the companions' nostrils as they searched, seeing an abundance of life.

The companions hesitantly explored the empty settlement, quickly identifying small grains of black dust which had settled on the wood of the houses. They pinched the sparkling grains between their fingers, which blackened their skin and rotted their nostrils with their smell.

Orla called to her companions, who stood on different sides of the fire, which had burned in the middle. She played with the dust between her fingers as she turned to her companions. "What is it? What is this?"

Darrel stated, wiping the dust from his fingers and onto his clothes, as he looked over at Orla and his other companions. "I witness this only once when the Necromancer's darkness spread throughout the earth. It is his doing!"

Ainsley exclaimed, "Why is it here?"

Darrel nodded. "He journeys further to the North."

"Where are the bodies?" Wylie asked as he searched the village

"The bodies burn and their ashes burn till they are black," Darrel responded bluntly as Orla quickly wiped the dust from her fingers and onto her trousers.

"Let us keep moving," Ainsley insisted with a shudder of her shoulders. "I do not want to be here any longer."

Orla and Ainsley trekked through the rest of the village quickly. Their heads bowed as the wind whistled through the eerie huts, echoing the creaks of the wood. The black dust which settled across the village was blown at their feet and stained their boots. Orla and Ainsley rapidly passed the last hut on the outskirts of the village, twisting to stop as they waited for Darrel and Wylie.

Ainsley and Orla sighted Darrel and Wylie from a higher point of the settlement, seeing their heads had turned the same way. Darrel and Wylie stared through the eerie huts of the village, hearing a sound echoing in the wind. The hairs on their arms stood, as they looked back at each other, sighting the tremors in their lips.

Wylie twisted on his heel and slowly stepped forwards, following the shrilling sound that was carried by the wind. His arm crossed over his body and grabbed his sword, wielding the shiny blade which had been hiding in his sheath and stealthily moving over the rubble on the ground. He searched the village, and Darrel lingered beside the diminished fire at the centre.

The screech became deafening when Wylie stopped in front of a hut. The hut was still intact, but there was a hole in the roof and the door was opened wide. There was faery dust covering the walls and roof, which was gradually blown away by the wind.

Wylie crouched in front of the door and peered into the darkness that had settled inside. His sword was stretched before him, as he shuffled towards the scream. He called out into the darkness and cried. "Who be there? Who screams?"

Suddenly, the screaming stopped. From the darkness, two white ovals with green circles inside, appeared, eyeing Wylie. The daunting eyes dazzled, as Wylie jolted back. He saw long, pinkish-red hair emerge from the dark, which fell over a blue tunic that covered a thin and bony body of a woman. The woman's cheeks sagged with circles and her lips were crusty and dry as she parted her mouth to speak from her parched throat.

She croaked. "Can thou help me?"

Wylie gripped his sword, tightly. He scowled. "Why dost thou need me?"

"The Necromancer came and he scorched my home," she whispered with a honeyed voice. "I am ill and cannot fend for myself until I am better."

"What dost thou expect me to do?" Wylie asked. "I have my own journey and do not want to be burdened by thee!"

"Please. Take me to the nearest settlement to seek medicine," she begged. "I do not have weeks to waste, as there are only so few days left until my passing."

"What shall I receive in return?"

"I do not have anything to give." She sighed. "If thee waits till I am well, then maybe I can be useful to thee on thy journey."

"Dost thou have any skills?"

"I can hunt and forage better than most," she declared.

"What is thy name?"

"Phillipa Thyme," she answered, proudly. "Pip is what my friends call me."

"I am Wylie Mint." He pouted, as he reached for her hand and lifted her from the hut, using his sword to balance their weight as he poked the blade into the ground. His hand released the balancing blade and hoisted Pip over his shoulder, before taking his blade and striding through the village towards his companions that waited.

Wylie returned to Darrel, insisting they return to Orla and Ainsley before any questions were asked. Darrel nodded, eyeing the woman that was flopped over Wylie's shoulder and paced to Orla and Ainsley.

Already, Ainsley and Orla had seen Darrel and Wylie approach with Pip on Wylie's shoulder, moving to greet them. Orla and Ainsley stopped a few feet from Wylie, scowling at the woman he carried.

Wylie lowered Pip to the ground, gently placing her on her feet and holding her tightly by the waist. He balanced her silently as she answered Orla and Ainsley's questions.

"Who are thee, girl?" Orla hissed.

"I am Phillipa Thyme."

"What dost thee need from us?"

"I wish to be taken to the nearest settlement. In exchange, I will hunt for thou on your journey ahead," she answered.

Ainsley spat. "There is agave on thy tongue!"

Pip shook her head.

Orla stated, "A deal cannot be broken. Yet, I must warn thee, we will slaughter thee, if thy lies are malicious. Be wary, friend."

Orla turned to pace ahead, tugging Ainsley behind, who stalled to examine Pip. Orla and Ainsley strode in front, quickly distancing themselves from Pip, Wylie and Darrel.

Wylie lifted Pip back over his shoulder. He gently grabbed her waist and flopped her belly over his shoulder, resting her as comfortably as he could against his collarbone. Wylie plodded after Darrel, who had already exited the village. He sighted Orla and Ainsley far in the distance, as Darrel stayed a few metres ahead.

Though Wylie had been distracted by Pip, in the silence of his mind, he had not forgotten the children he had fed to Bathilda. He fought to find questions to ask Pip, but his mind focused on the eyes of the young girl that Bathilda had released and saw an infinite sadness. Wylie's questions for Pip quickly faded and he was quiet as they headed to the nearest settlement, Winlock.

Winlock was a settlement of the East. It was an enormous village, further East than Elba and further South, too. Winlock was surrounded by fields of cattle, which the village sold and ate. There was no meat finer than Winlock cattle, with many travelling far to taste the succulent flesh that the village sold.

Just as Wylie carried Pip in his arms, she whispered to him. Her voice was chilling and her words were tormenting, speaking clearly from her throat. "Thank ye, but it is with great pain that I shall say there are swords pointed at your backs."

Wylie stopped and scowled at her. He examined her grimace and listened to her shrilling laughter that escaped from her lips. Wylie bore into her eyes, which were not weakened by any plague, as a cold and sharp point pressed against his back.

Gladly, Pip threw her body from his arms. She thudded onto her feet and twisted, sliding a dagger from her boot and pressing the blade against Wylie's neck. Pip smiled, overlooking Darrel, Orla and Ainsley who had also halted abruptly, as figures stood behind them and pointed their swords against their flesh.

Pip chortled as a striking figure strode between the companions and turned to observe them. Pip addressed the figure, still pressing her blade on Wylie's throat with a smile. "Hello, Pa. I told ye I would find wealthy travellers."

The tall and broad man rested his large hands on the handle of his sword. He was draped in armour and a cloak sat over his shoulders, which blew rapidly in the wind. His brown and grey hair grew to his chest, matching his tangled beard, as his green eyes bore alongside his cold expression.

The man's voice bellowed, as his chest puffed. "Well done, Phillipa. I sight much food and money from these foolish travellers."

The figures behind the companions stepped forwards, pressing their swords against the companions' ribs as they searched through the companions' pockets. The figures rummaged for money, throwing pouches onto the floor, where loose coins clanged and stripping the companions from what they had earned.

Once their money had been found inside their pockets, their weapons were taken and their rationed food was stolen. The figures returned to stand behind them poking their backs with their blades and holding everything they had taken from the companions, waiting for their order to return to their horses which stood a few feet behind.

The man stepped forward, ignoring Orla, Ainsley and Darrel and striding towards Wylie. He stood closely to Wylie, holding his gaze. The man chuckled, releasing his spoiled breath. "How glorious. It is Wylie Mint. We have tricked and stolen from Wylie Mint. Thy day could not be better! Word shall spread. The barbaric Klaus Thyme of the East has mocked the infamous Wylie Mint!"

"Klaus Thyme? I have never heard of thee!" Wylie stated.

"Oh, but thy name is so infamous that the rest of us are in the shadows of thy ego." Klaus smiled, as he stepped away from Wylie and observed the other companions.

Klaus paced towards Darrel, slapping his stomach with the back of his hand. He cackled. "Thou art a fat one!"

He plodded onwards and looked down at Ainsley, stopping as he examined sideways. "Art thou a dwarf? I did not know there were any left after the Necromancer slaughtered ye all for good."

Ainsley growled, but she bit her tongue and glared at Klaus as he trudged towards Orla.

Klaus stopped before Orla and remarked, as he squinted to observe her face and sniffed the sweaty aroma rising from her body. "Thou smell."

Orla pouted and stayed silent.

Klaus returned to the centre to view all the companions before him and with a loud and clear voice he questioned. "Where is thy company heading? Thou do not come from the East, so why dost thou venture here?"

Darrel answered, bluntly, "We do not wish to head East, though our journey has taken us there."

"Where dost thou head, then?"

"South!" Wylie declared.

Klaus twisted and scowled, stepping closer to Wylie and stopping a metre from him. "Thou wish to go South? Why dost thou wish to journey there? Dost thou wish for death?!"

Wylie shook his head. "My companions and I do not wish for death."

"Why dost thy company wish to head there, then? Thou shalt surely be killed as soon as thou step over the border." Klaus chortled nervously.

"The Southern heir is returning to the throne!" Darrel exclaimed. "We are the companions to bring the heir there and overthrow the Necromancer for good."

Klaus pondered, as his eyes examined all the companions. "A compelling story thou tell, but is it the truth? Does this companionship help the Southern heir? Or do they lie to escape between their teeth?"

Pip growled. "Pa, let us leave!"

"Hush, daughter," Klaus spat, twisting his head over his shoulder, as his eyes widened. "I am in deep thought."

Klaus paced before the companions, as his eyes squinted at the sky above, sighting a large bird of prey soaring above them. A small smile appeared across his lips, revealing dimples in his cheeks. His eyes flicked away from the bird and at Wylie.

Klaus stated, "Take us to the heir of the South and we may return thy belongings!"

"I cannot take thee to her. I do not know where she is." Wylie sighed. "My companions and I split after being hunted by Belladonna."

"Belladonna?" Pip cried, almost lowering her dagger from Wylie's neck and facing Klaus. "Pa, do not involve me in this companionship! I do not wish to encounter Belladonna again."

Wylie muttered, glaring at Pip, "Again? What do ye mean?"

Pip did not answer him. Her hand tightened around her dagger and she placed her blade to rest against Wylie's neck again, eyeing her father.

Her father stared at her, still. His smile faded slightly and he mentioned, "I wish to see the heir. Ye do not remember the South and King Moryn and Queen Gwendolen's reign. There was a time when creatures far beyond us roamed, such as dragons and giants. It was everything. A kingdom far greater than any other. A kingdom which needs to return."

Pip scowled, forcing her blade away from Wylie's neck and pushing him forwards, towards her father. She growled. "Fine! Follow him and his company. Surely we shall die."

Klaus smiled a little, as Pip stormed to return to her horse. He watched his daughter climb her horse and wait impatiently for him, as Klaus turned to his men and women, ordering them to release the companions.

Wylie, Darrel, Orla and Ainsley stepped forward, away from the figures that had captured them. The companions eyed Klaus as he circled them, slowly.

"Where wast thou headed?" Klaus questioned.

"My companions and I wish to fight the Necromancer and Belladonna, but if we are to do so, an army is needed," Wylie mentioned. "It does not matter who fights."

Klaus awed. "Indeed, follow me to my friends who wish to fight. My friends are settled further East, if ye wish to meet them. There be only two, but if ye were to witness them, ye would believe them to be ten."

The companions nodded.

"All shall share a horse. My daughter Phillipa can ride with the infamous bastard, to her great pleasure! I shall ride with the dwarf, whilst the fatty and the ugly one can choose from the rest of the flock," he declared as he strolled towards his horse and gestured the companions to follow.

The companions strode towards the group of horses, following Klaus and the men and women in front. They climbed the horses and rode towards the East, as Klaus strode in front and led the men and women behind him.

14

Almost reaching the borders of the South, a group stormed across the land, passing enormous swamps that wreaked with a foul smell rising from the black waters that filled them. The grass had disappeared and mud squished beneath their feet. There were few trees to be seen in the vast distance of the lakes, as low and grey clouds were resting on their shoulders. Warmth radiated around the ground, spilling sweat from the group as they marched on.

The group was being led by a woman with angelic sapphire eyes, as she rested on her horse, eyeing ahead. Her dark hair was perfectly placed on her shoulders, laying against her dark blue dress. Her skin glimmered, even in the absence of the sunlight. She rode before her warriors who surrounded four helpless figures with their horses.

The figures' hands were tied and they were forced to cross the land, stumbling as a group. Dark circles appeared to sag down their cheeks and their eyes puffed with crimson veins shooting towards their irises. Thick layers of dirt covered their faces and their clothes were soaked with sweat, as the wizard, the drunkard, the duenna and the child were kept captive.

A man led his horse beside them and eyed the companions with his golden eyes. He held a long, wooden staff in his hand, which he waved carelessly, inspecting the wood as he did. The man wiped away the stains of scarlet from the staff, flicking the liquid from his hand and onto the ground.

The man chuckled at the companions. "Hurry, my companions. The wizard's staff I hold will surely slap thee again!"

The duenna muttered, "Why art thou walking in the darkness, beside a woman and a man that are nothing but cruel?"

"For he is alone on earth," the wizard answered.

The drunkard slurred, "The only comfort he has found, is the darkness."

"He is lost," the child declared.

Just as the child spoke, the man stretched his arm beside his body and extended the staff. He whipped his arm and twisted his wrist, slapping the staff through the air and lacing the child's back. The child screeched, as the wood tore through her clothes and lashed against her back, knocking the child to her knees as blood gushed from a slash across her back.

Instantly, the companions stopped, hearing the wood smack against the child. They charged to the child and dropped to their knees to console her. The companions held the child, placing their hands against her lashing and applying pressure to stop the rapid flow of blood that flooded down her spine.

The riders stopped around them, as did the woman who led them. They turned to watch the companions nestling on the ground, as the man with the staff dropped the reins of his horse and strolled towards them, waving the staff in his hand. He stooped above them.

The man shadowed them, blocking the sunlight behind. He huffed. "I did not hit her hard. She barely bleeds."

The drunkard howled at the man. "Ye whipped her so hard! How could thou do so? She is a child!"

"Helen? Helen?" The duenna called to the child as she knelt before her. She rested her hands against the girl's cheeks and stared into her tearful eyes.

Helen nodded. "Tasmin. I am pained."

Tasmin heaved Helen to her feet, clasping Helen's tied hands and hauling her to stand. Tasmin held Helen, as Helen's knees tried to buckle underneath her slouched body. Tasmin continued to whisper to her, choosing the most consoling words, as her other companions raised to turn to the man stooping over them.

The drunkard hurled his spit across the man's face and cussed. "Ye dastard bastard! How could ye?"

As soon as the drunkard had finished speaking, the man stepped closer, pushing the end of the staff into the ground and gripping tightly. He stood closer. His fist clenched and his arm raised. The man's knuckles smashed into drunkard's face, hurdling him to the ground and bruising his nose.

The drunkard tumbled backwards, as his head rolled backwards and slapped against the ground. His hand raised to clutch his nose as his teeth ground together and he screeched through them. He creased the side of his trousers with his other hand and breathed deeply once he had stopped screaming.

The wizard stayed standing before the man that held his staff and declared, "We will kill ye, Nemo."

"Move, Ezra. Pick up your companions and keep moving!" Nemo ordered as he raised the staff and threatened the companions. "Otherwise, I shall hit ye till thee stops speaking."

Ezra lowered to Sir Terrence and raised him to stand as Sir Terrence still held his bruised nose. Ezra hauled his drunk companion, grappling his hand and hoisting him to his feet. He reassured Sir Terrence, before beginning to walk ahead and leading his companions, who followed to stumble behind him.

Once the companions began walking again, the horses were nudged to move by their riders and Belladonna continued to lead across the land. Still at the side of the companions, Nemo lurked and his watchful eye saw every trip and every shudder.

Soon, the companions were forced to stop, as Belladonna and the riders abruptly halted, with Nemo delaying his stop from focusing on the companions. It was moments after their captures stopped, did the companions halt also. Their heads raised from resting against their chests and their eyes gradually observed their surroundings. The companions' throats burned and their voices were unable to reach the ears of the riders to ask where they were. The companions focused on what was ahead, before eyeing every rider that sat motionless on their horse.

Ahead, there was a wall of trees that were wide and vastly stretched to opposite horizons. The trees wept and were too weak to hold their leaves and branches, which flopped over the trunks. A grey tinge settled on the leaves, plunging over pools of water with some stretching far and others being small and deep. Only darkness was seen between the trees, as a light raven colour shed from the mist and clouds above. An intense heat plummeted towards them and instantly poured the sweat from their bodies.

At the front, Belladonna continued to stall. Her blue eyes bore at the forest, searching frantically between their trees, as her eyes winced. Belladonna was quiet, tightly clutching the reins of her horse and breathing deeply. She heard a painful silence generating from the forest, hearing her heart pounding above the ringing, until she heard Nemo's voice shrill from behind.

Slowly, Belladonna turned her horse to face Nemo. Her grip around her reins did not loosen and her voice was quick and pitched as she ordered, "Nemo! Keep the companions together through the forest. Do not lose them!"

"Why do we stop?" Nemo questioned. "Do we need to leave the horses behind?"

Belladonna nodded, before hesitantly throwing herself from her horse and landing firmly on the ground. She looked at her riders with a stern stare and watched her riders dismount also.

When the riders dismounted, Belladonna ordered them to storm through the forest ahead. Without hesitation, the riders marched with their weapons and entered the forest, beginning to disappear amongst the fog.

The companions were pushed forward by Nemo. He grappled the rope which was tied around Helen and Tasmin's wrists and hauled them forwards to enter the forest. Behind, Belladonna followed with Ezra and Sir Terrence, dragging them without strain.

The companions were forced to step into the forest ahead, pushing through the drooping branches and leaves and stumbling beside the twisting rivers ahead. Their boots were smothered with heaps of mud, as they drowned in seas of sweat gushing from their pores. The companions' ears rang, as the infinite silence swarmed around them and a foul and earthy smell filled their nostrils. The mist mostly blocked what was ahead.

Belladonna and Nemo heaved the companions through, still holding onto the rope which was tied around their wrists. They dragged the companions towards the riders that waited motionlessly amongst the midst with drawn swords and waiting for Belladonna to arrive.

The riders surrounded Belladonna and Nemo as they appeared from the grey clouds, beginning to march through the forest. The riders moved swiftly, as Belladonna and Nemo alongside the companions, stayed in the centre, dodging the trees.

Gradually, the companions were led to the heart of the forest. The trees became gigantic, vanishing into the sky, as their branches extended to block the light, twirling around each other. Above, the drooping leaves fell like curtains, as the leaves flaked onto the ground and fell softly and delicately like snow emerging in a heavy heat.

Through a low curtain of leaves, which toppled onto the floor, the riders led Belladonna and the companions into a large clearing. The clearing was covered in the wispy leaves that continued to fall, as roots raised from below the ground and stretched in a circular motion, twining with others. There were no gaps seeping light from above and the clearing stayed inky.

Belladonna and the riders halted a few feet from the centre. The riders raised their swords, as their eyes scanned the trees. Belladonna scouted the trees also, as her eyes frantically moved to search between the leaves.

Nemo grappled the rope, which tied Sir Terrence and Ezra's hand, as Belladonna passed them to him. He stood between the companions, keeping them still as his golden eyes searched above and as the companions followed his wandering eye.

A faint rustled echoed throughout the forest, as the grey leaves began to fall rapidly to rest on their clothes and hair. As they searched the leaves, there was no movement, but they could hear light footsteps tapping from above and beginning to surround them.

Then, a voice bellowed through the forest and called to them. The voice was deep and close to where they stood. It asked. "Who dares to travel through the Forest of Thaddeus?"

Belladonna answered, ferociously, as her eyes glowed subtly bluer than usual. "It is I, Belladonna!"

The voice growled. "I know who ye are! I question whom thou bring with thee?"

She responded. "The men and women I bring are my prisoners. I wish to bring them to Cahercasey, the Southern castle!"

There came no reply from the voice. Instead, Belladonna's answer was followed by a rustle from above, which caused leaves to fall quickly around them.

Their eyes glared upwards at the swaying curtain, identifying figures hiding amongst the leaves, as their bodies twisted around the vines to be perfectly balanced. The figures lowered their heads towards Belladonna, the riders and the companions, moving like spiders. Their feet curled above their bodies and kept them afloat.

Too distracted by the mesmerising movement of the figures, they failed to see a figure standing at the centre. The tall figure had appeared from the vines above and had landed on the ground without a sound. Their long and blond hair fell over their broad and muscled shoulders, and they wore armour over their chest. The figure's intoxicating azure eyes eyed the group of men and women ahead, with their swords already drawn and waiting at their side.

Eventually, the figure was noticed. Their eyes were incredibly bright and were seen from the corner of Ezra's eyes, causing his head to turn. Ezra spun slowly to view the figure that waited for them and, parting his lips, Ezra asked. "Who art thou?"

All at once, everyone's eyes turned to eye the figure at the centre of clearing. They were bewitched by their eyes, which were large and electrifying.

Belladonna slid through the group and strolled towards the figure, stopping centimetres before them. She hissed, as her neck arched upwards and her deeper blue eyes dazzled the figure. "Sargon. Why dost thou stop me? Thou know the agreement I made with thy leader!"

Sargon's voice was light and musical. He smiled pleasantly at Belladonna and his eyes beamed brighter, as his stern face became animated. "I am aware of the agreement made with my leader. Of course, we shall let ye pass. However, it does not mean I cannot stop thee whilst present in the forest and inspect what thou have brought to us!"

"What I bring is no concern to ye!" She growled. "Now, let us through."

"Ye forget the forest ye are in. It is not an ordinary forest. It is alive." Sargon grimaced. "The forest has its own mind. Its own thoughts. There are so few that know the way out."

Belladonna's neck lowered and her eyes flicked away from Sargon, as her teeth ground together. She remarked, quietly, "I do not know the way. I will need help."

Sargon chuckled, forcing Belladonna's arm to loop with his, as he began to lead her through the forest. He confidently called for the riders and the companions to follow, as he took them through the oval passage covered with leaves, which was ahead.

Nemo and the companions were the last to follow Sargon. Nemo had released the rope from his grip, which had scorched his hands and pushed the companions ahead of him with his sword drawn.

The companions stumbled beside each other, pacing after the group of black-hooded riders and seeing Sargon and Belladonna in the near distance. The four companions stopped just before the oval, watching the riders enter through the thick thickets of vines and disappear onto the other side.

With a single shove from Nemo, the companions were hurtled through the passage, tripping over the long vines and hurdling through to the other side. Nemo had booted Tasmin and Sir Terrence through first, followed by Ezra and Helen. They grunted as Nemo's boots imprinted against their backs and spat the leaves they caught in their mouths as they passed through.

On the other side, there was a smaller clearing. The clearing was still shadowed by hanging vines that were much lower than the previous clearing, which blocked the sunlight and submerged the clearing in further darkness. The ground was rocky and uneven, and thick trunks rested around the edge with no other passage.

Yet, as the companions scanned the clearing, they could not see Belladonna or the riders. They had vanished, whilst Sargon stood in the centre and greeted the stumbling companions as they entered.

Before the companions could ask Sargon where Belladonna and the riders had gone, Nemo stormed into the clearing after them. Nemo entered with his sword and paced in front of the companions, already aware Belladonna and the riders had disappeared. He waved his sword towards Sargon, placing his blade against Sargon's throat and standing before him.

Nemo spat, as he locked onto Sargon. “Where is my mother? Where is Belladonna?”

“Ah! The bastard son of King Moryn.” Sargon cackled, slapping his hands together. “Thy mother is ahead. She waits in another part of the forest with her riders. I did warn that the forest moves with its own mind.”

“Thou art a traitor to us!”

“My leader and I are more interested in the persons ye have brought with thee.” Sargon smiled, tapping Nemo’s blade and lowering his sword. Sargon stepped around Nemo and approached the companions behind. “I am interested in the persons that stand behind ye, Nemo. The persons who know the Queen of the South. For years, we believed there was no heir. Now, there is. My leader and I wish to meet the heir and help her return.”

Tasmin croaked, “The Queen does not want to rule. She does not want the kingdom.”

“She does not wish to rule?” Sargon queried, still smiling. “Well, we shall show her what it means to rule! Now, my leader wishes to meet thee. I shall take thee to her. First, Nemo, please release the persons from their ropes.”

Nemo still faced away from the companions, staring at where Sargon stood. He paused before turning to the companions, slowly striding towards them and raising his sword. Sargon placed the edge of his blade against the rope and sliced his sword through to release the companions from the rope that had reddened their wrists.

The companions rubbed their itchy wrists as soon as the rope fell. They watched Nemo stand to one side after he had finished releasing all the companions, before turning to Sargon that came to stand closer to them.

Sargon gestured them to follow, as he quickly turned and headed to the other side of the clearing. The companions followed, with Nemo lingering behind, before stopping at the foot of a tree.

The tree grew above the curtains of vines with an enormous trunk and gigantic roots, which staggered above the surface. Its dark wood was cracked and knots appeared all the way up, as its long branches reached across the forest.

Sargon strode towards the tree, tracing the bark with his fingers, searching for something. His nails dug deep into the wood and tugged. The outline of a door appeared as Sargon heaved to open it, snapping small pieces of bark from the trunk that flicked through the air and towards the companions. Sargon leant against the door, keeping it open and revealing a passage through the tree.

The passage was pitch black and a cool gust whipped through the companions' hair. Besides the howling wind, the passage was quiet and seemed never-ending. The companions stepped forwards and stopped before the entrance.

Ezra snatched his staff from Nemo, grappling the wood and lighting the end of his staff with a white light. The light appeared as soon as the staff was reunited with Ezra. Its light was not enough to brighten to the passage ahead, but it was seen amongst the darkness, as Ezra bravely entered first.

Tasmin and Helen followed, with Sir Terrence tugging at Nemo's arm and leading him inside. The companions entered, as Sargon shut the door behind and consumed them in darkness whilst they began their journey through.

15

In the West, the skies were bleak, as water gushed from the sky and drowned the land, forcing mud to gush into streams. There were bright lights flashing across the sky with purple forks striking the land and deafening roars vibrating the ground. A chilling wind snapped branches and uplifted trees from their roots and caused them to tumble, as the leaves were torn from the wood and left the trees bare.

Barnabas, Tatiana, Free and Bidelia crossed the turbulent land. Their clothes were stuck against their skin, chilling their bodies, as they shuddered. In the wind, the companions' hair slapped across their faces and clung to their glossy, wet skin. Their hoods flew from their heads, as their cloaks flapped behind them. The companions' hands were covered by thick leather gloves, but their fingers were still frozen, and their noses reddened besides their flustered cheeks.

Barnabas led the companions towards the West. He strode ahead, distancing himself with his quickening pace, creating metres between them, even as the wind blew against him. Barnabas' green eyes scanned the land, searching for a sheltered and dry area to rest his painful legs.

Every so often, Barnabas' head clocked over his shoulder, as he continued striding. His green eyes looked back at his companions that stumbled far behind him. Though he saw their tumbles, as their throbbing feet tripped on uneven land, Barnabas continued, even as his eyes winced at watching them fall.

Free's pace kept him ahead of Bidelia and Tatiana, locking onto Barnabas through the falling rain. He balanced his weak body against the handle of his sword, gripping firmly to keep him afloat. Free heard very little as the rain beat against the ground, unable to hear his fellow companions struggling behind him.

Mostly, Bidelia's pace was strong. Her legs stealthily carried her forwards, charging to catch Barnabas and eventually staying by his side, though her teeth chattered and her cheeks became brightly flustered. She fought the hurtling wind and pushed her soaking hair away from her hazel eyes, helping Barnabas find shelter, as her feet splattered in the rivers of mud.

The last companion was Tatiana. Tatiana's back slouched over her chest, as her neck swung to lean from shoulder to shoulder. She saw through her brown eyes, which were nearly covered by her eyelids that whipped open as soon as they had closed. Her white messy hair was knotted from the wind and strands of hair continued to cling to her face. She was too weak to raise her hand and to push her hair behind her ears.

Tatiana's eyes had been watching the muddy ground, seeing flows of mud run around her legs, as her feet became lost in the deep streams with every step. She heard the crashing of raindrops plummeting to the ground, whilst silence filled the gaps of her journey.

Yet, her feet stopped in the mud, as the streams flowed over her boots. She listened between the rain, hearing noises that had replaced the quiet. Her body froze, as a strong shudder ran up her spine and shivered her shoulders. Tatiana's eyes widened, fluttering as she awoke from a daze, slowly drawing her eyes to look up.

Tatiana gazed ahead. She saw Bidelia kneeling against the ground, as clumps of mud and strands of grass stuck to her clothing from the pool of brown liquid she knelt in. Bidelia's hair clung to her face, as her mouth opened wide to yell, disturbing the silence Tatiana had heard. Both of her arms clutched something against her chest, keeping something dry and warm, as the wind pushed all her hair to cover her face.

A few feet away, Tatiana saw Barnabas running towards Bidelia, as she ordered Tatiana to hurry. Barnabas raced to her, as his dark hair blew behind him and as his feet splashed spurs of mud across his trousers. He slid onto his knees, landing in the pool of mud at Bidelia's side and reaching to clutch what she held between her arms.

Quickly, Tatiana hurried. The wind lifted her hair that was attached to her skin and blew her hair behind her shoulders, as her cloak followed behind, rippling in the wind. The rain still thudded hard and the lights from the sky continued to flash. She arrived at Bidelia and Barnabas' side, dropping into the pool and overlooking what they held.

Resting against their arms there was Free's muddy and wet body that had been buried underneath the waters they now knelt in. His eyelids covered his brown pearls and his hair was still beneath the pool. His body was limp, as his arms swung at his side and as Barnabas propped Free's legs onto his lap.

Tatiana gushed, resting to lay her hand on Free's cold and blue cheek. "What has happened?"

"Did thou not see?" Barnabas screeched. "He was in front of thee!"

"If thou did not walk so far ahead, maybe thou would have seen also," Tatiana snapped. "Not everything is my fault!"

"Stop!" Bidelia ordered, scowling at Barnabas and Tatiana. "Thy bickering does not help. Now, lift him. We must find some shelter immediately."

Tatiana removed her hand from Free's cheek and slipped her arms underneath his torso. She balanced on her toes and pushed with her knees, as Bidelia and Barnabas lifted also, growling through their clenched teeth. They carried Free onto their shoulders, as water drained from his clothes and poured onto them.

Once Free balanced on their shoulders, the companions charged from the pool of brown water, which had left their clothes stained with mud and grass. The companions carried Free, as water continued to fall from the sky and as flashes of light flickered.

Almost an hour had passed when the companions found shelter. The companions travelled with rocks growing beside them and hills becoming higher. Amongst the land, they found a collection of white stones building a small mountain on top of a hill. The stones shadowed above a small area of dry land that was enough for the companions to sit underneath.

Free was laid to rest underneath the roof of rocks, dropping to the floor with a small thud as he slipped from the companions' grip. They raised him to rest his back onto the stone behind, stretching his legs almost back into the rain, as the companions shuffled to sit beside him.

The companions nudged closely together, staring at the gloomy and grey hills they had crossed and watching the rain drip from the edges of the rock they hid underneath. Their bodies shivered, as the wind blew towards them and their wet clothes became frozen.

As the companions rested, Bidelia placed her crossbow to her side and began searching through her bag. She sought the blankets she had packed, throwing them onto Tatiana and Barnabas' lap and placing her bag to one side as she wrapped the blanket she shared with Barnabas around her cold and wet body. Tatiana shared with Free, tightening the blanket around him, as she tried to warm her body, too.

Immediately, Tatiana's eyes closed and her head rolled to rest on Free's wet shoulder. She did not glimpse at her surroundings after receiving her blanket, kicking off her shoes and socks and tucking her frozen feet underneath the blanket to dry. She warmed quickly, though her teeth chattered and her body shuddered, snuggling closely to Free.

Bidelia looked over at Tatiana, watching her fall asleep with a small smile. Bidelia removed her shoes with her feet and pulled her socks with her toes, leaning forwards to grab them and leaving them to dry on top of her boots. Her pruned feet slid underneath and curled around the blanket, letting them dry. She sighed with relief as her boots and socks finally came off and her feet were heated and dried.

Then, Bidelia removed Free's shoes and socks also. She wrapped the blanket over his feet before releasing his cloak from his neck and placing it beside his boots. Bidelia raised Free, slipping off his top and tucking the blanket around his cold and soaking chest, hoping he would warm quicker as she laid him to rest on the rock.

Finally, Bidelia leaned her aching back against the white stone, with a prolonged sigh of relief. Her hazel eyes watched the falling rain and she slouched further underneath the blanket, as her white swirls of air escaped from her lips.

Barnabas watched Bidelia rest with his spring green eyes. He remarked as her hazel eyes nearly closed. "Dost thou wish to rest whilst I keep watch?"

She shook her head. "No. Thou need to rest, as thou art our leader."

"I wish our Queen had the same spirit as thee," he murmured.

"Barnabas, please do not be disappointed by her. She is not like us. Her life has been cushioned and she has been safe. There are no scars on her skin," Bidelia explained, as her hazel eyes looked up at him. "What did thou expect? She is only young. Plus, the throne is not truthfully hers. If her brother Thaddeus had not been killed with King Moryn and Queen Gwendolen, she would not rule. I understand her fear and her loathe to rule. Truly, I do! Now, thou must also."

His eyes rolled. “I will not understand.”

“It is hard to understand when we have seen a world much different to the one others have lived through. There have been moments where we have not wanted to see the light of the morning sun. Whilst other days have been peaceful with an urge to hurt ourselves. We have been forced to consider other’s feelings, when we have suffered in agony to feel nothing but numbing!” Bidelia’s eyes flooded with pools of water, as her voice trembled. “Often, we have wished for a better life, wanting to escape the draining memories of the past and hold onto the goodness of the present.”

Barnabas glared at her, as tears streamed down her cheeks and rolled from her chin. Her nostrils flared and her nose had turned red, whilst her cheeks flustered pink. As her tears poured quicker and heavier, whilst snot ran over her lips, her breath was rapid and she gasped for any air that she could, clenching her hands together underneath the blanket and gazing at the rain ahead.

Barnabas’ arms wrapped around her and forced her to lay against his chest, though she fought him. He felt her heart racing and her chest beating, muffling her cries as he pushed her head into the material of her clothing. He hushed her.

A beautiful and melodic voice escaped from Barnabas’ lips, soothing Bidelia. “Stop those tears, Bidelia. There is an adventure ahead of us and we shall need all our strength!”

Bidelia’s eyes shut, as Barnabas continued to hold her. Barnabas remained awake and watched his surroundings. He felt Bidelia’s heart calm and her chest relaxed, as her hands clambered his clothing. Barnabas waited for the storm to settle before waking his companions from their slumbers.

After hours of resting, the storm finally ceased. The grey clouds still lingered above, but the rain had finished and the wind halted. The flashing lights and the roars from the sky had vanished, but the ground was still soggy and rivers of mud still streamed.

As Barnabas’ heavy eyes focused, his eyes locked onto something strange that stood in the near distance. His eyes squinted, as he noticed a shadow crossing the land with a stealthily stride and approaching fast. He saw a black material flowing behind and noticed armour strapped to the shadow's body, as long black hair flowed behind and a pair of golden eyes locked with his. Barnabas shuddered, as the shadow carried a deep darkness.

Rapidly, Barnabas' hands shook Bidelia's body. Barnabas frantically called her name. He heard her groans as she rose and pointed towards the approaching shadow in the distance that had strangely become closer than before.

Bidelia's tired eyes focused, trembling at the now clear sighting of a tall and broad man that glided towards them. She threw herself over Free's sleeping body and reached for Tatiana, beginning to shake her body ferociously and yelling as her throat cracked.

Tatiana's eyes flicked open after hearing Bidelia's shrilling voice and throwing the blanket away from her body to rise. She twisted to face Bidelia, seeing her trembling lip and her hand pointing to something in the distance.

Tatiana stared from the corner of her eye, sighting the figure instantly. From the figure's tall stature and dark existence, seeing his golden eyes, Tatiana already knew who the figure was. She grabbed her boots and her socks, darting from underneath the rock and beginning to race down the other side of the hill.

Bidelia grabbed her crossbow and began to fire her arrows, even as she crawled out from underneath the shelter. She staggered forwards, piercing her arrows against his chest, but seeing he did not even wince.

As Bidelia fired, Barnabas awoke Free. Free stirred slowly, seeing Barnabas as a blur. His back straightened and he rose from the rock he leant against. Free gazed at Barnabas, listening to Barnabas' rapid and squealing voice, as Barnabas dragged him underneath the rock and heaved him to stand.

Free stood without his shirt and without shoes on his feet. He scowled at Barnabas, but Barnabas slapped Free's shirt and shoes against his chest without an explanation. Barnabas pushed him towards the same direction that Tatiana had sprinted, still sighting her in the distance, as Free followed her.

Barnabas stayed with Bidelia, as the man staggered towards them and as Bidelia's arrows failed to wound him. He ran towards the man, pulling his sword from his sheath and lunging forwards as Bidelia continued to aim, missing Barnabas with her flying arrows.

Yet, the man stopped and his golden eyes locked onto them. Feverishly, the man grimaced. His hand covered with metal gloves rose and he spread his fingers apart, showing his palm towards Barnabas and Bidelia.

Abruptly, Bidelia's crossbow became stuck and was whipped away from her hands, landing on the ground beside her. She stepped forwards to grab her crossbow, but her feet were glued in the streams of mud. Bidelia growled as she squirmed her body, failing to move her feet.

As Bidelia's crossbow was thrown to one side, Barnabas' sword slipped through his fingers, pulled by an unknown force and thrown to the side. His feet were also stuck to the grass, twisting his body to move as he was screeching at the top of his lungs.

The man smugly strode towards them. He faced the rock behind Bidelia and Barnabas, looking at them from the corners of his eyes with a smile.

The man chuckled, before turning to face Barnabas. "Ah! Hello, Barnabas Mint. I am glad to encounter thee again. I believe thou wert just a boy when we saw each other last. Dost thou still have scars I gave?"

Barnabas' eyes rippled with water, as his teeth pushed together and he swallowed the lump in his throat. He stayed quiet, unable to clearly project his voice.

The man spun to face Bidelia, taking a step closer and examining her. He remarked. "Ah! The servant girl from the kitchen at Cahercasey. I guarantee it was thee who helped Tatiana escape from me and Belladonna."

"My name is Bidelia Lovet and thou art no King, Samael!"

King Samael grinned. "My name is the Necromancer. Listen well, Bidelia Lovet. Otherwise, thy death shall come soon."

The Necromancer snatched Bidelia's hand and squeezed. A puff of smoke appeared from her feet and swirled around her ankles, beginning to suffocate her. Bidelia disappeared as the smoke raised around her, as the Necromancer released her hand, which was pulled into the smoke. Bidelia held her breath, as the black smoke continue to spiral around her and blocked all air from entering the tube she stood in. She was unable to see the Necromancer and unable to see Barnabas, hearing only silence.

The same black smoke snaked towards Barnabas, rising from his feet with soft swirls. The puffs of clouds cocooned him, twisting above his head and absorbing every ounce of air he had once breathed. The twirling smoke churned Barnabas' stomach and his eyes closed, as his head spun. He heard the same silence as Bidelia, also unable to see the Necromancer and unable to sight Bidelia through the inky tornado.

Suddenly, a light appeared at the top of Bidelia and Barnabas' twirling prisons, as the grey smoke drifted to part. The ebony clouds started to disappear gradually, lowering to their feet and dispersing. Bidelia and Barnabas gasped, as air filled their lungs, collapsing whilst their minds rapidly spun.

As the raven cloud vanished and as Bidelia and Barnabas recovered from their nauseous stomachs, their eyes searched their surroundings through metal bars in a hanging cell that hung high over a dusty floor below. They were squished into their cells, as they hung beside each other, in a gloomy and dingy circular room with a set of spiralling stairs leading towards a door. A few torches sat in iron holders on the walls, which created enough light to see a figure glaring at them from below.

Barnabas and Bidelia met the golden eyes of King Samael. He stood tall and smiled at them, before his voice echoed through the room, welcoming them. "Bidelia and Barnabas, welcome! Welcome to Cahercasey. Welcome to the South. Welcome to the dungeons of the South. Here, thou will remain. Shortly, death shall come if thou do not prove valuable to me."

Bidelia growled, lunging at the bars of her cell and causing her cage to swing. "Thou wilt die, Necromancer!"

The Necromancer cackled. "Tonight, I unleash all my power into this world. A darkness shall spread that will destroy everyone and everything I do not desire, including Queen Tatiana!"

Barnabas muttered, as he leant into the bars of his cell, "She does not even want her throne!"

The Necromancer's smile faded and he paced to stop just before Barnabas' cell and scowled. His voice deepened and he questioned. "Why does she not want her throne?"

“She is a coward.” Barnabas’ eyes rolled. “She does not want any responsibilities. She does not want to rule. She does not care…”

“Barnabas! Be quiet!” Bidelia screamed as she turned to him and glared.

The Necromancer grinned, slowly stepping away and silently climbing the stairs. He opened the closed door and entered a dark passage, slamming the door shut and turning the locks that echoed in the dungeon.

Barnabas’ stared at the wall adjacent to him and avoided Bidelia’s stern frown. His head leant backwards into the gaps of the bars and flopped his arms over his knees. He stayed quiet, even as Bidelia’s voice shrilled through the silence.

“Barnabas! Thy temper is fragile. Thy temper shall get us killed, as it will allow thee to be killed also. Thy stupidity has left Tatiana vulnerable,” Bidelia declared.

“Dost thou believe Tatiana will bend to the Necromancer?” Barnabas shouted as his head rolled forwards with a raised eyebrow.

“The Necromancer will now do all he can to exploit her. For I will not blame her if she succumbs to him.” She hissed, “I saw the fear in thy eyes when thou saw the Necromancer; thou hath done his bidding also and succumbed to much more than doing his will.”

Barnabas’ eyebrow lowered, as his green eyes turned to look away from Bidelia, filling with water. His nose scrunched, stopping his tears from falling and pouting his lips. His throat became clogged and he fell silent, looking at a spot on the stone walls and relaxing his entire body that suddenly tired.

Bidelia watched from the opposing cell, seeing the reflection of the flames below in the water which filled his eyes and stretching through the bars to reach for him, rocking her cell. She called, as her eyes watered too, “Please, Barnabas! I do not dare say such words again. I promise.”

Barnabas’ eyes closed. His tears stayed under his eyelids and his mouth stayed pouted, as his nose relaxed. He breathed deeply, hoping to fall asleep quickly and wanting to drown Bidelia’s voice.

After a while, Bidelia stopped. She had called to him one last time and received no response, pulling her hand back through the bars and slumping into her cell. Bidelia leant back and rolled her neck to lean against one of the bars, as her eyes watched the black iron ceiling of her cell, disappearing into her thoughts, before falling asleep.

16

Riding across the East, galloping on their horses, which ploughed through the thick snow, there was a group of riders. The three horses at the front carried two people on their backs, whilst the rest only carried one. The front riders were closer together than the rest of the group, conversing through the light flakes of falling snow and above the wisps of the Easterly wind.

Leading the riders was a broad and tall man. Proudly, he rode his horse, as his long and black hair flowed over his shoulders with the gusts of wind. His small dark brown eyes searched between the flakes of snow, with a woman sharing his horse.

The woman riding with him was small and stumpy. Her arms were crossed over her body, as she held her cloak over her arms with her fingers. The woman's brown eyes were closed and her chin dropped into her neck, as her nostrils flared from snoring loudly. Her dark hair flopped over her face and her cheeks were reddened by frost.

On the horse behind, there rode a woman with deep red hair resting against her light green cloak. She lightly held the reins of her horse, as her green eyes eyed the white blanket which covered the grass. Her lips pursed, as the man that rode with her lay his head against her back.

The man behind had fallen asleep during the falling snow. His curly hair laced over his closed eyes, as his head dropped onto the woman's back, dribbling onto her cloak. His arms dangled at his side, as he breathed loudly and deeply, exhaling snores from his nose.

At the side, straddling from the group, there was a short and large man. He rode at the back of his horse with frost sitting on his long ginger beard and his cheeks turning pink. Between his lips, his wooden pipe sat, as he inhaled his burning weed and tobacco, staring amongst white land.

He rode with a woman, slightly younger than him, who was tall. She bore brown eyes and a fierce pout, as she was forced to lead her horse to follow the man at the front of the group. Her long blonde hair was matted, as white flakes clung to every strand and as she shivered, sharing the man's pipe of weed and tobacco.

The man at the front, which was Klaus, remarked with his loud voice bellowing over the silent land. "Ah! The Stars shall not watch over us tonight. There is far too much cloud for us to see them."

"The Stars always watch over us, even if we cannot see that they are!" the enormous-stomached man called after giving the pipe to the woman he rode with.

The woman he had passed his pipe to was Orla. Orla sniggered. "The Stars left us many years ago, when the Kingdom of Old was destroyed by the Necromancer, followed by the desolation of the South!"

"Forevermore, the Stars watch us," Pip declared, as Wylie slept against her back. "For I have seen a Star."

Ainsley, riding with Klaus, snorted. "Child, thou hath seen no Star!"

"Indeed, I have. The Star came to me with a message and ever since, I have spread the message!" Pip announced, proudly. "The Star told me there was an heir to the South, long before rumours spread."

Orla teased, "The Star told thee of the heir to the South and thou spread the message of the Star?"

Pip nodded. "Yes, I did."

"Thou art the reason for the Necromancer knowing of the heir's existence?" Ainsley questioned.

"It was not all me! The rumours came from the mouth of a drunkard from Cheslyn, whilst I told only the truths," Pip hissed.

"The drunkard is our companion," Darrel growled.

Abruptly, Klaus stopped his horse. The group of riders stopped behind him, as Klaus drew his blade to the side of his body, followed by the clangs of the riders and the companions grappling their weapons too. He spotted movement in the distance, which was unseen by the rest of his riders.

Slowly, Klaus led the riders and the companions forwards, marching through the snow. They rode quietly, despite the figures in the distance already sighting them. Klaus staggered in front of the group and approached the two figures that they met.

The two figures stopped before Klaus and the riders. They wore cloaks over their shoulders and hoods completely shadowed their faces.

On their hands, there were metal gloves, which held the reins of their horses, as black gowns draped over their bodies. Hanging around their necks, there were tight golden necklaces, with a clear and oval ruby dangling at their chests, which seemed to glow, as lines of metal entangled the gem.

The figure's necklaces were already recognised by the companions, sighting the emblem of the Southern kingdom, as the metal created the veins of a leaf starting from a single line. It was known as the Fire Leaf, containing the fire and made by the Stars.

One of the figures questioned Klaus, as their voice echoed across the snowy land. "Klaus Pontos, Phillipa Thyme and friends. We have met just on time, just as we planned!"

"Yes, Caspar Deorwine." Klaus smiled. "We bring great news!"

The other figure responded with a deeper voice than the first, leaning to one side and eyeing Wylie that continued to sleep against Pip's back. "Is that the bastard Mint brother?"

Pip's eyes rolled. "Unfortunately, so. He travels with us and leads us to the heir of the South. Thou must be excited to meet the heir, Asriel Power, after so many years."

Asriel answered, "Yes, Caspar and I have waited many years for her return. After seeing her flee the castle with the wizard, we had hoped she would come to Cahercasey again."

Asriel and Caspar turned their horses around, beginning to trot over the trail of horseshoe prints they had made and beginning to lead. Klaus followed, gesturing the riders and the companions to travel beside him.

As the companions rode through the snow, following the hooded figures, Caspar and Asriel, Wylie began to hear the small neighs of the horses and the whispers of voices. Slowly, his eyes opened, sighting the mountains in the distance and the bleak white ground from over his shoulder as a blur. Gradually he rose, seeing Pip's red hair and a dark patch on her cloak, as his hand wiped away the remaining saliva from his mouth. His head turned to view his surroundings, half smiling at his companions, before eyeing the strange, new figures that led them.

Wylie's voice croaked, as he started to speak, muttering in Pip's ear, "Who be those riders? Why do we follow them?"

Pip was not startled by Wylie's voice, feeling him lean away from her back and relieving her from leaning forwards as she rode. She mumbled with a chuckle, "Those riders are my father's companions. My father claims they befriended when Cahercasey was born, but the South was born thousands of years ago! Asriel and Caspar wear necklaces which only so few were given by King Moryn. Those few swore to bring the Southern heir back to the kingdom, promising King Moryn just moments before the Necromancer stormed through the castle gates."

Wylie looked over Pip's shoulder and yelled at Asriel and Caspar, "Where do ye lead us?"

Suddenly, the two cloaked riders halted, abruptly stopping the riders behind. The riders stared into the distance before looking over their shoulders and glaring at Wylie, though their faces still could not be seen.

Asriel asked, "Who interrupts the rhythm of our travels and the silence of our nature?"

"It was I, Wylie. Wylie Mint."

"Already we come to know thy name," Caspar responded. "The bastard thou art."

Wylie growled. "How dare thou speak to me like so!"

Caspar chortled. "Thou bring no fear into our hearts. For we are unlike mortal men!"

Wylie jumped from Pip's horse, slamming his feet into the snow and storming towards them. He stood between Caspar and Asriel, who remained seated on their horses, as Wylie scowled. Though Wylie stood close, still he could not see their faces, examining a black mask that covered their faces.

Wylie quizzed, "What are thou if not alike women and men?"

Simultaneously, Caspar and Asriel gloved hands reached to clasp their masks with their fingers and removed their black metal masks to rest on their laps. Their faces were not fully seen underneath their hoods of their cloaks, which they slowly lowered to rest on their shoulders, as Wylie examined their faces.

Wylie met Caspar's dazzling sapphire eyes that twinkled in the bleakness of the snow. Wylie saw Caspar's glowing and radiant skin, which was untouched by any pigments and scars, before following his long and golden hair that ran over his chest. A soft and warm glimmer surrounded Caspar and caused Wylie's knees to weaken, as Caspar revealed his large and white smile.

Wylie turned to see Asriel's long black hair reaching the bottom of his back and blowing in the small gales of passing wind. His truffle skin was soft, as his brown eyes dazzled Wylie. Asriel's smile was just as big as Caspar's with a bright light surrounding him also. Asriel's great height shadowed Wylie, as Asriel stooped above him.

Asriel and Caspar pulled long silver necklaces from around their necks which dropped over their chests with a small, rayed star covered in crystals with an oversized sapphire at the centre. The glorious chain sparkled and the sapphire glowed even in the dark.

Wylie stood speechless between Caspar and Asriel, as his companions saw the necklaces sparkle and whispered as they gushed with excitement, as Darrel's cheeks became wet with tears.

Orla was the first to speak into the overwhelming silence that had suffocated the companions. "O by such heavenly nights do the Stars appear! Before me, before my companions, the Stars are here. In all their glory and all their light, they shine ever so bright, as they watch us in the night. From the world above us, the guide to home, which is mine."

Ainsley grumbled, "The Stars which have fled and allow us to perish underneath the Necromancer and Belladonna!"

Asriel stared at Ainsley and mentioned, "Yes, the Stars have fled. Yet, I and my brother would not leave thee so helpless. We made a pledge to King Moryn and we have not forgotten. For we have gathered many to create armies beyond thy dream."

Wylie still stood between Asriel and Caspar, flicking between them and admiring them, as his stomach churned. His hands shook, but his scowl lightened and the corner of his lips turned upwards. Slowly, he retreated to Pip's horse, stepping backwards, as his eyes continued to lock onto the two Stars he saw.

He reached Pip's horse, clumsily climbing onto the saddle and slamming his chest against Pip's back. Wylie's eyes continued to lock onto the Stars, as did Orla, Ainsley and Darrel.

Darrel asked, seeing the riders had not flinched at the stunning sight of the Stars, as his head looked over his shoulders, "Have thou always known the Stars?"

Pip smugly smiled, as her green eyes viciously flicked over at Darrel, Orla and Ainsley. "Forevermore."

Caspar and Asriel twisted to face the front of their horses, beginning to move and continuing to lead Klaus and his riders through the snow. Their journey to the East would takes weeks, as the snow thickened amongst the ground and the winds strengthened. A bitter frost began to freeze their hands and the strands of their hair, as white flakes covered their clothes.

They rode their horses for as long as they could before having to seek shelter from the storm, detouring towards the mountains to the left and finding small clusters of rocks to nestle between. As they hid between and underneath gaps of rocks, sparsely populated at the foot of the tall and bewildering mountains above, they rested in pairs. Too frozen to move, they clambered around each other, as their bodies shivered and as the wind lashed against their faces, reddening their cheeks. They spoke through their chattering teeth with trembling voices, as white clouds blew from between their lips.

Resting inside a cave of rocks, with a small and landscaped entrance that the companions slid underneath, there were Wylie, Pip, Darrel, Orla, Ainsley and Klaus. They huddled together, as the wind entered and screeched. The companions saw a line of white snow at the foot of the entrance, as they gathered in darkness. Their legs were tucked into their chests, as their feet rested on the points of the rocks, huddling together and clutching their cloaks over their shoulders with their hoods covering their frozen skin.

Slowly entering the cave were Caspar and Asriel, crawling underneath the low entrance and shuffling towards the companions in the darkness. Caspar and Asriel sat across from the other companions, examining their flustered and cold faces, as they stayed warm and untouched by the frost which settled on the companions' eyelashes.

As they seated, Asriel's voice echoed through the cave and underneath the shrieks of the wind that entered. "In the years that the Necromancer has destroyed the old kingdom and the forgotten kingdom, he committed genocide of a thousand. Those that survived fled East. The creatures I tell of hide amongst many shadows and may not be found in the safest places."

Caspar continued, “With our light, we will guide thee through the darkness and keep thee safe!”

Klaus trembled. “Thank ye, friends. Be there a way to warm us?”

Caspar and Asriel nodded, pulling their bags in front of them and heaving blankets from inside. They raised to place the blankets around the companions’ bodies, as their hands were too cold to grasp them.

The companions were warmer as the blankets settled over their shoulders and as they shuffled closer together. They moved towards Asriel and Caspar, as their voices continued to echo through the cave, speaking louder over the wind.

Caspar announced, “As soon as the snow lightens, all must move ahead. If we are to wait till the snow stops all together, then we shall be waiting weeks.”

Darrel wiped away the snot running from his nose and questioned. “Where do thou wish to take us first?”

“Far in the East, a gathering of Seelie’s awaits us!” Asriel responded.

“Seelie’s?” Wylie quizzed. “True and living Seelie’s await us? Did they not die when the Necromancer and Belladonna came?”

“No,” Pip whispered, sternly. “The Seelie’s escaped with my father and I.”

“Thou have been shown more than any have seen. For none of my companions have seen Stars or Seelie’s!” Wylie groaned, as his eyes flared emerald. “How have thou seen so much when thou art so much younger than I?”

Pip’s tired eyes stared at Wylie, as her lips hesitantly parted and she breathed, brushing her hair behind her ears, which were strangely protruded and pointed sharply. “I am not like thee. For I am a Seelie.”

Wylie stayed quiet, as his eyes continued to shine green, scowling at Pip’s pointed ears, features found only in the Seelie race. His teeth ground and he bore at her, even as she turned to bow her head.

Ainsley spoke softly, calling Pip. “There be no shame, Pip, in being a Seelie. In fact, thou must be so proud.”

Orla added, “The Seelie children always came to thy village to play when I be young. How I miss such days before the Necromancer and Belladonna.”

Wylie twisted and spat. “Thou have seen Seelie’s?”

Orla nodded.

"Why is it I be the only one to not have seen a Seelie till now?" Wylie moaned, examining the glaring faces around him. "Why have I been left to sulk in darkness with my brother? Where have thou been to help us? My brother and I deserve to have seen the Stars and Seelie's, not the points of a thousand blades and burned with scars to last lifetimes!"

Wylie's words drowned the whooshing wind, as the companions focused on his clenched teeth and pouting lips. He searched for parting lips, ready to silence the voice that escaped from them, but his companions' mouth stayed firmly shut.

"My brother and I have been hurt more than anyone. Seelie's and Stars help those like us, but none of ye did," Wylie hissed, lowering his head and avoiding his companions' stares. "No one helped us."

Pip sat next to Wylie, sharing the same blanket as him and Ainsley, sitting between them. Her green eyes watched his tears drop and hit the grey, rocky ground, leaving dark patches on the ground. Still locking onto his tearful eyes, she reached for his hand that hung over his crossed leg and clasped his cold fingers, leaning her head against his shoulder. Pip's eyes closed, as she held Wylie's hand tightly.

For a moment, Pip and Wylie sat alone, before Ainsley, Darrel, Orla, Klaus, Asriel and Caspar gathered to comfort Wylie and stopped his falling tears.

Caspar gripped Wylie's shoulder firmly, as he shuffled closer towards him and glared into his hazel eyes. His lips parted to release a soothing voice to express encouragement, but all he voiced was an apology. "Truly, I can only express my dearest apologies for leaving thee in the dark."

Wylie's eyes flicked up at Caspar, as his lips trembled and his cheeks flustered. The whites of his eyes had now turned scarlet, as his tears stung his skin. His hazel eyes flared with anger, as all his muscles tightened. He filled his lungs and prepared to scream but released only a long exhale whilst he slowly fell backwards and rested his back against the frozen cave floor, glimpsing the black ceiling above before his eyes closed to sleep.

After watching Wylie fall asleep, the companions reclined also and rested their backs onto the rocky ground. The companions glared at the inky ceiling of the cave, examining the rigid and low rocks that were above them, as their eyelids fluttered shut and their shivering bodies slept.

17

Towards the West, crossing the bare land and trudging through the rivers of flowing mud that flooded fields of grass, two sprinting figures with long white-blonde hair raced across. Their cloaks flapped in the wind behind them, as they struggled to breathe. The figures were soaked from the pounding droplets that were thrown from the grey skies above, as air cooled their sweaty and smelly bodies and as their faces flustered.

The two figures abruptly stopped, after running beside each other and no longer being able to catch their breath. Their backs hunched over their bent legs, as they grunted, breathing heavily and quickly, whilst their jelly legs collapsed underneath them and dropped into the mud. The figures' necks rolled backwards and their warm faces were soothed by the icy waters that splattered on their faces.

The shorter figure with much longer hair and deep brown eyes was the first to catch their breath. The figure exasperated deeply, looking over at their companion. "Dost thou be all right, Tatiana?"

Tatiana turned to glare at her companion and nodded. "Yes, I be fine. Why did the Necromancer and Belladonna not follow us? Instead, they have taken our companions. Why leave us? Easily, they could have followed us and captured us!"

Her companion nodded.

"We will find them, Free! We must find Barnabas and Bidelia." Tatiana breathed. "Once our breaths have been caught and our lungs filled with air, we shall find them."

"Tatiana, do not lose the direction of our journey. We must journey West to the Nathair kingdom."

"Free! We cannot leave them!" Tatiana screeched, stumbling to her feet and standing above him, as she clenched her fists.

Free raised also, stamping his feet into the mud and staring at Tatiana, as he yelled, "Then, why did thou run?"

Tatiana shook her head, stepping away from Free, who had pushed his face towards hers. She stormed past Free and splashed her feet in the mud, charging towards the direction she had come from in the falling rain.

She sprinted fast. Her feet pounded in the pools of mud and her white hair flapped behind her. She started well, but her throbbing legs soon slowed and she stopped only metres away from where Free stood. Her eyes focused on the land ahead, searching far into the distance for the remaining presence of the Necromancer and Belladonna, but sighting only the falling rain and the gales of wind blowing through the trees.

Free paced towards Tatiana, stopping at her side and looking up at her stern face. His sparkling brown eyes glimpsed at her, as his hand clasped her wrist and gently tore her away and led her West. He heaved Tatiana through the mud and across the hills ahead.

They hurried to the Western kingdom, Nathair, passing small craters in the ground which released swirling and hot smoke, which spurted with a small noise as it was released. A sweltering heat forced Free and Tatiana to remove their cloaks and their boots from their sweaty feet, as the rain dried and as they stretched their toes on the cracked brown ground. There was a pungent and sulphuric smell swirling through the air, as Free and Tatiana stumbled further West.

In the distance, a stooping towered palace was seen through the low clouds and beyond the steam. Its stone walls had been scorched and were transformed black by the radiating heat and the large hot mountains that spurted orange flares. The palace was circled by deep and smoking waters which baked the guards who stood on the lowered bridge of the castle, as orange swirls cackled on the high palace walls. Despite the flaring orange embers, the palace stood mostly in darkness, though ear-ringing shrills gravitated over the land and from the palace dungeons.

Tatiana and Free stopped their throbbing and pulsating legs, examining the palace ahead as their hearts pounded and their palms sweated. They stood underneath its shadow, admiring the lights of the dancing flames and following the orange flares that exploded from the mountains behind.

Following the orange light, Free and Tatiana stumbled towards the bridge. As they approached, their skin melted and the guards drew their weapons, blocking Free and Tatiana, stopping them at the foot of the bridge.

A guard with an arrow pointed at them, yelled, "These days are very strange and dangerous times. We do not heed to strangers no longer. Thou must declare one's name and state thy reason to come to Nathair!"

Free announced, taking a small step forward and scanning the guards before him, "I be Free Stellam and I be accompanied by my companion, Tatiana Green. King Umut and Queen Ioana sent word of our arrival."

The guard hissed, as he slid his sword into his sheath. "King Adrion has awaited thee for many days! Follow me, at once."

The companions were gestured to step onto the bridge, as the other guards lowered their weapons. The guard in front swivelled on his heel and led the companions across the bridge and underneath the large gate ahead. The companions strode past the castle walls and entered the courtyard.

Behind the gate, the large courtyard was silent, as figures crossed the muddy grounds and held the leads of their horses that followed behind. The castle towers shadowed the grounds below, as the figures' heads stayed bowed and their faces were shadowed by their hoods. At the edges, there were a few stalls selling dried herbs and vegetables, which were brown and wrinkled with a strong stench.

The companions entered the courtyard and followed the guard through, stamping their feet in the mud that splattered on the back of their legs as they stormed after the guard they followed. The companions hurried underneath an archway and entered through the rest of the kingdom.

The archway led to a path with small houses on either side with walls made from stone and roofs made from concrete. The chimneys piped clear grey clouds into the dark sky above, where the sky smouldered from the erupting ash, as black sparkling dust trickled onto the companions' shoulders. The path snaked and led towards the castle ahead, heading to the castle wall where a raised iron gate was heavily guarded and led to another smaller courtyard on the other side.

The guards that guarded the entrance of the castle wall parted immediately as the guard leading the companions stormed through. The guard crossed the empty courtyard and towards the closed castle doors opposite, where two guards stood either side and opened the doors as the guard and the companions approached.

The doors opened wide, revealing an enormous throne room, which Tatiana and Free entered, following the guard. Tatiana and Free stepped into a dark room with the curtains drawn over the windows on either side of the room, as the heels of their boots echoed on the black marble floor. Free and Tatiana paced to the far side of the room, as goosebumps appeared on their skin and their hairs began to stand.

At the far side of the room, there was a black iron chair. A fur coat draped over the back, and a man sat upright against the throne. The man was proudly leaning against his chair and flopped his hands over the arms of the chair, as he glared down his nose at Tatiana, Free and the guard they followed. His crown shadowed Tatiana and Free, as his onyx jewels blinded their eyes even as they stood in the darkness of the throne room.

Tatiana and Free bowed, as the guard left the throne room and left them to stand before the King in silence. They rested on their knees and waited to be spoken to.

The proud man before Tatiana and Free scowled at them with a pair of jade eyes and pierced full lips that parted to release his light and melodic voice, which danced throughout the throne room. "Welcome, Queen Tatiana Green to the kingdom of Nathair! Thy arrival is late, but no less pinnacle. There has been great chaos from thy existence and what pleasures it brings me to have thee here."

Tatiana continued bowing, with her knee still against the cold ground. "Thank ye, King Adrion! The kingdom of the North has been most kind to us and I hope thou will treat us with the same warmth."

King Adrion grinned and raised from his throne, slamming his feet on the marble and yanking his trousers to sit at his waist. Proudly, he strode towards Tatiana and Free with his hands crossed behind his back. "Now, Queen Tatiana, whom hast thou brought with thee? A suitor?"

"This is Free Stellam. My companion. I will not depart from him and he shall not depart from me," Tatiana declared, scowling at King Adrion's smile.

King Adrion did not glare at Free, instead stepping down from his throne and stopping before Tatiana, where she felt his warm breath on the bridge of her nose. He stayed grinning and stretched one hand to lay heavily on her shoulder, as his chin lowered into his neck and as his breath caused Tatiana to crease.

"Both of us must converse, as the threat of the Necromancer and Belladonna increases greatly. For now, thou shall be escorted to the dining hall and thou shalt receive food most appetising." King Adrion looked up from Tatiana and gestured his guards that stood at the entrance of the throne room, with a small wave of his hand, to come forwards.

Instantly, the guards responded and quickly approached Tatiana and Free, stopping a metre behind. Tatiana and Free bowed at the King, before turning to the guards and following behind, as they were led from the throne room, feeling the eyes of the King watching them as they left and even as the throne room doors closed behind.

The doors slammed shut, as the guards escorted Tatiana and Free through a long hallway at the side of the throne room doors. The hallway was winding and narrow, as the marble floor shined and the dark stone walls remained bare. Tatiana and Free's footsteps echoed in the silent castle, with few people to be seen, except from the guards that dotted the edges of the hall, standing motionless.

Towards the end of the hallway, the guards twisted into an arched opening and entered a room, stopping a few feet inside. The room was without windows and lit torches flickered on the walls, as beams balanced along the ceiling and as the room stretched ahead.

At the centre of the room, there was a long, black table with benches either side. The tabletop was decorated with glowing black lanterns and ceramic plates already set with cutlery. There were few sitting at the table, but those that were ate from their plates in silence.

Tatiana and Free perched on the benches, sitting opposite each other, as they were gestured by the guards which left as soon as Tatiana and Free were seated. They watched the guards leave, before turning to face each other with wide eyes.

Free whispered, pressing his hands against the table and leaning towards Tatiana, locking onto her eyes, "Do thee feel the strangest?"

Tatiana nodded slightly, as her eyes scanned the dining hall and identified the few people that sat further along the benches of the table.

"I was chilled by a shudder of fear as I entered the castle and it has not ceased since," Free admitted, as he leant away from Tatiana and gripped his knees underneath the table. His eyes frantically searched the room.

Tatiana's eyes flicked over at Free, as her back slouched and her hand rested against her chin. She muttered. "If thou worry further, it shall be noticed! Stay calm, Free Stellam."

Free nodded, falling silent, as his leg juddered underneath the table and he picked his fingernails with his teeth.

Almost immediately after they had stopped speaking, from an archway at the corner of the room, two figures emerged carrying pots of food, which released steam and a sweet smell that travelled towards Tatiana and Free.

The servants carried the pots and dribbled the broth into the bowls which sat in front of Tatiana and Free. The broth was murky with roughly chopped pieces of carrots and potatoes, splattering against the sides of Free and Tatiana's bowls.

As soon as their bowls were filled, the servants left, as Tatiana and Free indulged to feed their rumbling stomachs. Free and Tatiana sipped the broth, calming their nerves, as they peered at each other through the rising white streaks of steam.

Free and Tatiana consumed their food, until they heard very heavy footsteps enter and echo throughout the room. Spoons were dropped from the hands of the men and women who sat farther up, as their heads turned to the entrance of the dining hall with wide eyes and beginning to bow.

Slowly, Tatiana and Free tilted their heads to face the archway, eyeing a man that stood above them and bowing their heads instantly. The man gestured the guard at his side to bring a spare chair to the head of the table, where he slumped down to join Tatiana and Free as they ate.

As soon as the man was seated, bowed heads were raised. Tatiana and Free glared at the man, wrapped in his black fur cloak with his silver crown perched on his head. His eyes squinted at Tatiana, as he leaned into his chair and began to speak with a light voice.

"Queen Tatiana, now thou fill thy stomach with warming food. It be time to converse. There be events and history that thou hast not been given. I feel as I am the one to give thee this information," he announced with a smile. "I be one of the few Kings and Queens that be alive when thy father was!"

Tatiana chortled, as her eyes rolled. She spoke with an unusually light voice and with a grin across her lips. "My King Adrion, do tell the great knowledge thee hold. I be needing enlightenment."

King Adrion's eyebrows raised and he leaned closer, beginning to speak with a quieter voice, which Free could just hear as he slouched over the table. King Adrion began. "The Lost Kingdom once belonged to Samael Cain. He and thy father were the most powerful. Some argued they were more powerful than any Star! The fellow kingdoms bowed before King Moryn and King Samael, including myself. Then, the war between the South and the Lost Kingdom began. The war be vicious and lasted for many years, till Samael Cain won. He came on the day thou be born and stormed Cahercasey, killing thy entire family, including thy brother, Thaddeus. Still, it be uncertain why the Necromancer attacked the South, after being companions with King Moryn for many years previous."

Free questioned, as he bore at King Adrion. "My King Adrion, would thou care to teach us thy reasons for the Necromancer attacking the South?"

"Indeed. I be happy to share my beliefs that the Necromancer and King Moryn's companionship ended after King Moryn refused to let Queen Tatiana marry the Necromancer's son, Nemo. Her cousin."

"I will marry no man or woman," Tatiana snapped. "Peacefully, I will rule alone."

King Adrion chuckled. "If thou rule alone, there be war, once thou produce no children to claim the throne."

Tatiana joked. "My kingdom shall die with me."

Free's eyes widened, as his head slowly twisted and eyed Tatiana's laughing face, seeing an unnerving glimmer in her eyes.

King Adrion gazed over at Free, before glaring back at Tatiana and laughing, loudly. His hand slammed down on the table, as water streamed from his eyes and down his reddening face. His voice was hoarse, as he began to speak. "A fine humour thou hath, Queen Tatiana! It be greatly welcomed in my kingdom."

Tatiana grinned, as her voice became stern. "Will thou aid us? Will thou be sending armies to the walls of Cahercasey?"

King Adrion's laughter faded, but a smile still glimmered across his lips. His voice deepened. "By the time the snow falls again, thou will have an army. Thou shall reign Cahercasey as soon as the snow has settled."

"Thank ye, King Adrion. I be most indebted to thee when I be Queen of the South!"

King Adrion pushed his chair back and raised abruptly. His green eyes searched the dining hall and observed the men and women that sat at the table with a small smile. He looked down at Tatiana, before spinning on his heel and leaving the dining hall, as glimmers of the torches made his eyes glow.

Before he left, King Adrion mentioned, "Thou be taken to my store of weapons, after thou has been satisfied by food. Choose what thou like."

Tatiana and Free glanced at each other, as the corner of their lips curled. By the time, Tatiana and Free looked up at where King Adrion had stood, King Adrion had disappeared through the archway and had turned the corner without a sound.

Free looked back at Tatiana, as Tatiana still stared at the archway. He added, "Can thou use any weapon?"

Without glaring at Free, still looking at the archway and into the dark hallway, she answered smugly. "My companions doubt me from the beginning, asking me no questions about my skills and only assuming. I be able to use a bow and arrow, better than thou can use a sword!"

Free's cheek flustered. His head lowered and his voice was soft. "I be sorry."

Tatiana turned from staring at the archway and looked down at her broth, using her spoon to scoop the warm running liquid into her mouth. She continued looking down until she had finished, aware Free's cheeks blushed and listening to his silence as she ate.

18

Ezra, Sir Terrence, Tasmin and Helen entered through the hidden door within the tree, as a white light appeared from crystal in Ezra's staff and as Sir Terrence held Nemo tightly in his grasp. The purple light of the forest vanished, as the companions watched Sargon gently close the door and as they waited in the hollow tree with Ezra's light being only bright enough to illuminate their faces.

After the door had closed, Sargon paced to the companions. He smiled, as he passed them and headed further into the darkness, stopping a few feet ahead.

Ezra raised his staff, as he stepped closer. The light of his staff revealed a downward wooden staircase, which spiralled to great depths below. From the staircase, there was warmth and a faint ray of orange light gleamed from around the bend.

Sargon lowered onto the first step and cocked his head over his shoulder, gesturing the companions to follow.

Hesitantly, the companions followed Sargon. Ezra followed first, using his staff to lower his body onto the steps in front, as the crystal in his staff started to fade and as flaming torches lit the staircase. Behind, Tasmin followed. Tasmin carried Helen on her back, as Helen's eyes stayed tightly shut and as her head flopped onto Tasmin's shoulder.

Sir Terrence plodded after Tasmin, grappling Nemo's wrist and hauling him behind. Nemo still smoked his pipe, flooding the staircase with an intoxicating earthy smoke, as he was forced to stumble beside Sir Terrence, following the companions and Sargon in front.

At the bottom of the winding staircase, which reached great depths below the hollow tree above, there was a wide, circular room, surrounded by soil, with beams poking the ceiling and ground. Hanging from almost every beam was a flickering black iron lantern, brightening the darkness. The room was bare, except from a straw bed pushed against one side of the room.

In front of the bed, there was a figure with long, raven hair resting over their velvet, plum cloak that was draped across their shoulders. Their large jet-black eyes glared at the companions, as their hands clasped in front of their body and on top of their deep purple gown.

The figure's eyes flicked at Sargon and asked with a soft voice, as he approached closer. "Be they the companions to be captured by Belladonna?"

Sargon nodded. "Yes, they be the companionship."

The figure looked back at the companions, noticing Nemo being grappled by Sir Terrence and continuing to smoke on his pipe. The figure called to Sir Terrence, "Thou can release the ass from thy grip. He will bring no harm."

Sir Terrence groaned. "Be not offended, but I be wanting to cling to the ass a little longer!"

The figure grinned, before staring at Ezra, where the figure's smile grew larger. "Ezra the wise! It be a while since we last met."

Ezra smiled. "Ponoma! Ah, times before the Necromancer and times when Belladonna be a friend! Times, when thou be with a Star."

Ponoma's smile faded, as her eyes filled with waves of tears. "For many years, I be forgetting those times. Yet, a new time begins. The time to restore the South."

"Who may thou be, except for Ezra's companion? There be darkness inside thee from a distinguished flame," Tasmin babbled.

Ponoma gestured Tasmin to place Helen across the bed, as she stepped to one side. She announced, "I be Ponoma Power. For when those escaped Cahercasey, after the Necromancer and Belladonna's attack, I sought to rescue the knights that came to me. Over twenty and five years, we be waiting to fight!"

"Thou be foolish to fight my mother and father!" Nemo declared, breathing white puffs of smoke from between his lips.

Ponoma cackled. "Thou be the foolish! Thou sides with mother and father when thou possess no power alike. A mere mortal man."

Nemo snapped, slapping away Sir Terrence's grip and charging towards her. His eyes flared, as his fists clenched and his feet pounded hard against the ground, stopping inches before her. "I be no mere mortal man, bitch."

She tittered, as she revealed the rayed star necklace that hung from around her neck. “I be not a bitch. For I be a Star!”

“Why be thou here if thou be a Star? Thou should be in the skies and be watching over us!” Nemo hissed. “Why be here?”

“There be few Stars walking amongst thee. The few Stars be in sight and have been since the fall of the Southern kingdom,” she explained, as her shoulders sunk and her eyes glazed over to watch Helen sleep. “Poor child!”

Sargon stepped forwards, as Ponoma continued to stare at Tasmin and the companions had fallen silent. He smiled, briefly, as he examined everyone. “It be time to leave. The time for us to be leaving for Cahercasey be now. Let us gather everyone and depart on our journey.”

Ponoma nodded, as she turned away from Tasmin and looked at the companions. “The journey and destination be no journey for a child. She must remain here.”

“No!” Tasmin argued. “If we be leaving without her, she be wondering where we be. She be so sad to depart from us in life and in death. She cannot be left here!”

Ponoma stepped closer to Tasmin and gently clasped her wrists, deeply looking into her eyes. “I be sorry, but I be not bringing a child with me.”

“How can we be leaving a child alone? She be safer with us,” Tasmin yelled. “I be staying with her. I be not leaving her.”

Ponoma released Tasmin, stepping back and heading towards the set of stairs. She waited at the bottom, as she looked over her shoulder and watched the companions parting from each other.

Tasmin turned to Sir Terrence and Ezra with a brief smile. She embraced them both tightly in her arms and whispered. “Do not hate me for staying. Do not call me a coward. I cannot leave her here. She be devastated.”

Sir Terrence added, as he and Ezra released Tasmin from an embrace, “Ye be far from cowardice!”

For a moment, Tasmin’s eyes gleamed at Sir Terrence, before they lowered to the ground. She twisted to step towards the bed and settled at the edge, just beside Helen’s feet, watching over her as she slept.

Sargon gestured Ezra and Sir Terrence towards Ponoma, as he mentioned, sweetly, "I shall be staying with them. Both shall be safe with me. Nemo be not harming them either, as he be staying here."

Sir Terrence and Ezra nodded at Sargon as they passed him. They strode towards Ponoma, following behind her, as they climbed the wooden staircase in silence. Ezra and Sir Terrence entered the darkness of the hollow tree at the top, watching Ponoma pace towards the door to push open, revealing the purple mist of the forest outside.

Ponoma, Ezra and Sir Terrence entered the humid clearing, with hanging vines and branches swarming above their heads, as roots circled them. The crisp leaves were crushed underneath the companions' feet, as they stepped through the forest and through the passage ahead that went through the wide trunk of a tree.

As they travelled through the forest, heading South, Ponoma twisted to Ezra and Sir Terrence. She sternly remarked, as she continued to walk ahead, "Belladonna be leaving the forest and she heads to Cahercasey."

"At least, she be not succeeding in capturing us!" Sir Terrence chuckled.

"Yes. Except she and the Necromancer succeeded in capturing thy companions, Bidelia and Barnabas. They be locked in the dungeons below the castle." Ponoma sighed.

"Where be Tatiana? Where be Free?" Sir Terrence exclaimed.

"I do not be knowing where they be, but they be not captured," she answered.

"Do they be wishing to lure Tatiana to the castle, if she finds her companions to be imprisoned there? Did they be making an attempt to catch her already?" Ezra asked himself.

"If all hurry, we can be at Cahercasey before Belladonna. Yet, it will be hard to distinguish whether the Necromancer shall be there. My men and women keep watch at the kingdom," Ponoma insisted.

Ponoma glanced upwards at the nearest tree and lunged for the lowest branch. Her hands grappled the bark and hoisted her body over with a grunt and a relieving exhale. She rose onto her feet, keeping her balance and overlooking Ezra and Sir Terrence. She breathed. "Come. Climb! The fastest travel through the forest be by climbing the branches."

Sir Terrence and Ezra stormed and lifted their bodies onto the branch. They growled as they fought to balance on their feet and joined Ponoma. They breathed deeply and followed Ponoma's eyes which wandered to stare at the branches above, which went high into the purple haze. Above that they began to climb.

Ponoma, Sir Terrence and Ezra heaved themselves high into the trees. They climbed till the forest floor became an inky abyss and the sunlight was seen through the leaves and glimmered onto their heads. The companions lightly stepped across a path of branches, which led them to the edge of the forest, a few miles from the Southern borders.

The companions saw a circular opening ahead of the path, created by the growth of leaves that was still high amongst the trees and overlooked the land ahead. The dusk sky was a deep blue, with Stars twinkling and the moon beaming, as the Southern borders stood in sight. There was a salty sea breeze drifting across the land, inhaled by the companions, as they examined the growing hills and the cliffs far into the distance.

As they squinted, there were swaying shadows marching over the land and heading South. The large group of men and women were clad in armour, and silver lights of the moon bounced from their metal shoulders.

Ponoma whispered, and her voice became deafening in the silence of the night, "Belladonna leads them South to greet the Necromancer. She returns alone and without the companions."

Sir Terrence mentioned without a slur, "Belladonna be punished for her failure to bring us to Cahercasey."

Ezra agreed, "Yes. She will be."

"Does our companionship follow them to Cahercasey?" Sir Terrence quizzed. "Does our companionship gather many forces to bring South, instead?"

"There be no one else to help us." Ponoma huffed. "There be so few, even half the Stars shall not help us."

"Was thou cast from the skies, for wanting to help us?" Sir Terrence asked, as he saw the twinkling pools of water forming in her eyes. "Can thou not return to the skies? Be this the only journey for thou?"

Ponoma breathed heavily, as her raven eyes lowered to stare down at the ground below. She stood at the edge and began to lower her body to the branch below, instructing Ezra and Sir Terrence to follow, as she climbed swiftly to the ground.

As soon as the three companions had reached the edge of the forest floor, jumping down with their feet thudding on the grass, they joined to walk beside each other and drew their weapons. Ponoma and Sir Terrence drew their swords from their sheaths, as Ezra held his staff, with his crystal brightly shining, as they headed South.

19

In the East, Wylie, Darrel, Ainsley and Orla rode with Klaus and Phillipa Thyme, travelling through the thick layers of snow that had settled on the ground with two Stars named Asriel Power and Caspar Deorwine. They had rested for hours underneath the large cavities of rocks that laid beside the mountains towards the East, sleeping and warming their frozen bodies till they trudged through the snow by foot, after their horses began to struggle through the ever-growing white blanket that layered the East.

Ainsley and Orla waded through the snow with Klaus at their side, travelling in the middle of the large group. Ainsley and Orla looped arms, hauling each other, as their teeth constantly chattered and their lips turned blue. Too cold to speak, they clung tightly and met each other's empty glares, as their cheeks burned red.

Ainsley gripped onto Klaus' forearm, as the falling flakes of snow began to blind them. Her skin was paler than the snow and cracks formed on the surface of her hands. She breathed slowly and shallow, as her eyes glanced at Klaus at every moment, watching the trembles of his lips, as he breathed white swirls from between them.

Ainsley stuttered to speak, moving her numb lips and disturbing her dry throat. "Be that thou love me? Will thou and I marry? Will thou and I be given children as precious as Pip?"

Klaus scowled, watching her eyes move slowly to examine him. He felt her arm tense, as her torso started to shiver and as he reached for her hand, which was frozen to touch.

Ainsley continued, "Oh Pip, I be thy mother. I be a mother to thou. Let me be a mother."

From the other side of Ainsley, Orla listened. Orla bore at Ainsley, hearing her rambles of delirium. Her eyes met Klaus' stare and Orla exclaimed, "What be she saying? I do not be believing her to be well! We must stop. She be not well to travel further."

Klaus retorted. "The rest happened only hours ago. There be no stopping if we be wanting to arrive at our destination!"

"Which be where?" Orla argued. "My legs ache and I shiver. I be travelling for hours without the glimmering sight of our destination."

Klaus huffed, before forcing Orla and Ainsley to stop. He shouted for Pip that staggered in front, with Wylie at her side. "Phillipa! Phillipa! Halt! Thou must halt."

Pip turned to see her father's arm waving at her. Instantly, she swivelled and paced towards him, gesturing Wylie to follow. She called, "Pa! Pa! Pa, what be the matter? Why dost thou halt?"

Klaus replied, as his daughter stumbled to stop before him, "Ainsley be not well to be travelling any further! She be frozen like the falling flakes of ice. Ainsley cannot continue."

"Would thou be wanting us to continue without thee, Pa?" Pip questioned, as her jade eyes examined Ainsley's shivering body.

"Yes, my daughter." Klaus sighed, gently letting go of Ainsley and reaching to embrace his daughter. "Be safe. Follow Asriel and Caspar. Do not stray from them! I be trusting only them to keep thee on this earth with me."

Pip nodded, squeezing her father tightly and parting from him. She slowly turned her back on her father, returning to Wylie's side and continuing to follow Asriel, Caspar and Darrel. Pip, Darrel, Wylie, Asriel and Caspar disappeared quickly into the distance.

Klaus stepped further away from Ainsley and Orla, crouching onto his knees and clawing at the heaps of snow with his red and stiff fingers. He scattered snow beside him, digging downwards and scurrying as he created a tunnel. Though Klaus moved briskly, his fingers were still frozen and his body refused to warm.

Underneath the layers of snow, Klaus, Orla and Ainsley scurried into the wide and shallow shelter that had been dug. They pressed their slouched backs against the snow walls, stretching their feet towards the entrance and as their heads touched the snow above. Klaus, Orla and Ainsley snuggled closely together, clasping each other's frozen and red hands, as they silently sat in the gloominess of their enclosure, watching the falling snow.

Ainsley had fallen silent. Her body shivered, as she sat between Orla and Klaus, with shallow breaths escaping from between her lips. Her pulse had weakened and her skin was like ice. She rested her head on Klaus' shoulder, as her face started to fade blue and as her eyes stayed glaring at the white flakes drifting from the sky.

Orla watched Ainsley, clasping her hands tightly and resting her head on Ainsley's shoulder. Orla's eyes closed, as the water droplets from her eyes froze and stung her cheeks, freezing to look almost like diamonds sticking against her skin.

Klaus saw the white sheets of flakes whipping in the howls of the wind, as his eyes became tearful. His stomach churned and his heart sunk into his chest, as he pictured his daughter's dazzling emerald eyes.

Phillipa's eyes squinted through the blizzard, as she and her companions held hands in the blinding snow. She squeezed Wylie's hand, unable to see him and clasping his frozen cracked fingers that were blue. Her whimpers were not heard above the screaming winds, as she fought the rapid winds and the whipping snowflakes that slashed her face.

She searched through the storm, as they came further East to find the Seelie's. Pip sought between the ice and into the grey voids, sighting balls of light. The orange light flickered between trees, at the edge of a forest, which was only a few feet away.

Instantly, Pip halted and tugged the rest of her companions to stop, also. She felt Wylie stop and felt his hand wrap tighter around her fingers. Firmly, Pip heaved Wylie towards the lights between the forest trees. As she hauled him, Wylie pulled the other companions behind.

Pip marched to the edge of the forest, seeing the bright lights becoming orange flames, which were further in the distance than she had thought. She led the companions between the trees and followed the flames ahead.

As soon as the companions entered, the roofs of leaves protected them from the heavily falling snowflakes, which had pelted their heads and blinded their vision. Few snowflakes slipped between the gaps of trees, but those that did fell gently. The wind screeched, but lightly grazed the companions as they paced between the trees, striding inside the minuscule warmth that the forest created. A thin layer of snow touched the ground, with visible strands of grass and sightings of grey leaves slowly dying as they crisped to curl.

Asriel, Caspar, Wylie, Darrel and Phillipa stormed towards the flames, which sat in iron around the trees and led to the centre of the forest, as more torches appeared. The companions released each other's hands and drew their weapons. Asriel, Caspar and Wylie staggered forwards with their swords, as Darrel wielded his axe and Phillipa readied her daggers to throw. The companions lightly stepped into the warming centre, as the forest became brightly lit in the orange hues of the torches.

In the centre of the forest, the companions saw lingering figures that stood together, forming a small circle in a small patch of ground that was clear from trees. The figures wore long, velvet plum cloaks, with their hoods raised and shadowing their faces, as their whimsical, whispering voices travelled through the wind. On their waists, visible to the companions' eyes, there were swords and daggers attached to their belts.

Slowly, the companions crept behind the figures. As the companions paced, certain they were not seen, they froze. The companions were eyed by the group ahead, which did not move to approach them, but glared indefinitely at them.

Instantly, Pip's daggers lowered and were placed into her belt. The group stared at Phillipa and dropped to their knees, bowing before her, as she staggered to stand in front of where they knelt to greet them warmly.

Pip smiled. "Please, rise."

The group of men and women raised, gently laying their hoods against their backs and revealing their sharp, pointed ears that were distinctly seen through the strands of hair. The entire group dazzled the companions with the same green eyes that Phillipa had, sparkling underneath the grey clouds, as the warm flames illuminated them.

Pip turned to the companions that gathered behind her, grinning and gesturing them to come forth, as the companions stayed frozen a few feet away. Her soft voice called, "Come, companions."

Asriel, Caspar, Wylie and Darrel came to stand at her side, glaring at the sharp ears of the men and women before them. They stayed quiet, as a woman at the front of the group, stepped forwards and spoke softly.

"The knight, Phillipa. Thy father told us to be waiting for thee."

"Yes. Thank ye. The snow fell too fast and we had been fighting stronger than we be imagining to," Pip responded, sternly. "I be glad to see ye all safe. Where be the others?"

"The others wait beside the Eastern borders, waiting for thy arrival and thy commands."

Wylie exclaimed, before either could speak any further and turning to Phillipa as his eyes widened and as his voice shrilled, "Thou be a knight? A seelie knight? Thou be leading the Seelie's towards Cahercasey?!"

Pip snapped. "Yes. It be so. I be a seelie knight and I be leading the seelie army to the South. Does that be creating an issue?"

Wylie stuttered. "No. I be shocked and confused, but I be having no issue!"

Pip twisted away from Wylie, as the group of Seelie's parted to create a path for Pip to pace through. Pip staggered through the forest, as the Seelie's raised their hoods and stealthily strode behind.

For a moment, Darrel and Wylie watched as the Seelie's staggered ahead and as Asriel and Caspar followed. They watched the black cloaks of the Stars and the purple cloaks of the Seelie's sway behind, as Wylie and Darrel rapidly moved to catch them.

20

On the Southern Sea, sitting in deep water, within sight of the shore, there was a castle. The white-stone castle was surrounded by sharp and tall mountains either side, with a long bridge stretching all the way to the beach, as waves slashed over the sides. Large, mossy green colours stained the glass windows of every room, with an enormous green-paned window sitting above the thick and tall white doors of the castle entrance.

Below the white castle, inside a gloomy dungeon, trapped inside the high birdcages hanging from the ceiling, two shadows rested against the iron bars. The iron rammed against the centre of their backs, as their heads rolled backwards into the small gaps between, keeping their eyes firmly shut and leaving them listening to droplets falling from the ceiling and crashing to the floor far below.

A shadow moved into the dim lighting of the torches, where orange hues illuminated the hazel eyes of a woman with a scar running through her brow. She glared at the shadow in the cell across from her, trying to see the shadow's face, which was covered by their cloak, as she looked over her shoulder. She grasped the cell bars and twisted her body to face the shadow, grunting, as her numb legs became heavy.

Just as the woman lifted her body to move, the daunting unlocking of the dungeon door at the top of the stairs echoed. The heavy metal door scratched against the stone floor as it opened wide and revealed a glimmering light from a corridor, where a foreboding shadow stood.

The shadow entered, slamming the door behind, as the metal screeched against the floor again. The shadow strode down the stairs, as it fixated on the woman, looking over its shoulder. It stopped at the bottom of the staircase and looked up at her with a pair of petrifying golden eyes that were wide and bewitching. The shadow, caped in black, smiled eagerly at the woman, whose stern stare had worn.

Suddenly, the woman's cage dropped, hearing chains rattling and beginning to lower. Slowly, she came to be level with the shadow that stood on the other side of the iron bars. Her cage hovered just above the ground, as the rattles of the chains halted and as she swung gently to a stop. The woman stared through the iron bars, grappling them, as she stopped just below the level of the shadow's eyes.

The shadow stepped forward with something jangling inside its pocket. Its golden circles bore at her as he removed a set of black, iron keys from his pocket and unlocked her cage with a skeleton key. The key turned, as the woman shuffled to the far side of her cage and moved away from the opening door of her cage.

The shadow lowered down to stare through, as the woman pushed against the iron bars, though she could not shuffle any farther away from the shadow that looked at her. Her heart thumped, but it did not race and her palms did not sweat. She scowled at the shadow, as the shadow ushered her to leave.

Hesitantly, the woman lifted away from the bars and shuffled towards the door. She dangled her legs over the side of the cage to touch the stone floor and slipped outside the cage. The woman straightened her back and gradually raised to balance on her lead legs, as the shadow stooped above her.

Abruptly, the shadow's hand launched forwards and clasped clumps of her dark hair, almost tearing strands from her scalp. Her neck arched back, as her abdomen leant forwards and her hands latched onto the shadow's hands. She growled, trying to shake the shadow, as the lower half of her body wriggled.

The shadow twisted, dragging the woman behind and forcing her to climb the staircase. The shadow captured the woman and slammed her against a wall of chains, grabbing iron cuffs and slamming the metal against the woman's wrists, clicking to lock. The shadow released her neck and reached for the chain hanging from a hook and locked it around her throat tightly.

The woman felt the frozen iron clinging to her skin, as the shadow restricted her legs with chains, too. She groaned, shaking the shackles around her wrists and hitting her back against the black walls of the dungeon, as she tried to escape.

She stopped, breathing heavily. "Do what thou wilt to me, Necromancer!"

The Necromancer smiled, turning to gaze at the shadow still trapped inside the cage above. The Necromancer grimaced at the sight of a man that slept and breathed deeply.

Continuing to look at the man above, the Necromancer growled. "Bidelia, thou shalt be weakening till Queen Tatiana arrives. When she does, thou wilt meet death!"

Bidelia exhaled. "I shall embrace death with warmth after the pain thou wilt force me to endure!"

The Necromancer turned back and lowered to press his frozen nose against hers. "Yes, but thou shall not be saving thy sister."

"Why be thou desiring her death?" Bidelia spat.

He chuckled. "As thou shall be dying soon, I shall tell thou. Queen Tatiana was born with no air breathing in her lungs. The wizard stood over her and he cast a spell to let air into those lungs, but her life was given by drawing my power. With each passing day, Tatiana grows stronger and I am weakened. For years, there are those seeking my death and yet they never knew how to kill me, but Ezra knew. He was informed by the Stars."

"Truthfully, loving fathers end themselves to bring life to their daughters," she hissed.

For a moment, the Necromancer lingered, continuing to press his nose against hers. His golden eyes flickered, as his chest deeply breathed air against Bidelia's lips. "Where be thy father? Where be Barnabas Mint's father? Thou be all fatherless!"

"My mother and father be resting amongst the soil of the earth, peacefully," she retorted with a small smile. "Soon, I be seeing them again!"

The Necromancer stepped away from Bidelia, flicking his cloak behind him and revealing a sharp silver blade attached to his belt. He reached for the blade, grappling his fingers tightly around the handle and raising the dagger through the air.

Bidelia screeched. Her stomach tightened and her shoulders flopped over her torso, as scarlet liquid flooded from a deep cut across her abdomen. Her head hung over the iron chain around her neck, as her eyes closed tightly and saliva drained from her retracted lips. Bidelia squished her fingers inside her palms, lifting from the wall and swarming in her shackles.

In the cage above, the eyes of the sleeping man opened. His eyelids lifted to reveal olive ovals, which opened to glare widely at the high walls, before looking down below. Lightly, the man moved in his cage towards one side, arching his neck and overlooking Bidelia and the Necromancer below. His olive eyes locked onto Bidelia, as her screams continued to shriek through the dungeon.

Instantly, Bidelia's screams halted. Her screeches were followed by whimpers, gradually raising to lean against the cool wall, as the blood from her torso started to trickle. Bidelia's head rolled to lean against the cold iron cuff, meeting the green eyes of the man above. Her hazel eyes began to water, as she released her fingers from her clenched fist and allowed the chains to catch her weight. Bidelia's body flopped and her head rolled to hang over her torso, as her tears dropped against the stone floor with a small splatter.

The Necromancer pondered, still holding his bloody blade at the side of his body and looking down at Bidelia. His stare was frosty, as he slowly returned his dagger to his belt, after wiping his blade on Bidelia's shoulder, using her cloak to clean the blood.

Once his dagger had been placed in the sheath attached to his belt, the Necromancer swivelled and glared up at the cage that held the man captive. The Necromancer's stare remained stern, even as he met the frozen eyes of the man above.

"It be a pleasure to have Barnabas Mint in my kingdom!" the Necromancer bellowed, as Barnabas scowled.

Barnabas mentioned, "This be not thy kingdom!"

"Does it be Tatiana's?" His eyebrow rose.

Barnabas growled. "Yes. It be her kingdom!"

The Necromancer twisted, flicking his cloak behind him and feverishly smiled at Bidelia. Bidelia's neck still hung over the iron collar, as the lids of her eyes rested heavily and as her lips parted to release shallow breaths.

Suddenly, she felt dots of pressure press her against her cheeks, as her jaw was lifted to meet the golden eyes of the Necromancer. With her hazel eyes, she looked past the Necromancer and locked onto Barnabas.

Now, Bidelia stared, Barnabas melted. Her wary stare made his heart ache, as the Necromancer's blade slashed diagonally across her face, listening to her cries that followed. Barnabas watched as the Necromancer released Bidelia's jaw and as her neck dropped to her chest. He saw blood dribble down her cheeks and drip onto the ground at her feet, as he heard the screams from her opened mouth. Barnabas witnessed Bidelia's floods of tears, which washed away her blood, but stung her wound.

The Necromancer wiped his blade against Bidelia's cloak, removing the blood and returning his sword to his belt. Afterwards, the Necromancer strode, pridefully, towards the door of the dungeon, leaving silently with a smile.

After the door of the dungeon was locked, it was not long before Bidelia's screams ceased. Still, blood ran down her face and dripped onto the floor, but slowly her head tilted upwards to lean against the wall. Her hazel eyes met Barnabas, faintly smiling at him and looking deeply into his olive eyes that glowed within the darkness of the dungeon. Her voice croaked as her lips parted to speak.

"Does this remind thee about thy youth? Certainly, this reminds me about mine."

Barnabas cleared his throat with a small cough. "What reminds thee about thy youth? Be it the pain? The darkness? The iron chains?"

"The first time I be entering this dungeon was when I be young. I be locked inside these cold and gloomy walls with shackles around thy limbs and neck, locked with many shadows that were worse than the Necromancer and Belladonna!" She sighed.

"Dost thou still feel those shadows inside thee?"

Tears formed at the corners of her eyes, as she trembled. "I be almost forgetting the pain I be caused. Until now, I be reminded by what be hurting me. The shadows still be lingering inside me."

The stern stare in Barnabas' eyes faded, as Bidelia's eyes looked away from him and searched the rest of the dungeon. Barnabas' softened glare watched Bidelia's head droop again and her weakening muscles relax. His abrupt and growling voice, lightened, as his lips parted to comfort Bidelia.

"Do not be letting shadows consume thee, when thou be stronger than I."

"I be not stronger than thou, Barnabas."

"Thou be hurt but be not harming others. Yet, I be hurt and be hurting all."

Bidelia's eyes raised to look at him with a small smile. "Yet, thou have not hurt me yet."

Barnabas' green eyes filled with tears and his lips began to tremble. His voice stuttered. "I be not wanting to hurt thee. Thou be kind to me."

"After all, thou be given a hardship and be deserving the kindest of things." She gleamed, as her voice spoke quietly.

He gulped. "If thou knew my sins and hardships, thou would not be wanting to give such kindness."

"Thou speak without knowing my sins and be comparing me to the Stars!"

"The face bestowed upon thou be glimmering like the Stars!" Barnabas smiled through his watery eyes and cleared the lump within his throat.

Bidelia blushed, as her eyes lowered to avoid Barnabas' stare and to hide the redness in her cheeks. "Thou be more beautiful than I be."

He chortled, listening to his laugh that he had almost forgotten and leaning back in his cage. "Beautiful? I be never called beautiful. Yes, I be called hideous."

Bidelia laughed a little, though her stomach pained her still. "I be believing they be jealous of thy features!"

A warm energy was created inside Barnabas, which made his heart race and his palms sweat. He wanted to smile, though he became nauseous and dizzy, resting his head back and closing his eyes. Barnabas stared into the darkness of his eyelids, hearing Bidelia's voice run through his mind, replaying her kind words that had not been spoken to him before. As he rested, Barnabas spoke often to Bidelia, comforting her in the frosty dungeons below Cahercasey.

21

Sir Terrence and Ezra had followed Ponoma towards the South, losing sight of Belladonna and the shadows that followed her. Sir Terrence, Ezra and Ponoma paced with soggy clothes sticking to their skin and their hair clinging to the sides of their faces, as water fell from the sky and as lights flashed within the clouds, followed by roars. Their boots were covered in mud, as they trudged through the brown puddles that drowned the grass fields ahead.

The companions' noses and cheeks reddened, as slime ran from their nostrils. Their teeth chattered, as their bodies shivered. Rapidly, the winds swirled towards the companions, removing their cloaks from their shoulders, as they fought the storms ahead.

In the screeches of the winds, the companions heard crashing waves, which were carried from the coast that was ahead. The waves were deafening, and the companions saw an ocean ahead, sighting enormous hurls of water crashing against grey grains of sand. In the air, the companions smelt hints of salt, which stung their eyes, but was refreshing to breathe. Amongst the water, there were sharp daggers rising high and surrounding a white castle at the centre.

The castle was sheltered by the grey mountains, with a long bridge sitting on the surface of the water as waves crashed at its side. The castle towers stretched into the clouds, as green stained-glass windows glimmered in the flashing white lights and as orange lights came from inside. The high castle entrance doors were closed and heavily guarded by shadows in black armour, which were lined towards the bridge in front.

Immediately Ponoma, Sir Terrence and Ezra stopped, staring at the castle ahead. The companions viewed the castle from far in the distance, slowly stopping their feet to stand in the rain. Their eyes glowed at the sight of the castle, taking deep breaths, as their legs shook.

Ponoma twisted to walk with the castle to the side of her, pacing through the short grass and leaving Sir Terrence and Ezra to linger.

Sir Terrence and Ezra stared endlessly at the castle before them, as their hearts ached and swarms of butterflies filled their stomachs. Their eyes were covered by a sheet of water, which blurred the outlines of the castle, as their knees weakened.

After a few moments, Sir Terrence and Ezra hurried after Ponoma. Ponoma stormed ahead, beginning to lead Sir Terrence and Ezra away from the castle and towards the furthest cliffs that still followed the coast. They travelled without being sighted, as they whisked across the Southern land.

The cliffs, which curved round and blocked the companions seeing the castle, ran with mud and grass, as stone remained still on the slopes. The cliffs sheltered the companions from the blowing winds, hearing the waves crash on the other side.

At the bottom of one cliff, in the centre of the curve that had been created, there was a burrowed entrance. The entrance was low and wide, tunnelling into darkness, with a strong gust of wind whistling through.

The companions stood at the foot of the cliff, staring into the darkness, as Ponoma pondered in front of Sir Terrence and Ezra.

Ponoma's lips parted and she called into the tunnel of the cliff, hearing her voice echo after she had spoken. "It be I, Ponoma Power! My friends, emerge from the dark to greet Queen Tatiana's companions."

Ezra clutched his staff tighter, as Sir Terrence reached for his sword resting at his side. Sir Terrence and Ezra locked onto the passage, as their muscles clenched and their breaths became heavy, waiting for what emerged from the inkiness before them.

Suddenly, from the passage, morphing from the darkness, there were slowly moving shadows entering the grey daylight. The shadows moved closely together and grouped outside the entrance, dressed in armour and armed with their weapons at their sides. They came out from the tunnel and towards Ponoma, bowing their heads.

Ponoma smiled briefly, as the figures bowed their heads and stood silently in front. She announced, "Hello, friends. Thank ye, for waiting thousands of days."

A figure addressed Ponoma with a soft voice. "Ah! We be waiting proudly and gratefully for thee. Thou be leading us to greatness before information be received about Queen Tatiana!"

"It be our destiny to fight the Necromancer," she declared, before raising her hands and introducing the companions behind her. "The companions be Sir Terrence Prisca, a knight of Cahercasey. Ezra Aulus of Cahercasey."

The figures bowed their heads at Sir Terrence and Ezra, as their grips loosened from their weapons and as they relaxed. Ezra and Sir Terrence gazed, as the figures raised their heads and glanced back to stare at Ponoma.

Ponoma stepped forwards. Instantly, the figures parted, as she began to head towards the dark tunnel ahead. She gestured Ezra and Sir Terrence to follow, striding behind, as the surrounding figures bore.

Sir Terrence and Ezra watched Ponoma disappear into the dark. She vanished without a sound, and they entered silently and became lost in the darkness also. They trudged through the damp and earthy-smelling tunnel, hearing waves crashing ahead and the sound of footsteps from behind.

It was a while before the companions saw any light. When light was seen again, Sir Terrence and Ezra fixated upon dots of lights, which lined the walls with marigold and dandelion hues that continued to illuminate the rest of the tunnel. In the glowing lights, they saw the soil walls and the beams that held the low roof above, seeing Ponoma in front and the group of figures behind them clearly.

At the end of the tunnel, Sir Terrence and Ezra stopped just behind Ponoma. She had halted slowly, before gazing over her shoulder to stare, as Sir Terrence and Ezra examined the soil wall of the dead end they had come to. Ponoma smiled at the scrunched faces of the companions behind, as she pressed her hand against the wall in front with a small push, before retracting her arm to rest at her side.

Immediately, a dusting of soil fell from the ceiling just above the wall, and a small rumble travelled through the tunnel. The flakes of soil continued to fall until gaps of light were seen around the edges of the wall, which became blindingly light. There was a creak and the wall opened like a door.

Behind the door, just outside, there was golden dust piled along the floor and stretched a few metres ahead. The grains met white foams of rolling waves from vast, grey depths of water that built enormous walls of water, slapping against the surface. A strong gust of wind swept towards the companions that still stood inside the tunnel, which blew their cloaks and hair from their shoulders, bubbling their skin.

Stretching into the sea ahead and before the tunnel, there was a rocky pillar that created a high archway above the sand with a wide ceiling, which sheltered the companions as they stepped onto the sand. The companions stepped onto the beach, which stretched for miles, running alongside the cliffs and beside the Southern Sea.

Ponoma, Sir Terrence and Ezra huddled with the figures that followed from the tunnel, creating a circle as they stood together.

Ponoma announced, as Sir Terrence and Ezra stood either side, touching her shoulders, "Cahercasey rests on the cliff above our heads. All shall await here, for the arrival of the Seelie's."

"Seelie's?" Sir Terrence exclaimed, as the surrounding figures nodded, as did Ezra. "There be Seelie's? Alive and well?"

"Yes," Ponoma stated. "There be Seelie's coming to join us, here. The Seelie's be joining us to fight! They be arriving in a few days."

Sir Terrence excitedly mentioned, "Such a sighting to be seeing Seelie's! Never I be laying eyes upon them."

Ponoma smiled briefly, as she ordered the group to disperse and seek rest underneath the archway. She insisted Sir Terrence and Ezra to wait beside her, as the group of figures spread to rest their weary muscles. Ponoma pulled the companions to one side, standing underneath the edge of the archway above.

Ponoma's voice was quieter and softer than before as she spoke to Sir Terrence and Ezra. She sighed, as her black eyes became lost from staring at the rough seas ahead. "There be a beast. A beast created from rumours, but truthful rumours. A beast, which be not breathing fire from its mouth like dragons, but with flames consuming its feathered body! A phoenix!"

Sir Terrence chortled. "Thou expects us to be believing Seelie's and a phoenix. I be barely seeing ghosts!"

Ponoma stated, "Such beings be not needing to be seen by thee!"

Ezra chuckled. "Ah! The phoenix. His name be Ra!"

Sir Terrence glared past Ponoma and stuttered, "Thou be seeing the phoenix?"

Ezra nodded. "Once, the phoenix lived amongst the walls of Cahercasey! He warmed the castle in the cold and flared light to fight the darkness. After King Moryn and Queen Gwendolen's death, the phoenix fled and be never seen since!"

"I be believing the phoenix never left. There be a cave in the distance, where an orange light be seen every night!" Ponoma explained, as she eyed a large and staggered entrance of a cave inside a cliff in the distance. "I be needing two companions to come with me. I be needing a wizard and a man who be needing to see a phoenix."

Sir Terrence and Ezra grinned, beginning to stagger in a straight line, following the edge of the cliffs, as Cahercasey overlooked them from the great height of the cliff the castle rested upon. Sir Terrence, Ezra and Ponoma paced quickly towards the cave, as nightfall slowly came and the rough seas refused to cease.

Swiftly, the darkness of the night was upon them. The moon and Stars were absent from the sky, leaving the world in oblivion. Shrieking winds whipped through the night, as the waves crashed onto the sandy shores that Ponoma, Sir Terrence and Ezra crept across.

As soon as darkness fell, an orange glow flooded the night, gleaming from the cave ahead of the companions. The light did not flicker like ordinary flames, constantly brimming with a tangerine flare and dispersing warmth into the frosty night, luring the companions further to the entrance of the cave.

Ponoma, Sir Terrence and Ezra arrived at the foot of the blushing light, stopping at the entrance and examining the daggered exterior formation, as the beach lessened and the waves crashed closer, spraying the companions. The companions' reddened faces were soothed by the heat that flowed from the inside of the cave, which deepened and stretched further than they could see, as their backs were stricken by the polar winds that came from the sea.

Before too long, Ezra inhaled deeply and stepped forwards into the cave, grappling his staff that he held before him, lighting his blue crystal. Ezra trudged along the wide path of the cave, where sharp teeth hung from the ceiling above and the path lowered into the fiery and warming light.

Swiftly, Ponoma and Sir Terrence came with their weapons drawn. Sir Terrence and Ponoma stealthily paced behind Ezra, following the same path into the fire and light that came from below.

The entrance of the cave soon disappeared and the whips of the winds became no more than echoes behind them. The ice, which reddened the companions' faces, was met by a sweltering heat, as water droplets rolled down their flustering cheeks. Though the blaze became blinding, there were crevices the light was unable to reach, as the path started to wind and the companions were shadowed by the moist walls that started to drip into the eerie calmness.

Far below, listening to the stillness of the cave, orange lights came from flames of fire surrounding a breathing beast. Its feathered body that did not burn, curled inside a gigantic circular clearing, as its neck twisted to lay its head against its back, sleeping undisturbed. The golden eyes of the beast were closed and feathers staggered into horns on its head.

The sound of footsteps bounced from the walls of the cave, as the beast slowly moved with the thudding movements that grew louder. Its large sparkling golden eyes whipped open.

22

Underneath the vast forest with drooping willow trees that grew into the clouds and surrounding swamps, where the air was suffocating and moist and where the companions had separated, there were Helen, Tasmin, Sargon and Nemo. They remained under the surface, inside a soil-walled room that was dark and damp, with a single bed pushed to one side, where Helen continued to sleep with Sargon, Tasmin and Nemo watching over her.

More than a day had passed since Sir Terrence, Ezra and Ponoma had left as Helen began to sweat through her clothes and soaked her hair. Her teeth chattered and her body shivered, but her body was hot. Helen's grey eyes were tightly shut and her face scrunched, as cool and wet towels were placed gently onto her forehead by Tasmin.

Watching over Helen, Sargon, Nemo and Tasmin conversed quietly. Tasmin rested at the edge of the bed, facing the tall Sargon and the muscular Nemo that stood a few feet away from the bed and glared at Helen as she laid.

Nemo hissed. "Soon, she be dead!"

Tasmin growled. "Thou be selfish and wicked! What dost thou be knowing?"

"There be no need for insisting death, when the girl be only becoming sick," Sargon explained. "Thou be needing to stay."

Nemo argued, "No. The girl be needing the clear air above the ground, not the damp air she breathes now! She be needing medicine. None of which thou be having. Let me take her. Let me take her, to my mother."

"Belladonna? Thou wish to be taking the girl to Belladonna?" Sargon spat. "No. Thou shalt not take her."

"Be there anywhere closer to receive medicine?" Nemo questioned. "I be not skilled in medicines. Nor be both of thee."

Tasmin pondered, examining Nemo's golden eyes. "Art thy mother at Cahercasey?"

Nemo nodded. "Yes. I be able to wander inside without questioning. I be taking young Helen to my mother and she be willing to help her, if I be the one to ask."

Sargon scowled at Tasmin, as she pondered. "Dost thou truly believe this to be an option? Thou cannot! He be betraying us."

She exhaled. "There be no betraying if there be no trust to begin with. If Nemo be giving the help to Helen, then there be no worries for us, even if he be throwing us at the feet of Belladonna and the Necromancer."

Sargon declared, "I cannot let this be!"

Tasmin rose from the side of the bed and looked down at Helen, as her body shivered and sweated. "She be mine to care for and I be insisting she be helped by Nemo and Belladonna. Though thou doth not wish for it to be so."

Sargon quietened with a huff. He saw the determination inside Tasmin's deep brown eyes and the firm clench of her fist at the sides of her body, pacing towards the foot of the stairs to wait.

Nemo stepped closer to the side of the bed, nudging Tasmin out of the way and leaning down, swooping his arms underneath Helen's hot body and whisking her into his chest. Nemo turned towards the stairs, where Sargon waited, calling Tasmin to follow.

Sargon led Nemo and Tasmin up the stairs of the tree, marching slowly towards the abyss above them. Tasmin, Sargon and Nemo climbed into the hollow tree, searching for the door amongst the darkness and leaving the hollow tree.

Sargon pushed the tree door open and left the tree, entering the purple haze of the forest and into a clearing. The companions travelled underneath the dangling vines of the leaves, which fell from the weeping and tall trees that surrounded them, as the crisp leaves crumbled underneath their feet.

As Sargon led Tasmin and Nemo across the clearing, a rumble vibrated the ground and shook the leaves above their heads. The thick and grey roots around the clearing slithered. The roots lifted and twisted to part, forming a narrow path ahead, with sheets of mist forming inside.

Sargon continued to pace ahead, even as Tasmin and Nemo stopped behind to admire the revelation of the path ahead, hesitating, at the eerie mist that formed. They waited till Sargon came to the foot of the path before moving again and following him into the clouds.

Tasmin and Nemo travelled behind Sargon along the path, as Nemo continued to hold Helen in his arms. Helen's throat tickled and she coughed into Nemo's chest, as her fingers wrapped tightly around Nemo's clothing.

The companions hurried through the mist, rushing to leave the forest underneath the dangling leaves and under the shadows of the branches. The clearing behind them disappeared as the mist they had cleared from passing through covered the air again. Above their heads, branches leaned and twisted, almost diminishing the spotlights of the daylight that shone between the gaps and submerging the companions in bleakness. Still, the air was warm and suffocating, as they moved quickly through the tunnelling trees that swayed towards them.

Through the forest, the companions paced, finally reaching the end of the path. At the end, there was no glistening light beaming through the branches and blinding the companions' eyes, as a refreshing breeze filled their lungs. The companions did not see the royal blue sky and did not sight the shimmering sun. The sickly companions' skin did not bask underneath the rays of daylight and they were not comforted by any warmth.

Instead, there was an abysmal sighting of water drenching the grounds that the trees did not cover, as rivers of mud flowed into pools, drowning the strands of grass in the fields ahead. A rush of splattering water was thrown against the trees, reaching the companions' ears, as they listened to the constant chatter of the rain, startled by the drops of water falling through the gaps and thudding against their shoulders. The companions entered a chilling air, which shook their bodies and trembled their lips.

Sargon, Nemo and Tasmin stood at the edge of the path, looking out at the dark grey land ahead, underneath the protection of the branches. They were sprayed by the falling sheets of water, which soaked their trousers and whipped against their faces, as the wind howled. The companions searched the darkness, hoping the rain would lighten.

Nemo stood behind Sargon and Tasmin, using them to protect Helen from the falling rain, still clutching her in his arms. He examined Helen as she shivered and sweated through her clothes, feeling her grip beginning to loosen around his clothing and feeling her muscles reflect.

Nemo's golden eyes flicked to stare at Sargon and Tasmin, as they stood silently in front. He whispered, "To be travelling through such a storm, when already near death, shall declare us to be fighting till the end."

Tasmin and Sargon agreed with deep breaths, lunging forwards and entering the storm. They stepped underneath the grey clouds inflicted by the cold and drowned by the falling water, losing their feet in the pools of brown liquid on the ground. Already, their hair clung to their wet skin and their hoods were too wet to keep them dry, so they wrapped their cloaks tightly over their shoulders.

A few seconds after, Nemo stepped out from underneath the safety of the branches and trudged into the pools on the ground, soaking his feet in the running mud. The water splattered him, as he leant forwards and shielded Helen with his shoulders and head, running down his spine. His dark hair rung with water, dripping at the sides of his ears and over his brows, as the rain from the clouds continued to fall. He stormed after Sargon and Tasmin, and Helen became soaked in his arms.

The companions marched through the endless storm, heading South and towards Cahercasey, quickly sighting the castle in the distance.

The white stone of Cahercasey was blackened by the thick and dark clouds that its towers disappeared into. Cahercasey rested on the cliff, beside the choppy seas, which slashed across the grains of sands that stretched for miles, following the cliff edge and blurring in the curtains of rain. The companions sighted the beacons of flames in the gloominess, focusing, as Sargon and Tasmin halted before Nemo.

Sargon and Tasmin turned to Nemo, as their feet planted into a pool of muddy water. Abruptly, they twisted and met Nemo's golden eyes, which had not moved away from watching Helen's tiring body until now.

Sargon pouted, as Tasmin held a small smile and raised her voice to speak over the howling wind and the deafening rain. She insisted. "Do take care. Take care of Helen. Ensure Belladonna be giving her the medicine she be needing, but mostly, be bringing her back to us. Please, Nemo. Promise us, thou shalt be returning her to her family."

Nemo nodded, as he pushed through Sargon and Tasmin, continuing to pace towards the bottom of the steep cliff, as Tasmin and Sargon waited. Nemo rushed towards the cliff and did not look back at the companions he left behind, reaching the bottom and staring up at the castle that cast a shadow over him.

As Nemo stood at the bottom, he sighted marching figures coming from the tall gates of the castle, dressed in shimmering armour and wielding waving blades that glimmered in the dark. The figures marched in lines and paced towards Nemo, circling him, wearing black cloaks and hiding their faces amongst raven clouds. The guards, stood eerily silent, locking onto him.

Nemo glared over his shoulders, as he pleaded. He called into the rain, "It be I, Nemo! I be the son of Belladonna. Let me pass through the gates, with my friend."

Nemo yelled into the darkness, again, as the guards remained motionless. "Let my mother be informed. I be here. I be returning, after being captured and separated from her."

The guards twisted away from Nemo but continued to circle him. They marched, forcing Nemo to walk, as the guards stormed towards the gates that started to open on their approach, taking Nemo inside.

Nemo carried Helen underneath the raised iron netting, stepping out from the rain and into the dry, long, tunnel, which was blurred by darkness at the end. The high and arched ceiling tunnel was warm, with few torches hanging from the white stone walls. The rain splattering on the stone walls outside deafened Nemo's ears, as the guards continued to surround him.

To the end of the tunnel, Nemo staggered with his wet clothes still clinging to his body and his skin still being bitten by the cold. He felt Helen shaking in his arms, watching her as she kept her eyes tightly shut and remained holding onto his wet shirt with the temperature of her skin, rising.

At the end of the tunnel, Nemo arrived at the edge of a circular courtyard, which was paved with the same white stones that built the castle walls. The courtyard was surrounded by inner walls with archways and the tunnel opposed a large set of golden doors, firmly shut. The courtyard was shadowed by the tall, white towers of the castle, as the dazzling stained-glass windows, sparkled green onto the wet ground.

In the centre of the enormous courtyard, there was a tall stone statue, crafted from grey stone. The grey stone formed a fierce beast with four long, muscular staggered legs, which stood on large talons. Long feathered wings stretched above the body of the beast, shadowing the courtyard and proudly raising its head. The beast's eyes had been carved for large and round rubies to fill them, and rain rolled over the sparkling gems. Its tail protruded as a whip, which swirled behind its body, as it faced to one side, standing on a rectangular platform.

The guards led Nemo into the rain and stopped just before the statue, still circling him. The rain poured onto Nemo, gushing onto Helen's shivering body, as her grip withdrew from holding onto Nemo's shirt and dropped onto her torso. Nemo rolled Helen closer to his chest, as the rain fell harder onto her limp body.

As Nemo waited, surrounded by the guards, a figure emerged from behind the statue. Eerily and briskly, the figure stalked around the statue, stopping in front and looking through the guards, locking onto Nemo with bright, blue sapphire eyes. Soaking, raven hair was tangled at the side of the figure's blueish cheeks.

From the figure's violet lips, a hoarse voice bellowed and silenced the storm. "At last, my son be returning. Step aside, so I can be greeting him!"

In unison, the guards slid to the side, shuffling to form rows and placing their swords at the sides of the belts. The guards twisted towards the tunnel behind and marched under, returning to stand outside the castle walls.

Nemo continued to stand in the same spot, as the figure slowly stepped forwards and stopped in front of him, meeting his gaze. The figure's blue eyes radiated in the darkness, as the rain lightened and the wind quietened, as the figure spoke.

"Who does he be carrying in his arms?"

"Mother, the young girl I be carrying, helped me escape from Sargon. She be imprisoned by them too," Nemo pleaded. "Please. Help her. I be carrying her for thee to help."

"How be it so that a young girl helped thee escape?"

"She just did," Nemo answered bluntly, widening his doe eyes that his mother could not resist.

The woman ushered Nemo to step forwards and to bring Helen before her. Hesitantly, Nemo walked towards her, raising Helen in his arms and stretching his arms outwards, showing Helen to his mother.

Nemo's mother examined Helen. She raised her hand and traced Helen's forehead with her long fingers, immediately soothing Helen's fever and stopping the rolling drops of sweat that were mixed with the falling rain. Helen's scrunched facial muscles relaxed, whilst her body stopped shivering and her shallow breathing strengthened calmly. Helen's hand that had fallen from Nemo's shirt twitched and raised to hold his clothing again.

A small smile appeared across Nemo's lips as he watched the pain withdraw from Helen's young face. He clasped her light body tighter, releasing one of his arms to stroke the sides of her cheeks, before raising his golden eyes to stare at his mother.

The woman's fingers lifted from Helen's forehead and rested to hang beside her body. The sapphire eyes of the woman looked up at Nemo with a frosty glare.

Nemo thanked his mother. "Thank ye, Mother. There be no one like thee. No one be more beautiful than thee. Thank ye, Belladonna."

Belladonna's head lifted, as she continued to hold her pout and stare. "I would do anything for my son."

"Soon, thou shalt be having Tatiana at thy feet, as promised by thee," Nemo declared.

"There be no needing to chase her. She shall come." Belladonna gleamed. "She shall come to be saving the companions that we be keeping in the dungeons below the castle! Her sister and Barnabas Mint be locked away in the dungeons. She be coming. The Queen of the South shall be coming!"

Nemo grimaced, after a small pause and after a sudden wrenching feeling he held in his gut. There was doubt in his golden eyes, which wanted to look away from the intoxicating blue eyes of his mother, but he continued to hold her gaze. "Yes, mother. Thou and I shall be sending her to her death."

Belladonna placed her hand on her son's shoulder with a firm grip, leading him towards the golden gates ahead, as she paced beside him. Belladonna led Nemo, who continued to hold Helen in his arms, underneath the shimmers of the emerald glass and towards the gates that slowly started to open, revealing a dim orange light from within.

23

Far outside the castle, in the distance, two figures had planted their feet in the soggy grounds. The first figure was tall, with long blonde hair and high cheekbones, and the rain pelted into the figure's bright eyes. The second, was slightly shorter, with large curls in their hair, which had been matted by the rain, sticking to the figure's skin. The figure glared ahead with deep brown eyes.

They stood frozen in the falling, freezing rain, focusing upon Cahercasey castle and its flickering, torch flames, standing closely to each other, as the day transformed into the night. The figures trembled, as their arms clasped over their chests and as gust of winds lashed against their faces. They had withstood the cold, long after watching their companions enter the castle walls.

From the corner of their eye, through the rain and gloom, they noticed shadows crossing the fields. The shadows rampaged across the land, charging towards the cliffs in the distance. The shadows were quiet as they crossed, travelling in sparse groups, creating moving black dots that travelled in the rain. There were many shadows being led by the few shadows that strode ahead of the others and carrying weapons on their backs that glimmered in the eyes of the two watching companions.

The first companions spoke over the falling rain, watching the figures continuing to storm over the land. "Be there no Stars above their heads! Yet, thou and I be watching them crossing the land in the darkness."

"Yes, I be watching them also, Sargon! Where dost thou believe them to be heading?"

"For I do not be knowing. Do thou and I follow them, Tasmin?" Sargon questioned, as his head peered over his shoulder to look at her and away from the shadow figures. "Does the figures cross as Seelie's, to be meeting Ponoma, Ezra and Sir Terrence?"

Tasmin shrugged, as she met Sargon's stare. "For I do not be knowing. Yet, thou and I shall be following."

Quickly, Tasmin turned from Sargon and uplifted her feet from the pools of mud she had been stuck in, trudging heavily, as the soggy ground tried to stall her. She turned her face away from the sea winds that had slashed her face and reddened her cheeks, tiring her eyes with salt, which also flooded her mouth. Tasmin shielded her face with her drenched hood, clasping the material at her neck, as the wind continued to twist the rest of her cloak behind her body.

The corners of Sargon's lips lifted, watching Tasmin storm in front. Swiftly, he followed her, holding onto the material of his hood also and turning away from the wind. He staggered closely to her, as his eyes flicked back to the crossing shadows that vigorously made their way towards the cliffs in the distance.

Rapidly, Sargon and Tasmin crossed unnoticed by Cahercasey castle that was now behind them, chasing the figures around the cliffs and watching the shadows darting into a cave.

Sargon and Tasmin stopped to examine the figures that slipped into the darkness of a pointed and low archway, which tunnelled deep into the cliff. The shadows disappeared into the darkness, as Tasmin and Sargon stepped to stand in front of the entrance, a few minutes after the last figure had been seen merging through the passage.

Above, the cliff shadowed Sargon and Tasmin, as they planted their feet at the inky entrance. They noticed streams of mud cascading down the cliff edge, dripping around and over the passage, as the rain continued to pour. Chilly winds whistled and crashing waves hurtled through the passage, as a fresh, salty, air was smelt, too. The footsteps and voices of the shadows they had seen enter, though, were silent to the companions' ears.

Into the passage, Tasmin entered first. Tasmin strode from Sargon's side, eagerly. She merged into the black cloud before her and drew her sword from her sheath, as she began to silently vanish from Sargon's sight.

As soon as Tasmin had disappeared, Sargon entered afterwards. Before taking his first step, Sargon whipped his blade from his belt and gripped the handle tightly at the side of his body, as his eyes focused on the passage in front. Hesitantly, he entered, chasing after Tasmin and searching for her amongst the growing oblivion.

Sargon called into the dark, hearing his voice echo through the passage and drifting further ahead. He waited for a response, still shuffling his feet along the moist soil and placing a hand on the side of the wall as he did.

Yet, Tasmin was not in earshot. Tasmin had sprinted through the tunnel, following the wall with her hands, sliding along the soil to guide her. Tasmin ran into the wind and tasted salt on her lips. She sighted the soil wall ahead, which had been revealed to her, seeing the gaps around the edges and stretching out her hand to throw open the door in front.

Blinded by the light behind the door and slamming open the door, Tasmin stumbled through. She met the daylight but did not feel spots of rain fall on her shoulders. Her ears were deafened by the rough waves, which she saw ahead and was whipped by the vigorous winds that arrived from beyond the sea. Tasmin's feet were covered in grains of gold and she was shielded by a cliff above her head that stretched into the shallow waters.

A few feet in front, Tasmin's eyes met the stares and blades of a hundred. She examined every person, as they rose from the ground and pulled their weapons from their belts and backs. Her entire body froze, as a lump formed in her throat and as her stomach churned. She sweated, as her lips parted and she attempted to call Sargon, only forming stutters.

Seconds after Tasmin, Sargon arrived. He stumbled to her side and adjusted his eyes to the brighter light, only sighting Tasmin at first. Sargon lowered to her, sighting the sweat that rested on her lips and then following her gaze.

From the corner of his eye, Sargon sighted the men and women with their swords and grinned. Sargon twisted fully and grappled Tasmin's wrist, stringing her forwards, as he approached the figures that lowered their weapons.

Sargon released Tasmin's hand, as he was embraced by some of the men and women that knew him, whilst others were strangers. He greeted his friends with large gestures, though only a day had passed since he had seen them last.

Cast to one side, Tasmin searched through the crowds and sighted sleeping men. The two cloaked men, slept against a large rock, at the edge of the beach. Their backs leant against the rock, whilst their legs stretched in front, sleeping against each other. One of the men snored loudly with his arms flopped over his lap and dribble running down his chin, as the other man rested with folded arms and breathed quietly.

Tasmin paced towards them, dropping to her knees in the space between the two men and reached out to touch their cheeks. Small tears formed in her eyes, as a smile reached her lips and as she stroked their soft, grimy skin with her thumbs.

"My companions, Wylie and Darrel."

As she whispered to them, Tasmin heard footsteps approach her from behind and was shadowed by a figure. Tasmin peered over her shoulder to see cold, gawking, green eyes and cerise hair being blown in the wind. She noticed the pointed ears of the figure and the soft skin the figure possessed, instantly recognising a seelie stood behind her.

The figure spoke with a brash and blunt voice, interrogating Tasmin. "Who be thou? Why dost thou be caressing them so? Be thou a lover to one?"

Tasmin chuckled, looking away from the figure behind to admire Wylie and Darrel that rested. "A woman be not a lover to man, but a friend. Merely, I be a companion to the men here. Which man has thou grown for?"

Underneath the figure's green eyes, their cheeks blushed, but their voice hissed, "Neither!"

Tasmin chortled, before her voice lowered and called for her companions to wake, shaking their shoulders. "My dear Darrel. My wonderful Wylie. Wake. For I be needing to witness thy eyes again."

The brown eyes of Wylie and Darrel fluttered to open, after their shoulders were shaken rapidly and heard the light voice that called their names. Wylie and Darrel raised slowly from the rock they leant against, waking themselves from their dreams.

At first, Wylie and Darrel saw Tasmin's frizzy blonde hair and chestnut eyes as a blur. It was a while before Wylie and Darrel saw Tasmin kneeling before them with a glimmering smile, as her wet hair dried against her forehead. Finally seeing Tasmin, Wylie and Darrel grinned, as tears seeped from their eyes and down their cheeks, hurling forwards to embrace her, almost knocking her backwards.

Tasmin wrapped Wylie and Darrel in her arms, melting in their warm embrace and holding them tightly. Her head rested between theirs with her chin sitting on their shoulders and glaring onto the rough surface of the waters. Darrel, Wylie and Tasmin held each other for a while, clinging to each other, as their hands fisted each other's clothing, holding tightly.

The figure behind watched the three companions. The figure's smile, which had grown after watching the companions embrace, started to fade. Instead, the figure scowled down her nose and her lips pouted. A small flinch in her fists was unnoticed by the companions that parted from each other.

Wylie looked up from Tasmin as soon as he noticed the figure behind. Wylie smiled at the figure's rolling eyes and laughed as the figure stormed away, joining the others. He looked back at Tasmin and Darrel, who stared at him with raised brows and smirks.

Wylie insisted to his companions, before their lips parted to tease, "There be no desire for her!"

"Who does the seelie be?" Tasmin grimaced.

"Her name is Phillipa Thyme," Wylie answered.

"Ah! I would have gawked seeing her, but she be speaking so abruptly that I be not able to admire her so." Tasmin shrugged.

Wylie laughed, as his eyes looked over at Phillipa, who was surrounded by Seelie's and Sargon's men and women.

Tasmin questioned, "Where be Sir Terrence and Ezra? Where be Ponoma?"

"The three companions be searching for the phoenix," Darrel responded, leaning backwards onto the rock and closing his eyes. "All be waiting for their return!"

"In which direction do they head?" she asked, rising to her feet and searching either side of the winding beach.

Darrel tilted his head to one side and announced. "The companions be following the beach towards the cave at the end! Dost thou be wishing to follow?"

Tasmin glanced over at the cave at the far side of the beach, searching through the falling rain and sighting a warm, orange glow, which was faint, radiating from within the darkness of the entrance. She saw the constant hues and stepped into the falling water droplets, pacing in the dark golden sand and fighting the wind.

Darrel and Wylie did not stop Tasmin. Instead, Wylie and Darrel rose and followed her into the rain. They rose from the rock they had slept against and trudged through the grains of sand, as the sea churned beside them.

Shortly after, Pip, Sargon, Klaus, Asriel and Caspar sighted the departing companions. They stood in silence, though conversations spurred, looking through the rain and at the companions growing smaller in the distance.

In the silence, Pip, Sargon, Klaus, Asriel and Caspar decided to pace from the voices of the men and women around them. They rushed after the companions, towards the cave in the distance and through the icy waters.

24

Inside the white stone walls of Cahercasey, Nemo held Helen in his arms, following Belladonna to the foot of a winding downwards staircase, which was lit by hanging torches in iron caskets. The white stone walls and marble staircase sparkled, even as Belladonna's twilight blue dress trailed across the steps.

Slowly and elegantly, Belladonna stepped, following the winding staircase round with Nemo following behind. Belladonna's black hair straggled against her back, as her sapphire eyes sparkled in the light of the torches. She walked quietly in her long dress, keeping Nemo close.

Nemo carried Helen in his arms. She had stopped shaking and her fever had died. Her clothes were still wet and she continued to clasp around Nemo, as her eyes remained tightly shut. He continued to embrace her, tightening his grip as Belladonna was in front and shielding Helen's face.

Mostly, Nemo had followed Belladonna and followed in silence. Yet, as they followed the twisting staircase, down into an inky abyss below, forever in silence, Nemo spoke.

"Where be ye taking us, Mother?"

For a moment, Belladonna halted. Her blue eyes glanced over at her shoulder, forcing Nemo to stop. She hissed, "Do not be questioning me, my son! Thou shall be following me into unknown depths without questions."

Belladonna continued to follow the staircase down into the abyss. Hesitantly, Nemo followed her.

At the bottom of the staircase, there was a black iron door. The door was narrow and tall, with a frozen sliding lock.

With a flinch of Belladonna's eyebrow, the lock slid open. The door creaked open, slowly, releasing humid air and a damp smell that wrinkled Nemo's nostrils. Barely any light came from inside the room which was behind the door, and it was not until Nemo stepped inside that he witnessed more.

The large circular room with an endless tunnel of darkness above was lit by only a few low-hanging torches. An infinite tunnel of inkiness stretched into a tall tower with no stairs to climb to the top. From the darkness, black, iron cages were strung from chains, swinging high. A small set of stairs led to the ground below, as the door opened onto a small platform.

As Nemo peered inside, his golden eyes glimmering in the orange light, he saw a man trapped inside the iron bars of one of the cages. The man's body flopped against the bars and the lids of his eyes were folded over, as his snores echoed.

Pinned to the wall at the side of the stairs, there was a woman hanging from iron cuffs. Her head bowed over her chest, as her long hair shielded her face. Crimson liquid ran into her clothing and trickled onto the floor at her chained feet. Her breaths were shallow and barely heard, even in the silence.

Belladonna followed the steps, passing the young woman without a glimpse and heading to the centre of the room. She looked up at the man with a scowl, as Nemo entered the dungeons.

Nemo stepped down the small flight of stairs. Slowly, he passed the woman that hung from the iron chains, stopping in front of her. Nemo's golden eyes examined the woman, glaring at her glazed hazel eyes that stared down at her own pool of blood.

He glanced over at Belladonna and quizzed, "Who be thy prisoners? Be they Tatiana's companions?"

Belladonna nodded. "Yes. The infamous Barnabas Mint and Tatiana's sister, Bidelia Lovet, but be not related by blood. Yet, both be loved by her."

"How does one be knowing she shall come for them?"

"Without doubt, she shall arrive," Belladonna remarked.

As Bidelia hung from the iron cuffs on the wall, her hazel eyes strained to stare into the cage above, where Barnabas slept. Then, her eyes locked onto Nemo, Belladonna and Helen.

Bidelia whispered with a husky voice, "How does a brother betray a sister?"

Nemo and Belladonna turned to Bidelia, as Nemo's stomach started to churn.

Bidelia continued to speak, stammering, as her voice gradually weakened, "Why does a brother kill a sister? There shall be no claims to the throne once the Necromancer has! Why does a brother wish to kill a sister? Spare me from thy lies, for I be taking thy truth to the darkness which follows soon."

Before Nemo answered, a voice muttered through the dungeon, as metal began to squeak. The voice was deep and came from above.

Barnabas' voice bounced inside the dungeon, as his green eyes locked onto Bidelia. His hands grappled the bars and he stuck his head through the gaps, muttering, as his voice rose.

"He be cowardly." Barnabas' throat cleared and he sighed. "Do not waste thy few breaths! Please, Bidelia. For thou should wait for meaningful words to be said."

"These are my final words." Bidelia smiled at Barnabas, as her final breaths slipped from between her lips. Yet, her smile faded and the expression in her face, dulled. A fluster pinched her cheeks, but her skin was frosted. The scarlet liquid from her stomach trickled, before fully stopping. The colour of her dark hair started to fade, as her head hung lower over her body and her hazel eyes lowered also. Her fingers still twitched, though her body had loosened and relaxed.

Into the dungeons, Barnabas called to Bidelia, though she could not hear or see him. "Bidelia? Bidelia. Bidelia!"

The warm glimmer that was in Barnabas' green eyes when he looked upon Bidelia was gone. His eyes did not return to his stern stare. Instead, his eyes filled with mourning and an endless sadness, which wrenched his heart. His green eyes darkened.

Belladonna smiled, as her eyes flicked between Barnabas and the lifeless Bidelia who was strung from the wall. She grinned, watching Barnabas return to the back of his cage, where he hid and locked onto Bidelia's body, staring endlessly.

After glaring at Barnabas, Belladonna's eyes glazed over at an empty hanging cage. With a flash of light within her blue eyes, the cage began to lower. The iron chains clang, as the cage lowered to the ground and hit the floor, lightly. The cage door opened with a squeak, as the chains stopped moving and as soon as the cage had stopped.

Nemo scowled at Belladonna, as she gawked at the cage with her shimmering eyes. He asked, "Why dost thou be lowering a cage?"

"Place the girl inside, my son," she ordered. "For I be knowing who she be. A companion of the queen."

"Then, why did thou save her?"

"All the more reason for the queen to come," Belladonna snapped. "Now, place her inside."

Nemo paused for a moment. His golden eyes looked down at Helen's young face, unable to see her bright grey eyes that flickered violet, as her eyelids remained closed. He clasped her tightly, shuffling forwards and towards the cage, which would hang beside Barnabas. Nemo forced himself to carry Helen towards the cage, as her wavy hair and her legs dangled over his arms.

At the foot of the cage, Nemo lowered to his knee, shuffling into the cage and placing Helen gently against the iron bars. Her tiny body fitted perfectly against the circular, metal floor of the cage, as she curled her knees and head towards her chest. As Nemo placed her down, his muscles were relieved to release her, but his golden eyes formed pools of water, which rolled into droplets down in his cheeks. His fingers ran through her shoulder-length hair, before tracing her cheek with his thumb and pulling away from her warmth.

Nemo clasped the door of the cage, pausing just before he closed it and looking through at Helen. He breathed deeply and retracted his falling tears. Quietly, Nemo shut the door of the cage and locked Helen inside, where she continued to sleep.

Still kneeling, Nemo watched as the iron chains rolled backwards and hoisted the cage above his head. Nemo rose with the cage, stepping back to sight Helen sleeping still, even as the cage hung beside Barnabas. He waited till the cage fully stopped and twisted on his heel to return to his mother's side.

He paced to stand at his mother's side with a bowed head, hiding his tears from her. Nemo stood silently, as his mother declared, "Outside, the darkness shall not cease. It shall worsen! Neither the moon, nor the

Stars shall be shining through! Then, Tatiana shall come. She be raising an army, but it be no match for what be to come."

Belladonna swivelled and stormed up the small staircase, passing Bidelia and ruffling her hand through her hair with a smile. Swiftly, Belladonna left the dungeon, ordering Nemo to follow, as she waited for him at the dungeon door.

With a sigh, Nemo followed. His eyes glared up at Helen, then at Barnabas and twisted on his heel to follow Belladonna. Sluggishly, he climbed the steps and arrived at Belladonna's side, where she led him through the door.

Behind Nemo, the dungeon door was slammed shut. The iron cylinder slid to shut across the frame, locking the companions inside. Nemo trudged away from the door and climbed the staircase with Belladonna.

Once the dungeon door shut with a deafening slam, Helen's body jumped and her grey eyes opened wide. Helen identified the iron bars that surrounded her and the dim lights of the torches that came from below, smelling the rotting walls. She raised her curled body, with the ceiling being far from her head as she shuffled to the edge and searched the dungeon.

Immediately, through the iron bars, she saw Bidelia. Helen saw Bidelia's lowered neck and her dangling hair that covered her face. Helen's doe grey eyes saddened, as a sharp pain ran through her heart. Tears formed in her eyes, searching through the dungeon further and sighting Barnabas through her blurred vision, seeing him stare constantly at Bidelia below.

Helen called to him, but he did not respond. For he did not hear her, as sadness swallowed and deafened him. She called again, but Helen heard only her voice returning to her inside the dungeon walls and laid on the iron again, sobbing, as her cries echoed.

Outside Cahercasey walls, the darkness continued. The rain continued to flood the land and the waves of the sea slapped onto the walls of the cliffs. Above, the clouds thickened and swiftly moved to cover the entire land in ink. The moon and the Stars disappeared. Their light was too dim to shine through the merging blackness that grew stronger, as the Necromancer and Belladonna's power radiated from the South.

Yet, as the darkness came and crossed the skies, there was a light. A silver light from something rayed in the sky. It was unusual and new, beaming brightly through the Necromancer and Belladonna's inky clouds consuming the sky and blackening the land. The light was seen by many as it appeared vividly and rapidly after the darkness had come. It taunted the Necromancer and Belladonna, as it gleamed onto the white castle walls of Cahercasey, shining from the North.

25

From the West, an army of a thousand men and women marched within the darkness of the land, dressed in golden armour. They crossed the land in a formation of rows, with horses and weapons, storming towards the South from the kingdom of Nathair. The army was silent through the inkiness with torches in their hands and sighting the glimmering rayed light above their heads, being led by three figures riding on horses.

At the very front was a wide man proudly riding a horse. The man sat upon his horse with a pipe in his hand and inhaling weed. His jade eyes sparkled, as he hummed from his slim lips. The man's cheeks flustered, as his ginger hair swayed behind hid with an onyx jewelled crown on top of his head.

Behind, a man rode closely. His brown eyes locked onto the man in front, pouting his lips and scowling. His long, white hair was hidden underneath his hood, shielding his angelic face from the fast-falling rain. He held the reins in a tight grasp but did not haul the horse's lowering head to rise. He said little, even though his companions rode beside him.

The man's companion was a woman with striking white plaited hair with wispy strands falling at either side of her high cheekbones. Her body slumped over the neck of her horse, as her eyelids covered half of her brown eyes, which blurred the darkness of the land and her companion also. She whispered to her companion, "What be the light which be keeping me awake?"

The hooded man cocked his head over his shoulder and looked up at the sky. His eyes met silver glimmers of a rayed Star, which twinkled inside the man's brown eyes. A small smile appeared across his lips as soon as he looked up. He replied, "A Star keeps thee awake. A Star I never be witnessing before! It be beautiful. Through such darkness, there still be a Star above us, Tatiana."

"A Star? Why be there a Star, when the others have disappeared, Free? Why does one remain when the others be deserting us?"

Free shrugged. “I be never sighting this Star before now. Who be knowing its name?”

Suddenly, the man at the front, called to the companions. “Ah! Often, new Stars be forming when the land be at its darkness.”

“King Adrion, the Stars be abandoning us many times. There be no trusting them!” Free sniggered. “The Stars allowed the old kingdom to fall and let Cahercasey become the forgotten.”

“I be a man believing in the Stars. There be many reasons thou and I cannot comprehend, so we must be trusting in what is unknown to us, but known by others,” King Adrion proposed. “Now, there be a price for my army.”

“A price? King Adrion, thou be already sending thy men to the South! King Adrion, how can thou be bargaining now?” Free declared.

“Ah! Yet, I be not sending them. For my army be not arriving at Cahercasey, if thou doth not bargain with I.” He cackled, turning back to the front of his horse and continuing to smoke on his pipe.

Tatiana rose from her horse, widening her eyes and looking over at Free. She asked King Adrion, “What dost thou want?”

“I be having no wife. No queen. I be wishing for thy hand, Queen Tatiana,” he insisted. “Thou and I shall marry before arriving to Cahercasey.”

“Where?”

“Currently, thou and I be not leaving the West. My kingdom be having a chapel at its borders. Thou and I shall be marrying there.” King Adrion grinned. “Choose not to marry me and I shall not be giving thee any army. Understood?”

Tatiana sighed. Her eyes flooded with tears and she returned to laying against the neck of her horse. She whimpered. “Yes. Yes, I be marrying thee. I shall be thy queen and uphold my agreement.”

“Yes, I shall, as soon as the marriage is consummated.”

Tatiana rose from her horse with wider eyes and a racing heartbeat. Her palms sweated and she sobbed quietly as she gazed over at Free.

Free’s eyes scowled at King Adrion, as his grip tightened on his reins and pulled the head of his horse to raise, hearing his horse neigh. Free turned to Tatiana, seeing the fear that had stricken her, as she sat frozen upon her horse. His eyes softened as he stared, stretching out his arm towards her and reaching for her hand that had turned cold, gripping her fingers tightly in his palm.

King Adrion laughed. "Ah! A youthful queen to be at my side, forever."

Tatiana grappled onto Free's hand, leading her horse closer to him. Her tears sparkled in the light of the Star, as her brown eyes became glossy with pools of water. She endlessly looked into Free's eyes, searching for hope, but not being able to find the glimmer he held. Her lips trembled as the rain seemed to fall heavier on her head and as the sky seemed to darken even further.

She mouthed, "I cannot. I will not."

He nodded. "I shall not let thee."

King Adrion trotted slightly ahead, as Free and Tatiana hung back. They dawdled amongst the army that parted around them and after their king, as they continued to hold hands and whispered through the rain.

Tatiana cried, "I cannot. I will not. I never will."

Free insisted, "Thou never have to."

"Does such a decision be making me abnormal for sustaining forever?" she questioned. "Does this decision be making me strange? Shall I be judged?"

"No!" He shook his head. "Anyone who judges thou for sustaining be narrow and blind! It be thy choice. If thou be looked upon by others as sustained, then they be not seeing the true beauty that I be seeing."

She trembled. "I do not want to be alone."

"Even acts of contact can make us feel alone," he mentioned.

"How do thou and I retreat? How do thou and I escape this bargain?" she begged. "Please."

"Somehow, thou and I shall!" he promised. "I shall not let anyone touch thee, if thou doth not want to be."

She smiled a little, as tears still rolled down her cheeks. "Thank ye, my companion."

"It be honour to be at thy side, as my queen and as my friend." He bowed, placing his hand against her cheek and stroking her skin with his thumb. He pulled his hand away and placed Tatiana's on her reins and ordered. "Have strength, my queen. Thou and I shall ride together."

Tatiana grappled her reins, as tears continued to fall. She waited for Free to speed ahead, before following him instantaneously. Their horses carried them from the middle of the army and into the open, striding ahead, chasing after King Adrion who had stormed forwards. The wind and rain battered against them, but their horses did not cease.

Tatiana held tightly onto her reins, as the rain poured down her face and hid her tears. The darkness shadowed her bloodshot eyes, as the wind punctured the numbness inside her heart. Her lips continued to tremble, as her brown eyes flicked over at Free for comfort, before returning to glare at the back of King Adrion, riding his horse in front.

An hour passed, as the flickering torches that the army carried and the Star that continued to light the night sky shone upon a small tower. The tower was built amongst a cluster of trees, with vines winding around its black stone walls. On the roof of the tower, there were few guards, which were seen in the flames of fire that burned in iron caskets at the top. The tower had one stained glass window at the front, which was circular and bedazzled with a purple light, sitting above a double door made from black, scorched wood.

As King Adrion led his army towards the tower, Free and Tasmin's pace lessened. Free and Tasmin lingered, as the army circled around the tower and as King Adrion turned to stare at Tatiana and Free, as he stopped his horse in front of the entrance.

Free and Tatiana stopped in the rain that flooded the ground. Their drooping eyes stared through the falling sheets of water at the tower ahead, as their hearts pounded fast and hard against their chest. They sat in silence mostly, listening to the pouring rain splattering on the trees and ground around them, hoping to find peace in its sound.

Free called to Tatiana, "If thou and I be going in there and thou doth not marry him, then thou and I shall leave only in death."

"Run," Tatiana ordered, as she quickly gazed over at him and pulled on the reins, twisting her horse around. "Run, Free!"

Instantly, Free spun his horse, as soon as he heard Tatiana's voice. He turned with Tatiana, away from the tower and King Adrion, as well as his army. His horse slipped in the running streams of mud, before charging after Tatiana.

As soon as Free and Tatiana had spun their horses, King Adrion called into the night. He yelled his orders, instructing his horsemen to ride into the night to chase after them. A large group of horses pounded against the ground, flicking clumps of mud against the back of their legs and bowing their heads as they fought the rain.

Tatiana and Free rushed into the night, hearing the gallops of the horses chasing behind them, stomping over the sound of the icy water that fell. They rode beside each other, as their bodies bounced on the backs of their horses, as they felt their horses slide underneath them. Their horses remained charging across the land, as King Adrion's men flew from behind, closing in on Tatiana and Free.

Tatiana and Free steered towards the East, as the winds veered them through a forest, where the leaves blocked them from the falling rain. The tall and thick trunks blocked Tatiana and Free from the gales that had slashed the land, as their horses whipped between the gaps. Tatiana and Free were thrown by their horses, holding on tightly, as King Adrion's horsemen surrounded them.

Suddenly, a light and loud swoosh ruptured through the forest. Shining white lights appeared from air, as blurred spheres passing between the trees. The lights snaked around King Adrion's men, pulsing brighter as they circled every horseman.

As the lights twisted around them, the eyes of every horseman disappeared and shone white, blinding them. The horsemen released their reins, reaching for their eyes and howling, leaning backwards and tumbling from the backs of their horses. Their bodies slapped against the grounds and against the trees, as the horses galloped astray.

Once the men had fallen and the horses had fled, the balls of lights whooshed above Tatiana and Free's head collectively. White lines followed the spheres, raising towards the sky and entering the black clouds above. The white lights still glistened even in the clouds, heading towards the large, rayed Star, which still shone. The lights shot into the Star, disappearing inside, as the Star twinkled brighter.

Tatiana and Free's horses stumbled to stop, as they pulled on the reins and halted to gape at the Star above. They gawked through the pouring rain, as their mouths dropped. Tatiana and Free inhaled deeply, as did their horses, blowing swirls of white air into the wind. They watched the Star continuing to spike, long after the balls of lights had vanished within it.

After a while, Tatiana and Free turned, facing each other in the rain. Tatiana and Free faintly smiled, as they reached to grasp each other's hands, clasping tightly.

Tatiana breathed. "Finally, the Stars be with us."

Free nodded with delight. "Yes. Yes! I be believing the Stars be with us, at last."

"Do the Stars be giving us a chance against the Necromancer and Belladonna?"

Free looked over his shoulder at the Star above. "The chance be given to us, by the Star thou and I be seeing now."

Tatiana and Free bowed their heads towards the Star, as the Star beamed brighter and rain rolled down the backs of their necks. Their eyes raised, as their hands released the reins of the horses with no destination to head for. They lingered, hoping for an answer.

As Tatiana and Free's horses stood in pools of water, which covered the land, the Star grew bigger. Its sharp points stretched across the sky, through the thick clouds and beaming over Tatiana and Free with an enormous spotlight. The bright, blue-white light illuminated their landscape, as Tatiana and Free's eyes searched their surroundings, which were lightly shadowed.

Through the shade outside the beaming light, Tatiana and Free saw nothing except from tall, sparsely separated trees. Thoroughly, they examined it, as the Star above stayed glowing. Tatiana and Free glared back at each other.

Once their starry eyes met, their brown eyes gleamed and widened with a thought. Free and Tatiana felt butterflies swarm in their stomachs and their hands beginning to sweat, latching onto the reins of their horses. They spun their horses and flocked away from the shining Star that shone onto their backs, riding through the rain.

26

In the North, the bright Star that flooded the land with a white light shone through mosaic windows, which dazzled with colours over grey stones. The windows colourfully beamed at different levels, as windows sat high on towers, low at the ground and decorated the tops of doors. Shadowing the beams of colour that shone through the glass, there were spires, raising to the sky with statues of women, men and children wearing crowns, made from the same stone. Surrounding the towers and spires there was a tall wall around a circular courtyard.

The iron lattice gate was dented and crooked. The black gate was raised from the ground and drawn halfway. The sharp metal at the bottom was stained with red and liquid dripped from the point onto the mole hills which leaked and laid still on the cold and flooded ground.

Past the gate, the hills continued to pile, leading towards the circular courtyard. The glass of the mosaic windows shone onto the cobbled floor and onto the gaps in the walls, as mountains of rubble laid at the sides. Amongst the cloaked hills on the ground, laying at their sides were sparkling, wielding metals and spheres of protection. There was an eerie silence whooshing along the wind that echoed through the crumbled archways around the edges of the courtyard.

Within the walls, silently wandering the paths, stepping over armour and shields of the bodies that layered the ground, there was a bloody and hunched man. His long, black hair smelled of iron and his face was slicked with red splatters. The man's cloak trailed behind him and covered his grey armour, which he stripped from his arms and dropped to his floor. He stumbled in his boots that were hidden beneath the water that ran as his toes became frozen. Already, his sword had returned to his sheath, hiding the blood that smothered the blade. His hands swayed beside his body as he searched the grounds and stopped underneath an archway leading to the courtyard.

Abruptly, the man halted. His dull brown eyes raised from below his eyebrows and glossed over the courtyard, sheltered from the rain as he stood underneath the archway. The man's knees buckled underneath him, then he crashed to the ground and tumbled to one side, smacking his head against the side of the wall.

Yet, his knees and head did not throb. He did not raise his head from the wall and continued to lay on his side, looking onto the courtyard. The ice that shuddered through his body disappeared as his limbs became numb. His mind flooded with images, though his face stayed still, though tears streamed over his cheeks.

The man trembled. His voice was quiet and croaked, barely heard underneath the patters of the rain. "My mother and my father be no more. My mother and my father, be not at my side. I be not with my mother and father. Yet, I be wishing I be. I be wishing I perished with them. I be not wanting to live without them!" he began. "What be the reason for my life to be continuing? I do not be wishing to be the king of the North yet."

Just as the man finished speaking, the Star in the night sky created a beam of light over the courtyard. The blue hue flooded over the hills inside the courtyard and caused the silver metals to sparkle. The light from the Star stopped the falling rain and halted the winds.

As the rain stopped and the wind ceased, the man's eyes twinkled, as he looked onto the courtyard that was piled with blood and bodies. The man's eyes filled with tears as he looked passed the mangled limbs to stare at the Star above him.

The man pushed his body to raise, stretching his legs before him, as he sat in the high, flowing waters. The blue light embraced him, as his dull eyes looked towards the Star and he muttered. "Why does a Star be shining over my kingdom? Never be the Stars our friends. Deserters of us all. Now, I be an orphan king. The orphan king of the North. I be King Hunter! As king, I be not trusting thee."

King Hunter huffed and raised to stand, still looking at the Star in the sky. He stepped out from underneath the archway and into the blue light, where the dark clouds still lingered in the sky, but where there was no rain, nor wind. King Hunter heard the water pattering and wind screaming in the distance, outside the light of the Star, which sheltered him and his kingdom.

He asked the Star, "Why dost thou come here after the Necromancer and Belladonna came? Dost thou taunt me?"

The Star's beam of light shifted. The blue haze lifted from the courtyard and stretched outside the castle walls. As its light moved and flooded the kingdom of Hanuli with darkness, the rain and wind began again.

Hunter stood in the darkness of the courtyard, as the rain poured and the wind blustered. He shivered, watching the Star shine through the broken gate and towards the darkness outside his castle.

King Hunter stepped over the bodies that laid beneath his feet and stood before the gates, searching into the dark.

Vividly, Hunter's mind returned to when his men swarmed towards the gate and to the thick doors that had been torn from their hinges, attempting to push them shut, as the Necromancer and Belladonna's army pounded with an enormous tree trunk that shattered the castle entrance. He remembered the courtyard walls tumbling around him and his men scattering throughout the castle, as the army climbed over the tops or knocked down the walls with a single thrust of the tree trunks they carried and surrounded the castle with. Howls and screams haunted him, seeing his men tumble to the ground in the pouring rain and in the darkness, which had replaced the daylight indefinitely.

After his men had been defeated in the courtyard, King Hunter hid. There was a secret floor door, camouflaged in the stone of the pantry, and King Hunter ran towards the empty kitchen, as faces from both sides passed him. He deafened the calls of his name, as his army watched him sprint into the safety of the castle walls. He removed the hidden slab, jumping down into the shallow pit and covering the hole with the stone again.

Inside the pit, he was in darkness. King Hunter waited till his castle had silenced, no longer listening to screams or howls that made him weep. He hid in the cold, sitting on the soil floor and waited, as he pulled his legs into his chest and rested his head on his knees.

King Hunter did not remember leaving the safety of his hiding place. Mostly, he remembered the bodies of King Umut and Queen Ioana, his parents. King Umut and Queen Ioana rested on the floor of the throne room. Their stretched limbs laid on the scarlet carpet that headed towards their thrones, as the bodies of their guards laid in the entrance of the opened throne doors. The gold and white banners that had strung from the ceiling flared with flames of fire and dropped to the ground once completely blackened.

King Umut and Queen Ioana bled beside each other with locked eyes. Their stares were dull and lifeless, as blood dribbled from their lips and eyes. Their bodies were frozen and their mouths remained parted from releasing their screams, after being struck by the blades of the Necromancer and Belladonna's army.

King Hunter resumed. He focused on the starlight ahead and paced through the tunnelled entrance. He left underneath the iron gate and continued to pace in the light. He stepped onto the soggy grounds outside his castle, as tears continued to pour down his cheeks. King Hunter bowed his head as he began to move away from the entrance and further into the mud, following the light.

Suddenly, he heard a noise in the silence that had swept over his kingdom. The sound echoed, though it was not loud and did not make him shudder or turn his skin pale. He twisted his head over his shoulder and looked into the darkness.

There, in the dark, was an inky four-legged creature. Its hooves clapped in the mud and splashed water to its sides. The creature galloped with a saddle on its back, and its long nose raised to greet Hunter. Its black eyes looked into Hunter's, stopping inches away and nudging Hunter with his nose.

The tears in Hunter's eyes stopped falling. Slowly, he turned to the creature and placed his hand on the creature's nose, stroking gently. The creature bowed his head, as Hunter's hand rested and as Hunter's other hand stroked its neck.

Faintly, Hunter smiled. "Midnight? Why dost thou come here? Why does Tatiana's horse come for me?"

Hunter looked back up at the Star and then at Midnight again, as they both stood in the light of the Star. They stood dry, as Hunter asked himself. "Do I be heading South? Be Tatiana my saviour?"

Midnight neighed.

King Hunter paced to the side of Midnight and placed a foot in the stirrups, lifting his body onto Midnight's back and sitting gently on the saddle. He stroked Midnight as his dull eyes stared at the light that pointed to the South.

Quickly, Hunter grabbed onto Midnight's reins and tapped gently. Instantly, Midnight burst into a sprint, and Hunter's grip had to tighten, fast. He reeled his body forwards, as his back leaned back from Midnight's sudden movement and curled over his stomach.

Midnight carried King Hunter out from the Star's light and into the pitch black that was beyond them. King Hunter and Midnight travelled amongst rain and winds, which worsened journeying towards the South.

27

On the Southern sandy beach, as the waves raged onto the shores, Tasmin, Sargon, Wylie, Darrel, Pip, Asriel and Caspar crossed. The companions fought the strengthening winds as they stormed towards the light that flooded from the cave ahead, arriving at its entrance.

The companions were embraced by the warmth that came from inside the jagged, pointed entrance, as their faces were illuminated with an orange glow, which was brighter than fire. The sea behind them continued to soak their backs and the wind carried their hair from their shoulders, as they stared down the sloping path of the cave, which darkened, even as the fire radiated from deep below.

Asriel and Caspar stepped onto the path where the walls of the cave sheltered them from the raging winds. They stopped almost instantly after entering and turned to the companions behind them, as they stood in the warmth and the citrus light, seeing their companions standing in the gloom of the storm outside.

As Asriel and Caspar locked onto the companions, Caspar and Asriel's eyes transformed. Gradually, their ocean eyes brightened. The blue hues around their black irises started to fade, becoming colourless, losing the pigments of navy that had once dotted their eyes. Like diamonds, Asriel and Caspar's eyes sparkled at the companions.

Once their eyes had changed, Asriel and Caspar were surrounded by a white light that beamed from their skin and darkened the honey light that came from below the ground. Their bodies shone towards the companions, as daggers of ray lights touched the companions with a warm embrace that shielded them from the biting cold.

From their hands, the brightest light was seen. White swirls emerged from the palms of their hand, which were slowly stretched away from their body. The curling light, slowly entangled and forged long and pointed, was silver that was grasped by Asriel and Caspar, despite being transparent and ghostly.

Caspar gripped onto his rayed star jewel that hung from his neck with his other hand and gasped. "A leader. A new leader thou and I be having!"

Asriel clasped his necklace also, flicking his eyes away from the companions and at Caspar with a small grin. "Yes! For us, thou and I be stripped from our strengths, afraid to be punished further. Yet, our, new leader, be rewarding us with our power again. Our swords be given to us again and there be no needing our mortal blades again. Blessed be the Stars!"

Asriel and Caspar wielded their lucid blades continuously in their hands, as the light around them faded slightly and allowed the companions to step closer to them.

Pip announced, as she approached them and as she laid her hands on Caspar and Asriel's cheeks, stroking their skin, "I be so glad thou be restored with power again. There be no needing for us to be wielding mortal weapons again!"

Tasmin, Sargon, Wylie and Darrel joined them, admiring the white light that surrounded them. They reached forwards, passing their hands through the light, which was warm and twisted around their fingers as their hands lingered inside. As soon as their hands retracted to their sides, the light released their fingers and the swirls around them disappeared.

Caspar and Asriel turned from the companions to look at the downward slope, where the path narrowed and the rocky walls darkened, as the light glowed. They twisted to pace along the dry rock and headed towards the light ahead.

Pip grappled Wylie's arm and hauled him to pace beside her. Wylie and Pip walked together and after Caspar and Asriel. They withdrew their swords from their sheaths, storming further into the cave and towards the tiger light.

Lastly, Tasmin, Sargon and Darrel came together to pace down the path and into the cave. As they walked beside each other, Darrel withdrew his axe, Sargon drew his dagger and Tasmin held her long, silver sword. They walked in silence after their companions.

Into the cave, down below the surface, the apricot hue strengthened, becoming so bright that it dimmed the grey rocks around them. The stones wagered the path, as the rocks widened, narrowed, pointed and blunted, spiralling the tunnelling path, as the ceiling lowered the farther they went. In the depths, the warmth, which had been comforting, was suffocating and sweltering as the companions sweated from their foreheads and upper lips.

Just as the companions deepened, the dark walls around them began to shake, as the ceiling above their heads vibrated. A rumble travelled through the entire cave and shook the companions' legs, stopping them on the path. The sound deafened the companions' ears, as they lowered from the ceiling that showered with rocks around them.

The rocks stopped and the rumbling halted, as the companions raised to stand. The companions flicked between each other, before hesitantly continuing their journey down the cave and holding onto their weapons tighter.

At the very bottom of the cave, at the end of a deep slope, there was a small and low opening. From the circular opening, a blinding orange light glimmered through the tunnel and engulfed the companions, as they headed towards the end. The light consumed the companions in heats of fire, which scorched their skin.

The companions walked through the fire and underneath the low opening, entering a spacious room. A bright, blinding orange light filled the circular room, though they were shadowed by something gigantic above them.

Before the companions noticed what was above them, they locked onto the figure that stood motionlessly before them. There were three figures staring upwards at what shadowed them, as their knees trembled.

Asriel and Caspar lingered in the opening of the entrance and gripped their transparent swords tighter. Asriel and Caspar hid their light from the orange fire and cowered in the darkness to watch the companions stepping towards the still figures.

Tasmin, Sargon, Wylie, Pip and Darrel stepped between them, turning their heads to view the faces of the figures. The companions stared into the eyes of the three figures, seeing images of fire reflecting in the glossy glaze that covered their irises. They stared at a man with blue eyes, a man with brown and a woman with black, all seeing the same raging fire as their necks arched to stare above.

The companions followed the gaze of the figures and looked above. Slowly, their eyes moved to lock onto what was shadowing over them and saw the same fires they had seen in the figures next to them.

Above their heads, the companions met golden and beady ovals that eyed them, with a black circular dot in the centre and staying eerily still. The golden ovals were position above a closed beak, which was sharp and pointed towards the companions. A long neck was attached to its head, flowing into an enormous body that was covered in thick, amber feathers. Its wings were glued to its body, as it rested on its four legs, both, being too large to move. The creature remained still, emitting fire from its body and blackening the walls with its flames.

The golden beak of the creature parted, wide. A high-pitched screeched was released, as its neck arched upwards. The scream shook the entire cave, as the companions shielded their ears and cowered towards the opening, hiding alongside Asriel and Caspar, as the creature's screams travelled outside the cave and across the land, silencing the storm. Its lark entered the walls of every kingdom and castle as it awakened.

Its screams stopped, as its neck lowered and its eyes resumed glaring at the companions that hid in the shadows by the opening. The creature examined them, lowering its neck further till it was only a few inches away from the companions, swarming them with its glowing embers.

Ezra was the first to lower his hands from his ears, stepping towards the feathered creature and examining its golden eyes. Ezra reached towards the bird's pointed jaw and rested his hand upon its soft feathers, stroking it as the creature remained calm.

With a loud voice, Ezra breathed. "Ra! How good it be to see thee again!"

Ra parted his beak, letting his soft, clear and melodic voice swirl through the cave, rolling his cheek into Ezra's hand. "My companion, Ezra. There be many years since thou wert last in my cave. For those years, I be alone."

Ezra vaguely smiled. "Ra, my queen be returning home! No longer be thou weakened by her absence. Those standing behind me be in her companionship, too."

"Where be my queen?"

Ezra's hand flinched away from Ra's cheek, as Ra's eyes grew and eyed the other companions ferociously.

Pip came to stand behind Ezra, placing her hands on his shoulders, after putting away her sword, and mentioned softly, "Hello Ra, I be Phillipa Thyme."

Ra's eyes glanced over at Pip and he hissed. "The Seelie traitor!"

Pip stepped back. Her green eyes lowered to the ground, as she clenched tightly around Ezra's arms, standing motionlessly in front of Ra. She heard Wylie's feet storming from behind, as he stood beside her, looking up at the creature.

"She be no traitor!" Wylie spat.

"Wylie Mint. The bastard brother of Barnabas Mint." Ra chuckled with a light and high-pitched laugh. "Dost thou not be wondering why a seelie general be not walking beside her queen?"

Wylie looked over at Pip and watched her avoid his gaze, as her green eyes continued to stare at the floor. Wylie scowled as he looked back at Ra, whose eyes looked over him.

Ra locked onto Asriel and Caspar and chortled. "Stars? Stars be inside the Southern kingdom? The Stars return to the kingdom that they let be forgotten, after watching King Moryn, Queen Gwendolen and Prince Thaddeus be slaughtered by the Necromancer and Belladonna?"

Asriel's sword disappeared and he yelled, "Recently, my powers returned. Caspar and I be punished after fighting our leader at the time Cahercasey be attacked!"

"Do not lie to me!" Ra bellowed. "I be seeing through every lie told. Thou and Caspar be revolting against their old leader and be using Cahercasey's destruction as an excuse to fight further. Why thy new leader be giving thy power back, be for reasons I be not understanding?"

Caspar admitted, "Well, Asriel and I be glad to be given our power back."

Ra's body sunk against the ground, vibrating the entire cave and shaking the companions' legs, as the walls began to crumble again. His tail dragged across the floor, as his body curled and he relaxed his head on his feet. Instantly, Ra shut his golden eyes and became still, stopping the rocks that fell from the ceiling.

He breathed. "When the queen be arriving, bring her to me!"

"Why?" Sir Terrence shouted. "Why we be bringing her to thee?"

Ra growled, keeping his eyes closed but causing the walls to tremor. "For she be needing me and I be needing her to be here."

Ezra, Asriel and Caspar twisted from Ra, slipping through the opening and pacing back through the cave. Swiftly, Ezra, Asriel and Caspar left Ra and the other companions, storming in silence to return to the Southern beach.

Tasmin clasped onto Sir Terrence and Darrel's hands, pulling them through the opening and through to the other side. She followed the path, with Sir Terrence and Darrel at her side.

Sargon followed after Tasmin, Sir Terrence and Darrel. He lingered to lock onto Ra, watching him sleep, frightfully and intriguingly. After a while, Sargon turned and slowly followed the other companions towards the beach, looking back at the beast one last time before leaving.

The last companions to leave were Pip and Wylie. Pip's eyes scrutinised Ra, as her eyebrows moved to closer to the centre of her nose and as lines appeared across her forehead. Her fists were clenched beside her body after releasing Ezra from her grip and slapping her arms against the sides of her body. She continued to frown at Ra as his eyes stayed closed soundly resting in front of her.

Wylie lingered beside her, watching her pout. She stood a few feet away from Wylie, planting his feet on the rocky stones and standing silently. He stepped forwards and reached for her wrist, lightly curling his fingers around her hot and flustering skin. Gently, Wylie tugged her away from where she stood, tearing her from Ra and forcing her to spin towards the opening behind, swinging his arm around her back and stopping her from turning to face the phoenix behind.

Wylie ushered Pip along the path, following Asriel, Caspar, Ezra, Sargon, Darrel, Tasmin and Sir Terrence. The companions' footsteps echoed through the cave, as they walked in silence towards the entrance and back towards the sea.

28

Over the land, the white sheets of icy water continued to be conjured from the sky. The pitch-black abyss that allowed water to fall and flood the flat meadows, held no moon, though the moon was shining brightly above the thick clouds. It was too dark to see the clouds shifting across the sky, and there was only one Star shining through the blackness.

The rayed Star located towards the North shone through the thickest clouds with its pure light. The Star was seen by every kingdom, but its beam led two riders through the storm and continued to brighten.

The two riders on their horses trotted through the grounds, being weighed by the thick mud that swirled around their horses' legs, as they slowly travelled ahead. The dark clothes of the riders glued to their skins, as their feet were submerged in a pool of water within their shoes. Their cloaks had been blown from their shoulders, lost in the winds, travelling as a dark phantom through the night, as the white hair of the two riders dripped.

The rain started to sting and their faces froze, as the water droplets landed on their cheeks as falling crystals. From the noses of the riders, fast slime ran over their lips and down their chins. Their eyes drooped and puffy sacks were embedded underneath, as their eyelids hung low. The two riders held onto their reins, as their bodies swayed on their horses' backs, falling weaker as they continued to ride.

The light of the Star shifted away from the two riders, shining ahead of them and over something in the near distance. The white light blinded the riders, as they stopped to glare.

Ahead, in the marshy grounds, they saw pointed and rocky boulders submerged in the high rising water. There were beige columns, crumbling and eroding in the rain, as some stood halfway above the ground and others stood taller than the trees. At the centre, stones had been stacked on top of each other, forming walls which had been destroyed, and rotten wooden doors and beams rested on the ground. The reminiscence of towers lingered, as thick roots twisted and climbed to the very top, cracking every remaining stone. The surrounding meadow had almost swallowed the remains of what had been a castle.

The two riders stepped closer to the rubble, stopping in front of what had been an arched opening and sighting seals on either side. Inside a carved circle in the wall, there was a tall and thick fir tree, drawn with every needle and root. From the seal, the two riders knew what they had found and what the Star shone upon. It was the fallen kingdom — Alder.

The riders jumped down from their horses, splashing into the waters below and swaying towards the destroyed castle ahead. They moved through the water and towards the archway, where the seals of the kingdom had been engraved on either side. For a moment, the two riders stared into the archway, before entering through.

The two white-haired riders entered the roofed tunnel and stepped out from the rain, leading their horses inside also. The riders crept into the cold dry tunnel, as water trickled between the grooves along the stone path.

The riders' wet shoes slapped against the crumbling stones, as water dripped through the cracks in the high roof above their heads, whilst the drops echoed through the silence of the castle. The tunnel was short, leading the riders into what had been an enormous throne room, stopping at the edge and staring out from underneath the dryness of the tunnel.

The throne room once had a high ceiling, with chandeliers and marble, but as the sky was seen above them and as the rain was thrown down, it was hard for the riders to imagine. The missing walls had been replaced by thickets of trees and fallen columns laid on the ground, crushing the stone that had been placed on the floor. Still, shattered glass laid on the ground, fallen from the high windows, which were now empty openings in the walls. Black scorched materials rippled in the wind, stuck underneath boulders and attached to rusty iron torch holders.

Before the riders could turn to each other, their brown eyes locked onto a crumbled archway ahead and sighted a black sheet moving in the wind. They heard shrilling neighs coming from the near distance, which shook the riders' horses behind, as they still held onto the leads. There were footsteps pounding on the slabs of stone, stomping louder and coming closer to the riders, as the black rippling material moved into the light, attached to a figure, leading a horse.

One of the riders stepped out from underneath the tunnel and into the rain, the rider strode towards the figure which stood in the blue-white light of the Star. The rider met the dull brown eyes of the figure, as the figure's raven hair blew alongside its jet-black cape that hung from its back. The rider was shadowed by the figure's height, as the figure released the lead of their horse, which waited at the archway, meeting the rider in the centre of the old throne room.

As the tired eyes of the rider and the figure met, they launched towards each other and squeezed the other, as their arms slapped tightly around their backs and embraced. From their crimson eyes, water swelled over their cheeks. The rider and the figure panted, comforted in each other's arms, as their hearts palpitated and their chests tightened. Their hands grappled around fistfuls of clothing, stepping closer to the other and resting their heads together.

The wet and black-cloaked figure cried, "My Tatiana! My father, mother and kingdom be fallen. I be alone if I be not having thee."

"Were the Necromancer and Belladonna the ones to destroy thy kingdom?" Tatiana croaked, turning her head into the figure and speaking over the rain.

The figure nodded.

"Hunter," Tatiana breathed.

Hunter's arms locked over Tatiana's shoulders, as his head drooped over his chest and dropped onto Tatiana's shoulder. Hunter placed his nose in the crevice of Tatiana's collarbone, muffling his cries and hiding his tears with her clothing. Hunter laid his head on Tatiana, as the other rider swiftly came to their side.

The long white-haired rider, bestowed with jewelled eyes and a bright smile, came beside Hunter and Tatiana. The rider's hands reached for Tatiana and Hunter's heads, comforting them with a soft and heavy touch. The rider smiled briefly. His smile faded after hearing Hunter's whimpers, which were barely heard above the plundering rain.

It was a while before Hunter raised his head from Tatiana's shoulder. His hair drained over the sides of his face, as his neck straightened. Slowly, he turned to the rider beside him, looking through the strands of his hair to gawk at the rider. His neck was still slightly bent, standing silently with Tatiana still in front of him.

The rider's hands still rested on the sides of Tatiana and Hunter's head, as the rider's eyes gazed at Hunter. The rider remarked with a deep and cracking voice, "Prince Hunter, why be there tears falling from thy eyes?"

Hunter gasped. "Free, my kingdom be destroyed. My mother and my father dead."

"Then, forgive me. For I did not address thee as I am to do so," Free admitted, as his head lowered and raised again. "King Hunter."

Hunter's neck raised. His lanky height stooped above Free, as his heavy eyes lowered to glance at the ground. His eyes dimmed further, darkening till the shining Star above their heads was not seen inside his eyes, like he saw in the reflection of Free and Tatiana's. Hunter's arms dropped from around Tatiana and he was deafened by the rain, as the cold consumed him.

Tatiana's arms were still locked around Hunter's waist. Her chin rested on his shoulder, as she peered at Hunter from the corner of her eyes and saw the light diminish within him. She felt his heart pounding through his chest and felt his shivering body halt.

Feeling his body stiffen, Tatiana released her grip and stepped away from him. Tatiana looked at him, as Free's hand pulled away from their heads. She lifted her hands to rest against his face, spreading her fingers across his cheeks, as she searched the darkness of his eyes, which were so dark that she could not see her own reflection.

As Tatiana rested her hands on his face, she breathed. "Hunter, can thou hear me? Dost thou hear my voice?"

Hunter only heard the rain, as his dull and lifeless eyes met Tatiana's. His tears dropped onto Tatiana's fingers, as he examined her face that beamed in the light. His head lowered, parting his lips and pouting, as he bounced forwards to press his lips against hers, closing his eyes. Hunter locked onto Tatiana's soft lips, pressing passionately against them.

Tatiana's eyes widened, as her lips were trapped between Hunter's. Her cheeks flustered and her hands pushed onto his chest, shoving him backwards. Tatiana's lips escaped from Hunter's, pressing them together, as she lunged backwards and away from Hunter, scowling at him.

Hunter's eyes flapped opened to examine Tatiana's red cheeks and the new tears that started to fill her eyes. From his parted lips, he stuttered, "Dost thou not wish to kiss me?"

She shook her head and twisted from Hunter, lowering her head to hide her warm and pink cheeks. The back of her hand wiped the moisture from her lips and removed the lingering taste of ale that had been left by Hunter's breath.

Tatiana's head looked over her shoulder and at the horse Hunter had been riding. She noticed its jet-black coat, camouflaged in the night and just seen in the starlight, shimmering. The horse neighed gently, as its onyx eyes glowed, staring at Tatiana, beginning to slowly trot towards her.

Her blushing cheeks faded and her moist lips dried. Tatiana's heart deeply beat inside her chest as she shuffled towards the horse and placed her hands on its nose. She smiled, as her hands stroked its soft and wet coat, before gliding towards its hair and running her fingers through the strands.

Tatiana sobbed, looking up at horse's deep black eyes and locking her knees before they buckled. "Oh, my Midnight. I be blessed to see thee again. I be loving thee dearly."

Hunter mentioned, as he looked over his shoulder at Tatiana and Midnight that stood behind him, "Midnight found me. He be taking me to thee, following the light of the Star!"

"My sweet, sweet Midnight. My horse from when I be younger," she whispered, as she laid her cheek on his nose and smiled, briefly closing her eyes.

Free gestured King Hunter to follow him towards the archway, where Free and Tatiana had left their horses. Free waved him over to his side, leading him to the shelter of the tunnel and stepping out from the cold tears of the sky.

Free and Hunter leant against the walls of the tunnel, sliding down to the ground and stretching their legs forwards. Their backs leant against the stone walls, as drops dripped down on their heads from the cracks in the ceilings. Free and Hunter's heads rested over the shoulders, looking at Tatiana and Midnight in the rain.

Tatiana's eyes opened, lifting her head from Midnight's nose and looking back into his eyes. She stepped back towards the archway, leading Midnight gently to the archway, as her hand continued to stroke the brow of his nose, squeezing the water that had soaked into his hair.

Tatiana led Midnight into the shelter of the archway. She led him deep inside the tunnel to where the two other horses rested and pressed her hand on his back, as he knelt gently on the floor. Tatiana lowered beside him, and Midnight's head moved to lay on her lap, as her back leant on the wall.

Midnight's eyes closed as Tatiana's hand glided through the hair on his back and felt his chest lightly chest lightly raise as her hand stopped half way over his stomach. Her tears had dried, as her lips formed a smile, almost forgetting Hunter had kissed her. She looked down at Midnight, watching him fall asleep on her legs, as her head rolled back, looking down her nose.

Free and Hunter rested a few feet away, relaxing closer to the archway. They felt the rain spit inside the tunnel, as the water splattered at the entrance. The spit landed on their clothes, but they did not shuffle their tight and heavy bodies from the cold. They listened to the raging winds, which howled over the rainfall, seeming melodic. The light of the Star reached the inside of the tunnel and caressed them in starlight.

29

Looking out at the Southern Seas, outside a staggered entrance of a cave, where an orange light beamed, there were some of the companions. The companions had stepped into the rain and away from the warmth of the cave behind, standing in the darkness where the light could not reach. They stood at the edge of rocks, at the bottom of a cliff edge, looking at the fierce sea waters, which splashed over the clustered rocks and ran towards their feet, which were planted in the sands. The companions stood in the light of the Star, which had caught their eye, as it hung behind them and lit the vast waters of the sea in silver.

In the middle of the companions, there was Wylie, with his back to the sea and his eyes locked onto the Star. He perched on the edge of a wet rock, as water from the sea splashed on his back and as the rain flooded the strands of his hair that hung at the sides of his face, which was slapped into the palm of his hands.

He mumbled to Pip, standing beside him and glaring at the sea with Ezra next to her, "Why be thou a traitor? Why does a seelie not be walking beside their queen?"

Pip's fixated green eyes tore away from the sea and frowned at Wylie, as she looked down at him from over her shoulder. She smiled. "Immortality. I be not believing Seelie's should live forever. Like the Stars, the Seelie's shall watch over the lands till the end."

Wylie lifted his face from his palms and stared at the Star above him, which flooded the darkness with its bright light. "Dost thou wish to be dead, then?"

Before Pip answered, Sargon huffed. He stood next to Ezra, listening and looking at the silver waves that crashed towards them. "She does not be wishing to be dead! Thou be not listening to her."

Wylie growled, as his eyes looked over at Sargon that stood motionlessly facing the sea. "I be listening. I be listening, well. I hear only death in her words. She be not wishing to live forever? She be not wishing for the dream that everyone mortal be wanting? Does Sargon be contemplating my reasons now?"

Sargon stayed silent, as Tasmin's voice shrilled over the rain and crashing of waves. "Do not persist further, Wylie. It shall be ending in heartbreak."

"Why? Why heartbreak? I be only asking for answers," He shouted at Tasmin, whose eyes glanced over at him as she stood with Sargon.

Ezra turned fully from the sea on his heel and looked down at Wylie. Klaus breathed heavily before speaking with a low and clear voice, "It be heartbreak, for thou cannot be with thy daughter. For she shall outlive thee. She shall outlive us all."

Pip's head lowered into her chest, as her green eyes formed tears to stream. She turned from Wylie, as his brown eyes bore at her, watching the drops run from her jaw and become lost in the wind and rain.

Sir Terrence chortled. "Did thou not know how long a seelie can live?"

"Hush," Darrel hissed, nudging Sir Terrence with his elbow, as he stood at his side. "Hush. Otherwise, I shall push thy head under the surface of the sea!"

Sir Terrence was silenced, as the companions twisted from the sea and formed a circle around Wylie and Pip. Their hearts thumped, as they witnessed the tears falling from Wylie and Pip's chins, listening to their sniffles. Wylie still looked up at Pip, who continued to hide her jade eyes from his stare.

Ezra remarked, as he pressed his staff in the sand and leant against it, "Do remember, thou can be together, if one can endure the pain when the other departs."

Asriel mentioned, "Do not think me to be rude, but let us return to the others."

"Yes. They be waiting long enough for thy return," Caspar added, as he started to march around the curve of the cliff that shielded them from Cahercasey castle.

Asriel followed.

Darrel and Sargon tugged the sleeves of Sir Terrence and Tasmin, who lingered to listen to Wylie and Pip, eagerly. Darrel and Sargon hauled them by their wrists, releasing them once they no longer had to force them to follow. Sir Terrence and Tasmin were reeled away by their companions, as they huffed and groaned, stuttering to create excuses to stay.

Slowly, Ezra turned from Pip and Wylie, pacing on the thinning sand, which ran around the corner of the cliff before stretching wide again. He pushed the end of his staff into the sand as he walked, using his long, wooden and blue crystal staff to balance, sliding on the wet avalanching sand.

Wylie lifted from the stone, facing Pip and examining her profile as she faced the sea. He saw starlight glimmering in her tears, as they continued to pour over her cheeks. She stayed glaring at the sea, even as Wylie yelled over the waves that crashed at the rocks at their feet.

"Does immortality dabble in decisions of love?" Wylie shouted, straining his voice and controlling his chattering teeth.

She nodded, but her green eyes did not move from watching the waves of water crashing down against the surface of the sea.

Wylie huffed, observing her jade eyes fixating on the sea, which did not flinch to move to look at his falling tears. He pressed his teeth together and allowed them to chatter again, stepping forwards and sluggishly moving from Pip's side to follow the bend around the cliff, following the other companions that were ahead.

When Wylie had left Pip's side, she gulped and wiped her eyes with a gentle twist of her fists. Pip glanced over her shoulder and her eyes scolded at the Star in the sky, which continued to shine over the sea and brighten her glorious pink-red hair.

Pip muttered to the Star, as the tears in her eyes vanished and as her voice deepened, "Dost thou watch to taunt? Thou can strip me from my immortality, but thou dost not. It be thee, who told me to leave my queen, long before thou knew to arrive in the sky! I be informed to leave, long before thou came. Yet, it be thou that told me to come here. How can thou tell me to come here, but taunt me with love that I cannot fulfil?"

The Star remained rayed, as Pip turned away from the sky and followed the other companions. Pip slumped around the bend, stomping her feet in the sand that stuck to her boots, curling her toes as water seeped inside her socks. She just saw the companions ahead of her, squinting through the rain and the wind that blew towards her.

The companions eyed Cahercasey ahead. The castle was almost in the darkness, if the torches on its walls had not been lit, blowing in the violent winds. Cahercasey was perched at the edge of a cliff, and a round arch formed below, standing a few feet tall over the sands of the beach.

Asriel and Caspar came to the arch, which was lit with a single torch that sat underneath the centre of the arch. The flame whipped in the wind, almost losing its fire and its orange light, as the rain poured diagonally towards its shelter. The torch light flickered, and the companions viewed still shadows laying on the sand, with their backs facing the winds. The shadows covered themselves in their cloaks, with the corners stuck underneath their limbs and stomachs, forming cocoons. They were soundless and motionless in the darkness and rainfall.

Caspar and Asriel stopped a few feet from the arch. Their white eyes surveyed the shadows ahead, as they continued to stand in the darkness and away from the flickers of the torch ahead.

Soon, Sir Terrence, Sargon, Tasmin and Darrel followed and approached Asriel and Caspar from behind. Their feet shuffled to stop and they gawked at the shadows that were just seen in the light of the flame.

Not long after, Ezra, Wylie and Pip joined them, stopping also.

The mouths of the companions gaped open. Their eyes glided over every shadow that was asleep on the sand, as the wind lifted their cloaks and revealed their faces for the companions to examine. The companions witnessed dull and still ovals, which were aimed at the Star and the sky that did not sight the glorious silver light above the companions' heads. The warmth of their bodies faded. Their skin was like ice.

Suddenly, the violent flames of the torch that had been planted in the sand was extinguished by the wind, followed by a puff of smoke. The shadows at their feet were lined with silver, almost disappearing in the pitch black, still sleeping soundlessly in their cloaks that were wrapped around their bodies.

Ezra stepped closer to the shadows, stopping as he embedded his staff in the sand and leant against the wood that was taller than his head. The blue crystal inside his staff gradually glowed to cast a pale coloured light over the shadows, as Ezra's eyes examined them further.

Asriel and Caspar passed Ezra, stepping over the shadows and lowering to their knees. Caspar and Asriel stroked their icy skin, before covering their faces with the materials of their cloaks, tucking the corners underneath their heavy heads. They covered every face of the hundreds that laid on the sandy shores of the Southern Sea, as scarlet liquid trickled into the golden grains.

From the shadows of the archway, from behind the rocks that staggered in the ocean, shining black armour emerged. Gigantic beasts sprung from the darkness, as silver blades sparkled in their hands underneath the starlight. The stumpy limbs of the beasts stepped over the rocks and the bodies, stamping towards the companions and vibrating the ground. The beasts stretched towards them, swinging their swords, as their faces were seen in the light of Ezra's staff.

The beasts had round faces and enormous mouths with large, sharp teeth rising from their drooping bottom lips, as drool dripped down their jaws. Their eyebrows sat low above their big, round eyes that scowled over their flat noses. The skins of the beasts were a light green, and they wore black armour over their large, stomachs.

Sir Terrence, Sargon, Darrel, Tasmin, Pip and Wylie swivelled on their heels in the sand and whipped their bodies to follow. They strung their legs forwards, rampaging across the beach and fighting through the rapid falls of rain, against the blowing winds. The companions heard the stomping feet of the beasts charging behind them, as they focused on the light of Ra's glow that radiated brightly from the cave in the distance.

It was too late for Ezra, Asriel and Caspar to run. The moment Caspar and Asriel rose and the moment Ezra tried to turn, the beasts' arms swung around their chests. Their feet were lifted from the sand and their lungs were crushed by the arms of the beasts. Ezra, Caspar and Asriel groaned as they were swept and captured by the beasts. They watched their companions vanish into the distance, as the beasts that held them carried Ezra, Caspar and Asriel towards the cliff edge.

The giant beasts stretched their long arms above their heads and grappled the ledges of rock, as their large feet crumbled the walls. The beasts climbed the cliff walls fast, taking Ezra, Caspar and Asriel to the white walls of Cahercasey.

The other companions still ran across the wet sandy beach, alongside the rough waters of the sea that crashed onto the shore. They sprinted towards Ra's light, which was still so far in the distance, as their feet stumbled underneath them. The beasts' long legs rampaged behind, quickly catching the companions' pace and swinging their arms to seize them.

Tasmin and Sir Terrence tugged each other through the shallow waters, separated from the other companions by a line of beasts, as they were chased by three. The beasts splashed the waters that soaked their backs and rippled the waters at their legs, sweeping Tasmin and Sir Terrence into the waves and falling under the black sea waters, which filled their lungs and pulled them further out to sea.

The beasts stopped and turned to follow the other companions that still ran along the shore, as Tasmin and Sir Terrence fought to swim underneath the water. Their arms grappled around each other, being spun through the waves like torpedoes and being chilled inside the freezing sea. Tasmin and Sir Terrence kicked towards the surface, feeling the winds flow through their hair, as their heads popped from underneath the water.

Tasmin and Sir Terrence were far from the shore, and the sea became calm. They floated amongst small waves that glistened silver and sighted the beach in the distance, where they saw their companions flee from the monsters that chased them.

Once Sir Terrence and Tasmin caught their breaths, their legs and arms slapped in the waters, swimming towards the shore. They were thrown back underneath the water, as the waves started to rise behind them and pushed them towards the sand.

On the sand, Sargon was the first to arrive at the orange glowing light of the cave. He had passed his companions that had been close behind and stumbled at the entrance, as he flocked inside. Sargon pounded his feet along the rocky ground of the cave and halted after the crashing waves had disappeared and after he heard his footsteps echoing around him.

Sargon stopped. His eyes glared at the pathway ahead, before twisting on his heel and looking at the entrance of the cave, as well as the empty path he had ran along. He searched the gap of the daggered opening, flicking his eyes to each side and hoping. Sargon shuffled forwards, hearing silence amongst the waves and the whistles of winds, panting, as his feet moved faster to the entrance.

Suddenly, Sargon leapt forwards and raced outside, returning to the storm. Sargon stepped into the battering winds and the icy falling water, sliding down the slanted shoreline, as he rushed around the bend of the cliff to search the darkness.

On the beach, Sargon's azure eyes sighted his companions' shadowed bodies rushing towards him. Helplessly, he ushered his companions to hurry, watching their legs almost buckle and their chests tightening to stop their breaths. He saw the beasts running dangerously close behind, feeling the quakes of the earth as the beasts pounded their feet on the shore.

Sargon stepped forwards and lunged, grabbing Pip. She was the first companion to arrive before him, as the others ran swiftly away from the beasts that still chased them. Sargon grappled her arms and swung her around the corner of the cliff, forcing her to run inside the cave.

Pip met the entrance of the cave as Sargon's hands released her and threw her forwards. She raced through the opening and into the warmth, as the orange light caressed her wet and cold skin. Pip slid across the downward path, finally halting, as her feet slammed down and stopped her from falling further. Pip sat with her knees still raised and she leant against the wall, breathing heavily and clutching her clothes tightly, as her green eyes closed, hoping the companions were not far behind her.

Pip heard footsteps pounding behind her but did not open her eyes to see which companion had entered. For the loud steps were not Wylie's, but Darrel's.

Darrel slammed his heels on the rocky ground of the cave path and sprinted downwards, grinding to a halt and stopping beside Pip as she sat on the floor. Darrel's torso lowered over his knees and his hands slapped on his knees, as his mouth opened wide and yellow fluid splurged from his gagging throat onto the ground. There was fluid still clinging to his chin, even after he had stopped and raised to catch his breath.

Pip's eyelids fluttered open, as her green eyes widened and her calm breath began to quicken again. Her ears loudened the sound of light and quick footsteps, which quickened her heart. She jumped onto her feet and swivelled to face the entrance of the cave, as she shuffled forwards before sprinting to a running figure.

Pip swung her arms over the figure and jumped onto her toes to place her head of the figure's shoulder. She pushed the figure into her chest, as her hand laced the back of his head and grappled a clump of hair. Pip panted, holding the figure, as her hand rested on his tensed back.

As she held the figure tightly, her green eyes saw the long hair and blue eyes of Sargon jogging into the cave, following the path towards them. She smiled briefly at him, before he passed her and stopped beside Darrel.

Still clinging to the figure, Pip watched the entrance of the cave and whispered into the ear of the figure she held. She breathed. "Wylie. Look!"

Pip released Wylie from her grip, as her hands fell down the sides of his arms and rested at his wrists. They turned to stare at the entrance of the cave, with Sargon and Darrel already glaring at the darkness between the jagged outline.

Just outside the cave entrance, the companions met the eyes of the beasts that had chased them. The beasts peered inside thc cave entrance, cowering, with lowered swords. They swayed in the orange drops of rain, silently. Their roars had ceased, slowly stepping back into darkness. Their green, grim skin and their sharp teeth vanished from sight.

Once the beasts had gone, Pip stated to her companions, still looking at the darkness and the rain outside, "The ogres fear the phoenix."

Sargon added, "Well, let us hide with the phoenix till Tatiana be arriving."

Darrel, Sargon, Wylie and Pip ventured down the cave path, returning to see the phoenix that warmed and lightened the entire cave from below. The companions slowly and quietly walked with each other as their clothes and hair dried in the heat.

30

In the East, from the skies, white, sparkling flakes still fell underneath the darkness that had grown from the South. Heavily, from the sky, the flakes fell and layered the land with a continuous white blanket, which continued to thicken rapidly. The winds gushed through the bare and black trees that filled the lands, shaking the branches and leaning sideways, as the howls wailed over the snow.

Below the layers of white sheets, amongst the snowflakes that had clustered together, there was a hollow cave, which was wide with a low ceiling and a tunnel leading down. The cave was dark, even as small, snow particles seemed to glow along the walls and across the crunchy snowy ground. The echoing winds swirled in the minimal warmth created by the shelter and the cave was untouched by the continuous snowfall.

Inside the cave, two women and a man pressed their backs against the flaky snow walls, looking through the tunnel and sighting the fast, falling flakes, which fell silently. The whites of their eyes were staggered with crimson veins, as large and black circles rimmed under their eyelids. They rested with their knees tucked into the stomach, turning into the woman in the middle, keeping their shivering bodies warm and holding hands.

The woman in the middle held onto those at her side, with purple and numb fingers gripping around the little warmth in their hands. Her kinked caramel hair fell to her shoulders, as her peached skin became blue and the brown in her eyes glowed. The woman's body did not shudder and her feet stretched in front of her body, as she wriggled her toes continuously and pain rippled through, and she clenched her teeth.

The tiny woman beside her, with stumpy legs and little arms, curled towards her like a puppy. The woman's eyes were closed, with a body that flinched as she slept. The woman's upturned nose sniffled and ran, as the colour of her lips turned into blueberries. There was still warmth in the small woman's body, as her skin continued to be perky and pigmented.

The dark-haired man with them was awake. With both hands, he held the woman's hand, shielding the purple fingers that laced on his skin. His knees were against his chest, as his head hung to rest on the top of his knees, as his hair flopped beside his cheeks. He hummed, quietly, as the women rested at his side, calmed by his soft voice. The man's lime-coloured eyes had darkened to be the same puffs of blue that slouched onto his cheeks.

The man whispered through his teeth, moving his frosty tongue in his dry mouth. "Orla and Ainsley! Can thou be hearing me?"

"Yes," Orla answered, as she woke from her light sleep instantly and looking over at the man who still lay his forehead on his knees.

After a while, Ainsley, who sat in the middle, spoke. "Yes, I be hearing thee, Klaus. I do not be remembering what I be saying before. I cannot be feeling my fingers."

Klaus and Orla grappled Ainsley's hands tighter, wrapping their other hand over her purple and frozen fingers, warming them, though there was no blood gushing through. Klaus raised his head from his knees and Orla shifted her neck to glare at Ainsley's expressionless face.

Klaus breathed. "Do not be worrying with what be said, Ainsley. Dost thou feel well to be travelling, soon? My companions and my daughter be arriving, if be not already, at Cahercasey. Thou and I must be arriving there, too."

"It be too dangerous to be wandering through the snow!" Ainsley declared.

"Thou and I must be moving, now!" Klaus argued. "I be needing to arrive at my daughter's side and know she be all right."

"She be having immortality. She be alive." Orla chortled.

"Yes, I be not having immortality!" He sighed.

Orla and Ainsley locked onto each other, as Klaus turned his neck and hid his face, muffling his tears, which instantly formed into sparkling diamonds that clung to his cheeks. Orla and Ainsley examined each other's softened eyes as they huffed together. Slowly, Ainsley and Orla looked back at Klaus, whose head was still tilted towards the shadows, as he whimpered.

Ainsley and Orla shuffled closer to Klaus. Ainsley tapped his shoulder until Klaus twisted to face them again. Softly, Ainsley and Orla smiled, as Klaus' tears crystallised on his skin.

Ainsley gripped his arm tightly in her hand and insisted. "Then, thou and I shall leave. If seeing Pip be stopping thy and his tears, then let us be on our journey to greet her!"

Orla lifted herself from laying on Ainsley's shoulder. Slowly, she moved her frozen legs, dragging them behind her and crawling towards the tunnel, beginning to slither through. Her numb fingers sliced into the ice and heaved her body with her weakened and cold hands. Gradually, Orla climbed to the surface, feeling the wind slash on her skin and being blinded by flakes of falling ice rapidly swirling around her.

Shortly, Ainsley released Klaus' hand and crawled forwards, unable to move or feel her fingers as her hand planted into the snow. Her knees dug deep into the white ground and she shuffled through the tunnel, brushing her back against the ceiling and dusting the ground. Ainsley reached the entrance, reaching for Orla, whose hands stretched towards Ainsley, ready to grab her hands and haul her from the tunnel.

Finally, Klaus wiped his tears and groaned to stretch towards the tunnel in front. Klaus pounded his feet and hands onto the snow, following Ainsley and Orla, seeing them at the end of the tunnel, looking through at him. Klaus moved quickly to Ainsley and Orla, exiting the tunnel and raising to stand in the strong winds and sharp flakes of snow.

Klaus clasped Orla and Ainsley's hands, before striding with them through the snow, which sat at their knees and continued to rise gradually. The snowflakes attacked their fragile bodies, slicing their faces and oozing blood from many, small cuts. Instantly, their blood froze reaching the surface of their skin, as the winds stung their newly formed wounds.

The companions stormed within the darkness, losing their feet in the mountains of snow and sighting only fragments of flowing snowflakes that gushed around them. They trudged slowly, with every step growing heavier, wading through and heaving their buried feet from the white sheets layering the ground. Their flesh was darkened purple, as their bodies shivered and their teeth chattered vigorously. Klaus, Ainsley and Orla's fragile and frosty ears, which burned, were deafened by the whaling winds.

Amongst the darkness, in the night sky, which the companions could not see, the single Star that glowed was not alone. Its rayed points stretched beyond its centre, as millions of smaller Stars joined. The dark sky was dotted with white lights, as purple and green hazes streamed, stretching for miles over the land. The Stars gleamed, fighting the blackness that covered the land, as thousands clustered and were seen from below.

Klaus, Ainsley and Orla halted to watch the Stars shine between the snow, at first glancing to the Stars, as still fragments of snow. The companions squinted as the snow continued to fly and as ice formed on their lashes, at the twinkling lights above, which caused the heaps of snow to glow and the land to brighten ahead of them.

The companions gasped. For a moment, their shivers and their chattering teeth stopped. The cold faded and the slashes on their skin eased. Their eyes glimmered, and they forgot their feet were buried in the snow and forgot their frosty, purple fingers they could no longer feel. Their existence melted the companions' hearts and gushed tears from their eyes, which crystallised and stuck to their cheeks. Klaus, Orla and Ainsley were warmed by the sighting of the Stars, which had returned to the sky, after leaving a blank canvas for over a hundred years.

As the companions fixated, the roaring wind silenced. The falling white flakes slowly dispersed and vanished before they hit the ground, until they disappeared indefinitely. There was warmth, as the wind, which continued to gush silently across the land, carried heat that warmed the companions, cocooning their icy purple and red bodies. The snow lowered, as the snow transformed into water and burst into streams of steam, till the companions' feet were revealed.

The companions observed their feet, which were free from the pockets of snow and now stood on a few thin layers of snow that still hid the grass strands. They saw their scuffed boots and lifted their feet from the ground, which were lighter now that they were not covered in heaps of snow.

Klaus, Orla and Ainsley glared back at the Stars that filled the dark sky above their heads, with timid smiles.

Klaus exclaimed. "O my Stars above! It be too long since my eyes be looking upon thee. My heart warms. My stomach flutters. Times before my birth and before my daughter's birth be returning, bringing us delight."

"Be the Stars helping us? Be they helping Tatiana?" Orla questioned.

Ahead, Ainsley stared. Her eyes had drifted from the Stars to examine what was striding quickly towards them. Ainsley's lips parted and quavered, whilst her eyes bulged with delight. She breathed deeply with relief, before squeezing Klaus and Orla's hands and gesturing them to look away from the Stars.

Travelling across the land and trudging over the thin layer of snow that had melted, a thousand black cloaks blew and a thousand swords sparkled, pointed to the ground. A shimmering hue, radiated from the black material that layered the bodies ahead. White oval pairs gawked at Klaus, Orla and Ainsley. Hanging from every neck, dangling over chests, there were long silver necklaces with rayed silver points. The thousands stepped lightly towards the companions, travelling in militant line formations and halting with a thud, a foot away from the companions.

Ainsley, Klaus and Orla panted, as their knees weakened and their hands trembled. Feverishly, they grinned, moving their stiffened and reddened cheeks, which ached. They stepped closer to the wall of thousands, hesitantly.

Orla uttered to the figures in front, "Thou be Stars? Thou be returning to us? Why? Why be thou returning to us now? After many wars and destruction, after many deaths, thou be returning now?!"

The Stars chimed, "Our leader be new. Our leader be different than those before. Our leader be sending us to thee."

"Why?" Ainsley questioned.

"Our leader be wanting us to take thee to Cahercasey! The seelie army be killed by the Necromancer and Belladonna. The Stars be the only hope for the Queen of the South."

"What be of my daughter?" Klaus demanded. "Be she alive?"

The Stars nodded, as Klaus sighed with great relief.

On the edge of their heels, which were planted in the snow, the Stars twisted together. The Stars turned to the South, pausing for a moment, before marching forwards to the forest and passing between the tall black trees ahead. They trudged silently and briskly to the South.

Klaus, Orla and Ainsley gaped at the thousands of Stars, holding their formation as they crossed the land and towards the forest. The companions followed them, dwindling behind, as the last row of Stars entered the thickets of trees. Klaus, Ainsley and Orla entered the forest with them and followed the Stars to the South.

31

In the heart of the land, in the kingdom of old, which remained in ruins with collapsed columns and crumbling walls, the tunnelled entrance of the castle remained. The tunnelling entrance, without any doors intact and vines clambering every stone like fingers, was pelted by icy raindrops that crashed from the sky, which had now been painted with sparkling, white dots and hazes of green and purple.

Inside the tunnel, a tall woman slept. She leant against the damp wall, as her head hung low over her chest and as the wisps of her white hair cascaded over her ageless face. Her long legs stretched forwards, as the head of a black horse rested on her lap with its eyes closed. The woman listened to the rain, sleeping lightly as she dreamt inside the tunnel.

Yet the woman was elsewhere. Her body was inside the tunnel, in the kingdom of old, but she had transported far into the distance. The woman felt weightless and the cold she had felt from the rain was numbed. Nor did she feel the warmth of the horse that rested its head on her lap, no longer smelling its damp, pungent coat. Still, she could listen, but the thundering rain instantly disappeared and her ears were eased by the sudden silence she experienced as she stood somewhere else.

The woman was inside a wide stone cylinder that stretched miles above her head into darkness. She stood on a damp and rocky floor, feeling cold air lift from its surface and swarm her. Hanging from above, there were metal cages, where two birds were trapped inside, sleeping for now.

Her eyes focused on the wall ahead, where a staircase led to a closed door and torches hung from iron holders. She saw the door from the corner of her eyes, as she locked onto a hanging shadow with its limbs locked in chains. The shadow's blue top was stained and a massive hole had been forced to tear by something sharp which had dug deep inside the shadow's flesh. Its dark hair covered its face, as the shadow stayed motionless in its chains.

Slowly, the woman shuffled towards the captive shadow, stumbling over her feet and feeling her heart burden heavily. Her breath quickened and her chest tightened, painfully squishing her lungs together. She stopped at the bottom of the stairs and leaned towards the shackled shadow, peering through the strands of hair that fell over its face.

Just as she examined, her eyes widening and her heart racing, she froze. A harsh and bellowing voice boomed inside the cylinder, shattering her ears and snapping the silence. Her eyes widened, slowly pulling away from the shadow and turning her head to gaze over her shoulder and above.

From one of the cages, a dark-cloaked bird eyed her with beady green eyes. Its wet hair was swept over its head, as it flopped onto the iron bars and rocked its cell, which creaked. The bird's claws clasped the iron, as its pouted face squeezed between to glare down at the woman and larked her name again.

"Tatiana? Tatiana! What be thou doing here? How can thou be here?"

Tatiana turned fully to face the bird above. Her eyes softened and a small smile parted her lips. With a croaky voice, she remarked, "Barnabas? Barnabas! Thou be living."

"How be thou here?"

Tatiana shrugged and stuttered. "I be not knowing. I be dreaming of my sister, Bidelia. I be imagining thee, too."

"Thou art in the dungeons of Cahercasey!" Barnabas exclaimed, leaning further forwards and tipping his cage. "How can this be? I still be not understanding."

She shook her head and shrugged. Tatiana twisted from Barnabas to glare back at the shadow in chains, curiously. She turned her body first, before letting her shoulders and head follow. Her eyes were the last to move, locking onto Barnabas still and watching his face scrunch with pain.

As she did, Barnabas shrilled, "Tatiana! Do not look behind thee! Please, I beg."

She stopped. Her eyes still deeply stared into his, watching his eyes flare. Tatiana's body had turned from him, but her face continued to look upon him. Fearfully, she asked, "Why? Who be behind I?"

"Thou need not worry. No one important." He smiled, faintly. His eyes looked over at the cell closest to him, where a small girl laid curled inside, sleeping. "Return to where thou be and save Helen. She be here with me. She was captured by Nemo, thy brother! She be well, but she be not alive for much longer if she stays. Take her with thee."

"I cannot." She admitted, as she glanced at her hands. Her ghostly hands glimmered, seeing the floor through them, as if they were disappearing. "I believe I be only here to witness, not to alter."

"Then, arrive quickly here! Save Helen," Barnabas insisted. "Do not save me. I be saving myself!"

Tatiana chortled.

Suddenly, the locked door at the top of the stairs, clicked, after the rattling of keys. A thud pounded on the centre of the wood, as the door was heaved opened. Slowly, the dungeon door was opened, as a figure slipped through the small gap, before the door slammed shut again.

At the top of the stairs, after the door had shut, a man stood at the top of the stairs and stared down at Tatiana's ghostly body with a pair of golden ovals. The man stood slightly shorter than Tatiana, with dark hair pulled away from his face and revealing the aged lines that permanently sat on his forehead and by his eyes.

The man trudged down the steps, but Tatiana's eyes did not follow him. She was afraid to meet the shadow still hanging in chains and looked back at Barnabas till the man came slowly to stand before her.

He stopped in front, stretching his hand towards her and grazed her shoulder, gasping, as his fingers fell through her ghostly body. His hands lingered in the space inside her shoulder, twisting his hand and watching the white sparkling light swirl between his fingers and thumb, till he pulled his hand to rest at his side.

"Tatiana? How…"

She huffed, as her eyes briefly glanced to one side. "How could my cousin betray me? How could thee, Nemo?"

Nemo breathed. "I cannot fathom the words that need to be spoken to thee. However, I be truly sorry. I be only wanting to protect my cousin that became my sister."

She sighed. "I do not believe thee."

He nodded. "Yes, I understand thee do not. Yet, I never led the Necromancer or Belladonna to thee. I led the Necromancer and Belladonna to thy companions, yes, but I be only luring them further away from thee. The safety of thee be all I caring for."

She growled. "Keep my companions from harm! Do not be letting the Necromancer nor Belladonna touch them. Ensure my sister be well, too."

Nemo forced his eyes to stay locked onto Tatiana, tempted to look over at the still shadow that hung in the chains on the wall. His eyes quickly lowered from her gaze, as sudden swirling water filled his golden eyes, bowing his head and watching his tears drop to the ground at his feet.

Though Tatiana saw his falling tears, she did not ask why. Coldly, Tatiana stood with a straightened back and an icy glare. She scowled down at Nemo, as a new and sweet voice echoed shallowly in the dungeon.

Curiously, Tatiana's eyes looked above. The lines of her face faded as her expression lightened. Tatiana's eyes met a bright pair of grey eyes, which were flooded with sparks of violet. The corners of Tatiana's lips lifted, sighting a young girl, trapped in the birdcage next to Barnabas'.

"Tatiana?" the girl called.

"Yes, Helen?"

"Thou be not an ordinary Queen, nor an ordinary person," Helen claimed, as she shuffled to the front of her cell to view Tatiana further. "There be more to thee than what be thought. Maybe, it be how thou can defeat the Necromancer?"

"I do not be knowing anything other than what be happening now. In the many years thou and I be travelling, be this the first and only strangest time."

"Well, thou shalt search for answers," Barnabas ordered from his cell. "Do not dare be here, till thou be having answers for the questioning strength thou be possessing. Do not dare go to Cahercasey unless thou be having the strength to destroy the Necromancer and Belladonna! Dost thou understand?"

"Barnabas, thou and Helen shall die here if I do not be arriving soon!" Tatiana argued. "I be not leaving my companions to be tortured."

"Do not dare," he hissed. "Do not dare here. Otherwise, thou shalt be useless to all. Dost thou understand?"

She gulped. Barnabas' stern stare choked her, and she continued to lock onto his green eyes, despite water filling her own.

Suddenly, Barnabas disappeared. Helen and Nemo vanished as Tatiana's vision blackened. She saw the black canvas of her closed eyelids and felt the weight of her body again, as something on her lap rested heavier. Tatiana felt the shrilling winds whip around her and shivered as her body felt the cold, hearing the rain crashing above her head, but her body kept dry. She listened to her deep breathing echoing, before catching whimpers of breath that were close to her.

Tatiana's eyelids lifted. She saw a stone wall sitting a few inches away from her feet with vines spreading across and moisture trickling downwards, trailing between the gaps. Tatiana followed the wall both ways, sighting the entirety of the tunnel she sat inside and seeing the small glimmers of raindrops in the darkness at either end. Her eyes glazed over the two men that slept against the opposite wall, before flicking her eyes onto the long face of the horse, which rested on her lap, reaching to run her fingers through the strands of its hair.

She smiled, as her hands ran through Midnight's soft hair that was still slightly damp. Though she smiled, Tatiana remembered meeting Barnabas, Helen and Nemo in the dungeons of Cahercasey, still unsure how. Tatiana rested quietly, turning her head to glare down the tunnel, as her name was calmly called.

Tatiana met a man's amber eyes, surrounded by enormous dark circles and thick lumps where his eyes were tired, hung from the bottom of his ovals. His long and black hair was sleeked behind his ears, still wet from the rain, as his roots became matted and damp. His back was against the stone wall, sitting beside a man that continued to sleep, as his voice softly played like music, calling to Tatiana.

"Tatiana? Be thou well rested?" he asked.

She nodded.

"I be sorry."

"No, Hunter. I be not wanting to be reminded," she snapped, pressing her lips together soon after she had spoken.

"My heart aches. My heart pains me. I be wishing for my mother and father to be here, again." He sobbed, muffling his tears as he wiped his nose on his sleeve. "How did thou survive without a mother and father? It be impossible."

She growled. "Despite the love thou be given by a mother and father, thou had been blinded and sought love from elsewhere. Though thou be given love, thou be filled with emptiness! Do not cry to me, for missing a mother and father, when I be knowing my parents, but be not sharing memories with them like thou can."

Hunter gulped, watching Tatiana's head lower and her eyes glancing away from him. "How can thou be like ice? How can thou dismiss my pain easily?"

Tatiana ignored Hunter, continuing to stare at the end of the tunnel and into the darkness. She clenched her torso, as a burning sensation swarmed inside her stomach. Tatiana groaned, as her arms wrapped around her waist and as her legs flinched, waking Midnight from his sleep. She slid sideways against the wall, crashing onto her shoulder, as Midnight raised his head and stomped onto his feet. Tatiana rolled onto her stomach, her body continuing to spasm. Her groans turned into screams, as sweat poured from her forehead and as her entire body scorched.

Hunter darted and crashed to his knees beside Tatiana, examining her and hesitant to touch her. He called to her, but she could only scream.

Soon, Free awakened. He was shaken by the high-pitched screams echoing loudly inside the tunnel walls and silencing the shaking thunder and the heavy rain outside. Free's body tightened and his eyes flashed open, widening, as he searched over his shoulders down the tunnelling passage and finally seeing Tatiana and Hunter.

He locked onto Tatiana, seeing her limbs stiffen and bend, curling on the ground and watching as Hunter helplessly loomed over her with his hands hovering above her body. Free listened to her screams and pounced to sit with Hunter, landing on his knees and sitting beside her face, which he could not see before.

Tatiana's face was red and moist, smelling sour, as her sweat soaked her hair. Her neck was blushed from her screams, as veins and bones popped to the surface of her flesh, straining. Yet her brown eyes caused

Hunter and Free to be concerned, since they were no longer recognising her bright and green sparked eyes, which had transformed.

Tatiana's eyes burned, bulging from their sockets and she used her fingers to claw at them. Her eyes watered, as faint white swirls raised from her irises and as her green sparks faded, alongside the vanishing of the brown shade that filled them. Her eyes brightened and glowed with colours of fire, burning brighter than any Star, seeing clearly into the pitch black outside the tunnel and watching every tear fall from the sky, which her companions could not. She saw surrounding trees and every shimmer of light, never mind how small. The flowing water flourished into steam and her body remained hot, but Tatiana's muscles relaxed and she loosened, stretching her limbs outwards, which had become cramped.

She gasped for air and reached for Free, who sat on his knees and overlooked her with Hunter. Her fingers, which were red at the tips, grasped the material of his trousers, and warmed Free's frozen knees with a single touch.

She begged, "What be happening to me?"

Free's hand wrapped around her fingers that clasped his trousers and held her warm, sweaty hand in his cool palm. His penny eyes locked onto her, lowering down to her and stroking her hot cheek with his thumb. He smiled faintly, as Tatiana latched onto him tighter and as tears poured from her eyes but diminished into steam after touching her skin.

"What be happening to me?"

Free and Hunter glanced at each other, as Tatiana's eyes flicked between them. Hunter and Free looked back down at Tatiana, watching her tears steam on her skin and staring at her unrecognisable, fiery, amber eyes, which glared at them. They stayed seated on their knees until Tatiana was able to move again.

32

Inside the grand walls of Cahercasey, along the cobbled path that looped tall towers and turrets, gigantic, green-skinned, heinous, ogres were patrolling with lit torches, as their feet stomped on the slabs of stone. The tall towers and turrets emitted light and from every window a shadow crossed, as the castle bellowed with screams and as the rain crashed down.

Below the castle and inside the cylinder walls of a tower which was made from stone, a gloomy and dark mist sat high at the ceiling. From the darkness, black chains hung and held small iron cages, which hovered high above a dusty, rocky floor, with a set of stairs attached to one side of the wall, leading towards a locked metal door. The wide tower was humid and flames burned the wood of the torches that sat in iron holders on the walls.

The small iron cages held figures that were squished against the bars, as their legs were squished into their torsos and their heads rolled back to lean in between the gaps of the cage. The figures were quiet, as they undid the top of their shirts and cooled their chests, as sweat waxed their faces and their hair. Their breaths were shallow and their eyes were almost closed, swinging their cages as their bodies shifted slightly.

In total, there was four figures inside four cages. Except a cage was lowered to the ground and a figure was missing. The cage door had been left opened and it stayed sitting on the ground, as the other figures remained in their cages.

The first figure cooped inside one of the cages was a tall man. His knees were pushed against his chest, as his back pressed onto the iron bars. He struggled to inhale the sticky air to fill his lungs and his deep chartreuse and large eyes, tiredly looked over at the cage on the floor, waiting for the figure that had been inside, to return. Though his eyes were tired, he still held his arrogant and stern pout.

In the cage next to him, there was another man. He was slender and skinnier, dressed in a navy-blue robe that clung to his sweaty body. His long and greyish-white hair was straggly and stuck to his back, as the man's head hung over his torso. There were lines at the corners of his bright, blue eyes that were surrounded by crimson veins, as he stared endlessly at a long, wooden stick with a crystal intact, which leant against the closest wall, sparkling.

The next cage held a white-eyed man that was cloaked in black, with a rayed star necklace hanging from his neck. His tight, curly brown hair was braided into a ponytail, where his curls frizzed against his back. The man's hood was shadowing his face, as his head hung over his broad and muscled chest, as he slept, sweating through his clothes.

The last man also had white eyes. He also had curly hair, which was sandy with a curled fringe over his forehead. His skin was golden and his cheeks were bronzed, as water droplets lingered on his face and dripped from his jaw. He breathed slowly and leant on his side against the bars, looking over at the other men, as his hand rested where his sword had been, before it had been taken from him.

As the men lurked inside their cages, a shrilling screech raced and bellowed through the castle, filling the dungeon tower and bursting their ears. The scream was piercing and came from every direction, being so loud that it seemed extremely close, as small fractures of pain were heard in the howling voice.

Their spines straightened, awakening from their sleep or their daze, flapping their eyes open and glancing at each other. They searched the dungeon tower, even glaring into the oblivion above them, as the tower tunnelled upwards, pinpointing from which direction the screams came. In the heat of the dungeon, their skin bobbled and a patch of chilled air uncomfortably rested at their back of their necks and made them shudder.

The cry was short. Resonating echoes did not follow. Nor did the voice howl again. The dungeon tower was quiet, quieter than before.

Soon after the screams had stopped, the door of the dungeons unlocked, following a clang of metal. The door of the dungeon was slowly opened and was pushed wide, scraping the floor at the top of the staircase. A bright light from the hallway from outside shone into the dungeon and shadowed a miniature figure paused in the entrance, as a guard stooped over.

The miniature figure was shackled in chains across their wrists. The figure stumbled inside the dungeon and dropped onto the steps of the stairs. The figure's hair was scarlet and wet, with patches of strands missing. Their face was blue and brown, and the figure's nose sat crookedly above a set of purpled and swollen lips. The eyes of the figure were grey with sparks of violet, but the whites of their eyes were filled with pools of crimson and bulging.

The small feet of the figure slowly climbed down the staircase, being followed by the guard behind and headed towards the lowered cage cell, passing a woman shackled in chains. Gradually, the figure lowered, as their body tightened and their face scrunched, groaning. Their knees bent down and the figure crawled inside the iron cage, where the door was locked immediately after their toes were inside.

Once inside, the tiny figure collapsed. The figure's hands slipped underneath their body and their chest slapped on the metal floor as the figure grunted. The figure whimpered and flopped onto their side, curling their knees round into their chest and burying their face.

The men watched the iron cage begin to raise, as soon as it was locked. The chains rattled, lifting the figure inside the cage to sit level beside the men. The guard left the dungeon through the dungeon door, after climbing the stairs, slamming the heavy door behind and locking it with a click.

As if the men had lost their voices and had forgotten words, they stayed in the silence of the dungeon, listening to the white noise from the rest of the castle. Their eyes either fixated on a random spot, or continuously searched the circular room, submitting to the silence. The men's eyes streamed with water and convulsed, struggling to breathe, as their chests tightened and a wrenching feeling deepened inside their stomachs.

After a while, once they had finally stopped the tears falling over their cheeks, their trembling voices spoke into the silence of the dungeons. Their voices croaked and whispered inside the tower, breathing their words, which forced tears to fall immediately from their eyes, without touching their cheeks and landing on their jaws to drop.

The chartreuse-eyed man bellowed, as his hands wiped his dry eyes. He called to the figure inside the cage, breathing deeply "My Helen! My little Helen! Speak to us!"

Helen whimpered inside her cell. Her ears bled, muffling the man's words, down the sides of her neck and rolling to stain her clothes. She curled her legs further into her chest, though it pained her and she groaned every time she moved. Helen tucked her chin into her neck, as tears cascaded from her grey and violet eyes, which hurt with every drop. Her hair toppled over her face, hiding her bruises, as all the strands of her hair were covered in her blood.

Helen soothed her tears and pain with a trembling voice, singing into the dungeon, barely hearing her soft voice hitting the notes of the song she sang.

The men around her listened to her quiet and broken voice, which echoed inside the tower. The men's tears swelled down their faces, overwhelmed, as her voice penetrated their ears and deepened the pit inside their stomachs.

The green-eyed man addressed the men, as Helen continued to sing, but lower, "Tatiana shall not come."

"Barnabas. Be calm." The elderly man with blue eyes looked over his shoulder and at Barnabas behind him, scowling. "Tatiana shall arrive soon."

Barnabas tutted and shook his head, glaring at Ezra, Caspar and Asriel inside their cells, as they all turned to glare at him. "Dost thou really be believing she shall come. For many years, she be knowing her destiny to rule here and yet she did not attempt to seize the kingdom!"

"Stop, Barnabas!" Caspar hissed. "Thou be not knowing her heart."

"I dreamed Tatiana was here. I dreamed she came and told me that she was coming to save us, but my dream was only a dream," Barnabas mentioned, grappling the bars of his cell and raising his voice.

"Barnabas! She will come and when she does, thou shalt kneel and apologise," Asriel ordered. "By the Stars, thou will!"

"Look at Helen. Why does she hurt for Tatiana?" Barnabas questioned, looking over at Helen and sighing. "Too young to be here with us. Tortured till she be dying. Waiting for Tatiana."

Helen's singing stopped, as the door of the dungeon unlocked again. The clang of metal was loud, as the lock slid open. The handle was twisted and pushed, as the door swung open and as the bottom of the door, screeched on the floor, carving lines in the stone. The light from the stone hallway, beamed inside and brightly shone onto the companions inside their cells, radiating from a flock of burning, orange torches, as the companions almost sat in complete darkness. The door stopped halfway, as a man slipped through the opening and down the staircase of the dungeon.

The man rushed across the dungeon, passing the shackled woman on the wall of the staircase and storming to the centre, stopping to stare at the companions locked in their cells. His golden eyes glowed, though they watered, panting below them. The man's full lips trembled, meeting the eyes of the companions and beginning to speak. His voice was wary and he sniffled, grappling the handle of his sword for comfort.

The man closed his eyes, unable to bear looking at the companions any more and unable to witness their tears. His trembling voice addressed the companions, as his palms sweated and his heart belted on his chest. "I be terribly sorry. I be sorry to all, especially to Helen. She cannot hear me, but I beg for her forgiveness. The Necromancer and Belladonna tortured her, for pleasure and no other reason. I be faulty, as I be watching from afar and be unable to stop the pain inflicted upon her. I be betraying my cousin and hurting a young girl, but I be not disappointing the companions, yet. Let me help. Let me help thee escape."

"How?" Ezra quizzed.

Just as Ezra asked, the stomachs of the companions lifted and sickened them. The iron chains lowered, loudly. The cages slowly lowered with the chains and dropped closer to the stone floor of the dungeon, as the companions gripped the iron bars tightly. The iron chains stopped and the cages tapped the dungeon ground, which was cool compared to the warm air the companions had choked in above.

One by one, Nemo came to the cages with a key and twisted the lock, unlocking the doors for the companions to open. He started with Ezra's and ended with Helen's. The companions pushed open the creaking doors of their cells and crawled onto the dungeon floor, toppling on their stomachs to lay on the cooling floor.

The man that had opened the cages and had opened Helen's opened the cage door and peered inside. He examined her bruised and blood-ridden body, as her fractured and weakened limbs curled at her stomach. He watched her violet and grey eyes dimming as they fixated on the iron floor of her cage, with tears still falling and her voice whispering the song that comforted her.

The man reached inside the cage and gently brushed strands of her hair away from her face, pushing her hair over her head. Gently, the man laid his thumb on the side of her cheek, slowly and timidly stroking her soft, painful skin. She winced and the man lifted his thumb instantly, hovering his hand above her. He lowered to touch her again, but stopped, as her grey eyes moved to look upon him.

The man froze, as Helen's violet sparks shot through the greyness of her eyes. His heart thudded and his palms watered, as his pulse raced. His lips trembled and tears splattered from his jaw onto the floor, with a tiny echoing drip. The man's golden eyes gandered at Helen, pressing his lips together.

Helen's tearful eyes stopped watering, though water remained swirling inside her grey eyes and her swollen lips parted to smile. She winced as her cheeks raised and her glimmering teeth were gone, as crusted blood rested on her gums. Helen smiled a little, before she relaxed her lips and hid her missing teeth, letting tears resume falling down her cheeks, as her face began to throb.

Softly, Helen's voice escaped from her lips, which she moved only a little to form her words. "Nemo. Nemo, I be in too much pain to move."

Nemo hushed her, instantly. He lowered further into the cage, carefully sliding his hands underneath her small body and rolling her onto his arms. Nemo hugged her into his chest and lifted her from the cage, as she growled in pain from Nemo touching her agonising wounds. He cradled her in his arms, raising to his feet, as her tiny body rested on one arm and held her, strongly. His other arm stroked the strands of her bloody hair, lightly. Adoringly, his golden eyes glowed.

As Nemo held Helen in his arms and as Ezra, Caspar and Asriel lingered, watching Nemo's golden eyes melt, Barnabas strolled towards the chained woman that hung from the wall at the side of the staircase.

Barnabas came to the foot of the stairs, slowly stepping on the stone slabs, as his eyes fixated upon the woman on the wall. He paused at the bottom of the staircase, eyeing the scarlet pool that stained her abdomen and darkened her clothes, before stepping on the first step. His green eyes followed the trail of blood that had dribbled down her trousers and onto the stone floor, as a pungent smell of iron lingered from the pool at the woman's feet, slowly drying on the ground.

He stepped higher, until he stopped directly in front of the chained woman. His eyes raised from the pool of blood that he now stood in and examined the dark strands of hair that covered the woman's sweet face. Barnabas lifted his hand and ran his fingers through her knotted hair, gently pushing her hair to glimmer at her face and tucking the strands behind her ears.

Barnabas' bright green eyes swirled with water, as he locked onto the woman's face, sickened by the ache inside his heart and stomach. He examined her face through the water that blurred his vision and saw her blueish skin, remembering the pink pigments that blushed her cheeks. He ran his finger over her blackened and crusted dry lips, already feeling an icy chill redden his fingers, as his hand hovered closely in front of her face. Barnabas' fingers sparsely opened and he laid his warm hands on the sides of her face, tilting his neck to look into her hazel eyes with a white glaze covering them, as the woman's eyes rested on a spot on the floor. He squished her face in the palms of his hands, as every finger stroked her frozen dead skin.

Ezra hurried to gather beside Barnabas. His head hovered over Barnabas' shoulder, locking onto the woman in chains, as his blue eyes began to water. The woman's blueish skin and black lips had made her unrecognisable to Ezra, as her decaying skin seemed to flake from her bones already. Ezra's wrinkled and aged spotted hands rested over Barnabas', holding him tight and stroking the woman's frozen and dry skin. He wept behind Barnabas, looking into the young woman's hazel eyes, which had glazed over.

Ezra forced his hands and Barnabas' away from the woman's skin, though their hearts had fallen into their stomachs and ached deeply. Ezra and Barnabas twisted from the woman, as tears flooded from their eyes and they marched towards the dungeon doors. They climbed the staircase, too pained to look back at the woman in the chains and rushing to wait by the door that had been left opened. The bottoms of their shoes were thickly covered in blood, creating a red set of footprints behind them.

Asriel and Caspar climbed the staircase afterwards, avoiding the pool of blood at the foot of the woman hanging from the wall, as they stepped over to land on the step above. Their white eyes glanced over her and joined Ezra and Barnabas at the dungeon door.

Nemo and Helen were the last to climb the staircase and head to the dungeon door. Nemo carried Helen, stepping on the staircase steps, as their eyes continued to lock. He stepped over the pool of blood that remained on the step and passed the woman in chains without glaring at her. His feet thudded on the steps, as Helen stayed resting lightly in his arms.

He joined the other men at the dungeon door and looked up from Helen, looking at the companions that waited for him. Nemo slipped between the gap of the door with Helen in his arms and into the brightly lit hallway outside, waiting for the other companions to step out from the dungeon.

Asriel and Caspar stepped into the hallway after, pulling Ezra and Barnabas, who lingered behind, looking at the woman from the sides of their eyes, as tears continued to fall. Asriel and Caspar heaved them from the dungeon and into the hallway, forcing them to leave the woman in chains behind.

Asriel, Caspar, Ezra and Barnabas followed Nemo into the hallway, as he continued to hold Helen in his arms. The brightly lit hall, made from black stone walls, wound towards a staircase at the end of the wide path. The hall was silent, and so was the rest of the castle, as the companions flocked to escape from castle walls.

33

Along the shores of the Southern Sea, waves roared and rose to gigantic heights, crashing onto the sand and bringing frosty winds. The dark waters, which sat underneath the diamond filled night sky, stretched for miles into the distance, continuing to rise and blocking the horizon.

Trudging the beach, surrounded by cliffs and beside the cliff where Cahercasey stood, a man and a woman crossed the wet mountain sands. Their clothes were wet and clung to their bodies, even as gales of wind lifted them off their feet and as their hair whipped behind. The man and woman's eyes squinted ahead, as they stormed towards the cave with a glowing light in the near distance. The rain had ceased, but the man and woman spurred water from their lungs, from falling underneath the strong waters of the sea after being chased by ogres and losing their companions.

The man and woman moved together, stepping with the same foot and at the same time, as their arms swung at the sides of their bodies. They could just hear their voices above the screeching winds, looping arms and listening closely.

The man called to the woman at his side. His voice was abrupt and his words were vicious, but his eyes gazed upon her lovingly. "Doth thou be having a plan if thou and I cannot be finding our companions? Or do thou and I wander the beach until death?"

The woman's dark eyes scowled and she spat. "Sir Terrence, be there no rum to silence thee?"

"No, Tasmin Berry. Thou shall be needing to buy me some, as soon as Cahercasey be reclaimed." Sir Terrence growled. "I shall be asking for rum till thy pockets be clear!"

She chortled. "If thou be not careful, thou shalt meet death by drink. At least blinded by it. Or lose taste for food and wither. Oh, how joyous I would be!"

“I be not believing. I follow a loon! I be asking an aloof woman for a plan.” He snickered.

“I do hope thy death be soon.”

Tasmin and Sir Terrence scowled at each other, as smiles appeared across their lips. They laughed together, underneath the diamonds that dotted the black canvas above them, marching onwards to the cave and storming to the orange, glimmering light.

They arrived at the cave, stopping at the jagged entrance and looking along the path that was inside and deepened. Tasmin and Sir Terrence paused in the wind, being embraced by the warmth that generated from inside, as the freezing sea breeze slapped their backs. Tasmin and Sir Terrence searched inside the cave, watching the orange light flicker like fire, rising from below their feet and from the end of the path.

Tasmin and Sir Terrence stepped inside the cave, still looping arms and entering the warmth, instantly being suffocated. Their bodies sweated into their wet clothes and droplets formed on their foreheads, as water rested on the bridge of their lips. They strolled inside and followed the path towards the orange light and downwards.

The two companions stumbled down the steep slope at the very end, losing sight of the entrance and moving away from the cold that attempted to enter the cave. Tasmin and Sir Terrence followed the path, as it swerved around sharp-edged corners of high walls and brightened as it deepened further. There was moisture dripping from the walls, echoing in the stillness of the cave, gleaming in the orange light that Tasmin and Sir Terrence continued to follow.

Tasmin and Sir Terrence held each other tightly as they stumbled along the dark rocky floor and sweltered in the warmth of the cave. Their hands tightened around the material of their clothing around their arms, even as their clothes began to stick together.

Tasmin smiled through her sweat and her dark eyes flicked over at Sir Terrence, after yawning loudly in the silence of the cave. “Terrence, dost thou not be having any drink to swig? My throat hurts.”

He shook his head. “I be sorry, but I be having nothing to soothe us. Currently, unfortunately, I be sober!”

She chuckled. “After all this, thou and I shall be pissed till thou and I fall into a deep sleep, not waking till ‘morrow. Thou and I shall dream sweetly in the warmth of thy home. What shall thou and I be dreaming?”

Sir Terrence pulled Tasmin closer and she toppled over her feet, as Tasmin was clasped by Sir Terrence. His eyes gazed deeply at her, admiring her onyx skin that glistened with yellow hues and was soft to touch.

Sir Terrence grinned and halted, stopping Tasmin at his side and mentioned, “After all this, I be asking thee to dance with me, till the end of all time.”

With a gleam in Tasmin’s eyes and a smile forming across her lips, her abrasive voice sweetly added as her hand raised to briefly caress his cheek, “Yes, I be dancing with thee, forever.”

Tasmin’s hand lowered to her side and she guided Sir Terrence forwards, still looping his arm and leading him along the path. Sir Terrence’s eyes still lingered on her, even after Tasmin’s eyes had turned to stare down the path ahead of them and even after her smile faded. Though Tasmin turned away and her smile ceased, her face was brightened by Sir Terrence, becoming brighter as his eyes continued to look upon her adoringly.

Tasmin and Sir Terrence strode down the path, heading deeper as they held each other. They twisted around the corners and walked through narrower paths as their shoulders pushed against the walls. They walked until they came to the deepest depth of the cave, arriving at a circular and narrow entrance, where the orange light they had been following glowed brightest, stopping in front.

Through the narrow entrance, they saw into a circular room, which was wide and tall. The light swayed like flames across the room, sweltering and burning the stone walls, as moisture that ran down the walls fizzled from the heat and morphed into swirling steam. The fiery heat scorched Tasmin and Sir Terrence, even as they waited outside.

Inside, amongst the auburn lights, Tasmin and Sir Terrence spotted figures that were shadowed by the dancing flames. Sir Terrence and Tasmin sighted three men, standing behind a woman who fiercely held her sword, which reflected the light of the surrounding flames. The woman’s pinky-red hair rested on her back with soft curls, as her sparkling green eyes looked up at something above. Her ears were pointed and she glistened with immortality, with youthful skin and undying strength.

The man that stood closest to the strong and immortal woman was bestowed with bronze eyes that glanced over the woman, multiple times, before returning to fixate upon the same thing that lingered above. He stood directly behind her, as two other men that were slightly further back waited at his side.

A plump man waited motionlessly behind the woman, grappling two axes at the side of his body. His cornflower eyes scowled underneath his thick ginger eyebrows above. His stance was broad, as his legs were parted and planted underneath his wide shoulders, tightening his grip around the handles of his axes.

The last man at their sides, was tall and slender with long, whitish-blond hair, which laid straight over his shoulders. His electrifying blue eyes were bewitching and his porcelain skin was sickly, glistening in the orange glows that swarmed inside, staring at something above also.

The top of the passage, stopped Tasmin and Sir Terrence from seeing what was above. Yet, through the passage, they witnessed the body of a beast with long, but soft feathers, in dark shades of orange and red. A slender and long tail wrapped around its gigantic body, and its enormous wings were cramped against the sides of its body. The orange glows were emitted from its body and circled the beast with warmth and fire. Its long neck stretched above, as it stood on its long front and clawed legs, as the passage blocked the face of the beast.

Tasmin and Sir Terrence entered. Hesitantly, they walked through the passage, together, with their arms still looped. They approached the figures that stood a few feet from the entrance and stepped underneath the passage, stopping short from the figures ahead. Sir Terrence and Tasmin eyed the face of the beast, which froze their feet and shuddered their spines.

The companions met bulging, golden eyes that sparkled at them, which sat above a sharp-pointed beak that stayed closed. The beast's soft feathers covered its face, being smaller than the feathers on its body, but having the same orange and red hues. Its face was round and it stared down the companions, and the beast's eyes flicked between the figures and the companions that entered.

The beast's eyes gawked at the companions that entered, turning the faces of the figures, which were revealed as Sargon, Wylie, Pip and Darrel.

Tasmin and Sir Terrence shuffled forwards and quietly came to stand beside them, as the other companions turned back to scowl at the beast. Tasmin and Sir Terrence stood quietly, fearfully locking onto the beast that shadowed them.

Phillipa addressed the beast with a stern voice and asked. "Ra, what hast thou done to Tatiana? I be sensing a deepening wrench inside my gut that be making me sick."

The beast replied with a bellowing voice, "I be doing nothing. She revived."

"From where did she revive?" Pip questioned.

"Death," Ra breathed.

"Death? How be she reviving from death? Dost thou be explaining her power had been revived from death?" Tasmin babbled, pulling Sir Terrence as she stepped forwards to stand with Pip.

Ra's golden eyes flicked over at Tasmin and hissed, "How be the babbling woman be the smartest?"

"Be that true, Ra?" Darrel called. "Be our queen powerful?"

"Our queen, Tatiana be more than a simple being. Bestowed with power beyond imagination," He declared. "She be unstoppable. She be the immortal queen!"

"How? Do explain how she be immortal!" Wylie demanded. "How be she so lucky to be immortal?"

Ra snapped, "Being immortal be not lucky, nor fun. A never-ending life be draining and lonely. As thy queen, Tatiana shall outlive all of thee. Well, except for the seelie."

"Please. Explain to us, how it can be." Sargon begged. "All of us wish to be understanding."

"Thou, need to enter the walls of Cahercasey and see the walls of the queen's tower," Ra insisted. "For thee to understand, thou must see the walls."

"How does one believe we shall enter?" Pip quizzed. "The walls of Cahercasey be heavily guarded and we have no army!"

"Do not be worrying. An army be coming."

"What army?" Wylie asked.

"An army of Stars," Ra announced.

Pip, Wylie, Sargon, Darrel, Tasmin and Sir Terrence glanced between each other, scowling, before looking back at Ra. The companions looked up at Ra, who still looked at them with his golden eyes, as the companions stared in silence. The companions stepped closer together, as Ra's head lowered and so did his legs, which he tucked underneath his body.

The companions looked at the resting phoenix, as his eyes closed and he breathed deeply, feeling his breath blow through their hair and flutter their eyelids. Their cloaks briefly blew from their shoulders and rippled behind their backs, as they lowered their weapons and placed them inside the sheaths on their belts.

Sargon, Darrel, Tasmin, Pip and Sir Terrence lowered to the ground. Pip and Sargon pulled their legs into their chests and wrapped their arms around their shins, resting their heads on their knees, as Tasmin and Sir Terrence pressed their backs together and rolled their heads back onto each other's shoulders. Darrel curled onto his side and kept his knees bent, as he slid his legs towards his stomach.

As the other companions rested, Wylie paced back and forth. His feet pounded on the ground and echoed inside the cave, as his head hung over his chest and watched his feet move. With every swivel of his foot, throwing his body to turn and lap again, Ra's eyes flickered and opened to watch Wylie, until Ra was forced to watch him.

Ra huffed, as his head stayed resting on his front feet. "What dost thou brood upon?"

Wylie responded, still pacing in front of Ra and without raising his head, "When do thou and I meet the army of Stars? And where?"

Ra's golden eyes rolled.

"Be the Stars enough? Be them enough to help Tatiana conquer Cahercasey?" he spurred. "Be thou helping, too, or dost thou reside here for reasons unknown to us yet?"

"Ignorant and poor words form from thee!" Ra growled.

Wylie stopped pacing and twisted to look at Ra, gawking at his bulging and terrifying eyes that constantly scowled. "Well?"

"Thou and I shall meet the Stars in three days. The Stars shall venture here. The Stars shall be enough. I shall help, too," He barked. "Now, stop pacing! Lay down and sleep. For I be weary and so must thou be too."

Wylie held Ra's gaze for a moment longer, before joining his companions. Slowly, he turned on his heel, leaving his eyes lingering on Ra until he had fully spun. Wylie paced to Pip's side, flopping closely and gently next to her, keeping his back turned to Ra. He shuffled his legs to sit crossed-legged, dropping his hands onto his lap and sighing, deeply, as his shoulders and back slouched, following the lowering of his head.

Ra's eyes closed as soon as Wylie was seated, blissfully sleeping, resting his heavy eyes and keeping the cave warm for the companions that also began to sleep. Ra and the companions were motionless inside the cave, with soft sounds of breathing underneath Sir Terrence's snores, drifting towards the entrance and meeting the sound of splashing waves and screaming winds.

34

Wylie, Pip, Sargon, Darrel and Sir Terrence slept peacefully, beside Ra's enormous body that was pressed against each side of the cave wall, even as his body curled. The companions sweltered in the heat, which dragged their eyelids to shut and soothed them into a deep sleep alongside Ra. Pip, Sargon, Darrel and Sir Terrence, comforted by Ra's warmth, slept incredibly well.

Yet, Tasmin's eyes stayed wide awake. Tasmin heard the wailing winds screaming from the cave entrance and felt the slashing waves pound against the beaches. She had rolled onto her side and laid beside Sir Terrence, watching him sleep. His snores were deafened by the waves and the winds she heard from outside, which trembled her lips and shuddered her spine. She watched Sir Terrence, wishfully wanting him to wake and wanting to look deeply into his eyes, losing herself amongst the dazzling brightness of his gaze.

Tasmin laid with her arm stretched out underneath her head and her knees curled into her torso. Her hand hovered above Sir Terrence, wanting to trace his face with her fingers, but realising a single touch would wake him from his dreams. Her hand fell lightly back to rest at her side and she continued to gaze at him, hoping her eyelids would fall over her eyes and she could join Sir Terrence in his dreams.

As Tasmin waited for her eyes to close, she scowled. Her eyes danced around the room, listening to faint thuds that echoed around her. Tasmin searched the cave that Ra kept warm, rolling onto her stomach and checking behind at where Darrel laid and Sargon laid. Her head tilted over her shoulder, looking over at Ra, then at Wylie and Pip, before landing on Sir Terrence again.

The thuds kept sounding through the cave, rising above the sound of the wind and the waves. The thudding quickened, as Tasmin rapidly rose to her feet and looked over at her companions who could not hear the pounding sounds which ran through only her mind. Her eyes flicked over at the passage ahead, clenching her fists and storming forwards on light feet, so she would not wake her sleeping companions.

Tasmin paced into the passage, stopping short. She examined the winding and narrow passage ahead of her, which was shadowed by Ra's powerful light. Tasmin glared down the black stone path and at the sharp turning walls at the very end. The ceiling stood high above her head, as sharp shards of stone hung above and as the rocks morphed into shapes and figures recognised by the imagination. Tasmin still heard the thuds, overpowering the winds and the waves of waters that were still entering the cave entrance and flowed to only her ears, as she stepped forwards.

Slowly, Tasmin paced along the steep path. She trudged towards the thudding sounds, climbing to the sharp turning and shuffling her feet, as her heart raced. Her palms sweated, grabbing her sword from her sheath and holding her silver blade to one side. Tasmin's breath quickened, as tears sweltered amongst her brown eyes that eyed the darkness ahead.

Abruptly, Tasmin twisted around the corner of the path, squishing the handle of her sword in her palms and raising the blade higher. Her teeth ground together, lunging and striking her sword forwards into the orange light that shadowed the walls and path, but lingered in the centre of the path. Her arm jolted with her sword with a grunt, followed by her whimpers.

Tasmin met a pair of bright lime eyes that sparkled with shades of chartreuse that rested underneath a fringe of curly hair, which was wet and frizzed in the heat of the cave. Strangely, she was soothed by the brash stare that she collided with, as her heart eased and as the grip on her sword, loosened. She lowered her sword, which she had just tugged away from the figure in front, before slicing their torso open. Tasmin placed her sword in her sheath and cowered towards the towering figure, wrapping her arms around their back and slamming her head into their chest. Her embrace was not returned, but she continued to hold onto the figure, melting in the warmth of their body despite the wet clothes they wore.

The man she held stared ahead, as Tasmin's curly hair tickled his chin. His arms remained limp at the sides of his body, refusing to hold Tasmin and refusing to push her away. His green eyes closed, hiding the water that rushed towards the centre of his irises and breathing deeply, as his heart fluttered with warmth and as his lips pressed together, suppressing his tremble.

He breathed. "Out of all our companions, thou be the one to wake and hear my steps? Ah, the babbles from Tasmin still be remaining."

"Oh, Barnabas! Barnabas, Barnabas, Barnabas." She laughed. "Underneath, such sarcasm and brashness I hear thou be kind! For, my companions and I be missing thee greatly, also."

Tasmin squeezed Barnabas' torso, before releasing him and sighting other figures that appeared from the darkness behind him. Her arms dropped to her sides and she smiled, as water streamed from her tears and she hurried to greet them.

She met the face of a wrinkled man with dazzling blue eyes, whom she greeted with a large embrace. She wrapped her arms around his damp clothes and held him tightly, as his hands fell to rest on the back of her head and as his fingers became tangled in the curls of her hair. The aged man held Tasmin for as long as she wanted him to, only releasing her when she began to push against his chest and watching her step back, where he met her gaze and smiled.

Tasmin looked over the shoulder of the elderly man that was dressed in a dark blue robe and locked onto two striking figures that strode towards her. She eyed their long and white hair falling over their shoulders and met their colourless eyes that glimmered. Tasmin sighed with relief, as she stepped between them and wrapped one arm around each of their backs. Their arms reached over her shoulders and patted her back, softly.

Just as Tasmin stood between them, Tasmin's locked onto a timidly, moving man that followed the path down towards them. Immediately, Tasmin's smile faded and her lips pouted. The tears in her eyes dried quickly, as her cheeks flustered and as her stomach tightened. She met a pair of dark yellow eyes, which glimmered, but they did not make Tasmin beam. Instead, her fists clenched and she broke from the two men, pushing through and charging towards the man behind.

Tasmin stopped an arm's length away from the man, as her nostrils flared and as her fingers clicked, curling into her palms. She growled at the man that shied away from her, as his golden eyes looked to the side of her and as he stopped before her with shaking knees.

Yet, her eyes were drawn to what the man held and her flustering cheeks faded, as the strength in her fingers was released, relaxing at her side. Her straightened back, slouched, as her feet slid forwards and as her hands shook, reaching for what he held. Tasmin's pouting lips relaxed and trembled, as her entire body weakened. The tears that had dried after seeing the man approach, suddenly gushed down her cheeks again and her mouth opened wide, as she struggled to catch her breath.

In the arms of the man, there was a girl dressed in an oversized shirt and belted trousers with boots covering her small feet. The thick hair on her head had been snatched from her scalp, and crispy red clusters clung to her bare skin. Her body had been punctured and burned with scarlet pools staining her clothes and bruises covering her face. She was motionless, with her arms tucked into her chest and her head resting in the armpit of the man. It was hard to see the pain she suffered in the glow from the violet sparks in her grey eyes, as she was comforted by the young man that she gazed upon.

Tasmin scurried to the young girl, as her fingers hesitantly clasped around her brown and painful hands. She lowered down to the girl's face and waited for the girl's grey eyes to lock onto her, before Tasmin smiled a little. Tasmin's tears still fell from her brown eyes, softly landing on the girl's clothes and breathing deeply to control the croak in her voice, whispering to the girl.

"My dear Helen. Dost thou be hurting? Dost thou be in tremendous pain? Please, do not be hurting too much, my dear Helen."

The corners of Helen's lips turned upwards. "I be well now. I thank ye, Nemo, for helping me escape."

Tasmin's eyes scowled at the man that held her, before looking back down at Tasmin as she continued to speak in a low and husky voice, as her throat began to hurt. "Do not be cruel to him. Please. In the moments that I be seeing, he be having courage and strength unknown to us."

"Helen, dost thou not see him? He be cowardly and unwell, wanting to be with a child!" Tasmin hissed.

"How old dost thou believe me to be?" she asked.

"No more than three years above ten!"

Helen shook her head. "I be nearly ten years older than that. My small stature and my childish demeanour confuse the minds of many."

Tasmin stepped away from Helen, as the glamour of her childish appearance vanished. Finally, Tasmin viewed Helen as the small woman she was and not the young girl that Tasmin had made her to be. Tasmin sobbed, as her chaotic mind had foolishly deceived her from wanting a child of her own.

Tasmin twisted from Helen and lowered her head into her chest, as tears continued to fall from her eyes. She cried, "I be incredibly sorry, Helen. Always, my mind deceives me."

Before Tasmin sobbed for too long, she heard her name being called. Loudly, her name was spoken with a growl which abruptly stopped her tears from falling. Tasmin's eyes looked up at the companion that had called her name with wide eyes and gulping away the lump in her throat, as she met Barnabas' cold glare.

Barnabas gestured her to step forwards with a small movement of his hand that stretched towards her. Quickly, he ushered and stated, "Come, let us greet the other companions! The companions must be resting, otherwise they would be filled with glee and greeting us already."

Tasmin nodded and shuffled towards Barnabas, as he led Ezra, Asriel and Caspar through the cave. Tasmin followed behind and left Nemo to walk with Helen in his arms, alone.

Barnabas followed the path and entered through the passage, after peering in at the sleeping phoenix and his sleeping companions for just a moment before entering. Barnabas stepped inside and stopped a few feet from his companions, looking over them as they slept, slightly smiling after glimpsing his brother Wylie sleeping.

His green eyes looked over at Ra, seeing he had already awakened and meeting his round, golden eyes and the small black irises in the centre of them. Barnabas nodded at Ra, before stepping over towards his companions to lower beside his brother, where Wylie rested with Pip.

Barnabas lowered to his knees and became level with his brother, examining him as he slept. Barnabas observed his brother's straight hair that fell over his shoulders, as his bun sat matted on top of his head. Barnabas watched his brother's lips part as he began to breathe deeply from his mouth and as the nostrils of his button nose, flared. Barnabas looked at his small, squinted eyes, imagining them opening and seeing his reflection in his brother's beaming, dark brown eyes.

He whispered, reaching for his brother and squeezing his brother's shoulder, "Many days have passed, brother. My heart aches and I be needing to tell thee why."

Wylie heard Barnabas, listening to the tremor in his voice and opening his soft and sweet brown eyes. The corner of Wylie's lips turned upwards, revealing his sparkling white teeth, as he sighted his brother. His smile quickly faded, as his eyes met his brother's.

Barnabas' head bowed, as his curly hair flopped over his face. His stern pout relaxed as his bottom lip shook. His hand clutched the left side of his chest, stricken with pain that stiffened his arm and back, as his fingers curled around the material of his clothing. The brightness in his peached skin dimmed, as the green in his eyes seemed to blacken. Gushing, like waterfalls, there were tears flooding down his cheeks and falling from his chin, soaking the floor at his feet and creating a puddle. From his nostrils, running down the bow of his lip, clear slime ran rapidly over his lip and dropped inside his mouth, falling from his mouth as he gasped. His struggle to catch a breath of air, transformed into screams that deafened the storm outside.

Wylie lunged into his brother's chest and raising Barnabas' head with his shoulder. Wylie squeezed his brother so tightly that he squished Barnabas' ribs in his grip, causing pain, but being too weak for Barnabas to feel, as his heart hurt. Wylie's eyes widened, as a few tears fell from his eyes.

Barnabas cries awakened the sleeping companions. Pip, Sir Terrence, Darrel and Sargon abruptly arose from their sleeps, hearing Barnabas' screams destroying the drums of their ears. The companions raised to see Wylie holding Barnabas, as they sat quietly looking onwards.

So distracted by Barnabas' tears, Pip, Sargon, Sir Terrence and Darrel did not notice the figures that entered. They did not see their fellow companions, as they watched Barnabas' suffering. Pip, Sargon, Darrel and Sir Terrence were motionless as they watched Barnabas sob.

Their fellow companions, Ezra, Asriel, Caspar, Helen and Nemo, also watched. They entered the cave and stopped shortly after entering through the passage, looking upon Barnabas, as Wylie embraced him, trying to muffle his screams.

Wylie questioned, holding his brother and speaking over his screams, "What be so heart-breaking that I be seeing my brother cry?"

Barnabas' words were muffled by his screams, struggling to form the words that he needed to say, but did not want to.

The companions stayed silent, as Caspar shuffled forwards and knelt behind Barnabas, lowering to meet Wylie's eyes and bowing his head with a sigh. "Bidelia be dead."

Wylie sighed and tucked his head closer to his brother's, as his brown eyes closed. "My brother, I understand the breaking of the heart, all too well."

The companions swarmed towards Wylie and Barnabas, falling to their knees and stretching their arms across each other's backs. They huddled together, as they encircled Wylie and Barnabas, muffling Barnabas' cries. The companions remained kneeling and holding on to each other until Barnabas eventually cried himself to sleep on his brother's shoulder.

Once Barnabas had fallen asleep, the companions parted and gathered away from Barnabas, as Wylie placed him gently against the floor, still crying as he slept. The companions clustered in front of Ra, standing in a semi-circle as they looked upon the golden eyes of the phoenix that continued to relax, even as the companions questioned him.

Away from the companions that grouped around Ra, Nemo sat against the far wall with his knees propped up and Helen laying across him. Nemo's arms stayed underneath her body, as she lay still with her violet eyes watching the companions and Ra, listening to their raised voices, whilst Nemo overlooked them and gazed down at Helen, instead.

Asriel insisted, "Caspar and I must meet with the leader. An army be heading this way and we must be sure of the plan."

"Yes, the leader shall arrive with the army and be informing us how to defeat the Necromancer." Caspar added, "It be easy enough to kill Belladonna, as soon as the Stars can be close to her."

"What?" Sir Terrence chortled. "Thou cannot leave so sudden. Who dost thou believe thyself to be?"

Darrel shook his head. "I be believing in the Stars, but now that thou be deserting us, should I be believing?"

"Cowards," Wylie muttered.

Sargon shook his head and tutted. "Why cannot thy leader come here? Dost thou not believe we should know how to kill the Necromancer, also?"

Ezra gripped his staff tighter and growled. "Selfish. Selfish. Selfish! Do not keep such information from us."

"Truly, thou be cowards," Wylie mumbled.

"Tell thy leader to come here!" Sargon demanded. "Tell us how to be killing the Necromancer."

As the companions argued, as Ra rested silently and as Ezra bit his tongue, Phillipa stepped to stand beside Ra and faced all her companions. She declared, silencing their shouting voices, instantly, "Fine. Caspar and Asriel may go to their leader. Yet this companionship shall be following them and this companionship shall meet their leader. Does this please all of thee?"

The companions scowled at Asriel and Caspar, as their fists clenched and as they stayed silent, listening to Pip's lingering commands. The companions flicked to glare at Pip, nodding slowly at her, but they did not release their clenching fists and their flustering cheeks did not cease.

Pip asked both Caspar and Asriel, as she turned her head to look at them, as they stood diagonal from her and surrounded by the other companions. "When does thy leader arrive?"

Caspar and Asriel smiled.

"Do not be smiling!" Pip hissed. "If anything, I be agreeing with my companions and would not be wanting thee to meet thy leader. It be best if thou kept information sweet and sharp."

Caspar answered. "The leader be already entering the borders of the South. The Necromancer and Belladonna's army be prepared for their arrival and shall march towards them as soon as they have crossed."

"Then, all the more reason to be meeting thy leader!" Pip spat, as she began to dart through her companions and head towards the entrance of Ra's lair.

Wylie's hand grappled her upper arm, forcing her to stop and look down at her, as he halted her just to the side of his body. He met her emerald eyes and quizzed. "What be the fate of my brother? What be the fate of Helen?"

Pip's eyes avoided Wylie's stare, as her head sunk into her neck. She huffed. "Barnabas and Helen be not fit enough to be fighting with us. Both must rest here."

Wylie's eyes fixated over Ra. "What be the phoenix? What be his fate? Does he be watching us from the safety of his cave?"

Pip's head remained lowered and she did not answer Wylie, breathing deeply, closing her eyes and shutting down her tiring mind.

Ra announced, lifting his head slightly away from his feet and looking over at Wylie as he continued to grip Pip's arm. "I shall be in the safety of my cave, till Queen Tatiana needs me. I be not here to protect thee. I be here to protect her and only her. In the meantime, I shall watch the staying companions."

Sir Terrence twisted on his heel and headed to the path, slipping through the narrow gap and muttering, "A phoenix, as useless as a pigeon!"

Tasmin was to follow Sir Terrence as soon as she had said goodbye to Helen. Tasmin strolled towards Helen, who still laid in Nemo's arms and crouched before them, peering over her and gazing at her bruised skin and her squinting, blurry eyes. Tasmin examined her small and fragile body, as her dainty legs flopped perfectly over the side of Nemo's arm and as her head rested in the crevice of his armpit.

Tasmin sighed. "Why did I see thou being a child? Why be it that I did not see thee as a woman?"

"I be seen as the daughter thou lost. The babe thou had when thou wert younger. Though, thou be never expressing such pain, I saw that pain, from the moment thou rescued me and those other girls. A pain that starts with love and excitement, but creates emptiness inside the heart," Helen squeaked.

Tasmin sniggered. "Was my pain too obvious, then?"

Helen smiled a little. "Yes, but I be grateful for the love I be receiving. I hope thou continues to love me all the same yet treats me like daughter much older than before."

Instantly, Tasmin nodded and leaned down to Helen, pressing her lips gently against her bruised forehead. Her lips lingered for a while, unable to push pressure in her pierced lips and laying her soft lips gently on her skin, until she felt it was time to pull away.

Tasmin lifted her lips that were moist from Helen's sweaty forehead and lingered above Helen for a few moments more, gazing down at her with a small smile. Tasmin viewed the young woman once more, before drawing away and rocking onto her toes, rising to stand. She spun from Helen, before she stayed too long and followed Sir Terrence, chasing after him.

Ezra's blue eyes eyed Ra, as he snapped and tightened his grip around his staff, "Do not be leaving us to fight alone. Arrive to our aid as soon as my companions and I be needing thee. Do not allow the Necromancer and Belladonna to win."

Darrel stepped beside Ezra and growled at Ra, "Do not let us all become fallen."

Ra's head rose, but before he could answer, Darrel and Ezra had turned from him. Ezra and Darrel raced beside each other, leaving Ra and the other companions and stepping into the narrow passages of the cave. They followed the passage to the entrance, following after Tasmin and Sir Terrence.

Sargon moved from standing beside Asriel and Caspar, pacing to the far side of the cave and halting at Nemo's feet, stooping above him. With a small tilt of his head, he forced Nemo's eyes to glance at him for just a moment. Sargon met Nemo's golden eyes that had torn away from Helen, waiting a few moments more before speaking.

"Come, Nemo. Come, fight with us. Come, thou be not injured and thou not be unwell. Leave Helen here, where she be safe, and come with us, now."

Nemo's eyes flicked down at Helen again. He gawked at the violet sparks in her grey eyes, which beamed brightly even as she resided in agony, laying still in his arms. Nemo cradled her, leaning down to softly graze her nose with his and grinning as tears streamed down his cheeks, dripping onto Helen's bruised skin, where she winced as every drop fell onto her face.

Nemo whispered, as his warm breath lightly touched her face, "I shall return for thee soon. Do not be trying to move. Do not be trying to fight. Stay here."

Helen's hand slowly raised to Nemo's face, tracing the side of his cheek with the tip of her fingers and feeling the warmth of his skin run through her veins. She slid her palm to rest on top of his cheekbone with her thumb resting just underneath his eye and gently stroking his soft skin and smiling, even though her cheeks felt like they were breaking.

"When I first sighted thee, I hated thee. I thought thee to be cowardly and cruel. Instead, I be seeing thee as brave and kind," Helen breathed. "For thou must return to see what shall be happening next between us. Yet, for now, thou must go with Sargon and my companions. For, thou be a companion now."

Helen's weak hand slid down his cheek and dropped onto her stomach again, flopping over her other arm. She gasped to catch her breath again, as her grey eyes closed and her body lay still again.

Nemo squeezed Helen in his arms, almost hurting her as he tucked her closer into his chest and wept. He rocked forwards, lifting Helen's body from his legs and placed her down on the warm floor of the cave, tucking his legs underneath him and kneeling over her. Nemo's hands slid from underneath her body and rose to lightly lace both sides of her jaw, as his thumbs ran over her soft and blackened lips. His golden eyes closed and he stayed with Helen for just a few moments, as Sargon waited just a few centimetres away, watching them.

Eventually, Nemo tore from Helen and lifted his nose from hers and straightened his back. Nemo's hands were pulled from Helen's face at the very last moment, before he rose to his feet and shuffled to Sargon, drifting towards the narrow paths that were ahead of them and towards the cave entrance.

Asriel and Caspar's eyes flicked between Helen and Barnabas, who laid on their backs and had fallen asleep, resting on the ground, motionless. Caspar and Asriel looked over at Ra, nodding their heads at him and spinning to follow the rest of the companions through the cave, chasing after them and leading them to their leader.

Helen and Barnabas slept peacefully inside the cave, just a few feet apart, resting on their backs with their arms laying at the sides of their bodies. From the corner of their closed eyes, water trickled down the sides of their faces and rolled into the edges of their hair. Barnabas and Helen rested in the warmth emitting from Ra's body, as they slept beside him.

Ra kept his head resting on his feet and his golden eyes watched over Helen and Barnabas sleeping inside the cave. His feathered body continued to emit flames and warmed the cave, as he began to hear the roars of war.

35

Outside the walls of the cave, at the front of Cahercasey castle, chains were rattling from the iron gates, which started to rise. The rising metal gate moved slowly and was deafened by the banging of drums that came from inside the walls of the castle, as the metal of swords clanged against metal shields, sounding alongside thousands of footsteps.

Emerging from the black gate there was shining armour covering bodies and helmets covering the faces of many. There came thousands flocking through the iron gate and marched down the cliff, towards the field in front, as rain poured from the jet-black skies, where white diamonds twinkled through the thick, grey clouds. The thousands marched with their swords banging against the shields that stuck to their chests, beating with the sound of drums.

In the second wave, enormous green legs stepped over the walls of Cahercasey and trudged down the mountain, as their heads hung over their torsos and as their arms swung across their bodies. Their greenish-yellow eyes glowed in the darkness, as drool drooped from their chins and as their teeth grew like mountains from their gums and out from their mouths. The monsters followed the first wave onto the battlefield.

In the distance, towards the North, a bright and white light glimmered across the horizon. The bodies of thousands, dressed in white, stormed the landscape with drawn weapons, heading towards Cahercasey. They came in silence, lightly crossing the field with large strides and moving closely beside each other, approaching the oncoming army. The light that was emitted by the men and women clothed in white became brighter with every step.

The army, travelling from the North, was led by a figure draped in a long, white, flowing gown that trailed behind. The figure paced a few feet in front of the army behind, with a stern glare coming from a pair of hazel eyes that eyed the black mist of the army in front. The figure stormed as their long and dark hair clung to the sides of their face, as the rain poured from the pitch black. The figure came with a white glow surrounding their body, being brighter than the lights that came from the army behind and illuminating their skin. In the light, their hazel eyes dazzled with a deep green rim blazing around the edges of the golden brown that dazzled.

Behind the glowing figure, there was a woman striding between a dark-haired man and a stunted woman, heading towards Cahercasey and separated from the army behind. The three figures were lost amongst the brightness emitted from the army and the figure in front, as their bodies did not glow at all, but merged into the darkness, even as the blades of their swords glittered.

All at once, the white-cloaked figure and the army behind abruptly stopped. The army's stomping feet thudded gently, as their feet planted in the ground and stood motionlessly, whilst drops of rain pounded onto their heads. The army locked onto their leader, who stood still just a few feet ahead, as the man and two women that disappeared amongst the darkness continued walking until they stood with the lead figure, stopping at their side and staring at the Necromancer and Belladonna's army that had also halted, halting their beating drums and halting their roars.

The battlefield had fallen silent after both armies had stopped on the land in front of Cahercasey. The rain thudded louder and the wind screeched higher, as the waves crashed harder on the shores of the beach in the near distance. The land darkened, as both armies stretched both far and wide, preparing to march towards death.

The man and the two women stopped beside the leader of the army, eyeing the army ahead and just making out silhouettes of the opposing army with squinted eyes. Their pulses were heard thumping inside the drums of their ears and their bodies warmed quickly with sweat, though the water pouring from the sky was icy.

The stunted woman croaked, "Barely can I see the Necromancer and Belladonna's army! I cannot fight in the darkness. Instantly, I shall meet death."

The leader stated, confidently, "Soon, there shall be light above the sky, guiding thee upon the battlefield."

"Suddenly, why dost thou be deserting?" The man questioned.

"I shall be returning, swiftly. I be not deserting thee for long and be returning with more than an army of Stars." The figure smiled. "Do not worry, Klaus. Do not worry, Orla and Ainsley."

Klaus asked, "Why does my daughter have to lead the army of Stars? Why dost thee ask my Phillipa to do so?"

"Please, Klaus. An honour it shall be for Phillipa. Happily, I entrust her to lead my army across a playing field for death."

Ainsley insisted, "Go! Leave. Orla and I shall ensure Phillipa leads us to battle. Please, bring our queen home."

The figure nodded, as their eyes glanced over Orla, Ainsley and Klaus. The figure's dark and wet hair lightened in colour, as strands lifted from their shoulders without the help from the winds. The strands of hair dried and eventually whitened, disappearing into tiny specks of light that swirled upwards. The figure's white clothes were brushed by a gentle wind and their cloak was blown to vanish and grow into the balls of floating lights. The body of the figure dispersed into thousands of lights, which flew into the night. Lastly, the figure's hazel eyes became lost in the growing whiteness, separating into small balls and following the rest of the rising lights that twirled higher towards the Stars, merging amongst them.

Ainsley, Orla and Klaus watched the Stars flow to the skies with small smiles, as their eyes twinkled underneath the lights of the skies. The companions glared up at the sky, long after they had lost sight of the small white balls that the figure had dispersed into, just admiring the painted lights.

Just after the figure had left in balls of light, the companions followed the rapid movement of the thick clouds that raced far into the distance. The puffs of grey, fizzled, as the darkness ceased. The sky became an inky blue and the Stars shone blindingly across the land, dazzling every shadow with a cool white light to reveal the Necromancer and Belladonna's army that stood amongst the yellow strands of the meadow before the companions. The winds had died, but did not cease and the rain had lightened, gently splattering onto their heads, as they heard the waves of the sea travelling towards them.

The companions eyed the army ahead, seeing ogres stooping above the armed men and women, stepping aside and creating a path that ran through the middle. The army and the ogres parted, continuing to glare at the companions, even as two striding figures stormed the bottom of the cliff that Cahercasey castle sat upon.

A tall woman strode along the path that had been created by the surrounding army, wearing a long navy dress with tattered seams and revealing her bare feet splashing in the mud. Her fingers traced the tips of swaying wheat strands, draining all colour as she passed and creating a black path behind her. The woman's eyes were the colour of oceans and her smile dazzled at the companions like the sun.

She stormed with a shadow at her side. The shadow towered above her and staggered closely beside her, scowling at the army of Stars in the distance. Its body was black, with flickering shades of grey and broad shoulders. The shadow paced without eyes or lips, being a silhouette amongst the fields, seeming to disappear at times, as if it was made in the imaginations of the companions.

The woman and the shadow came to the front, as the army stepped sideways and closed the path behind them. They stopped just a few feet from the front line of their army and darkened the white light shining from the Stars in the sky, shaking the bodies of the companions and tiring their hearts, as the Necromancer and Belladonna stood before them.

Klaus, Orla and Ainsley shivered, standing closer together and looping arms, continuing to stand in the light of the Stars that stood behind them. The companions' eyes were glued to look upon the Necromancer and Belladonna, as their breaths were sucked from their lungs their hearts heavy. Orla, Ainsley and Klaus gripped each other, huddling together, as they still held their weapons in their hands.

Amongst the gentle winds and the light falling rain, there was a shrilling voice crossing the land. The voice awakened the companions from their fears as their heads turned to look slowly over their shoulders to glare at the meadows towards the East. The croaking squealing voice inhaled deep breaths of tears and gasped, loudly.

In the distance, the companions saw a sprinting figure, running through the meadow and alongside the army of Stars. The figure's feet pounded in the muddy fields and they raced to the companions, as tears fell with the falling raindrops. The figure's dark pink cloak rippled behind them, as their arms stretched above their head and waved at Klaus, Orla and Ainsley.

Behind the calling figure, a group of men and women followed. The group ran quietly behind, holding swords and even a long, wooden staff with a blue crystal attached to the end. Their hands raised, also, waving at the companions, as their eyes glanced at the Stars, grinning.

Once the figures had staggered closer, Klaus tore from Ainsley and Orla, charging towards the first figure that had been calling. Klaus met the figure's green eyes and saw their pinkish-red hair that was swayed behind them and was ringing wet. His arms whipped to his sides, as he stumbled to a stop, catching the figure that bolted into his chest and locking his arms around them. Klaus' knees bent as he buried his face in the figure's shoulder, sobbing with the figure which clambered around him. His heavy heart had lightened slightly, as a sharp pain slithered in his chest and warmed him for a few moments, as he held his daughter, Phillipa.

Ainsley and Orla sprinted towards the oncoming figures, passing Klaus and the figure he held and running into the arms of the others that came. Ainsley and Orla grasped the men and women, stopping to create a tight and cosy embrace, as their arms lapped over shoulders and their heads were pressed together. Ainsley and Orla met many, familiar eyes and smiles, which poured with tears and fell from their jaws, quickly. They wept with their companions, holding Ezra, Tasmin, Sir Terrence, Wylie and Darrel, alongside Caspar, Asriel, Nemo and Sargon who they embraced too.

Ezra, Tasmin, Sir Terrence, Orla, Ainsley, Caspar, Asriel, Darrel, Wylie, Nemo and Sargon joined Klaus and Phillipa, as they released each other from their tight embrace to form a circle.

The Necromancer and Belladonna locked onto Nemo with scowls as he stood amongst the companions. Nemo hid behind Darrel, shielding his flustered cheeks and gasping for air, as his hands grappled around Darrel's arms and as his head flopped onto the back of Darrel's neck, whilst the companions flicked between the Necromancer and Nemo.

Willingly, Darrel hid Nemo and whispered, "Come now, Nemo. Do not be afraid. This companionship shall protect thee. After all, thou be a companion now."

Nemo snapped. "My father and mother shall kill me and they shall kill my cousin Tatiana, too. It be best, to end our lives peacefully, whilst there be time still."

"Nemo, thou must be strong," Ezra said encouragingly. "In times of war, our hearts show whether we be strengthened or weakened by our endings."

Nemo shook his head. "When the time comes, I shall not be taken by the hands of another, but by my own hands I shall control the fate of my life!"

"Ye dastard!" Sir Terrence growled.

"Certainly, it shall be completed by Barnabas!" Nemo hissed.

"Where be Barnabas? Where be Helen, too?" Ainsley quizzed as she searched amongst the companions

"The companions be safe. Helen be too weak to fight from being tortured by the Necromancer and Belladonna when she be captured. Yet Barnabas' heart be broken and he weeps, constantly," Darrel explained.

"The love and joy he received be taken from him," Tasmin mentioned.

Ezra sighed. "My Bidelia. My granddaughter, not by blood, but by heart."

Ainsley, Orla and Klaus exchanged glances, as their brows frowned. They stood quietly for a moment, as they saw the heads of their companions lower, mourning Bidelia.

"Where be the leader of the Stars?" Caspar asked, as the other companions fell quiet.

"Yes, the new leader should be awaiting us! It be what ordered by the leader," Asriel declared.

Ainsley gulped. "Well, the new leader of the Stars be asking for Phillipa to lead the army into battle."

"What? Why must it be I?" Phillipa quizzed.

"Ah!" Caspar smiled, turning to her, as she stood next to him. "Then, Phillipa, the Stars shall follow thee."

"How does the leader know I should be the one to lead?" Pip croaked.

"There be confusion amongst us. For I, Ainsley and Klaus be seeing Bidelia," Orla answered.

"She be not dead!" Ainsley exclaimed.

"Bidelia be alive," Klaus added.

"How?" Ezra spat. "How dost my granddaughter live, when I be seeing her body decay?"

Klaus, Orla and Ainsley raised their necks to look up at the sky, as their eyes landed on every Star they could see with smiles forming on their lips.

The companions followed their gaze, looking at the Stars, which brightly twinkled across the navy canvas above them. Their saddened frowns lightened, as the bright lights flickered constantly, talking to the companions.

Pip lowered her eyes to look at her surrounding companions, nodding at them, though their eyes gazed at the Stars. She cleared the lump in her throat and nodded at the companions surrounding her. She gestured them to line up alongside the Stars, turning to face the Necromancer and Belladonna, as they drew their weapons from their belts.

When the companions' weapons had been drawn, they heard thousands of swords slicing from sheaths, as the Stars drew their weapons too. The Stars waited for Pip's command, as she stood further in front of the Stars and the companions, eyeing the Necromancer and Belladonna.

Pip and the companions behind exhaled deeply, as their hearts palpitated and their palms secreted sweat. Already, sweat rested on the bow of their lips and their bodies produced uncomfortable amounts of heat, fearing it was the end.

Before Pip gave her orders, she heard the soothing words of her companions behind, as they yelled loud enough for the Stars to hear.

Klaus began. "In the name of King Moryn and Queen Gwendolen, we fight!"

"In the name of Prince Thaddeus Green, who be deceased," Darrel added.

"In the name of Queen Tatiana Green, let there be hope," Tasmin cried.

Sir Terrence declared, "For Cahercasey, we strive."

"For the South, we suffer!" Wylie yelled.

"For the companions, we be losing!" Ezra screamed.

Ainsley and Orla chanted, "And for the home we wish to reclaim!"

"Praise be to the Stars!" Asriel shouted.

"Praise for their return," Caspar called.

"Praise they shall help," Sargon insisted.

Nemo breathed, "Help us win."

Finally, Pip exhaled. "Let us fight."

Patiently, the companions waited and grappled the handles of the blades of their weapons, as they locked onto the Necromancer and Belladonna ahead.

36

As the lights of the Stars prevailed over the land, their lights shone over piles of rubble and pillars of stone that had fallen to the ground, hiding amongst an overgrown forest, as vines and branches covered remaining crumbling walls and forgotten entrances. Fading stone turrets, with dislodged beams and staircases still intact but plunging down from the walls they were nailed to, towered above the tall and wet trees. The glass still inside the windows sparkled in the light of the Stars, forming beams of colours inside the walls of an ancient kingdom that was buried by debris.

Inside the castle, in the hallway leading to the throne room, which now stood without a roof, pressed against the cold walls and stretching on the damp, stone floor, there was Tatiana. Tatiana's head leant to one side, as she gawked at the opposing wall, where Free and Hunter sat staring at her new, glorious amber eyes that glowed in the darkness of the hallway. She breathed deeply, as her body burned like fire and she sweated like pigs. On her lap, Midnight's head rested, as he waited with Tatiana and as Tatiana's hand ran through his ebony hair.

Free and Hunter watched Tatiana indefinitely. Free and Hunter leant against the frozen and damp wall of the passage, at the edge of the hallway and sitting at the side of the beaming lights that came from the high glass windows of the tower. Their legs stretched across the path, as their hands flopped onto their laps and as their mouths gaped open, breathing deeply, unable to form any explanations for Tatiana's saffron eyes that glowed brighter than the Stars, which had suddenly appeared in the night sky.

In the silence, Tatiana breathed. "What has happened to me? What be happening?"

Hunter and Free croaked from their throats but did not answer her. They continued to stare at her.

Tatiana's glowing eyes looked down at Midnight, frowning. Her eyes squinted at the top of Midnight's head, where something long and pointed appeared growing from its hair. Twisting grooves formed around the midnight blue and glassy horn which grew from his head.

Tatiana's hand stopped running through Midnight's hair and raised to his horn, wrapping her fingers around the soft, shiny and twisting bone that protruded from his head. Her fingers examined every curve, as she saw the reflection of her glowing orange eyes, raising her fingers to the very top.

"Midnight, when be thou having a horn? All this time, did thou conceal this from me? Why? Why did thee hide from me? Why dost thou reveal thyself to me now? A rare and an extraordinary breed, thou be. For I be seeing many unicorns but be never seeing one born with black hair!" Tatiana looked up at Free and Hunter, exclaiming. "Dost the both of thee be seeing his horn, too? Am I turning mad?"

Hunter and Free looked over at Midnight, as he laid his head on Tatiana's lap. They observed Midnight, sighting his horn and seeing their reflection in its blue shining surface. Free and Hunter's mouths gaped open further.

Tatiana shrilled at their expressions, "Thank ye, I be not mad!"

Free and Hunter shuffled towards Midnight, crawling on their hands and knees to kneel beside him and reaching for his horn. Gently, they traced Midnight's sparkling horn, following its grooves that spiralled down from the tip and to the bottom, where their hands ran through his soft and black hair. Their eyes looked up from his horn and stared at Tatiana, stuttering to speak.

"How did we be not seeing?" Hunter asked Tatiana. "Midnight be with thee since thou wert a child! How did we not see?"

Free cleared his throat and questioned. "Why did he be deceiving us?"

As soon as Free asked, from their corner of their eyes, there was a flash of lightning. The electrifying strobes flickered from the throne room, striking through the hallway that Tatiana, Hunter, Free and Midnight sheltered in. The lightening appeared without noise and no thunder sounded afterwards. The light dimmed, but did not disappear, as a sparkle continued to glimmer at the edge of their eyes.

The companions turned and stared down the tunnel, towards the centre of the throne room, focusing on the glimmering light that gathered underneath the starry night. The white cloud of light, beamed from a proud figure that slowly stepped towards them and walked amongst the beams of stained-glass windows that glowed in the light of the Stars in the sky.

The white robes of the figure fell to their feet and their sleeves gaped over their hands, which swayed at the sides of their toned body. Around their neck, a silver necklace hung low with a rayed star pendant hanging just below their chest. Resting on their forehead and on their scalp were jewelled chains that connected to a headpiece that sat on the figure's mousy brown hair with individual silver pins stretching outwards and encrusted with diamonds, keeping their hair cascading down their back. The figure's colourless eyes became infatuating, as a rim of green circled a golden-brown colour.

The companions were glued to the ground, fixating on the gleaming figure that penetrated them with a dazzling light. Their eyes were almost blinded, as tears swirled inside their ovals and wetted their cheeks. The companions' lips pierced into smiles, as the approaching figure nestled beside them and placed their hand on Midnight's side.

The figure glanced firstly at Hunter, then Free and lastly, Tatiana, smiling at each of them. The figure addressed the companions with a soft and gentle voice, playing like music. "Ah, Midnight! I be glad that thou be revealing thyself. For a while, I and thou be separated. For Midnight, we be living centuries before all those that surround us. Dost that be strange?"

Tatiana sobbed. "How doth thou be here? I saw the decay of thee."

The figure chuckled, lifting her hand from Midnight and reaching to caress Tatiana's cheek with the soft touch of her fingers. "My sister, Tatiana! I be glad to see thee again. For I did not be knowing how long it be, till I saw thee again. In the sky, I be watching thee. I be watching as a Star! Protecting thee. My grandfather be wondering how his granddaughters had such extraordinary fates, when we be not related by blood."

Tatiana pushed the woman's hand away and hissed, "Sister, if thou be protecting me, then what be happening to me?"

"Please, help her!" Free begged.

"Tatiana, thou be not needing help," the woman insisted, reaching for her hand and clutching her tightly. "The burning sensation running through thee be only the power that be given to thee from generations before. I must take thee to Cahercasey, for the castle be empty as war begins."

"Why, sister? Why now? Why tell me now, Bidelia?" Tatiana snapped.

"Please, Tatiana. Thou must trust me!" Bidelia cried. "The last hope to kill the Necromancer and Belladonna be thee. First, thou must know how and must understand the past to restore the Southern kingdom."

"I do not be wanting the kingdom. It can burn."

Bidelia sighed, as her eyes closed and she leant away from Tatiana, dropping her shoulders as she breathed. "At least, put an end to the war. Then, I be showing thee how to release the throne to someone who be worthy."

Tatiana agreed. "I shall end the war by killing the immortal, but after, I be not taking the throne. Nor shall I rule the Southern kingdom. I do not be wishing for this. I did not wish for any of this."

"Thank ye, sister."

"How does one be the Queen of the South and be having a black unicorn to ride?" Tatiana wondered, as her eyes looked down at Midnight resting on her lap.

"Please. Let me take thee to Cahercasey," Bidelia insisted, releasing her fingers from her fist and stretching her hand forwards towards Tatiana. "I shall take all thee there, including Midnight."

Tatiana's glowing eyes flicked up at Bidelia, reluctantly placing her palm against her sister's hand and feeling Bidelia's grip lightly hold her. Tatiana rested her other hand on Midnight, brushing his hair, as Hunter and Free shuffled closer to Bidelia, laying their hands on her shoulders.

Bidelia glanced at each companion and at Midnight, too. She remarked with a grin, "Close thy eyes. For Stars shine with a blinding light."

Free, Tatiana, Hunter and even Midnight closed their eyes. Through the skin of their eyelids, they saw darkness, which quickly transformed into the pink shades of their flesh and eventually became white. The companions still felt the ground beneath them, and they continued to hold onto Bidelia without a jerk or the slightest breeze as she transported them.

The companions did not witness Bidelia's skin glowing and blurring as the light from within her was emitted into the tunnel. Bidelia's eyes saw the companions in her blinding light, smiling at them, as everything around her became white and killed the damp and dingy darkness that came from the passage. The light that radiated from her skin brightened to shine brighter than the diamonds on her headpiece, being intoxicating and warming as Bidelia sparkled.

After a few minutes, Bidelia's light began to fade. The colourless glow surrounding the companions gradually dimmed and shrank. Her body absorbed the hue, as pink pigments returned to her skin and as her hair darkened brown. Her eyes stayed white, observing the companions, as their eyes fluttered and opened after seeing the skin of their eyelids become black again.

Tatiana, Hunter, Free and Midnight opened their eyes as soon as Bidelia's light had ceased. Their eyelids whipped opened to stare at Bidelia, before observing their strange surroundings.

The companions had arrived in the centre of a long rectangular room, with a tall, golden ceiling, as chandeliers hung high above. They were positioned in the same resting places as they had been in the tunnel, inside the kingdom of old, resting on a warm, light green carpet that ran along the top of a white marbled floor. The carpet ran from a set of tall and thick, golden double doors and towards a set of arched stained-glass windows that captured the light of the Stars glistening outside.

In front of the tall windows, standing in the colours of beaming light, there was a chair. A grand chair, made from the same exact marble as the floor with thick armrests. On the seat, there was a green plush cover, as the veins of a leaf had been carved into the back of the chair, with gold filling the grooves. The chair stood on high legs and sat upon a stage with steps surrounding each side, as the stage was pushed against the wall, below the windows.

Once Tatiana sighted the throne ahead, she gently nudged Midnight's head from her lap and slowly stood on her feet. She eyed the throne in the light, as it glimmered at her. Tatiana stepped forwards, following the green carpet and shuffling towards the stage ahead. She stopped just before the steps, locking onto the throne, as her heart pumped and as her knees shook, looking at every corner of the chair before her.

Stuck inside a trance, she forgot her companions had risen also and paced along the carpet, with Midnight following behind. Tatiana's companions lingered behind, as they shortly halted and observed her as she was flooded by the light of the stained-glass windows.

When Tatiana and her companions had finished observing the throne, their eyes drifted to the stained-glass window, which painted a picture with many colours. Most of the windows were filled with dark blue square panels creating a night sky and radiating with blue lights. At the centre of the middle window, which was the largest, there were white strokes lapping each other and creating five points like a star that shone with a creamy white light onto the throne.

Tatiana turned from the Star and faced her companions, but her eyes looked up at the ceilings, eyeing every figure that had been drawn and coloured. The ceiling was filled with pictures to every corner, leading towards the centre where she saw the veins of a leaf, running with gold, just like what had been carved in the throne. Tatiana's companions followed her stare, admiring the paintings as their eyes dotted and their heads turned to view every colour.

As Tatiana stared, Bidelia's eyes quickly glanced from the ceiling and at Tatiana. Bidelia watched Tatiana as she tilted her head to view the paintings from the right angles and as her eyes wandered all over.

Bidelia headed towards Tatiana, following the green carpet and stopping in front of Tatiana. She reached down to hold Tatiana's wrists and raised her hands, as Tatiana met her gaze by lowering her eyes from the ceiling and looking deeply into Bidelia's eyes.

Bidelia's voice was soft, echoing across the throne room, though she whispered her words. "This be the throne room of Cahercasey castle. The walls be so thick that thou cannot hear the raging war from outside. Before thou can join the war, thou must understand the paintings above us."

Hunter and Free took a step forward, just hearing Bidelia's voice and just seeing the sides of Tatiana's face. They viewed Bidelia and Tatiana as they stood motionless together in the centre of the green carpet and in front of the throne. Free and Hunter stood quietly, watching them and scowling.

Tatiana and Bidelia's palms overlapped and their fingers tightly gripped, as a white ball of light seeped from between their hands, gluing them together. The light remained inside their palms, as Bidelia's white eyes stared at Tatiana's blazing amber pair.

Bidelia explained, softly, "King Moryn and King Samael be brothers by blood. King Samael be the eldest and ruled the South when their father be dead. Quickly, King Samael be needing to be thrown from the throne, after dealing with power far beyond his control and turning dark. He be thrown from the throne by King Moryn and Queen Gwendolen, who raised an army to conquer Cahercasey, but were too weak to kill the Necromancer, who fled. Before the Necromancer be overthrown, he had a child. A daughter. A daughter born in autumn and be given a tower in Cahercasey. He cherished her, but she be taken from him by King Moryn, who gave her to a wizard to keep her safe. The daughter be thee. The Necromancer's daughter be thee."

Part of the light that radiated inside their palms, transformed into an orange hue, penetrating from Tatiana's hands and growing around them. Her eyes gleamed like fire and her skin sweltered with small dews of sweat appearing on the creases of her collarbones.

She stuttered, "I be not the daughter of King Moryn?"

Bidelia shook her head. "No. The Necromancer be thy father! Nemo be thy brother. Not thy cousin."

Tatiana looked down at the orange flames that wrapped around her hands and almost diminished Bidelia's light. "Does my power come from him?"

"As well as the phoenix, known as Ra! Him and thee be connected by power and life," she insisted. "He be the source of all thy power."

"How do I end all this all?" Tatiana questioned.

"Thou must be willing to kill the beast that gives thee life." Bidelia sighed. "Yet, thou must kill the Necromancer, before thou and I be succumbed to his darkness."

Tatiana's hands unglued from Bidelia's, as the orange light that grew from her fingers and palms strengthened and created a comfortable heat. She lifted her hands closer to her face, inspecting them, as she turned them till she was satisfied. Tatiana watched her hands drop to her sides that continued to glow, dimming ever so slightly as she relaxed.

Bidelia grinned, dropping her arms and diminishing her light with a squeeze as she created clenched fists at the sides of her body. "Now, there be weapons just outside those golden doors, ready for thee, if thou art ready to go to war?"

Tatiana's eyes flicked over at Hunter and Free, as their scowls lightened and they gawked at her. She faintly smiled at them, as they nodded in agreement. She breathed deeply, pressing her lips together and stopping the boiling water drops from falling down her cheeks.

Free and Hunter hurried to Tatiana, standing with Bidelia and stretching out their hands to guide her along the carpet and towards the golden doors ahead. Bidelia paced in front, taking Midnight to her side and leading them to the doors.

Bidelia came to the set of doors and reached for the hooped iron handles with both hands and tugged the doors open, shifting backwards as the doors opened wide. The doors widened with a heavy metal clink and a small squeak, as the doors swept dust upwards and clustered to form a cloud that covered the companions, forcing them to sneeze and choke.

The doors opened to reveal an enormous hallway which ran alongside the throne room, with enormously tall and narrow, painted glass windows. The hallway path was wide, as blue and green beams shone through and led to darkness at either end, where the walls curved.

Bidelia, Hunter, Free, Midnight and Tatiana lingered in the hallway, looking down the hall in both directions, before eyeing the windows and staring through the glass.

The companions peered through the blue and green squares, overlooking the circular courtyard, at the front of Cahercasey, seeing the raised golden gates of the castle, which faced the downward slope of the cliff. The white stone walls and slabs of the courtyard were unguarded, and pinnacles of orange were spotted in the near distance, alongside a glowing stream of white light. They heard nearby roars and screams loudly travelling through the castle and deafening their ears as shivers crawled along their spines.

Bidelia stepped from the window and gestured the companions to follow her through the hallway, crossing through the shining lights. She waved her hand at Hunter and Free, as Hunter guided Midnight to follow beside him. Their feet echoed through the hall, but were deafened by the clips of Midnight's hooves, which seemed to bellow.

As Bidelia led Free and Hunter, as well as Midnight, Tatiana lingered in front of the tall narrow window, standing amongst the light of the blue and green glass, as her face was illuminated by the blue panel she stared through. Her bright eyes fixated on the courtyard, but she did not stare at anything in particular, as her ears heard something peculiar.

Through the hall, echoing through the castle and from somewhere afar, a voice called to Tatiana. At first, the voice was no more than a murmur, like the whispers of the wind brushing through the leaves. Yet, the voice grew to be heard and a silvery demand was wailed into her mind by her own voice.

Burn the castle.

Tatiana twisted from the window and with her face still gleaming with the blue light of the glass, she looked over her shoulder and at her companions down the hall. Her companions had stopped a few feet from her, scowling at her as they looked back.

She met their gaze with a faint smile and announced. "Go. Take Midnight. I shall join thee, soon. Do not be weak until I can be there to save thee!"

Instantly, Bidelia nodded and twisted, grabbing Free and Hunter's wrists, as they started to step towards her. Bidelia heaved them to stop and forced them to spin, hauling them behind her, as Free and Hunter clocked their heads to look back at her, as she became a shadow down the hall and eventually disappeared as they whipped around the corner.

Tatiana stepped back from the window and stood in the centre of the hallway path, turning from the window and sprinting in the opposite direction of her companions, running down the hall. Her footsteps thudded in the silence, as she raced along the marble, strangely knowing the layout of the castle already and intuitively choosing the right paths.

37

Inside the walls of Cahercasey, sprinting through the white marble walls and grazed by the blue and green lights of the stained-glass windows, there was Tatiana. Her white hair had fallen from its plait and swayed against her back, as the front strands clung to the sweat on her forehead. She chased the sound of the voice she had heard echoing through the castle and was carried to a set of closed doors, at the bottom of the turret.

The golden doors were closed, but through the small gap underneath the door, a gust of wind swept towards her feet. The wind shrilled and rattled the doors from the outside, which remained closed no matter how strong the wind blew.

Tatiana stepped forward and grabbed the handles of the door, wrapping her hands tightly around the metal and heaving the doors open. She threw the doors open, impaled by the strength and frozen wind that slammed the doors against the walls, blowing Tatiana's hair and cloak behind her, as her arms remained stretched at her side from holding the door handles. Her eyes watered as the wind fluttered her eyelids and as she focused on the darkness.

She stepped onto a path which ran through the middle of grass and stretched towards a building, which shadowed her. There were high walls either side, and turrets stood behind. A long time ago, the flaking vines on the walls would have bloomed with roses and the weeping plants would have dazzled with many colours, as they remained planted in the ground. The Stars twinkled above her, and she spotted flickers of light coming from the turrets, shining through the blue and green panels of glass and creating spotlights along the path towards the building ahead.

Tatiana slowly paced towards the building, which was a tall and white cylinder with a pointed roof. There was an arched window without any glass at the very top with a golden door at the bottom of a tower, standing in darkness, as Tatiana strode along the path to the tower entrance.

She paced slowly along the long path ahead and towards the small door, which grew above her as she came closer and stopped just before the golden double doors. She stopped to glare at the intricate swirls that ran through the doors, running her fingers along the grooves and following them to the round handles, grappling around the metal and pushing the side of her body against the door, falling into the gold and heaving the stiff door to open.

Tatiana fell through. She stumbled into the tower, as the door slammed against the wall and entered darkness. She released the handle and wondered into the centre of the tower, glancing at the abyss above her head. A wooden staircase twisted to the top, disappearing halfway into the blackness. Her footsteps echoed through the tower, even after she had halted to stand still.

In the centre of the tower, she examined the walls that circled her. The walls were painted with faded bright colours to the very top of the tower, under a thick brown layer of grime which was brushed away with a sweep of her hand, revealing the painted images.

She stood before the wall at the foot of the wooden staircase, glancing at the largest painting in the tower, which had been painted with strokes of orange and red. Gentle brushes had guided the walls to create enormous, feathered wings and had sharply placed ink against the walls to paint yellow claws that were close to the bottom of the tower. A beak had been filled with deep golden paint, and an oval had been painted just above and to the side with a sparkling and brighter gold that dazzled in the dark. The red and orange strokes that created a breast and wings were drawn through the staircase that was attached to the walls, covering almost all the walls inside the tower, as dust laced every crevice.

Tatiana leaned backwards to stare up at the beast, arching her neck upwards and spotting the golden eyes of the beast which seemed to follow her. She rested her hand against the chest of the beast, after wiping away the dust to form a cloud that reddened her eyes and clogged her throat.

She whispered into the tower, as her eyes watered before turning quickly into hot steam. "Why did the Necromancer be my father? Why did he tie my life to thee? Why did he tie my life to a phoenix, who can never truly meet death and shall always rise again, even if it not be willing to? The Necromancer once cherished me but be wishing to kill me now. Am I strange to be laughing? I be needing to see what my father built for me and so I must climb the staircase to see."

Her hand slipped away from the wall and dropped to her side, with dust lingering on her fingers and palm, as her hand slapped against her leg and the dust puffed into a small cloud. She spun on her heel and faced the bottom of the staircase, following the steps round that twisted above her head.

Tatiana stepped onto the staircase. Hesitantly, taking another step and freezing before moving again. Her eyes still glared at the staircase above and eyed the painted phoenix, sighing. She tore her eyes away and stared down at the steps she began to take, hurrying around the tower and towards the top.

Tatiana climbed rapidly, slipping on almost every step, as the thuds of her feet radiated through the tower. She brushed the dust from the walls, which exploded behind her, and the brown sprinkles fell silently as she whipped past, stamping on the creaking wooden steps.

At the very top of the tower, Tatiana sprinted onto the last few steps and onto the landing in front, gently thudding her feet to stop in front of a closed and wide door. The door was locked, with a circular glass window pane that had green panels, which glowed and beamed onto the iron landing. In the wood of the doors, there were deep grooves forming swirls and flower patterns, which were barely seen under the thick grim layers of yellow-brown dust.

She eyed the illuminating green glass that dazzled in her eyes, as she stepped onto the small landing. She moved away from the dusty walls and into the glowing beams, tiptoeing closer and pressing her nose against the glass and peering through. Her hand reached for the golden circular handle and twisted the lock, hearing a *click,* as the door opened slightly.

Tatiana felt a small draft whip around her legs, dispersing the dust that settled at her feet. She pushed the door wider, smelling a musty and damp aroma escaping from the room on the other side fill her nostrils. Tatiana pushed the door further, sighting a white light flooding the dark wooden floorboards that she spotted through the widening gap and watching clumps of dust float from the ground.

Finally, Tatiana nudged the door to rest against the wall and stood in the doorway, glimmering in the white light that streamed from an arched window directly before her, seeing the brightly lit Stars gleaming inside the room of the tower.

Standing in the same light, at the centre of the room, was a wooden cot. A cot that rocked, with untouched blankets and useless dolls, collecting dust and mould. A small blow of air twitched the cot, which started to squeak as it moved eerily from side to side, being the only object in the room.

Tatiana paced towards the cot and rested her hand on the ledge, stopping the cot from rocking and rattling side to side. Her hand gripped tightly around the wood, layering her hand with the sticky dust and leaving a clean print amongst the dirt, once her hand had let go and dropped at her side. She looked down at the tightly folded blankets, as tears from her eyes rolled from her jaw and dribbled onto the white sheets, splattering onto the dust.

As soon as she had sighted her falling tears, she released the cot and stepped backwards. Her eyes flicked upwards at the dark ceiling and she felt the streams of her tears falling down her cheeks. Tatiana's eyes lowered to observe the rest of the remaining empty room, which shook her lips.

Then, her orange eyes stared through the window and at the Stars. Her fingers curled into fists and she panted, loudly. Tatiana's body began to burn and water rolled into droplets of sweat, as fire swept through her and an orange light radiated from her hands.

The light scorched and stretched across the room in rays, darkening the white from the Stars. An auburn hue burst from her body and covered the room with heat, sparking flickering flames on the floorboards and burning through the walls, as a black line crawled around the woman and as snow peeled from the wood of the cot, slowly disappearing.

In the night, the tower became a torch of light. A firelit lighthouse that was seen by both armies, which still prepared on the battlefield, facing each other. The armies locked onto the flames quietly inside the tower, with large pieces of rubble spurring into the rest of the kingdom.

The eyes of the Necromancer and Belladonna widened, watching the tower burn in the light of the Stars, as they stood at the front of their army.

Their army continued to roar, even after seeing the tower covered in flames.

The Necromancer stormed through his army and returned to the castle. His army parted for him, as the Necromancer darted to Cahercasey. His shadowed body faded, flowing into grey streaks that took flight in the wind and stretched away from his body, as he disappeared amongst his army.

Belladonna watched the Necromancer drift and vanished before twisting from the tangerine flames burning the tower and spinning to face the white light from the army of Stars and the few companions that stood ahead. Her arm flicked above her head, where it hovered, before gliding down and arching before her.

At once, she heard thousands of marches vibrate the ground. Dark silver armour, the green eyes of ogres and the clanging of metal swarmed around her, shifting forwards towards the Stars and companions on the other side of the battlefield.

With her dark pink hair tied and her sword stretched at the side of her body, Pip dauntingly eyed the approaching army, standing fiercely in front of her companions behind. Deeply, she breathed and lifted her sword above her head, marching amongst the tall fields of wheat.

Behind Pip, storming with her, were the companions. Closely following her was Klaus with his sword, as Nemo paced ahead of Pip and charged towards Belladonna with his eyes blazing. Darrel, Tasmin and Sir Terrence wielded their weapons and shortly came after, with Wylie, Ainsley and Orla following.

Then, the moving feet of millions shifted the vibrations of the Necromancer and Belladonna's army, as the Stars glided behind the companions. Instantaneously, the Stars reached for their glimmering silver swords that rested inside their white sheaths and grappled the handles of their blades, as they carried the weight of their weapons at the sides of the bodies, shuffling forwards.

Both armies, once closer, stepped longer and faster, sprinting to collide. The armies pounced between each other, whipping their arms to slice their blades through the air and cutting flesh to spray scarlet liquid onto the yellow strands that grew at their feet. The armies roared and screeched, as the ogres stomped through, knocking both sides from their feet and swinging enormous branches, shooting bodies into the air. Sudden bright sparks rapidly lined the land, spurring and wrapping around the armies, frying their skin and burning to fall.

The battlefield was filled with spurs of flames and rising clouds of smoke, as white light radiated from the figures of the Stars merging with the dark silver figures. The cries of war were deafening, leaving the rest of the world silent.

Amongst the battle, the companions had been displaced from each other. As soon as they had collided, the companions were whisked across the meadow, taken with the tide of weapons that crashed towards them. The companions were lost, battering the waves of soldiers that crashed to them, whilst searching for their beloved companions in the chaos, trampling the bodies that had already fallen under their feet and forgetting the burning tower inside the castle.

The tower flickered in flames, as Tatiana still stood inside, standing amongst the dancing embers and the falling ash. The roof above her head revealed the night sky with a gaping hole in the middle, as the tiles melted into a runny golden liquid that dribbled into the fires below, sparking more flames to grow around her. She did not feel the blazing heat around her or burn her skin, though the flames whipped at her flesh.

Inside the tower, between the flames, a soft voice travelled amongst a wailing wind that almost diminished the flames which faded with the sound of the deep and bellowing voice. The voice chilled Tatiana's spine and her auburn eyes looked up, as a dark shadow appeared over her head.

She gazed into the hole in the roof, as the golden tiles still dribbled and the Stars still glistened above. Closely, she met golden ovals at the side of a face and a large protruding beak, surrounding by growing tangerine feathers that graced a body, transforming into saffron at the edge of grand wings that stretched across the twinkling sky. Its feathery body blazed with hues of orange light and swirls of fire, as Tatiana was stroked with heat.

From its beak, its voice was released from deep within. "Queen Tatiana Green! A pleasure it be to be finally meeting thee again. When I saw thee last, thou wert a babe and now thou art finally submersed in thy power."

Tatiana breathed, as her hand reached forwards and rested on either side of its beak, running her fingers through its feathers and gazing into its eyes. "Ra! Be thee, the one to tell me to burn the castle?"

"Yes," Ra answered. "Dost thou wish to live in a castle made from the blood of slaves and crafted by a man?"

She shook her head.

"The Necromancer comes this way. Thou and I need to leave, but not for the battlefield. For thou need to restore the faith of a companion, who be lost and be not at war," Ra replied. "Climb my back. I shall take thee."

Tatiana nodded.

Ra pulled back from the tower, stretching his wings wider across the sky and directing his four legs at the tower. His yellow claws reached for the remaining golden tiles, grappling the beams and stone tightly and lunging backwards.

In his claws, Ra heaved the tiles he clung to and crumbled the stone walls, tearing them from their foundations. Ra lifted the roof and part of the wall, releasing the stone and metal as soon as it began to tumble, falling down the sides of the tower and crashing below.

Tatiana hurried away from the cracked and falling tiles that fell in front of her. She watched the walls of stone become displaced, reclining to rapidly descend the side of the tower, just hearing the rubble crash on the garden below. She hid underneath the remaining tiles and against the side of the few standing walls, as some tiles and walls began to crumble after, landing in the fire where the cot burned in the centre, as other fires swayed around her.

Ra lowered, turning his body and becoming level with the floor of the tower and stretching out his strong and thick wing towards her. He stretched his long neck round and faced her, eyeing her stillness with his golden eyes at the sides of his face. He hovered, with his bright flickers of fire, unhurt by the flames that Tatiana had created inside the tower and waiting.

Tatiana examined her burning surroundings, bewitched by the auburn fires, before striding through them and towards the edge of Ra's wing that laid on the floor of the tower. She stared at Ra's thick wings and the long feathers that decorated them. Her foot lightly stepped onto a feathery bed, which did not sink as she pushed down against his wing and lifted her other foot away from the creaking tower floorboards, which would soon break beneath her feet.

She gulped, standing on the edge of Ra's wing and looking down over each shoulder at the depths below her, which tingled her hands and weakened her legs, seeing the fallen rubble that was spread across the garden and at the tiny paths forming around the turrets. She froze on Ra's steady but gently moving wing that threw her balance, feeling the ripples of the wind raise her like the waves below a still boat.

Ra locked onto her, as the colour in her skin faded and the fire from her hands darkened to a glow lining her fingers. He questioned, without startling her, but waking her from her thoughts. "Queen Tatiana, be thee scared?"

Tatiana looked over at Ra, quickly flicking her eyes from the depths that spun her vision and staring deeply at his warming golden ovals. Slowly, she nodded at him and she trembled. "Yes. I be not afraid of the Necromancer or Belladonna, but I fear falling from such heights."

Ra chuckled. "Do not fret. If thee falls, I shall catch thee and wrap thee inside the warmth of my feathery wings."

Tatiana wielded her feet forwards, as every step shook her legs and as her fingers tingled til they became numb. She closed her amber eyes, biting her shaking lips to stop as she moved across Ra's stealthy wing and felt his feathers rippling in the air, which formed waves inside her stomach. The steps towards Ra's body seemed to be infinite, desperately rushing to him against the fast pace of her heart and falling to her knees to crawl the rest of the way.

She crawled on her knees, quickly crossing the remainder of his wing and hurrying to his long body, clutching his feathers and throwing her legs around his body. Tatiana buried her face, slamming her stomach down and clenching her thighs either side of his spine. Her grip pinched him, as she kept her eyes closed and as her tears dried against his feathers.

Ra stayed hovered by the side of the tower, clocking his neck round and watching Tatiana clambering to his body. He called to her with his deeply soothing voice, "Queen Tatiana, ease the strength in that grip. Keep those eyes closed!"

Ra's body tilted from the side of the tower and glided gently away before flapping his wings. He slapped his feathers against the wind, gaining speed and spinning between the turrets of the castle, as air blew along Ra's streamline body and swept Tatiana's cloak behind her.

Tatiana's ears became frozen, as the wind brushed them and screamed inside them. Her hair rattled on her back, as her cloak rippled behind and tugged at her neck, lifting her head away from Ra's feathered body. Her neck arched but she kept her eyes closed, as the wind blew her tears to roll over her cheeks and into her scalp. She grappled Ra's feathers, feeling other strands tickle her hands as they brushed over them.

Ra whipped upwards and darted towards the white dots of light in the sky, as his body became vertical and Tatiana felt her legs slipping downwards over his feathers. Her grip tightened and her teeth ground together, as she became colder from Ra's ascending height. The winds strengthened around her, but the air she breathed became thinner and harder to catch.

Tatiana rode on Ra's back to heights beyond clouds, rising above them and slicing through the air, as his body glowed like the sun. Tatiana was carried by Ra, as the war below raged on.

38

Ra flew above Cahercasey and darted towards the dark blue waves of the sea, gliding alongside the yellow beaches and just above the tall cliffs. The circular white sphere of the night glowed above him, reflecting on the waters of the rough seas and lighting his way towards the very edge of the cliffs ahead of him. He glided through the salted breeze of the winds that came from the Southern Sea, protected from its frosty bite by the fire sprawling from his body.

On his back, Tatiana still clung to him, pinching his feathers in her grasp. Tatiana's face was buried beneath his soft orange body, smelling the salty sea breeze and hearing the waves slap against each other. Her body tightened as Ra continued to fly, hiding underneath the hood of her long green cloak that she pinned with two fingers, as the rest of her hand continued to grapple Ra. Her eyes remained shut and her stomach swished, waiting for Ra to land.

It was not long till Ra landed. Swiftly, Ra's claws arched forwards, dropping gradually towards the heaps of golden grains that rested beside the vast waters. Steadily, his feet touched the cold and soft sand, as his wings stretched backwards, catching the blowing wind to balance himself before tucking his wings at the side of his torso. Ra landed lightly on the shore and looked round at Tatiana who was still clinging to him.

A while after Ra had landed, Tatiana's hands uncurled from around Ra's orange feathers and her fingers unpinned her hood, which now rested on her head without being abruptly blown by the strength of the wind. Her stomach stopped churning and she lifted slowly, keeping her eyes closed until her back had straightened.

As soon as Tatiana's eyes opened, she met Ra's gaze. Tatiana glanced at him for only a moment before she was drawn to the sea that she heard crashing at the side of her.

Tatiana's head turned to looked over her shoulder, staring at the rough waters and being memorised by the silver twinkling dots and the silver sphere that was seen sparkling on the surface of the fiercest waves of the Southern Sea. Even as the waves slapped together and as the night darkened the baby blue sea, the waters were still so clear, as Tatiana spotted the grainy and golden, sandy bed in the shallows.

Before too long, as Ra examined her still body sitting on his back, he called to her. He stated, as he eyed her, "Most beautiful."

Tatiana's lips pulled into her cheeks, chortling. Once more, she glanced at the sea, before turning to face Ra again and forcing her smile to fade.

She met his golden gaze and flung her legs to one side of his body. Tatiana pushed against his soft feathers and slid down his torso to plummet her feet into the sand. She hit the sand with a thud and a small tumble, bending her knees and catching her balance, before her torso rolled over them. As soon as she was still, Tatiana rose.

She observed the cliffs in front, shadowing her as she stood at the foot of them, just seeing the toughs of grass poking over the edge of the black rock walls. Tatiana looked over her shoulder, following the winding beach, as Ra and Tatiana stood hidden by the bends of the cliff, unable to be seen from Cahercasey, which sat in the near distance. She twisted to Ra, following his gaze, as he turned his neck to look down upon an opening in the cliff.

A jagged and pointed entrance, which was pitch-black, had been carved into the black walls. The tall entrance, which widened towards the bottom and created space to be entered through, led deep into the cliffs and deep underground with a path following the curves and twists of the rocks inside.

Tatiana paced to stand before the entrance, peering into the darkness, as she was consumed by the icy breeze that came from inside. Her body shivered as she stood underneath the archway, breathing white swirls from her parted and trembling lips.

Ra looked down at Tatiana, as she stood at the foot of his body looking into the cave in front. He eyed her and hissed, "Inside the cave, there be thy companions. A child, who be hurt. A man that be saddened. Dost thou hold the power to save them? Dost thou hold the power to save them all?"

Without hesitation, without a second thought, Tatiana strode forwards. She entered the darkness, as her pink blemishing skin became apricot and radiant. From her body, swirls danced with warmth and light, just like embers of fire. Her orange glow dazzled the cave and covered the black walls with sparkles. She glided down the path, banishing the inkiness and thawing the ice, almost forgetting Ra, who watched her from the cave entrance and saw her ignite.

As she followed the path deeper, the walls behind her continued to sparkle. Her light ceased to fade, even after she was far from the cave entrance, continuing to bedazzle the walls with her orange hues of light.

For a while, Tatiana wandered the caves, with her light booming around the cave, as she moved deeper into the cave and arrived at the circular opening, which sat at the end of a steep path. Tatiana examined the opening, staring into the darkness on the other side and hesitating before entering, as her light refused to stretch inside.

After a while, after searching the ink clouds that covered her eyes, Tatiana stepped through the opening. Tatiana paced inside, just able to see her feet stepping onto the hard, black ground with her auburn light, which was tamed by the thick blackness that suffocated her and grazed her flames with frost and flickering blue.

She moved further into the darkness, stepping slowly, as her head turned to look over her shoulders, searching. Tatiana listened to the crushing clusters of rock underneath her feet, which echoed inside the opening, pacing to what she believed to be the centre and stopping shortly, after hearing nothing but silence over her own breath.

Tatiana was motionless amongst the jet-black clouds, stopping directly before the entrance, but watching as her glow was forced to stay at the edge and leaving her to stand in the dark. The flickering embers around her body became colourless and then blue, as the ice from the clouds started to smoulder her.

Tatiana stuttered, calling into the darkness, as her voice bounced from every wall. “Be there anyone here? Respond to my voice, please.”

Almost instantly, Tatiana heard a sweet, but croaking voice responding to her and snapping the silence. “Tatiana?”

Immediately, Tatiana swivelled on her heel and turned to look behind her, gasping. She recognised the voice that had answered. Her heart thumped in her chest and the flickers of light around her body sprouted.

Within the dark, Tatiana's bright eyes saw a ghostly figure pressed against the wall, sliding to one side and leaning on their elbow as they eyed Tatiana with sparks of purple sparring inside the grey circles of their eyes.

At first, it seemed the darkness was covering the figure's face, but as Tatiana looked closer, the dark purple patches were formed deeply over their skin. Wispy strands of fair hair poked from their shiny scalp, as crusty mountains of dried red liquid formed on their head. Their bony legs were curled against the floor, as one arm shook to raise and their index finger struggled to point at Tatiana.

Just as Tatiana shuffled forwards, she stopped and realised that the pale figure was not pointing at her, but something resting at her feet. Her toes bounced from something squishy and light, which was long and stretched across her. The object was easily overlooked and easy for Tatiana to step over, but her eyes looked down her nose, as her light illuminated what was on the ground.

Below, she saw a body stretched across the floor and motionlessly resting with their arms at the sides of their torso. She saw a body wrapped in clothes and a head being covered by a hood of a cloak, shadowing a set of sparkling lime ovals surrounded by crimson veins in the whites of the eyes. Tatiana saw strands of dark brown hair curling from underneath the hood and sticking to the sweat that remained on their forehead, even though the cave had suddenly turned cold.

Slowly, Tatiana lowered and sighed. She knelt beside the body, as her hands reached forwards and laced the sides of their cheeks with her fingers, wiping away water droplets from their skin that had fallen from their eyes. Tatiana held their icy stare, which thawed as soon as she grazed their skin with her soft touch.

After wiping away the figure's tears, Tatiana's hands locked around their fingers and laid their hands to rest on their stomach. She squeezed the figure's frosty and peached skin, as tears started to roll onto her cheeks and steam.

Tatiana trembled, as the figure below her stayed laying on the floor, motionless and silent. "How far thou and I be fallen? How can both hearts be aching? Yet I need thee. For I need my companion."

She looked over at the ghostly figure leaning against the wall and admitted, "I need all my companions."

The ghostly figure stated, "I would help thee, if only I be not wounded so."

Tatiana breathed. "I can heal thee!"

The figure huffed. "Then, heal me. For I be seeing death."

Tatiana looked down at the figure and released their hands, gently. She placed the figure's hands down on their stomach as she climbed to her feet and stepped around the resting figure, towards the person against the black walls.

She approached the leaning figure and knelt on one knee in front of them. Her golden eyes locked onto them, as her hands stretched forwards and cupped the person's jaw. Tatiana lifted their head gently away from their shoulder and softly positioned the figure to straighten.

As soon as Tatiana's warms hands pressed onto the figure's jaw and squeezed her thumbs into the figure's cheeks, an orange haze emerged from her palms. The figure paused before screeching, as the growing flames from inside the palm of her hands scorched their skin. The figure pulled from Tatiana, but Tatiana's hands were stuck to the figure like glue, burning through the figure's flesh.

Tatiana sent small, intense flames to bubble the blood inside the figure and warm the figure's body, as sweat dripped from their forehead and armpits, creating dark, wet pools in their clothing. Tatiana watched the figure's purple eyes tightly shut and saw deep into the figure's throat, deafened by the screech that vibrated from inside.

Suddenly, the purple smudges on her skin lightened and transformed brown, as the edges puffed and brightened to be yellow. The figure's skin glowed with a white light, clearing remaining blood and closing opened wounds, as thin layers of skin stretched to cover the injuries. The figure screamed, as their fair hair that had been removed from their head protruded from their scalp and fell beside the sides of their face, glowing golden.

The force plummeting from inside Tatiana and to her companion shook her hands and revealed the whites of her eyes. Falling from her forehead were dews of water, rolling down her skin and steaming, before rolling into bigger droplets. Waves of water seeped into her clothes and clung to her moist skin, as her hair stuck to the sides of her face, straightening her curled strands.

Suddenly, Tatiana's hands melted the glue from the figure's face and her heavy hands dropped onto her lap. The glow from Tatiana's hands faded and the light from her body stopped radiating. She tumbled onto the back of her feet, as her eyes lowered from the back of her head and glared at her companion.

Tatiana's companion flourished with a glow to their skin and their new hair shining brightly over their chest. The violet sparks inside their grey eyes glimmered and violently crossed like bolts of lightning, as the companion's face beamed, clear of any bruises and spot blemishes appearing on her cheeks like before. The fire that had streamed through the companion's veins had ceased, but warmth still pumped her blood.

The companion lunged forward and swung their arms around Tatiana's warming and brightly lit body, squeezing her. The companion clutched onto Tatiana, as tears rolled down their cheeks and dropped onto Tatiana's shoulder, burying their face into Tatiana's collarbone and muffling their cries.

For a moment, Tatiana's arms stayed limply at the side of her body and she stayed slumped on the back of her calves. Her eyes drooped and she gazed at the wall behind her companion as her vision blurred. Tatiana gasped and brightened the flames around her body again, which had darkened after releasing the power within her.

After a while, Tatiana's arms strengthened to raise and wrapped around her companion's back. Tatiana embraced the warm body of a young woman, feeling the woman's golden strands of her hair streak across her face, as Tatiana placed her head on her shoulder. She placed one hand over the back of her companion's head and gently pressed down, clumping a soft handful of hair. Tatiana panted, as water streamed from her eyes and dried instantly after they had grazed her cheeks.

Tatiana sobbed. "Oh, my Helen. Helen Hobbart. What happened to thee?"

Helen cried, "I be happy thou be here, Tatiana! Thank ye, for coming to us."

"Almost everything be well." Tatiana sighed, pushing Helen away and staring down at her face with a small smile, seeing Helen's eyes beaming.

"Where did such power come from?" Helen asked.

"Always, I be having power. Its origins be dark, but I be wanting to only shine light," she declared, holding onto Helen's hands and guiding her to her feet.

"The other companions be already at war! Be us to join them?"

Tatiana nodded, before looking over her shoulder and at the still figure on the floor. She stated, "Yet, thou and I be not leaving until the last companion be joining us."

The figure tilted their head to face Tatiana and Helen stooping above. The figure's green eyes gleamed, catching the light of Tatiana's flames in the tears filling their ovals. Their lip trembled and their hand lifted from the floor, reaching for Tatiana and Helen, who knelt beside the figure and clasped their hands together.

Tatiana and Helen leaned down to their companion with small smiles, as they gripped his hand tightly and as tears also swelled inside their eyes.

Tatiana begged. "Please. Please, Barnabas. I be not able to fight without all my companions. I be the Southern Queen and I be needing my companions. Wilt thou fight alongside me? Wilt thou fight for my sister?"

Barnabas stretched his other arm over his body and slapped his hand on top of Tatiana and Helen's. His frosty hand held onto the warmth of their skin, as Helen and Tatiana yanked him to his feet and huddled around him. Barnabas' arms reached around their backs and clambered onto them, finally letting his tears fall down his cheeks.

Tatiana rested her head on Barnabas' shoulder, pushing her forehead against his neck and resting the palm of her hand on his chest. She locked onto Helen's gaze, as Tasmin stood in the crease of Barnabas' armpit smiling and wrapping her arms around the lower part of his torso.

Tatiana, Helen and Barnabas held onto each other for as long as they could, before they dropped their arms, dispersed and headed through the opening to begin following the path to the entrance of the cave and meeting Ra on the Southern beaches.

39

Tatiana, Barnabas and Helen stormed beside each other through the cave, pacing along the steep path and towards the entrance of the cave. Barnabas and Helen walked closely beside Tatiana, being warmed by her flickering flames and searching the crevices of the cave that she illuminated with her light. Tatiana, Barnabas and Helen saw the staggering archway.

Through the archway, they saw the midnight-blue sky with twinkling spots of light and glimmers of the waves, just seen through the gaps of a creature's legs. They saw rows of orange feathers growing from a gigantic beast, as its neck curved down to peer inside the gap, revealing its golden eyes and its golden beak.

Tatiana quickened ahead of her companions after seeing Ra through the gap and hurrying to him with a smile. Her companions were quick to catch Tatiana, sticking to the warmth of the flames that flickered from her body.

Tatiana stepped out first onto the sandy shores, as Ra's face pulled from the entrance and his neck rose to look down at her and her companions that exited the cave just a few seconds after. Tatiana was nudged by Barnabas and Helen as they stumbled to her side and stopped to stand within her flames, as they all stared at Ra.

Ra's neck lowered to them. Just as he did, his head jolted to one side and his golden eyes searched the darkness of the shores. Ra checked the sandy beaches, elongating his neck to stare over the cliffs and at the beaches just before the Cahercasey, seeing the tower still burning. His wings twitched and his feathers erected with a shiver as his feet clawed at the sand.

Tatiana trudged from underneath Ra's shadow and through the sand, heading towards the curve of the cliff. She searched the night, hearing silence underneath the crashing waves at the side of her but feeling something twist her stomach. Tatiana's eyes flicked from side to side in the darkness. The flames around her body ignited brighter as an unnatural breeze battered her face and shivered her companions' bodies.

Tatiana yelled for Ra without twisting to face him or her companions, pulling an arrow from her quiver and removing the bow that rested on her back. "Ra! Take Helen and Barnabas, now! Take them to the battlefield. I shall be fine."

Quickly, Ra laid his wing onto the sand, stretching his wing towards Barnabas and Helen. His neck lowered and his head dropped to stare down at the companions that stood side by side in his shadow, watching Tatiana.

Barnabas and Helen saw Ra's wing swoop down towards them, lying flat against the sand and creating a steep path to climb onto his back. Helen and Barnabas did not move to step onto his feathery wing and eyed Tatiana as she readied her bow and arrow, blankly.

Barnabas called, "Tatiana, what be wrong?"

"Leave! Leave, before he comes," she howled, twisting her neck over her shoulder and glaring at her companions who waited motionlessly.

Barnabas grabbed Helen's small hand and tugged her feet out from the plumes of sand, taking her to the edge of Ra's wing. He lifted Helen onto his wing and pushed her forwards. Barnabas insisted for Helen to climb Ra's wing, watching her clamber on his feathers as Ra lifted his wing level to his body. Helen crawled onto Ra's back, quickly looking over her shoulder and seeing Barnabas still standing on the sandy beach.

Ra jumped into the air, pushing from his feet and lifted above the cliffs. His wings flapped rapidly as his body arched upwards and as his tail flickered below. He straightened his neck and darted forwards, sweeping over the tops of the cliffs and carrying Helen, as she looked down at Tatiana and Barnabas, to the battlefield.

A strong breeze rattled through Tatiana and Barnabas' hair as Ra's wings slapped the air. Their legs shook when Ra's feet pushed from the sand and vibrated the land, flickering small particles of golden at the backs of their legs. The warmth and orange light of Ra's glow disappeared, which had been much brighter than Tatiana's light and had dazzled her and Barnabas' eyes.

Barnabas joined Tatiana, trudging through the sand and standing in the brightness of her seemingly small flames. The unusual wind that had flourished, had disappeared, but an icy chill crawled along their spines and across their arms. Barnabas withdrew his sword, holding his blade at the side of his face and watching the moonlight hit the surface of the crashing waves, standing closely to Tatiana in silence.

As Barnabas searched the darkness, he felt frost growing behind his neck and staggering into the lines of his hair. Barnabas' grip tightened around his sword, planting his feet deeper into the sand and standing closer to Tatiana as a swirling wind encased him.

Abruptly, Barnabas' eyes rolled backwards, seeing the dark sky above him. Barnabas' back followed, tumbling over his legs, which lifted from the sand. He flew into the air, thrown taller than Tatiana and dropped onto the sand, slamming onto his back and smacking his head. His sword had remained tightly in his grasp until he plummeted onto the floor and hit his wrist, releasing the handle as his sword rolled onto the sand. Barnabas' eyes darkened, just glimpsing the Stars, before his eyes closed and his head rested to one side.

Tatiana looked over her arrow, seeing Barnabas rise silently above her. She felt his body thud on the sand, vibrating underneath her feet. Tatiana screamed for Barnabas, still pinning her arrow and string as sand was flicked at her from his fallen body.

Suddenly, as Tatiana's feet were planted in the sand and she held her bow, while a shrilling and eerie voice thumped her heart. She continued to point her arrow in front of her and checked her surroundings as Barnabas laid unconscious beside her. Tatiana's grip tightened around her bow and her fingers pulled her arrow further towards her cheek, listening to the voice that sent curls of ice down her back.

"My daughter, Tatiana. At last, thou and I reunite. Years, it be since I saw thee last." The voice hissed all around her, bouncing from the walls of the cliffs and riding along the waves of the sea. "My, my, what strength thou possess. I be giving thee such power. Thou must be thankful."

Tatiana spat, looking over her shoulders and behind her back, searching for the shadow of the Necromancer. "I be not thanking ye. Thou disobeyed the Stars and turned the unruled Southern lands into blood and darkness!"

Suddenly, as Tatiana turned to face the front, a dark cloud rapidly dashed towards her and swirled around her neck. Tatiana was launched from her feet, dropping her bow and arrow onto the sand below as she was thrown in the air and slammed against the cliffs, bashing her head. She howled, cracking the surface of the cliff, as her feet floated just above the sand and as the cloud still grabbed her.

The cloud curled around her neck like fingers and clasped tightly as Tatiana gagged. Her arms raised to the cloud, which she was able to touch, wrenching the hand from around her neck as her feet wriggled. She shook the arm that stretched from the cloud, which slowly blurred pairs of eyes and a hollow mouth. The puffs of cloud formed pairs of legs and wide pair of shoulders, creating a tall and stooping shadow over Tatiana.

As the cloud morphed, the grip around her neck burned her flesh with ice, diminishing her flames. Tatiana skin swirled blue as the light in her eyes started to fade and her flames started to die. Her lips started shiver and her toes became numb. Her eyes struggled to stay open as she stared into the dark ovals of the Necromancer.

"Before I came, the kingdoms fought over the Southern lands. There was blood and darkness before I even fell from the Stars! Taking claim to the land and building walls turned enemies into allies, but they became my enemies." The Necromancer hissed. "King Moryn and Queen Gwendolen led an army against me, too weak to defeat me, but strong enough to take thee. Where be thou hiding all those years? All this time, was thou truly hiding in that small village? Who protected thee? The stupid servant girl?"

"She is my sister!" Tatiana howled.

He cackled. "Ah, be Barnabas Mint thy brother? Did he be telling thee what I be doing to him when he be just a child?"

Tatiana's eyes widened, but not because she heard what the Necromancer had said. Just at the side of the Necromancer's head, she saw the limbs of the figure laying on the ground, twitch. Discreetly, she eyed the waking figure, who slowly rose. She watched the figure look over their shoulder and at their sword, reaching for the handle, as their eyes glanced up and met Tatiana's wide stare.

Instantly, the figure jumped and charged towards the Necromancer. He raised his sword, roaring, as he plunged his sword into the clouds of darkness and through the Necromancer's back, hearing his blade squelch against his flesh. Barnabas grappled his sword, pushing deeper, as the Necromancer's head arched and strung backwards, loosening his grip from around Tatiana's neck, but not releasing her.

After a moment, Barnabas stepped back from his sword, seeing the Necromancer become still. He scowled at Tatiana, looking past the Necromancer who stayed still and staring at her eyes. Barnabas saw her fluttering eyelids and her lashes flapping over her cheeks, as her eyes swirled with water and as the light from her amber eyes vanished all at once.

Then, the Necromancer's head lifted slowly. His head raised to gaze back at Tatiana, as a small laugh escaped his lips. The Necromancer's body shifted through the side of Barnabas' blade and through to the other side without a hint of pain. He continued to hold onto Tatiana's neck, looking over his shoulder at Barnabas and now standing to the side of Tatiana.

Yet Barnabas' blade did not fall. His sword remained, even after the Necromancer had moved through the blade. His silver handle sparkled and where the Necromancer's body had been, scarlet liquid did not stain the metal.

As Barnabas' eyes followed his long blade towards the end, Barnabas dropped to his knees. The point of his blade had disappeared through thick layers of flesh and pushed into the cliff wall. On parts of the blade that could be seen, there were dribbles of blood, which ran to the centre of the sword and down towards the handle.

Barnabas flicked to look back at Tatiana's face. The light in her eyes diminished and Starlight sparkled inside them, as tears fell over her cheeks and poured down her jaw. Her chest jolted and from her mouth, she spluttered red liquid across her lips and down her chin, which dripped onto her clothing. Tatiana's hands had lowered from the Necromancer's arms and clutched the sword that had been struck into her stomach. The flames around her body fizzled and Tatiana's glowing skin faded.

The Necromancer laughed, as Barnabas sobbed on his knees and as Tatiana gargled the blood in her mouth. "Thank ye, Barnabas. Thank ye, for doing what I be needing too. It saved me all the effort."

Barnabas shook his head. From his nostrils, snot ran over his trembling lips and down his chin, as his bright eyes formed water droplets that poured like waterfalls. His fingers clawed the material of his trousers, as his nails dug into the skin on his thighs and drawing red vertical lines across his flesh. Through his tears, Barnabas gawked at Tatiana with his lime eyes as her eyes bulged.

The Necromancer continued to babble and laugh, as his hand stayed around her neck. "The throne shall belong to me, forever!"

Just as Barnabas watched Tatiana and as the Necromancer continued to glare at Barnabas, there was a flicker of orange light grazing over Tatiana's eyes. Barnabas scowled as the orange light faded over her dark brown eyes and ignited a rim of orange around them. The blue blemishes across her frozen skin brightened with pink hues covering her cheeks and creating pigments across her skin. A small auburn glow lined her body, as her hands released the sword that was pushed into her flesh and softly withdrew to her side. The blood stopped gushing from her mouth and her lips curved into her cheeks, revealing her red-stained teeth.

Barnabas scowled.

Rapidly, Tatiana's arms raised and slapped onto the Necromancer's arm. Her hands squeezed his shadow arms, almost disappearing amongst the darkness of his body. Tatiana's nails dug into his flesh, striking pain through his arm and towards his shoulder, twisting the Necromancer's head and hearing his screams.

At once, Tatiana's skin started to glow. Her pinkish flesh transformed, peaching brown with a glowing and golden tan. Tatiana's straggly white hair unravelled from her plait, slowly falling around her head, as if she had been whooshed with a gushing wind. She stayed smiling with blood on her teeth, as the line of light around her body beamed with long and thick rays. Instantly, she emitted warmth, which reached Barnabas and the Necromancer, scorching their faces.

Tatiana looked over at the Necromancer with her eyes that had brightened from a deep brown into flares of orange. She grinned at the Necromancer, listening to his screams as her nails stayed deep in his skin and drew bubbles of blood. A blinding honey light, which was almost white, generated from her hands and gradually brightened, sizzling the Necromancer's arm.

The Necromancer howled, releasing Tatiana's neck. He was stuck in her grasp. Even as his knees buckled underneath his body, the Necromancer was held and forced to stand. He wiggled his body, tearing from Tatiana, as his feet flicked and flew particles of sand that reached Barnabas and scratched his face.

As Tatiana's hands held the Necromancer, his shadow melted. The darkness receded, crawling away from Tatiana's hands like millions of ants flocking across his body. The Necromancer's hand at the end of the arm that Tatiana clasped revealed white flesh underneath his shadow appearance, which was sickly and frosty with long fingers and sharp nails. The dispersing shadow revealed plain silver armour covering his arm and across his entire body.

Then, the darkness lifted from the Necromancer's face. The Necromancer's eyes, which almost resembled Nemo's, were revealed to Tatiana as the millions of ants retreated. Thick and long eyebrows rested above his large golden eyes, which widened, fearfully. Shoulder-length colourless hair rippled at the side of his pale face as wispy strands straggled over his forehead. His full lips remained parted as he howled, with wrinkles appearing at the side of his eyes and creases sitting at the sides of his mouth.

Tatiana's eyes quickly flicked over at Barnabas. Her golden eyes locked onto his lime eyes that bulged, eyeing the Necromancer's human skin. She waited until Barnabas noticed her staring, seeing his head turn after catching sight of her glimmering eyes and nodded at him.

Somehow, Barnabas knew. He knew what she asked and what he needed to do. Barnabas' lips trembled more and his tears stopped falling, but his eyes did not cease to water. Barnabas growled, as he forced his body to rise. He stomped his feet into the sand and straightened his back, locking onto Tatiana and stumbling over the dips in the sand.

Hesitantly, Barnabas trudged to Tatiana. His hands lifted in front of his chest and stretched forwards, shaking as they moved. Barnabas looked down at Tatiana's stomach and the blade that was wedged inside her body through the water in his eyes.

Slowly, his trembling hands wrapped around the silver blade of his sword and over the blood that had dribbled down the blade, which splattered in his grasp. Barnabas clenched the metal handle of his sword, as he dug his feet into the sand and locked his arms in front of his torso. He kept his eyes locked onto Tatiana, as she reassured him with a large smile.

Deeply, Barnabas inhaled. His hands wrapped even tighter, beginning to blister, around the handle of his sword. With his arms, he yanked his sword and pushed his teeth together as he screeched. He felt the sword loosen from Tatiana's stomach and stumbled a little, before heaving the sword further.

Barnabas stayed watching Tatiana, as her scream shivered his shoulders and her eyes tightly shut. From the bottom of his eyelids, Barnabas could see streams of blood running over the clots on her skin, flooding down her chest and along Barnabas' sword, running towards his hands and smothering them.

Yet, Barnabas continued. He took another deep breath and clenched his reddening and blistering hands even further, cutting his flesh on the metal rims of his handle. Barnabas released his tightened jaw and widened his mouth, howling hoarsely. Barnabas tugged the handle of his sword against his chest with a thump, after catching his blade on the intestines of Tatiana's stomach and slashing them open, splattering blood from her chest.

He shuffled backwards with his freed sword and watched as Tatiana's body slipped down the cliff wall. Her limp feet touched the tops of the sand, as the Necromancer's strong grasp continued to hold her. Tatiana's legs shook as she weightlessly stood, still leaning on the cliff wall and silencing her screams, as the hole in her stomach became bearable and numb.

There was one thing that Barnabas still needed to do. Barnabas lunged forwards with his red sword wielded in his bloody hands into the sand depressions, rapidly. He stretched his sword in front of him, slicing his blade through the cold, sea air and across his body towards his side. His lime eyes still focused on Tatiana, but at the corner of his eyes, he could see his sword swooping.

Across Barnabas and Tatiana's face, they were dotted with dark ruby and thick splatters that was thrown towards them as Barnabas sliced through flesh. The warm blood smeared into their eyes, as they winced and heard a thud on the sand.

Finally, the Necromancer's hand released Tatiana's throat with twitching fingers and retreating from her. The Necromancer's arm distanced, falling to his side limply. His back leant away from Tatiana and slanted, as his feet lifted from amongst the golden grains of sand. The Necromancer's body slumped into the ground.

He fell just at the side of his head. The Necromancer's golden eyes were covered in an icy glass and he stared into an abyss of darkness. His mouth remained parted, but there were no more screams, as his head laid on its side and as his thick, black strands of hair straddled across his pale blue face.

As soon as the Necromancer's hand lifted from Tatiana's neck, Tatiana fell beside him. Her legs plummeted onto her knees, slamming them into the sand. Tatiana clutched her stomach, as her torso leant forwards onto her arm and on her hand that was amongst the grains of gold.

Tatiana grunted, as she shifted her weight to crawl along the sand. She slapped her hand and her knees in the sand, moving towards the Necromancer. She shuffled in the sand, as grains clung to her clothes and as the sand froze her warm hands. Tatiana stopped beside the Necromancer and leaned over him, as she raised to slump on her knees and sunk in the sand.

She overlooked the Necromancer as his headless body rested by her knees and as his head laid on the other side and just a few inches away, with his face turned from her. Tatiana reached forward, stretching her fingers and laying her palm to rest on the middle of the silver armour covering his chest. She pushed heavily and dented the metal.

Brightly, her eyes burned, as she glared down at the Necromancer's body. Her skin still glimmered and scorched. Orange and red flames flickered around her and illuminated the Necromancer, as well as warming Barnabas who crept and stooped to shadow her.

From under the palm of her hand, a light hue of yellow blazed across the armour of the Necromancer, moving gradually over his body and flaring brightly. The lemon glow lifted with pointed and small flames, rising. The flames danced over the Necromancer, melting the armour around his body, burning through his clothes and scorching through his skin. A boiling inferno expanded around the Necromancer, as white flakes were whisked from his flesh and taken by the wind.

After a while, Tatiana lifted her hand from the runny silver liquid of his armour that was stuck to her palm. She pulled her hand out from the fire and dropped her arm at her side, as she slumped further into the sand, rolling backwards and seeing the Stars.

The light in Tatiana's eyes still flourished, as did the flames igniting her body. From her wound, only dribbles of blood poured from her open stomach as her body filled with warmth. There was still blood sitting on her lips and her teeth, but it dried and she could speak freely.

Instantly, Barnabas rushed to her side and skidded onto his knees. He knelt behind her back and rolled her into his chest, cradling her in his arms. He pressed the side of her torso into his chest, as her neck rested on his forearm and as her legs still laid in the sand. Barnabas glanced down at Tatiana's bloody mouth and the layers of grime that covered her face with a quavering lip, as his free hand caressed the sides of her cheek.

Barnabas remarked, fluttering his eyelids to dry his tears, "Truly, thou be immortal."

Tatiana smiled and said with a croaking voice, "Thank ye, Barnabas, for everything!"

"The darkness be nearly lightened," Barnabas cheered. "The battle still rages behind us. Thou and I must join the companions."

"Yes, Barnabas. Soon, thou and I shall join them. Let a small amount of time to pass, for I be needing to heal," Tatiana insisted, lifting her hand to cover Barnabas'. "Again, thank ye, Barnabas."

He nodded.

Tatiana's eyes moved away from Barnabas' and glanced up at the dark midnight-blue sky, just past his head. She watched the twinkling rays, which covered the sky, as they glimmered in her eyes. Tatiana rested comfortably in Barnabas' arms, warming him with her light, as he comforted her with his strong hold, listening to the peaceful crashes of the waves that flooded the sandy shores.

40

Standing on the cliff like a torch, the tower inside Cahercasey still blazed. The tower had shrunk as stone and wood crumbled down the sides and snapped, hitting the ground. The dancing orange swirls were pulled by the winds, stretching higher towards the twinkling sky and widening over the tops of Cahercasey Castle. The surrounding turrets and towers ignited, as flames swarmed around the kingdom and blazed.

In front of the burning kingdom, men and women dressed in amour and bestowed with swords, axes and bows sprinted to fight, and their blades clashed as arrows fired through the air. Their feet stomped in the meadow, splattering pools of red running liquid and over lumps that hid between the yellow strands which grew. They roared, fighting with injuries, as blood squirted from their wounds and as bruises layered their skins.

Amongst the war, there were Tatiana's companions, battling through the meadow and plunging their feet into the scarlet pools soaking into the ground. Her companions marched with torn and bloodstained clothes, as deep slashes sliced across their bodies and faces, oozing and bubbling with crimson. The wind whipped their hair across their faces, slapping red lines onto their skin. The companions dripped in sweat, panting, as their arms and legs felt like lead.

Fighting side by side, standing just a few inches behind each other, were Pip and Wylie on the outskirts of the battle. Pip's dark red hair flicked across her face as her green eyes scanned the battlefield. Her face was layered with mud and blood, and a raised slash stung her ear and cheek from a swinging sword. From her deep wound, blood gushed and trickled down her neck. Her arms ached, holding two swords in a tight grasp standing in blood.

She stood with Wylie as Wylie fought with his sword and as his black hair rippled in the winds. His glowing and golden skin, clear from blemishes, was destroyed with gashes that would scar. His deep cuts burned, as yellow heaps of pus squirted from inside his wounds and as his skin began to swell. The whites of Wylie's eyes sparked with crimson lines, as his eyelids hung over his dark brown eyes that examined the men and women in front of him.

Wylie and Pip pressed their backs together as warriors from both sides swarmed around them. They eyed oncoming opponents, lifting their weapons and tightening their grips. The ends of their blades pointed forward, and they braced their feet in the blood-ridden ground and waiting to be attacked.

Further amongst the fighting warriors, running between, there was Darrel. Darrel's feet thudded and crushed the meadow, charging towards the ogres storming the battlefield and killing figures underneath their feet. Darrel raced with his hands stretched out at his side and gripping two long metal axes. His blades sliced across backs and stomachs, flicking drops of blood across his face and into his eyes, as he headed towards the feet of the ogres, slicing their flesh and forcing them to drop to their knees.

Just as Darrel ran towards the ogre that stormed towards him, Sir Terrence and Tasmin sprinted across, just missing the ogre's legs and heading deeper into the battlefield. Sir Terrence and Tasmin disappeared quickly after Darrel had glimpsed them, flocking towards their oncoming opponents, glued to each other's sides.

Sir Terrence sprinted to Tasmin's side and grabbed his sword that rested at the side of his body, jumping over the bodies lying at his feet. He darted between fighting figures, waving his sword across their necks and sprinting back to Tasmin's side.

His brown eyes sought Tasmin's dark frizzy hair swaying behind her, as she threw her axe forwards and chased after her spinning weapon, which hacked through her opponent's forehead. Tasmin heaved her axe from their flesh with a grunt as her opponent fell beneath the pools of blood in the meadow. Her dark eyes searched for Sir Terrence as soon as her opponent had fallen, scurrying to find him again.

Deep in the battle, with their backs pressed together, were Klaus, Orla and Ainsley. Their opponents circled and charged as Klaus, Orla and Ainsley held their swords in tight grips. Klaus, Orla and Ainsley's feet shifted, wanting to sprint from their oncoming enemies, as their hands blistered around the handles of their swords. Their ears were deafened by roars, as thick, scarlet liquid oozed from their deep wounds.

Suddenly, a trail crossed and blazed across the sky, lighting the battlefield and reflecting on the surface of the pools of blood in the meadow. The tangerine light spread across the night, forming flames and flying above the battle, which paused for only a moment to gaze at the fire and duck underneath puffs of heat that swallowed their heads, before continuing to fight again.

As the fire flourished in the sky, a shadow glided within the light and above the fighting figures below. Two curved blades lined the sky, spreading the fire and igniting the meadow, turning the yellow strands black as flickers of orange started to line the ground rapidly and scorching figures that fought. The enormous shadow came with a gust of wind, as its blades flapped in the air and dived to the ground.

Its clawed feet thudded on the ground as its skinny legs bent slightly and caught its heavy body. The shadow blazed with fire and raised its long neck as its long tail flung approaching warriors with a single whip. Its wings slowly stopped flapping, still brushing air and whisking men from their feet, even as its feet stood on the ground. The shadow lowered one of its wings and created a ramp, and a figure rose slowly from holding its feathers.

The tallest shadow was hidden underneath a deep purple cloak, holding two daggers at their sides of their thighs. Their long, golden and shiny hair was whisked from laying on their back and their grey eyes that sparked with violet bolts observed their surroundings, before sprinting down the shadow's wing and jumping into the bloody meadow.

The figure splashed in the crimson pools, which splattered on her clothes, and straightened her bent knees, standing tall. Their head turned to look over their shoulder and at the shadow behind. The figure spoke softly, "Ra! Can thou set fire to the land?"

"Of course, Tasmin. I shall be happy to do so," Ra replied, as his golden eyes looked to the sky.

Tasmin stormed from the edge of Ra's wing and pounced into the battle, clasping her hands tighter around her daggers as she raised them from the sides of her thighs. Tasmin raced into the chaos, using the small blades of her daggers to shred through flesh.

For a moment more, Ra stayed, eyeing Tasmin running towards the mass war ahead. Ra glimpsed Tasmin slicing the blades of her daggers across necks and squirting blood into her hair and onto her face, which she smeared with a rough wipe of her sleeve. Eventually, Tasmin was washed deeper into the battle, and her hands majestically crafted the wield of her daggers, plunging and stabbing her opponents.

As Tasmin vanished, Ra's eyes turned back to the sky. His golden eyes locked onto the twinkling rayed dots that lit up the night, seeing them through the thinning black clouds that disappeared. The Stars sat across a deep midnight-painted sky, as streaks of pink shimmered beyond the East, and the head of a golden ball began to rise from the horizon.

Ra's claws released the reddened soil. His legs crouched, pressing heavily on his feet, and he hunched his body lower to the ground. Ra's neck stretched towards the Stars and his tail swept across the tops of the meadow, clearing the last few warriors that ran to attack him. He leapt into the air, pushing from his feet and rapidly flapping his wings, slapping the pools of blood with gushes of wind.

Ra took to the skies. His slender and long body whipped through the air with ease, as his wings angled and his body slanted. He twirled around the battlefield as his fiery streaks burned through the night and trailed behind him. Ra lowered. His fire followed and spiralled in thick sheets, cooling into grey swirls of steam ever so slowly.

Ra dipped and flew inches above the battlefield, dragging his flames behind him. His flames rippled and flared, sparking the meadow with orange flecks and frazzling strands of hair as he crossed over the land. His light forced eyes to shut and his heat forced faces to be shielded, though he passed quickly.

The flecks of orange that clung to the stems of the meadow sizzled. The bright dots steamed through the yellow strands and ignited them. At first, small flickering flames raised from the flecks and swarmed upwards, growing larger, as the flames consumed the rest of the wheat. It was not long until every strand in the meadow was bursting with flames which grew over the pools of blood, catching the warriors in cocoons of fire.

Ra swooshed high into the sky, twirling his body to overlook the swaying flames that rapidly travelled further and further, burning brighter. He hovered as his flames entrapped the dark silver armoured warriors of the Necromancer.

Yet Ra's golden eyes searched for someone amongst the shadows of the flames. He deafened the rising screams and focused his search, scanning for the bright blue-eyed woman that bewitchingly dazzled amongst the warriors.

Just as Ra lingered above the battle, his red feathers shuddered all over his body. His golden eyes bulged and his head twitched. A deafening vibration boomed across the South, shaking the ground and wobbling the legs of the warriors below. The sound rippled from the nearby distance and silenced the land with a roar.

Ra twisted to the North, scanning the darkness of the night and sighted a gigantic shadow floating towards him. At first, he saw a pair of glimmering Stars, but as the shadow came closer, he met a callous stare. The shadow came rapidly from the North, with a wide and heavy body, which was laced with white glimmering scales. Its wings heavily slapped the air as its four clawed legs hung from its body, waiting to land. A funnel of fire was released from deep within its pinkish throat as daggers hung from its gums.

The beast dropped lower to the battle, sweeping above and blowing vast quantities of fire that resonated inside its chest, which flared with every breath of flame. The beast swooped into the land of fire, landing on its four muscular legs and clearing a piece of meadow with fear.

The beast eyed the last few ogres that were dotted amongst the battle and had not been yet inflicted with Ra's flames, throwing his legs forwards and pouncing ahead, forming a small flight towards them. The beast flew elegantly and quickly, spurring tunnels of fire and circling the large stumbling ogres, until their flesh had been scalded and they fell against the burning meadow.

For only a few seconds, the companions stopped to glare at the fire-spurring beast and watch the fall of the remaining ogres. The companions stood within the heat and the blaze of the meadow, as water droplets fell down their faces and as their hair glued to their scalps. Their shallow breaths were masked by shouting and screaming, as they were scorched by the dancing flames that circled them.

The only companion that held their gaze dangerously longer was Wylie. His knees wobbled, rippling the pools of blood he stood in, as his heart fell into his churning stomach. Wylie's sword slipped from his grasp and dropped into the liquid, sinking beneath the red surface with what was a silent splash amongst the falling bodies of the dead.

Behind Wylie, Pip dug her sword into her opponent's throat and kicked their chest to draw out her sword with ease. Pip saw Wylie from the corner of her eye, twisting on her heel and rushing to stand before him. She grappled his shoulders and rattled his body, screaming his name.

Pip's voice was muffled and blurred by his vision as he eyed the white-scaled beast. She halted the shaking of his body, rapidly lowering her hands down the sides of his arms and releasing him with the hand she still held her sword in. Pip's other hand locked around Wylie's, swirling round and searching the battlefield.

Desperately, as her eyes frantically moved, she searched for a gap within the war and waded through. Pip stretched her sword at her side and tugged Wylie behind, forcing him to duck underneath swinging swords, pushing him to dodge flying arrows and nudging him away from the rising spurs of fire. Pip held him tight, even as she lunged to use her own sword, battling towards the outskirts and towards the fields of meadows that were free from fires.

Pip tore through the outskirts of the battle, heaving Wylie behind her. She hopped over the strands of meadow, dragging Wylie away from the battle and swinging him in front of her as she stopped. Pip placed Wylie before her and glared at him as she released his hand and slapped her palm onto his chest, throttling him with a slap. She yelled at him as Wylie followed the flying beast.

Just as Pip shouted, she felt the ground thud and vibrate through her legs. She heard screaming roars and the sound of chains whipping to spin something heavy through the air. The screeches became louder, but her stomach sunk, knowing the grouped warriors of the Necromancer were already too close for her to win.

With an extended exhale, Pip's heels dug into the ground and she swivelled. The strands of her red hair stretched and twirled with her as her sword glided round. Pip locked onto the warriors that charged to her, raising her blade to the side of her cheek and creeping forwards. She jabbed her sword forwards and her blade collided with the warriors that swung for her, whilst Wylie stood motionless behind her and continued to watch the enormous beast that tackled the ogres.

Pip howled as the warriors fought against her. They swung their spiked ball and chains over her crouching body as their swords slashed near her neck. Her feet stumbled quickly, stepping backwards and away from the warriors, and she stretched out her arms and protected Wylie as she pressed against him and shoved him away.

The black-armoured warriors staggered as they paced to her and continued to swing their balls and chains. A black metal ball spiked Pip's hand and knocked her sword from her hand as a sharp blade stabbed through her palm. Her sword flung into the strands of the meadow, as Pip cowered and slapped her hands together, screeching and lowering to floor. She knelt in front of Wylie, shuffling between his legs and eyeing the warriors, weeping at Wylie's feet.

Wylie was still bewitched by the white-scaled beast. In his trance, Wylie could not hear Pip's screams as water streamed from his brown eyes and rolled over his cheeks.

Yet as Wylie gazed at the beast, he met the beast's wide-eyed stare. The beast had its teeth clenched around an ogre's neck, tearing its flesh and snapping its head from its body. The beast flapped its wings and lifted itself from the ground, loosening its jaw and rolling the ogre's head to tumble next to its fallen body. The beast listened to Pip's shrills, which travelled across the battlefield, and saw her cower at Wylie's feet as the warriors feverishly surrounded them.

The great, white-scaled beast darted and whipped over the battlefield, flying towards Wylie. The beast parted and roared, tumbling fire from its throat and blazing the air just above the battlefield. The ferocious white creature swiftly flew, flapping its heavy wings and roaring louder, revealing its sharp and long teeth that sat either side of its forked tongue.

Wylie was frozen amongst the strands of meadow, with Pip still sitting and crying on his feet as the beast swooped towards him. Wylie's knees shook and his hands wobbled, glaring at the beast that flew. His eyelids folded over his watering brown eyes, closing them so tightly that wrinkles appeared at the sides of his face.

The beast leaned to one side, gliding one of its wings on top of the meadow strands as the other flicked towards the sky. Its long neck floated a few centimetres above the ground as its mouth widened and its teeth arched backward while its tongue stretched. It released hot air from the fire it had breathed, but its mouth passed Wylie and Pip as its wing glided over them.

A gush of air rattled through Wylie and Pip's hair, as a *swoosh* whistled through their ears. Through Wylie's eyelids and Pip's tears, they saw the shadow of the beast's wing brush over them as the beast silently passed.

Wylie's eyes flicked open, searching the battlefield for the beast. His brown eyes looked round at the meadow and sighted the beast. He saw the beast standing on its four, with its long neck stretched upwards and its wide mouth shutting as it gobbled. Wylie's knees buckled as his back slanted and his head rolled, tumbling backwards into the meadow and catching himself with his hands that he planted in the ground just at the side of his body. His chest tightened and he breathed shallowly, panting, as his eyes glared up at the Stars.

Yet, as Pip's tears dried, she saw an empty patch of meadow before her. Pip rolled onto her knees, looking where the warriors had stood and seeing only yellow strands of wheat. She cried her last few tears as her head turned, seeing the beast swallowing and hearing it gulp. Her green eyes looked over at the beast and she smiled faintly.

Pip twisted on her knees and crawled to Wylie's side. She gazed at him with her watery green eyes that searched his bruises and burnt and braised face. Pip leaned and clambered her arms around him, hoisting him into her arms and holding him tight. She lifted his rolled neck, supporting his head with her palm. She stayed silent, at his side, listening to his breaths and feeling his chest thud against hers.

She looked up from Wylie and at the beast that stood to observe them. The beast turned its head to face them, and its neck and body followed, while it closed its wide wings. The beast plodded and squashed the meadow strands, striding towards them. Its tall and large body shadowed them, stopping a few centimetres away. The beast curled its neck and its head lingered above them, looking down with its black eyes and breathing warm air through the strands of their hair.

Pip trembled, though she sensed the beast would not hurt her. "What do I call ye?"

"Bathilda," the beast snarled.

"Thank ye, Bathilda. Thank ye, for saving us."

"There be no need for thanking. I be in great debt to Wylie," Bathilda growled.

Pip smiled, as her green eyes lowered down to Wylie, and remarked softly, "What good deed did thee do for such a magnificent beast?" Bathilda mentioned, as her black eyes looked over her nose and down at Wylie.

Her stare still caused him to tremble, as he rolled closer into Pip's chest and as his lips shook. "Wylie, there be no reason to worry. I consumed what was the last after hearing Queen Tatiana's return and deeming thee trustworthy. May thou and I be friends in the future!"

Instantly, Pip's head flicked upwards and she said. "I believe him and thee shall be friends for a lifetime."

Bathilda exhaled before turning her neck and overlooking the battle that seemed to be quieter. Her black eyes scanned the burning tower inside the castle and looked up at Ra that still hovered above the battle, searching as well. Bathilda's long tail swooped along the meadow, knocking down the strands of meadow and curling around Pip and Wylie, until Wylie had recovered.

41

On the Southern beach, large and bright dancers swarmed around a dark shadow laying on the cold grains of sand. The shadow burned and illuminated the walls of the cliffs, resting a few feet away from the crashing waves that hit the shore. The orange dancers were blown to circle the shadow by the strong sea breeze.

Beside the burning shadow, a woman was nestled on the sand. She rested on her back and glared up at the Stars. The woman felt the rapid brush of the breeze circling her feet, as a sweet salt smell entered her nostrils and the sand grains clung to her clothes. Her glowing white hair was spread across the ground and her body was illuminated with an orange light. The woman rested her hand on her stomach, with dry and crisp red clots sticking to her palm, as the wind blew through the hole in her top and blew on her fiery skin. She relaxed beside a man overlooking her.

The man was knelt on his knees. His back was slanted, shadowing her. He examined her with lime eyes and dry pouted lips, breathing deeply. The man was silent, as his hands clasped together on top of his lap and he twiddled his thumbs with sweating palms. His curly hair was blown across his face by the sea breeze, as his shoulders shuddered and he shuffled closer to the warmth of the woman's body.

The man moved to warm himself in her flames and asked. "Now, thou be well rested? Shall thou and I begin walking into the battle? Tatiana? Queen Tatiana?"

Tatiana's blazing eyes wandered over to Barnabas with tears swirling inside her irises. She croaked, "I be ready. Help me to my feet!"

Barnabas unclasped his hands and leaned over her to grab both of her hands. His fingers tightly curled around her wrists and his palms laid over the top of her hands. He squished his flesh and fastened his grip, slamming one foot into the pits of sand. He pushed on his foot and lifted, straining his muscles, as he raised to Tatiana to stand with him.

Tatiana's eyes shut and she shrieked, clenching her fists and raising her back from the sand. Her stomach curled and her knees arched, dragging her feet inwards and slowly sitting upwards. She planted her feet into the golden grains and pushed, as Barnabas lifted her.

Tatiana's body slowly unravelled to stand, straightening and holding onto Barnabas, balancing herself. She kept her eyes closed until the pain in her stomach had ceased and after a small tear fell from underneath one of her eyelids. Tatiana exhaled, deeply, opening her eyes and seeing Barnabas before her, who still held her wrists.

Tatiana smiled at his slumped but pouted lips and his wide eyes, which sat underneath his scowling eyebrows. His face was relaxed, with a few specks of her blood on one side of his cheek. She grinned at his wavy hair blowing in the wind and over his face, as he stood completely unaffected by the cold that bobbled his skin.

Suddenly, Tatiana's head slanted to one side and she looked through Barnabas' strands of hair, witnessing a bright light. Tatiana's eyes twinkled, catching the white sparkle that rayed on the sandy shores, shining in the near distance. Her bottom lip dropped and parted, as her eyes started to water. Then, she smiled again.

Barnabas' eyebrows scowled and his chin raised. His eyes squinted, looking down at Tatiana, as she bewitchingly stared over his shoulders. Barnabas gently placed Tatiana's hands at her side and released her wrists, as his arms swung back to his sides. Slowly, he turned to his head. His heart fluttered inside his chest and his cheeks flustered. Barnabas' eyes widened and his pouted lips parted, releasing a deep shallow breath. His eyes turned to the sea and then round to the shores behind him, twisting on his heels and tightening his chest.

Barnabas' legs began to shake. He eyed the sparkling white light in the distance, which floated motionless above the sand. Barnabas' scowl lightened and the strain across his face faded. For the first time, the corners of his lips rose higher into his cheeks and for the first time, there were waterfalls falling from his eyes.

His heart fluttered faster and his shaking legs moved along the sand. His fist tightened and his arms lifted and curved, shifting his torso to the beat of his sprinting feet. Barnabas flicked grains of sand behind him, as the wind blew his gushing tears from his cheeks and into his scalp. His smiled faded, as his lip rattled, but his eyes gleamed like never before, growing and brightening in colour.

Barnabas charged to the light, crashing into its rayed points and swinging his arms around its body. He heaved the white and twinkling body of the light into his arms, holding the glow in his chest, as tight as he could. His fluttering heart ached, feeling the light's warmth swarm through his body and melted the ice running through his blood. He felt warm arms slip around his waist and clasp behind his back, holding him still. Barnabas held the head of the light with his hand, stroking soft strands of white hair and pushing its head into his shoulder, as his other hand rested on the centre of its tender back. His head curved into the crevice of its collar and smelled its sweet lavender scent excreting from its skin.

For a while, Barnabas wrapped the light in his arms. His surroundings darkened and he saw only the light he held. Barnabas closed his green eyes, clinging to the light and almost forgetting the war that raged on the other side of the cliffs, as well as just remembering that Tatiana still stood on the shore with him.

The light released Barnabas, nudging him gently and stepping back to view Barnabas, whilst his hand still rested on the back of its head, caressing its hair. The light looked longingly at Barnabas, with a pair of hazel eyes that simmered with water. The light faintly smiled, as the light placed its hands on his cheeks and stroked his wet skin with its thumbs, catching his tears that continued to fall.

Barnabas' knees buckled underneath him, as his cheeks slipped through the light's palms, crashing onto his knees. His head bowed over his chest and his jaw buried into his neck, closing his eyes and feeling his tears fall, which were too heavy for the cool sea breeze to carry away. Barnabas slanted forwards and leaned his head against the stomach of the light.

The light gently pushed Barnabas' head from its stomach and lowered. It perched before Barnabas, lifting its hands to rest on his neck and underneath his jaw, lifting his face. The glow shuffled closer to Barnabas, as its eyes viewed Barnabas from only a few centimetres away.

The glow remarked with a soft voice. "My dear Barnabas! How far thou came! Do not cry any more, I be here now."

Barnabas looked at the light and examined its long white dress that fell to the floor. He observed its jewelled star crown that was on their head and smiled at a long necklace falling from its neck, with a sapphire attached to the end. He stated, as his eyes locked onto the rayed star necklace that fell on its chest. "A Star? A Star be what thou be now?"

It chortled. "Every night, I watched thee. Every night, I hoped thou would sleep. I be not just any Star, Barnabas Mint. I be their leader."

Barnabas sniffled his flaring nostrils. "The leader? The Stars saved thee to make thee their leader?"

It nodded.

"Oh, Bidelia!" Barnabas exclaimed. "Forever can thou stay by my side?"

She nodded.

"Do not be leaving again!"

Bidelia sighed. "I cannot promise. For I do need to return to the skies once the battle be ceased. Once I return, it shall be some while before I be here again."

"Let me return with thee!"

"No!" she hissed. "Thou cannot come to the skies, yet. There shall be a day when thou can, but not till such day."

"Be that day the day of my death?" He chortled.

"Yes." Bidelia huffed. "Do not try to be leaving any earlier, either. Otherwise, thou and I shall not sight each other again."

Barnabas nodded. "Then, please watch over me until such time. For, I shall always be looking up at the skies at night, searching for the twinkling light that I see before me, wanting its warmth again!"

She nodded, leaning into Barnabas and hugging him one last time before lifting to her feet. She stretched out her hands towards Barnabas and guided him to stand, taking his hand and striding towards Tatiana across the grains of sand.

Tatiana grinned at her sister's blinding light and her beaming expression, stepping closer to Bidelia and Barnabas, as her arms folded across her chest. She stepped before them, as her eyes flicked between their bright and happy faces.

She remarked with a fading smile, "One day, shall I be happy like thee?"

Bidelia and Barnabas stepped forwards, reaching across Tatiana's back and pulling her to stand between their chests, holding her tightly. Bidelia and Barnabas laid their heads to rest on her shoulders, as Tatiana's hands reached to lay on their backs and as her head squished between their shoulders.

Bidelia sighed. "I be not knowing, sister. I be not seeing all!"

Barnabas declared, "Yet I shall be staying with thee until thou be happy!"

"Yes." Bidelia sighed. "Until Barnabas stops breathing, him and I cannot be. Yet I shall watch over him till his last breath. I pray for him to be at my sister's side, until such day."

Tatiana breathed deeply. "Then, let us return to the battle. Belladonna be still amongst the battle."

Bidelia pulled from her sister, as Barnabas released Tatiana too. Bidelia's hand rested on her sister's shoulder and she shook her head. "She be the reason why I came. No longer she be on the battlefield! She flees to the forest on the Southern borders."

Tatiana's parted lips closed and pouted. "She must be killed!"

Feverishly, Bidelia and Barnabas smiled, as their faces tilted towards each other and locked onto the glimmers they both held. Bidelia and Barnabas turned their angled jaws to glare at Tatiana, who stared with her pouted lips growing into a smile.

Bidelia's hand slid down her sister's arm and grasped Tatiana's hand. Bidelia's eyes closed, still smiling, as her exceptional light that formed around her body, flickered. Her white haze of light beamed from her already radiant skin, blurring her features. A blaze of heat was released from Bidelia, stronger than before and swirling around Tatiana and Barnabas, as Bidelia's light became blinding, too bright for Tatiana and Barnabas to keep their eyes opened.

As Bidelia's white light encased them, fumigating them with warmth, Barnabas and Tatiana still felt as if they were standing on the lumpy grains of sand underneath their feet, still feeling the salty breeze of the ocean and feeling frozen. Yet, Barnabas and Tatiana knew they were moving, though they could not feel it, nor could they see it, continuing to smile as Bidelia transported them.

Through the pink casing of Barnabas and Tatiana's eyelids, they witnessed Bidelia's light starting to fade, as their eyelids darkened. The warmth was whisked from them and returned to Bidelia, as the white haze around the outline of body dimmed. Her features became structured and the blur of the light disappeared, as her gleaming white hair, became caught in the wind.

Barnabas and Tatiana opened their eyes. First glancing at each other, then at their surroundings. Barnabas and Tatiana no longer stood on grains of grass, but between strands of yellow. The salty sea winds still lingered, but the crashing waves were not seen, nor were they heard. Instead, there were faint roars far behind them, coming from the meadow they had been taken to. At their sides, they were shadowed by tall, drooping trees, which clustered together and grew thickly along the Southern borders. A humid and unbreathable heat was released from the long forest they now stood before.

Bidelia released their hands, dropping them gently to their sides and turning her head to gaze over her shoulder. She scanned the fields behind her, which stretched into the distance and led to the roars of war, waiting eagerly, as the fields remained untouched.

Tatiana moved from Bidelia and Barnabas' side and stepped further into the meadow, turning her back on the high trees of the vast forest behind her and readying her sword. She searched the meadows, watching the winds trail the long grains of wheat all around her. She barely heard the screeches from the battle in the distance and heard only whispers of the winds, as she waited.

As Bidelia waited behind with Barnabas, she snatched his hands and twisted to face him. Bidelia forced him to step closer and hushed him as he began to speak. Bidelia's skin rayed with light again, as the outline of her body blossomed and her skin flawless shone.

She whispered, "Thou and I shall go to war. She be not needing us here."

Barnabas looked over his shoulder and watched Tatiana standing amongst the strands of meadow, looking out in the distance. He observed her, as Bidelia's light brightened, until his eyes were burned by her light. The light rinsed over Barnabas' eyes and he lost sight of Tatiana, closing his eyes as soon as he could no longer see her, disappearing with Bidelia and heading to the battlefield.

42

Tatiana waited. She waited in the meadow and stared across the yellow strands. Her hair was whisked by the wind which travelled quietly from the sea. She was chilled underneath the black night sky, just being able to see ahead with the brightly lit moon and the glimmering Stars above her. Tatiana readied and aimed her bow and arrow into the distance, searching for a dark shadow to appear and listening to silence of the night, hearing the forest leaves sway behind her.

After sighting a flashing twinkle in the corner of her eye, she had realised Barnabas and Bidelia had left. It was a while since Bidelia and Barnabas had left and she wondered how all her companions were. Tatiana hoped all her companions were still alive.

Suddenly, as Tatiana's amber eyes gawked into the distance, she saw something stagger up a hill of the meadow. Tatiana locked onto the fast-moving shadow that knocked down the swaying yellow wheat strands, which paced towards her. Its head was cocked over its shoulder, glancing back at the battle which was too far behind the figure to be seen. Its bewitching ocean eyes glimmered amongst the darkness, glowing as bright as the moon and finally sighted Tatiana ahead.

Abruptly, the shadow stumbled to halt. Its deep-sea eyes gazed at the motionless Tatiana, who stood in the far distance, seeing her tensed arms holding her bow and arrow. The shadow's body fell limp, dropping their arms at their sides and bending their knees, almost dropping to the ground. The shadow exhaled, releasing the tension in their chest and slowly walking through the meadow, towards Tatiana.

Tatiana stayed still, as the oncoming shadow approached. Her heart started to flutter, as the shadow's hands stretched beside its body and its fingers ran along the tops of the wheat strands. Tatiana's grip tightened around the wood of her bow, as her fingers pinched her arrow further. Her amber eyes and the flames wrapped around her body, flaring as she glued her feet on the soil.

The shadow swayed towards her with a smile, stopping metres away and being clear enough for Tatiana to identify the dark moving figure that approached.

Tatiana had already seen its glorious eyes glimmering in the night, but as the figure stood closer, she examined the long, raven hair falling at their shoulders and their straggly strands blowing in the wind. She scanned the blueish cheeks of a middle-aged woman, seeing the woman grin with rotten and rigid teeth, as blood clustered on her dry and thin lips. She shuddered, as the woman's rasp and crisp voice shrilled across the meadow.

"Truly, thou be powerful." Her hands raised and clasped just below her chin, stretched in front of her chest. "I be sorry, Tatiana! I be not meaning to cause harm."

Tatiana spat. "Belladonna, I believe not thee. Thou entered my kingdom, took my throne and captured my companions. How can thou convince me?"

"Please. Let me go!" Belladonna begged, hesitantly stepping forwards, as Tatiana kept her arrow aimed at her. "I beg thee. Please, before he finds me. Let me return home."

Tatiana pondered. Her eyes lowered and her heavy eyelids fell too. She sighed, relaxing her tensing arms and lowering her bow. Tatiana slowly released her fingers from pinching her arrow and stretched to place her arrow into her quiver on her back. She lifted her bow overhead and placed it to sit gently around her, as her head raised and she opened her eyes.

Belladonna crept forwards, unclasping her begging hands and exhaling with relief. She tiptoed quickly on her bare feet, widely passing Tatiana and thanking her as she did. Belladonna sprinted towards the warm and dark forest behind, slowly stopping to walk to enter.

Before Belladonna entered, Tatiana twisted and called to her, "Pray thou and I shall not meet again."

Belladonna stopped at the edge of the forest, taking a moment to stare into the darkness of the forest with a smile before turning her head to look over her shoulder. Belladonna laughed. "Once I be through the forest, thou and I shall never see each other again."

Tatiana sighted Belladonna's blue eyes for the last time, as Belladonna turned her head and peered into the bleakness of the forest again. Belladonna stepped between the stumps of two tall, thick trees, wriggling her toes amongst the mud and between the brittle brown grass. She lunged onto her foot and took another step forwards, almost vanishing amongst the dark if had not been for her sickly skin.

As Belladonna entered the forest, Tatiana strode towards its outskirts and stood at the edge, promptly after Belladonna had disappeared into the dark purple haze between the trees. Tatiana searched for Belladonna, as far as she could see, but through the trees and over the thick uprooted roots, Belladonna had gone. Tatiana huffed, pressing her hand against the tree beside her and leaning, as her head clocked to one side.

Suddenly, from the palm of her hand, a light penetrated the bark, glowing a deep burnt orange. The brown wood beneath her hand scorched and sizzled black, smelling sweet and musky like a bonfire. The small patch that her hand burned crawled along the sides of the tree, crumbling the bark and rising towards the grey leaves, which decayed and browned, splitting from the branches and gently swaying to fall around her. From the tree, grey swirls smoked and travelled through the forest, before rising towards the Stars. Tatiana lifted her hand away from the wood of the tree.

Suddenly, from the roots of the tree, flames zapped along the trunk and swirled around the branches. The tree was consumed by a blinding orange glow, which incinerated the wood that fell like flakes of snow, trailing after the fall of the leaves, but being whisked away by the wind, as their amber embers burned.

The embers spiralled through the forest, gliding on a sudden gush of wind that chased Belladonna and shuddered her shoulders. Belladonna stopped amongst the darkness, eyeing the falling grey flakes lined with an orange glow, which cascaded around her and diminished at her feet. Her palms faced upwards, as ash swayed to land across her flesh, burning for only a few seconds, before she clenched her hand and crumpled the ash into miniature flakes, releasing them into the wind.

Belladonna chuckled and glanced over her shoulder, looking back at the way she had come, as if she were able to stare back at Tatiana and witness the ash that had been created. Belladonna turned back, breathing deeply, shuffling her feet across the mud and bursting into a sprint. She threw herself forwards, stretching her hand before her and clearing her path, pulling back the moving trunks and roots that slithered to block her way.

At the edge of the forest, Tatiana stood beside the tall and burning tree. She smiled at the bright whipping flames, curling up the sides and spinning around the branches. The scorching heat caressed Tatiana's flesh, catching a flame that danced across the grooves of her palm, which staggered strangely towards the centre of her hand. She guided the flame towards the tree on the other side of her shoulder and placed her palm onto the bark, letting the flame escape.

The escaping flame latched onto the bark and rinsed it black. The tip of the flame curled inwards, rolling around the sides of the tree and flying towards the branches, swarming to the leaves and sizzling them into thin sheets of grey, which tore from the wood.

At the end of the branches, the fire launched into the air and swooped onto the following tree. The orange swirls danced along every branch and shrivelled the leaves, which crisped into clustering grey flakes and drifted over the treetops, carried by gentle winds, sprinkling across the forest floors and lighting the ground.

Inside, Belladonna darted between the trees with her hand stretched before her, moving the trunks that slithered and lifted to form openings for her ahead. She sprinted from the bright orange horses that galloped behind her and scorched the flesh on her back, as they smoked the forest with thick cloud puffs. Belladonna witnessed the herd merging to the corners of her eyes, even as she slid underneath thick roots, which perished in the heat, crumbling behind her.

Belladonna crossed through an opening and flicked her hand to lift the roots of the compact trees in front. The roots curled from the soil, tearing from beneath and standing on the sharp ends of the thousands that had laid below, shifting like spiders and parting for Belladonna, as the trees behind did the same, creating a path.

She raced along the clear path, as she moved the trees, hoping to see the other side of the forest through the grey puffs that cocooned her. She searched for the exit, as her blue eyes reddened and tears drizzled her cheeks. Belladonna wheezed after almost all the air in her lungs had escaped her, falling to her knees and gasping to breathe again as her eyes looked at the burning low branches above and stopping the moving trees, as she dropped her arm.

Softly and slowly, the leaves curled with embers of fire, parting from their branches and drifting around her, as the flame disappeared in the fall. The leaves left the branches bare, which tangled and grew high above Belladonna, where she saw the Stars resonating.

Her blue eyes glanced at every twinkle, as the leaves fell and as the fiery heat drew closer to her back, penetrating through her clothes and scarring her flesh. The horses circled and she was trapped within their glow, with sweat pouring from her pores and heavy, falling, eyelids. The Stars above her warped as her head rolled forwards and she flopped onto her side. Belladonna looked at the dancing horses around her, without seeing anything through the gaze of her beautiful blue eyes.

The horses pranced over Belladonna, consuming her and swallowing the rest of the forest, as the sun began to rise in the horizon.

Tatiana stepped away from the ignited forest as the first glimmers of daylight tore through the prolonged night. She sighted the orange and pink streaks painted in the distance, as the sky above her head remained dark, with Stars still shining and the moon still glowing. The cool morning eased the frosty night she had fought through, as the flames on her body desisted and created a haze around her. Her eyes still shined amber and her hair was still white, clutching her strangely formed palms in front of her body, taking a few more steps away from the forest and into the meadow.

Tatiana twirled from the mass fire that stretched as far as the eye could see, hurrying into the strands of the meadow and releasing her clasped hands, as she returned to the battlefield. She ran with flooded eyes and water running over the banks on her face, streaking over her filthy skin. Tatiana sprinted with snot running over her lips and dropping down her jaw, desperately catching the air she needed to breathe and wanting to arrive quickly at the battlefield.

43

On the battlefield, the Stars and the companions fought the remaining members of the Necromancer and Belladonna's army. Both sides were covered in heaps of dirt and sweated through the blazing fires that ran through the meadow, which scared and blistered their skin. Their limbs grew heavy as they fought and dragged their weapons at their sides, thrusting their blades forwards with all the strength they had left. Amongst the battle, there was less noise, but screams still travelled, as Ra and Bathilda chased the Necromancer and Belladonna's warriors away from Cahercasey and dispersed them.

A while had passed since Bidelia and Barnabas had left Tatiana alone at the borders of the South, racing into battle as soon as Bidelia had transported them in front of Cahercasey castle. Bidelia and Barnabas whipped their swords from their sheaths, sprinting towards the Necromancer and Belladonna's knights, who were dotted across the meadow, still fighting against the companions and the Stars. They ran to their fighting companions and relieved them, as their agonising arms raised their blades to a clashing weapon, groaning with strained and clenched faces.

When Tatiana arrived at the battlefield, sprinting through the meadow and stopping at the edge, glancing at the fighting figures on the outskirts of a large, clustered circle of warriors, she burned brightly. Her amber eyes searched between the dark armour of the Necromancer and Belladonna's army for her companions, watching their arms tire and seeing faults in their steps as they lunged towards their opponents.

Tatiana dashed forwards, taking her bow from around her back and pulling arrows from her quiver, aiming into the battlefield. She sprung her arrows just above her head, as the fire from her hands spurred around them and brilliantly lit up the sky, before curving down and plunging through dark silver armour and piercing flesh, as her arrows sparked bodies to ignite. Tatiana marched to the outskirts, putting away her bow as warriors rampaged towards her and drawing a small sword from her waist.

As Tatiana appeared at the battle, striding towards the clustering warriors that were before the burning castle of Cahercasey, her bright light dazzled the eyes of one of her companions fighting amongst the Necromancer and Belladonna's army. Tatiana's light blinded a pair of golden eyes, which saw her above the heads of the battlefield, standing amongst the strands of meadow. Her companion smiled at her, hearing silence amongst the battle, as their arms weightlessly fell and released their sword. The companion watched her stride forwards, and even as a blade stayed lodged in the centre of the companion's stomach, they were no longer feeling its agonising pain.

Just as the companion tumbled back and as the sword was wrenched out from his stomach by his opponent, the companion met her amber eyes that grew wide and saw her eyebrows raise into her forehead. The companion's eyes fluttered as she sprinted and as the light around her body flared with flames. The companion grinned, unable to hear her screech their name, but seeing her mouth move to form it. They plummeted into the strands of meadow and thudded their body into the reddened soil, soaking their body in the pools of blood, as their head turned to the side and saw Tatiana's shoes running closer.

All the companion felt was a blaze of her fire blasting the warrior from her hand that slapped onto his chest, seeing her cry. The companion's blurring vision saw Tatiana scorch the flesh of the warrior that burst into flames, witnessing the pain across the warrior's face as the flames incinerated him. The companion saw the dark figure fall at their feet, falling to the ground and continue to burn.

As soon as the warrior fell, Tatiana dropped to her knees beside her companion. She swooped her arms underneath and cradled her companion onto her knees, tucking them into her chest. Her warm hand pushed away their hair from their cooling face, as her companion's golden eyes gushed. The sounds of the battle around her faded, only hearing the sobs of her companion and seeing only her companion's blood pouring from their stomach and bubbling from their mouth.

Tatiana stroked her companion's cheeks, wiping the falling tears and laying her hands on their icy skin, seeing the colours fade from her companion's fading hot cheeks. She ran through her fingers through their wet and sweaty hair, playing with strands and soothing her companion to sleep, as tears dropped from her amber eyes. She locked onto her companion, whimpering, as she saw the golden specks of her companion's eyes, fading and glossing over with dull and white glass.

At her side, she felt someone push against her side and roll their head onto her shoulder. Tatiana turned to see long and golden strands of hair laying across a woman's muddy face, as tears streaked through the heavy grime and fell from her violet eyes. The woman's hands clasped around Nemo's, holding his grey and cold skin in the palms of her hands and locking his icy fingers between hers. Through her sobbing, she released a sweet and melodic voice, breathing every word and holding back her tears.

There be a place for thee
Among the land and the sky
There be a place for thee
When thou shall sleep to fly

There be a place for thee
Where people do not lie
There be a place for thee
That life cannot deny

A place I cannot be
A place I cannot see
A place I do believe
A place to be relieved

There be a place for thee
For thou to watch over me
There be a place for thee
Where thou shall safely be

As Tatiana listened to Helen sing her last words to her companion, Tatiana and Helen felt their wriggling companion stop. They felt their companion become still, as the companion stopped choking on the blood that had risen to their throat, hearing the companion's whimpers falling silent. Tatiana and Helen felt the icy skin of their companion through the flames that surrounded Tatiana, as they struggled to hold their companion's weighted body in their grasp. They bowed over their companion, sobbing against their face, as their tears fell onto their frozen skin and away from their cheeks.

Tatiana cried. "Do not try to be forgetting what happened between us. I be not hating thee for betraying me. Nor, do I be hating thou for putting my companions in danger. For thou be the only person, who held the same wish for me; to live simply and to never rule. Already, do I miss thee. I miss Nemo!"

"I shall struggle to like anyone more than thee. Truly, did thee find a place in thy heart." Helen sobbed.

After a while, Tatiana's companions stepped closer and surrounded her. They had put away their weapons after killing the last warriors of the Necromancer and Belladonna's army and gathered to silently witness Nemo's passing. The companions' tears fell alongside Tatiana and Helen's, as their heads bowed, listening to them scream for the only companion to have died alongside the Necromancer and Belladonna's army.

Bidelia ordered her army of Stars to infiltrate Cahercasey, wanting to cease the fire that burned down the tower. Her army obeyed, as Bidelia kept a handful of Stars at her side, walking them over to the huddled companions and stooping over them. She stood silently, watching the companions cry beside Nemo's frozen body, before giving her orders to the Stars behind.

"The sun be nearly upon us, thus take Nemo's body from Helen and my sister!" Bidelia declared. "Carry him to the sea and prepare for his burial."

The handful of Stars staggered behind her, marched forwards and forced their way through the companions who bordered Tatiana and Nemo. The companions fought hard to stay in their positions, but the Stars stealthily pushed through and reached Tatiana almost instantly.

The Stars lowered and reached for Nemo's body, even as Tatiana and Helen slapped their hands from him and screamed at their faces. The

Stars continued and whisked their arms under his body, taking him from Tatiana and Helen, throwing their clambering hands off him. They lifted him above their heads and carried him on their shoulders, as he glowed under the twinkle of the Stars in the sky, storming towards the beaches of the Southern Sea.

As the Stars carried him away, Bidelia met the scowls of her fellow companions — Barnabas, Pip, Wylie, Sir Terrence, Tasmin, Darrel, Free and Helen, who rose to their feet. Her eyes overlooked them and gazed at Barnabas' frown and then at Helen's hateful stare, lowering her eyes to then glance at Tatiana still sobbing on the ground. Bidelia was deafened by the voices of her companions that screamed at her and bellowed over each other, questioning her, as she bowed her head and closed her eyes.

She stood there, silently, drowning their voices and waiting for their silence, unable to quieten them herself. From under her eyelids, crystal dews plummeted down her face, as the rims of her eyes reddened and so did her nose. She breathed shallowly, hoping the whistling winds would mask her sobs, as the companions continued to shout.

Just as the companions shouted, slowly, Tatiana pushed from the ground and lifted her wet and red clothing from the pool of blood she had knelt in, raising without her companions noticing. Tatiana placed her hands on the ground behind her and rolled onto her toes, jumping to her feet, looking down at the shallow pond where she had sat and where her boots were now sunk beneath, listening to her companions' voices.

Tatiana's lips parted, releasing a deep breath of air, before raising her lowered head and glancing between Bidelia and her companions. Tatiana projected her voice over her companion's, which shrilled and echoed over the silent meadow that was covered in mountains of dark silver armoured bodies. "Stop! Stop thy foul words and just be silent!"

Immediately, the companions heard Tatiana's pitched voice and stopped their yelling, as their sentences trailed into silence. The companions stared at Tatiana and back at Bidelia, finally hearing her muffled cries that she had been hiding from them and feeling something pull at their stomachs.

Tatiana waltzed to Bidelia and stopped in front of her. She stretched her arms over Bidelia's shoulders and laid her hands on her back, pushing

Bidelia into her chest, as Tatiana stood on her toes. Bidelia's head fell on Tatiana's shoulder, as Tatiana leaned her head down to hers and hushed her crying sister.

At once, the companions paced forwards and circled Bidelia and Tatiana. The companions' arms stretched to the sky and overlapped each other, leaning their chests and heads onto Tatiana and Bidelia, squeezing each other tight. The companions closed their crimson and dark-circled eyes, listening to Bidelia's fading cries and hearing the still land around them.

The companions stepped away from Tatiana and Bidelia, after a while, as Bidelia and Tatiana parted from each other. The companions still formed a circle, standing closer to Tatiana than Bidelia, as Bidelia gazed individually at the companions around her.

Bidelia huffed. "Nemo be my family, too. Swiftly, the sun be rising and I shall be leaving. . . for good. Only, do I have time to say my goodbyes in what be left of the night."

Helen stepped towards Bidelia and looked up at her with her grey eyes that sparked with violet lightning bolts. Helen placed her bloody and filthy fingers on the strands of Bidelia's flowing white hair, pushing them behind her ears and finding a perfect place for them to sit. Faintly, she smiled. At first, she was avoiding Bidelia's stare and looking at her hair, until lowering her eyes to meet hers and stating, "Barely, I be given a chance to know Nemo more than I be knowing. Barely, did he be knowing me. Dost thou believe, he shall be waiting for me, though he did not get to love me yet. For, I do love him and shall continue to do so."

Bidelia nodded. "Love be not measured in how long thou be knowing someone. It be measured in how much thee gives. So, I do believe he shall be waiting for thee. I believe he feels the same."

Helen looped her arm through Bidelia's, twirling her to the direction of the sea and feeling the wind blow directly against their faces. She insisted, "Let us say our goodbyes, before all us shall have to leave."

Bidelia smiled briefly, as Helen walked at her side, heading towards the Southern Sea. Bidelia and Helen paced through the strands of the meadow, and Helen's dark purple cloak and as Bidelia's white cloak swayed behind them. They headed to the beaches, and the wind whisked their tears and carried their tears behind them as they admired the Cahercasey, which had ceased to burn and the cliffs behind.

Tasmin whisked Darrel and Sir Terrence in her grasp, following Helen and Bidelia, striding against the winds and leading them to the beaches. She held their bloody and warm hands in hers, as they ventured through the still meadow, stepping over the masses of bodies on the ground, storming to the sea.

Behind, Pip and Wylie came together. Pip and Wylie followed the line of companions ahead and towards the beach. They travelled closely beside each other, colliding into each other as their aching legs wandered. Wylie had not fully awakened from seeing Bathilda, but was comforted by Pip's words, as she spoke softly to him on their way through the meadow.

Lastly, Tatiana followed the rest of her companions into the distance. Tatiana strolled into the pools of blood and eyed the sea, just seeing the waves crashing on the sandy shores. She stepped forwards, with Free and Barnabas walking at her side, but with onlookers thinking they did not know each other at all, as sparse gaps stayed between them, heading to the Southern Sea.

The companions arrived at the edge of the meadow, as the soil gradually formed into grains of sand and the meadow of wheat transformed into long strands of grass, looking over the wall of sand dunes that sat at the start of the beach and at the sea. The tide was high, and the white foams of the waves lingered on the sand, as the crystal-clear waves flooded back, after crashing rapidly on the shores. Above, the sky was in darkness towards the West, with the Stars and the moon still glimmering, whilst the East started to grow with bluer and brighter skies, shadowing the Stars that were no longer seen.

Together, the companions waited for each other and slid down the sand dunes, stumbling onto the flatter white grains of sand and strolling towards the darker side of the beach. The companions sighted the small handful of Stars, waiting closely beside the sea and paced towards them, walking in a horizontal line across the beach.

The companions gathered in front of the Stars, who parted and stepped to one side, revealing Nemo's body. Nemo had been laid on his back against a thick plank of wood settled on the white sand, with his trousers rolled and his boots removed from his feet, which had been placed to the side. He still wore his bloody clothes, but his hands had been placed to cover his wound on his stomach and had been drizzled with oil, which matted his hair and lingered all over his skin, just seeping into his clothes. He lay peacefully, and his glassy eyes twinkled with starlight.

The companions surrounded and lowered around Nemo's frozen and still body, grappling the wood with their hands and lifting Nemo, holding him low at their waists. They looked down at Nemo, examining his body, as tears streamed from their eyes and their hearts ached again. The companions turned to the sea, trudging onto the wet sand and pushing against the crashing waves, entering the cold water, carrying Nemo over the waves.

The companions fought the crashing waves and staggered from the shallows, as the water raised and lifted to their stomachs. Their feet still touched the soft and sandy seabed, as they waded through calmer movements of water and laid Nemo's body on the surface of the water, holding him still on the surface, then they halted.

They glanced at each other's watery eyes, then down at Nemo's still body, taking a deep breath. The companions leaned down and grappled the edges of the wood, pushing the wood against the flow of the water and into the deep. They released their grips from the around the edges of the wood and forced Nemo out to sea.

Just before they pushed the wooden plank that Nemo rested upon, Tatiana, who loomed above Nemo's head, placed her index finger on his frosty forehead. Her falling tears steamed as soon as they touched her cheeks. Her index finger was surrounded by twisting flames, lowering down to the patch of oil that rested on his skin and bubbled the liquid, until a flame burst onto his flesh, rapidly journeying across his body. Her flames followed the drizzled line of oil, catching quickly and swarming instantly around Nemo's body, until the companions could no longer see him resting and pushed him away.

Even as they released Nemo into the bright waters, as the sun began to rise in the East and sparkled on the surface, the companions stayed in the cool waters. The companions eyed the flaming orange cluster that drifted ahead of them, as it became just a single dot of light floating on the water of the seas and under the remaining night sky.

Suddenly, the sun rose higher and Nemo's body had disappeared beyond what they could see of the sea. The companions lingered for just a moment more, looking at the spot where the pinnacle of light had last shined, before turning and trudging back to stand on the white sand, being thrown by the forces of the waves.

The soaked companions trampled the sand, pulling their weighted and wet feet from the sea and approaching the Stars that had waited on the beach. The companions stood before them, as Bidelia parted and headed to stand in front.

Bidelia stood at the front of the grouped Stars that staggered behind her and looked upon the rising yellow haze of the sun, before staring at the companions with a smile. Her hands clasped together and her clothes dried quickly, as the companions remained wet still. She addressed the companions, as Tatiana stood in front with Free and Barnabas at her side, followed by Tasmin, Sir Terrence and Darrel, then Wylie, Pip and Helen. "The time for us to leave be now. The sun be nearly upon us and the Stars cannot be when there be daylight. I shall only return once more. Then, I shall never be able to walk upon the earth again. My destiny be written many years before my birth and I accomplished my destiny, helping the Southern Queen claim her throne. From the skies, I shall watch over all of thee. I shall be there on all the adventures. If thou be ever lost, consult me, by staring up at night. I shall answer. . .What an extraordinary adventure, thou and I be having. I shall not say farewell, for thou and I shall see each other for one last time, very soon."

As the companions tried to speak, Bidelia and the Stars behind were circled by a gust of wind, blowing their white hair from their shoulders. Their skin illuminated with a colourless glow, as their clothing radiated and their faces shone with a blinding light that stretched to the companions' feet. The eyes of the Stars shone like pairs of torches, with each Star having a different coloured set of eyes, as the light from their bodies wrapped around them. The Stars' faces began to blur amongst the powerful and fast-growing light, shutting the companions' eyes, as they waved goodbye to them.

In a few seconds, the Stars vanished. Their light had fizzled into small balls of light, which hovered for a moment, before climbing towards the sky. The bulbs danced above the companions' heads, as they opened their eyes and watched the Stars fly into the night, gradually disappearing amongst the thousands of lights already painting the sky.

The companions watched the last sightings of the balls of lights, dropping their waving hands and finally seeing them vanish amongst the remaining dark sky. They stood at the edge of the beach for a while longer, just looking up, even as the sun began to move over and warmed their wet clothes, blinding them with a new and yellow light, making their eyes squint.

Eventually, the companions stopped staring, as the Stars disappeared, shuffling along the beach, towards the sand dunes and crossing the meadow ahead.

The first companions to cross the beach were Pip and Wylie. They moved from the sea with smiles across their faces, feeling relieved as they fell down the sides of the sand dunes and finally laughed with ease. Pip and Wylie's laughter was infectious for the other companions, who cackled with them. Pip and Wylie waltzed from the sand dunes and into the meadow, playfully pushing each other as they headed to the castle, still laughing freely.

Following Pip and Wylie's laughter there was Tasmin. She stormed up the sides of the sand dunes with Sir Terrence following, twisting around and pushing him down with the sliding sand, crying with laughter as she watched him tumble onto his back. Tasmin raced into the meadow, and Sir Terrence charged after her and tackled her, tickling her sides.

After, Darrel guided Helen to the side of the sand dunes, stepping first and stretching his arm behind him, taking Helen's hand. Darrel tugged her gently, helping her miniature size climb the dune and leading her into the meadow. Darrel swung his arm over her shoulders and cuddled her at his side, as tears still fell from her eyes and her heart still ached inside her chest. He consoled her by promising the making of his sweet-tasting and rich cakes inside the castle kitchen.

Barnabas and Free turned to Tatiana, as she stared at the sparkling blue sea and watched the waves fall along the shores, listening to the soft crashing of the water hitting the sand. Barnabas and Free stepped to either side of her, turning their heads over their shoulders and gazing at her stern expression, as the fire around her body continued to blaze. They stood with her until she was ready to return to the castle with the other companions, standing in silence, as the sun caused their eyes to glisten and as their hair blew in the sea breeze.

Barnabas and Free were unsure as to why Tatiana stood for so long looking at the sea, as their stomachs twisted and told them it was not because Nemo sailed along the water. Their twisting guts opened their arms to lay over Tatiana's shoulders, holding her and hoping to comfort her, as she stared endlessly and painfully at the sea.

At least an hour had passed, since the other companions had returned to the castle, when Tatiana decided she was ready to go as well. Finally, her eyes tore from the sea and she turned to smile at Free and Barnabas, lifting her arms and patting their backs, gesturing them to release her. She turned on her heel, with Barnabas and Free slowly looking from the sea and following behind, as her half-smile did not cease, and she returned to Cahercasey alongside her other companions.

Epilogue

Just a few days had passed since Tatiana and her companions fought the war against the Necromancer and Belladonna, but the South continued to blossom in the bright sunlight during the day and underneath the Stars at night, as the wheat meadow became ready to harvest and was cleared from the blood that had stained the soil. The Southern Sea continued to have soft waves hitting the white sand on the beaches behind the dark cliffs, as a light breeze skimmed across the sapphire water.

In the South, Cahercasey still stood on a steep cliff which stretched across the shallow waters, as the white stone that built the castle walls shone. The white turrets and tower still stood tall, except from the tower towards the back of the castle, which had been burned halfway down by Tatiana with fallen rubble inside. The golden gates of Cahercasey had been opened and lifted at the top of the cliff, as the stained glass in every window gleamed and golden statues glimmered along the white marbled paths that curved through the castle.

In the castle, inside the throne room, with a marble floor and painted ceiling, a woman wandered before the white throne that sat on a small stage at the far side of the room, in front of tall and narrow stained-glass windows. The woman walked between the white columns, following a long green carpet that led from the golden front doors and towards the throne, running in the centre of the room.

The woman wore a long gown with a small train dragging behind her as she strolled into the throne room and along the carpet, staring at the painted ceiling above her. Her emerald dress was decorated evenly with white lace, and her bodice was decorated with the same lace and with diamonds. Her muscled arms were covered by a sheer cloak that wrapped around her shoulders, as her hands crossed and clasped in front of her. The woman's hair had been pinned neatly into a long plait that fell down her back, and wisps of hair sat at the sides of her face.

Just as the woman strolled inside the throne room, she heard a light tap echo through the room and twisted slowly, pinching the sides of her dress and spinning to face the golden doors behind. The woman called, "Freely enter!"

After she had called, one of the golden doors was pushed opened from the other side and a figure entered the throne room, closing the door behind. Immediately, the figure stopped at the doors once inside and gawked at the woman, as she dazzled in her dress.

For a while, the man waited at the doors, just watching the woman stand before him with a timid smile across her lips, as she stood in the centre of the room and mesmerised him. His brown eyes glimmered at her beauty, slowly beginning to step forwards in his nicest clothes and wearing a light green cloak on his shoulders, without a sword hanging from his belt.

The man rushed towards the woman, as the woman stretched out her hands and beckoned him. He clasped her hands, admiring her, as his eyes examined every detail in her green dress and gushed, "Today, thou shall dazzle everyone, my Queen Tatiana."

"Thank ye, Sir Free." Tatiana grinned a little. "When shall the last guest arrive to the castle?"

"Everyone be arriving promptly, except for King Hunter," Free answered. "He be forwarding no reasons for his lateness."

Her amber, glowing eyes rolled. "Just for one day, he be needing to stop rebuilding his castle. Once today be over, I be able to aid him and it shall take a shorter period for Hanuli to be restored."

"It be assumed he be still arriving, as no word be given for an absence," Free mentioned. "At least, the most important people shall be watching thee."

She smiled. "Yes, my companions and my sister! Be it so strange that my coronation be at night?"

"Here, in the South, everything be accomplished differently," Free stated, gripping her hands tighter. "Now, the flames around thy body cannot be seen, but I still feel the heat in thy hands, which make mine sweat! Hopefully, in the night, thy flames can be seen again."

“Yes. I want to shine bright like Ra does, as he flies the Southern skies and sleeps in the cave he found along the coast, residing with Bathilda,” Tatiana exclaimed. “I shall hope I shine again.”

Free smiled, releasing her warm hands before his palms became too hot and dropping his arms at his sides. “The sun shall set in half an hour. Then I shall be leading our guests here, inside the throne room and I do not wish for them to see thee yet. Ah, I shall take thee to Barnabas. No one shall disturb him, not even the other companions. Come, my Queen.”

Tatiana laughed at Free and roughly looped his arm, spinning him to face the golden doors of the throne room and forcing him to walk beside her. She pushed down on the handle and opened the door, playfully pushing Free through first and following him into the hallway, looping arms again and pacing down the hall in the light of the green and blue glass that was in every window along the corridor.

Free and Tatiana headed down the corridor outside the throne room and came to a winding staircase, which led to the top of a small tower that was attached to the main building of the castle. Tatiana climbed the staircase first, as Free lifted the back of her dress from the floor and carried the train gently in his hands, following her to the top of the tower and stopping on the last step.

At the top of the tower, after climbing the stairs alongside the emerald and sapphire panelled windows, they came to a tall and dark wooden closed door with a black iron latch. The door had been placed just above the last step of the quiet staircase, with a window at one side, as the last shimmers of daylight entered through the stained glass.

Tatiana looked down at her hands, eyeing her strange palm lines that grew outwards from the centre and curling her fingers inwards. She dropped one of her hands, using the other to tap her knuckles against the hard wood, as the sound echoed throughout the tower and through the room on the other side. She knocked only a few times, before lowering her arm and awaiting an answer.

In a few seconds, she heard feet shuffling along creaking floorboards from on the other side, moving closer to the door. Tatiana saw a shadow seeping from underneath the gap at the bottom of the door, standing in the orange light that came from the inside. She heard the latch unlock and saw the door opening, revealing bright lighting as the door opened wider.

At the entrance of the door, once the door had opened, there was a tall and broad-shouldered man, shadowing above Tatiana, just ducking his head underneath the frame. The man's chartreuse eyes sparkled in the green and blue light, widening, as his eyes fixated upon her dress and followed the white lace and diamonds to her face. His lips formed into a smile, gazing at her face, with large infrequent drops of tears falling from the corners of his eyes, instantly falling from his high cheekbones and dropping from his jaw.

Though the man stood with an opened mouth, Tatiana's bottom lip, dropped lower. Her chin fell into her neck, as her amber eyes flicked up at him and eyed his face. His previous tangled hair had been brushed and sleeked behind his ears, with shining highlights on his cheeks and his peached skin glowing, whilst his lips were glossed and no longer crusty and dry like before. Her eyes looked down at his thick green cloak sitting on his shoulders. He wore a clean and bright white shirt underneath with a pair of beige trousers and a pair of shiny boots. He was armed with a sword, hanging from his belt, with a glimmering silver handle poking from its brown sheath.

Tatiana stuttered. "T-t-thou be so pretty!"

He chuckled, wiping the tears that were just underneath his eyes with his finger. "In all my life, I do not believe I have been called *pretty.*"

She grimaced, as her cheeks blushed, still eyeing his face. "It be the only word I thought! I apologise, Barnabas. Yet, I be never seeing thee looking so beautiful."

Barnabas' eyes stared from her face and looked over her shoulder, seeing Free standing just around the corner, still holding her dress. He called to him. "Brother, Free! Dost thou send her here to hide?"

Free nodded. "Yes! Endlessly, she wanders the castle and she cannot be seen by the guests yet. For the last few minutes of daylight, she shall stay here with thee."

Barnabas stretched out his soft hands and guided her into his room. Free released her dress at the frame of the door and rushed down the steps of the tower before Barnabas had even shut the door. He closed the door as soon as Free had turned the corner and as soon as Tatiana's train had passed him.

Tatiana entered Barnabas' room and stood at the centre, underneath his high iron chandelier that dangled from the pointed ceiling. She gazed over the dark walls and floorboards of his room, caressed by the light streaming through the two stained glass windows on either side of her. Tatiana turned to view Barnabas' enormous bed, which had been neatly made with the edges of the green sheets tucked underneath the mattress and white, plump pillows sitting on top. A bedside table sat on both sides of the bed, with a chest of drawers pushed to one corner and a mirror just beside one of the windows.

After she had observed his room, Tatiana twisted and saw him leaning against the door with his arms folded and staring sternly at her face. Tatiana grinned at him until he smiled back and moved from the door, approaching her and dropping his arms to his sides. She was joined at the centre of the room, as Barnabas smiled at her, glaring at her face.

Barnabas admitted with a small sigh. "Ye look beautiful!"

Tatiana's eyes rolled, continuing to grin at him. "Look at ye, Barnabas! Look how handsome ye be. I never seen thee look so mesmerising. Yet, I do not think thou shalt look better than my sister."

"Of course, not. I shall just look better than thee." He chuckled.

Tatiana flicked the back of her hand against his opposite shoulder, slapping his skin as she scowled. As soon as she did, her hand dropped and her head lowered. Her scowl faded after a long sigh, as water flooded her amber eyes, turning her head to one side and hiding.

Barnabas stooped lower and pressed her fingers against his jaw, turning and lifting her face. He moved her to look at him, even as her eyes continued to stare away and insisted, "If thou cannot find another Queen to love, then be lonely and love the Queen thou already be."

She nodded, flicking her eyes back to him and not letting her tears fall.

"Until the day I die, I shall never leave thee alone and I shall help thy loneliness," Barnabas stated, laying his hands on her shoulders and lightly rocking her torso, as he faintly smiled.

Suddenly, they heard faint voices yelling over stomping feet, which echoed inside Barnabas' room, bellowing from the other side of the door.

Underneath the gap of the door, shadows appeared and shifted closer, as the voices became louder, but not any clearer than the muffling sounds that they had heard before. The latch lifted and the door swung open, slamming against the wall.

Charging inside Barnabas' room, three men stumbled to halt in front of the door, freezing before Barnabas and Tatiana. The three men gaped, as Tatiana and Barnabas eyed them.

The first man to enter the bedroom was the tallest of the men and wore the same clothes as Barnabas, with the same thick, green cloak sitting on his shoulders. His young and clear skin, gleamed, as his heart-melting, deep brown eyes looked upon Tatiana. He gasped, with his white teeth smiling and his hands raising to cover his mouth, beginning to chuckle nervously.

The second man entered wearing the same uniform, and stopped his tumbling feet, as his dark green eyes saw Tatiana standing before him. His long dark hair fell softly into waves and fell over his shoulders, with white streaks running through, sitting with his thick and tidied beard. There were scars across his face, which had been stitched, but were still red around the edges, running into his scalp. He grabbed the metal cannister from his belt, swigging his drink, before his eyebrows rose and he stood silent.

The last man came in with his forest cloak swaying behind him, pushing through the other two men and stopping, before heading towards Tatiana. The man's light blue eyes glimmered at Tatiana, as his ginger hair flowed into two plaits and rested on his back. He marched forwards, with a smile across his full lips, and his freckled cheeks gleamed with a shine. He plodded to Tatiana and rested his hands gently on her blushing cheeks

His soft voice worsened the tears in Tatiana's eyes, as his thumbs quickly wiped her tears before they hit her cheeks. "Beautiful. A beautiful young woman, my Queen be!"

"Darrel, thou look dashing as always!" Tatiana sniffled, as her eyes looked over his shoulder and at the other two men. "Sir Terrence and Wylie! How smart thou be dressed."

Sir Terrence and Wylie smiled, stepping closer to Tatiana and standing either side of Darrel, examining Tatiana's dress further.

Sir Terrence teased with his breath reeking of alcohol, "Ye be looking no different. Still as ugly as when I met ye."

"No, Sir Terrence. She looks even more ugly than before." Wylie smirked.

Tatiana laughed, as Darrel hands dropped from her cheeks.

As she laughed, Tatiana and her companions heard small and shrilling gasps. Tatiana looked over her companions, as they twisted, staring at the door of Barnabas' room. She and her companions sighted three figures standing together inside Barnabas' room, looping arms and wearing the same green cloaks and clothes as Darrel, Wylie, Sir Terrence and Barnabas, with swords at their sides, gushing at Tatiana.

The woman in the middle of the two figures was the youngest and smallest of all the companions, Helen. Helen's eyes popped with fluorescent shades of violet, dimming the shades of light grey that were seen before. Her golden hair flowed beside her face, and her plump and reddened lips formed a smile, with her pale skin shining.

Helen rested her head against the shoulder of the woman next to her, who staggered above her. The woman beside her was Pip, with her red hair sitting in a plait on her shoulder, which fell to her stomach and rested in soft curls. Pip's glimmering teal eyes observed Tatiana, briefly flicking at Wylie with her smile, before staring back at Tatiana again.

On the other side of Helen, wearing the same cloak and clothes, there was a woman with frizzy, curly brown hair. The woman's umber skin was glowing amongst the green and blue lights, as her deep brown eyes clocked Tatiana from underneath her thick and arched eyebrows. The woman was Tasmin, smiling at Tatiana, as she looped Helen's arm.

Tasmin, Helen and Pip rushed forwards, pushing through Wylie, Sir Terrence and Darrel, wrapping their arms around Tatiana. They gushed, squeezing her tightly in their arms, as Tatiana stretched her arms around them, unable to embrace Helen, who laid against her chest and between Tasmin and Pip. Then, the companions released her, stepping back to view her, as Sir Terrence, Darrel, Wylie and Barnabas came to stand with them.

Helen clasped her hands in front of her and beamed. "Everyone shall swoon! So beautiful."

“How jealous I be!” Pip muttered, as Wylie came to her side and swiftly wrapped his arm around her, smiling at her.

“So, shall our Tatiana find the woman she desires? Does she be needing a woman? No! She be with us. She shall never be alone.” Tasmin gulped, after Sir Terrence passed her his flask, which she drunk quickly from. “Thou be not needing a woman. Thou be the only woman thou need.”

Tatiana smelt the alcohol already lingering in Tasmin’s breath and rolled her eyes, asking Sir Terrence also. “Be both of ye already drunk? There be a celebration afterwards!”

Sir Terrence argued. “No. No, yet. Tasmin and I drink so much that it be hard for us to be drunk.”

Tatiana smiled at him and Tasmin, and her eyes moved to glance over the companions that stood before her. Her smile grew larger, seeing the gleams in their eyes and the happiness across their faces, even when they did not smile. She breathed. “Tonight, my favourite part, shall not be my coronation, but afterwards. Afterwards, I shall perform my first duty as Queen of the South. Tonight, I shall knight all ye.”

“I cannot wait for the companions to become knights alongside me!” Sir Terrence announced, raising his flask, which spilled over the sides as he lifted his arm. “After King Moryn gave me my knighthood, I be alone for some time, but not any longer!”

The companions cheered with Sir Terrence, as he passed his flask between the companions and gesturing them to drink the strong alcohol inside. The companions’ eyes widened and closed, as his bitter, yet sweet liquid ran through their mouth and along their tongues, which they spat between their lips after his alcohol had burned their throats.

Barnabas coughed. “What ye be drinking?”

Sir Terrence chuckled.

“Only the finest!” Tasmin cheered.

“It be disgusting.” Helen gagged, as her tongue was seen poking from her parting lips.

Wylie’s eyes fluttered and he stated, “I need to sleep.”

Pip yelled, clutching her neck, “Terrence, why did ye not warn us? My stomach be in knots. How does ye be drinking with ease?”

"I be not able to even bake with such a drink!" Darrel yelled. "Where did thou brew such a drink?"

"Do not be like that!" He huffed, as his flask was returned to him and he stepped forwards, passing his drink to Tatiana. "Let the Queen drink! She be the only opinion I need."

Tatiana snatched the flask from Sir Terrence, as the companions bickered after Sir Terrence had enraged them. She lifted the flask and knocked her head back, putting the metal against her lips and running the liquid through her mouth, feeling the cold alcohol surround her tongue. She tasted the sweet golden liquid, gulping hints of apple, which scorched her throat, as she closed her eyes and stepped back, bringing the flask away from her lips and wiping her mouth with the back of her hand. She gasped, cooling her throat, as she passed the flask back to Sir Terrence and looked at her companions with a raised brow.

Her companions stopped bickering and laughed, as joyous tears fell from the corners of their eyes, struggling to breathe.

As Tatiana raised her eyebrow at her companions, watching them laugh, her eyes caught a white spark flaring just in front of the doorway of Barnabas' room. Tatiana's eyes widened, scowling across the room and pushing through the companions, seeing a glowing figure standing a few feet behind the companions.

She rushed towards the figure with long white hair, wearing a silver crown on their head with small, twinkling stars sitting on silver rods, stretching outwards. The figure's chestnut brown eyes, were surrounded by a deep, green rim, dazzling, as their skin shone in the very little daylight that was left, subsidising through the glass windows of Barnabas' room. The tall and curvaceous figure wore a thick and heavy white cloak over their shoulders, as their hands poked through two holes inside the material, wearing their cloak over a long, white dress that sparkled. The figure's hand stretched to welcome Tatiana, embracing her tightly into their chest.

Tatiana slammed into the figure's chest and rested her head onto their shoulders, as the figure's arms wrapped over her. She whispered the figure's name. "Only a few days passed, yet I missed thee dearly. My sister, Bidelia, I be excited for thee to return. How be thou only here for a night?"

Bidelia looked over Tatiana's shoulder, seeing the companions gawk and eyeing Barnabas, hugging Tatiana tighter. "Truly, I missed thee! I watched thee from the sky, only to wish I could be with thee."

Tatiana released Bidelia, taking her hands and walking backwards, guiding Bidelia to the companions. Tatiana stopped and stepped to one side, standing beside Bidelia and presenting her, lightly tapping her back, pushing her forwards.

Bidelia paced to the companions, opening her arms, as they rampaged against her chest and wrapped their arms around her. The companions closest to her chest, kissed her cheeks and squeezed her torso, as they smiled and asked her many questions.

However, Bidelia did not respond. Her eyes were drawn to the companion that did not rush to hug her, fluttering her heart with his stare. Bidelia's lip trembled, as her grip around the companions loosened. Her eyes poured with small diamond droplets, falling from her cheeks and dropping onto the shoulders of the companions that were closest to her, as she longingly locked onto the companion's green eyes that swarmed butterflies in her stomach.

Suddenly, the companions released Bidelia, hearing her whimper. The companions stepped back and parted, creating a path between Bidelia and the companion behind. They gathered on either side of the path, flicking between the two silent companions that looked lovingly at each other.

Bidelia and the companion stepped forwards, slowly walking towards each other and meeting in the middle of the path. Bidelia smiled as she came closer to the stern stare of the companion, whose lime eyes streamed with slow falling tears, rolling over his cheeks. The companion's hands lifted to rest on Bidelia's shoulders, before heaving her into his chest and wrapping his arms around her warm body. She lifted her chin onto his shoulder, as her fists clenched his shirt, letting him melt into her and holding him as his legs shook.

Bidelia whispered softly, to her companion that was always speechless around her, "When thou be frozen, I warmed thee in the night. When thou stood at the window and spoke to me, I heard every word. Barnabas, I miss thee. Tonight, shall be our last night together, for a very, very, long time."

Barnabas nodded, sinking his face into her shoulder and weeping into her cloak.

At the door, Free knocked and entered Barnabas' room, dispersing Tatiana and the gathered companions, as well as parting Bidelia and Barnabas. Free strolled inside, as Tatiana and the companions watched him enter, passing them and heading to Barnabas and Bidelia.

Free waltzed towards Bidelia and Barnabas, stopping in front of them, as they stood closely together and looped arms. Free smiled, quickly wiping away their tears from underneath their eyelids with his thumbs, before turning and facing Tatiana and the companions behind.

Free asked Tatiana, "There be some time before the coronation still. Would thou wish to start early?"

Tatiana chortled and shook her head. "Be there enough time for me to take flight? Be there time, for me and Ra to take a quick flight through the sky?"

Free nodded.

Tatiana stretched out her arms and gathered her companions to stand in front. Her amber eyes fixated on the men and women waiting in front of her, smiling, as their eyes glistened and their faces radiated with grins. She gawked at their scars, which lined some of her companions' faces, whilst seeing stitched gashes across their hands, but seeing her companions still grimacing at her.

Tatiana cleared her throat and softly projected her voice. The more she spoke, her voice trembled and eventually she spoke through her tears. "My companions, if thou had never convinced me to return to the throne, I cannot imagine what would have become if the Necromancer and Belladonna continued to reign. At happy times, such as today, I remember what thou did for me and the loss of my brother, Nemo. Sometimes, I be seen bursting into tears, because I be happy and yet, saddened. Tonight, my companions, the people I cherish most, shall be the knights of Cahercasey. Already, I be lucky to be having one knight already and I wish for all to join Sir Terrence, as well as to stand by the side. My companions, thou shall be knights of Cahercasey, even in death. For I shall outlive all ye and I shall not be able to replace or forget the companions that I fought beside. Forever, my companions shall be the knights that be mine. Thank ye, for everything."

Tatiana bowed her head, as her tears fell from her eyes and steamed against her boiling cheeks. Her eyes flicked from her companions, who gushed with tears, seeing Helen burying her face in her hands and watching Pip cover her mouth and nose with her hand. Tatiana tore from Sir Terrence and Tasmin, who cried through their smiles, as Wylie, Free and Darrel avoided staring at Tatiana for too long and moved their eyes around the room.

Yet, Bidelia and Barnabas' eyes remained dry, as they stood taller than most of the companions, looking over Helen, Tasmin, Darrel and Sir Terrence and at Tatiana's bowed head. Bidelia and Barnabas pushed through their companions, rushing towards Tatiana and overlapping their arms over her shoulders.

Free joined them, standing in front of Tatiana and lifting his chin to rest on the top of her head. He wrapped his arms around her waist, gently squeezing her, as her chest expanded against him. Free pressed Tatiana's face to rest in the crevice of his neck, which quickly became wet from her falling tears, muffling her cries against his skin.

Helen ran and slipped between Free and Tatiana, ducking underneath Free's arms and wiggling between. She comfortably stood below the top of Tatiana's chest, feeling heavy droplets falling from her chin and landing on her head with a small thud, as Free hugged them both from behind. Helen laid her head on Tatiana's chest and rested her hands gently on Tatiana's stomach, fiddling with the lace and diamond embellishments on her bodice.

Darrel plodded around them and placed his hands on the sides of Tatiana's arms, rubbing the sheer material of her cloak. His head turned to one side, as he pressed his face against her back, with his head just sitting below Tatiana's shoulders. Darrel closed his eyes, listening to her quiet cries and feeling her back jolt.

Sir Terrence stepped between Darrel and Bidelia. He laid his arms over their backs, resting his hands on their shoulders, leaning forwards into the huddle. His head rested in Bidelia's shoulder, lowering his eyes and exhaling deeply, blowing his pungent breath away from his companions, turning from Bidelia and looking down at Darrel.

Tasmin joined the huddle alongside Sir Terrence, standing on the other side of Bidelia and between Free. She rested her head against the side of Free's shoulder, towering just slightly above Helen, whom she could see through the gap between Free and Tatiana. Tasmin's hand, closest to Free, reached to rest on Helen's shoulder, as Helen faced her with a smile. Her other hand, rested on Bidelia's back, laying on top of Sir Terrence's.

Pip filled in one of the last spaces, shuffling between Barnabas and Darrel. Her arm wrapped fully around Darrel's neck, almost choking him as she did. Pip's head leaned on the side of Barnabas' curved back, as her arm wrapped around the lower half of his torso. Her green eyes looked over at each companion, sometimes meeting their gaze and other times just watching their watery eyes glistening.

The very last companion was Wylie. He huffed and slowly joined the rest of the companions, pushing between Barnabas and Free. His back curved inwards, placing his muscular arms over Free and Barnabas, just reaching Pip's head and ruffling his hands through her hair, as his other hand grappled the top of Free's shoulder. Wylie lowered his head, peeping down at Tatiana, as she continued to cry against Free's throat.

The companions embraced each other for a very long time, even though their necks stiffened and their arms cramped. They were silent, comforted by the warmth and the sounds of their beating hearts, being so comfortable beside each other that they could have fallen asleep. The companions did not release Tatiana until she had stopped crying, which was just in time for her coronation and the knighting of the companions.

Finally, Tatiana Green took her place on the Southern throne, staying with her companions until their final days. She would rule for centuries, making new friends and fellowships, but never forgetting the friends, the family and the companions she once had long after they had passed.

The End